# Be Not Thy Father's Son

by

# Howard Gordon

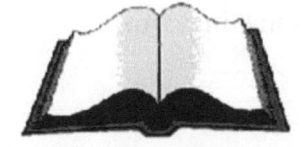

**CCB Publishing**
**British Columbia, Canada**

Be Not Thy Father's Son

Copyright ©2011 by Howard Gordon
ISBN-13   978-1-926585-21-5
First Edition

Library and Archives Canada Cataloguing in Publication

Gordon, Howard, 1942-
Be not thy father's son / written by Howard Gordon – 1st Ed.
ISBN 978-1-926585-21-5
I. Title.
PS3607.O59365B46 2011   813'.6   C2011-906335-2

Publisher:   CCB Publishing
             British Columbia, Canada
             www.ccbpublishing.com

# Be Not Thy Father's Son

# Preface

In developing civilization from chaos, we seek order. This ordering comes from the cultural heritage that has been handed down by our forbears from the beginning of time. While some ideas preserve our essences, survivals, and identities, they also serve to tell us we are better than others. Religious and nationalistic rivalry has driven the young and vital of our generations to gory and senseless destruction. Is this the civilized order we seek?

To establish an ordering we must question the patterns to which we have become acclimated and formulate a plan that fits our life. Our parents showed us their love by passing their survival techniques and customs. We are not them, nor is our life experience theirs. Hence, we have to alter or discard some of their teachings. The elder generation perceives this as a threat to their survival. Facing the concept of change sometimes means standing alone with our decision. Mom and Dad are not there to support us. The new template we stamp out will create either a new cultural pattern or self-destruction.

Mark Engler and Kiona Almederson are a representation of the tendency of young people to strike out new territorial imperatives that results in incorporation or annihilation. In evolutionary terms, these young people are an expression of survival by adaptation to changing needs within the organism. By engineering this alteration, the domain of humankind is expanded because man is controlling cultural norms, not being regulated by them. I believe that this is how progress occurs. In theocratic terms, we are moving to a closer relationship with God. We were created in God's image to develop the fruit of his labor.

The aforementioned ripening of the fruit requires courage to move away from the stultifying and stagnating aspects of our social structure. The driving force behind the solitary stance we must take is a belief in the rightness of our cause. Sustenance of this self-belief has its origins in trusting our judgments because we were loved to experience their outcomes in a protective setting.

If this has not been sufficiently available, a precedent might serve as a motivator. For this reason, I created the persona of Gideon Retta.

He was a man from a by gone era that fled from one culture striving to impose itself on another, stood firmly in his beliefs, and risked ostracism to build a life of his own.

The transgression that Mark and Kiona were embarking upon was that two people of differing racial backgrounds could build their own happiness together. Their belief in the love they shared needed an impetus to give it time to grow and become firmly cemented. This dislodging force was Gideon Retta, a figure out of Ethiopia of the Middle Ages and the Spanish Inquisition. He discovered he had to reconstitute his culture to survive in a New World. This restructuring served as a template for change.

This alteration of societal prerogatives is not essential or even desirable for all people, but it needs to be available to those, who require and/or want it. Thus, did Gideon Retta and later Mark and Kiona venture into self-actualization?

History is full of men and women that became sensitized to human shortcomings and iniquities. They were impelled to adjust their lives according to their percepts, stood their ground, and impacted upon human relationships. These are the Galileos, Spinozas, Ghandis Mandelas, and Martin Luther Kings of our planet. They have brought us closer to God's light. Such is my goal, such is my life, and such is my book.

# Acknowledgments

Many people have helped me to engage in this momentous task. My dear departed wife, whom I will cherish the rest of my days, set the stage for me and shared a love with me that went beyond racial boundaries. Belita Tisder Gordon, this is for you. Please look down on me and smile. To my five children Kelvin Tisder, Jarvis Tisder, Eric Tisder, Stephanie Tisder, and Almeda Tisder and to all of my grandchildren I want to express my gratitude for being patient for my isolating myself from you to rebuild my life, in part through this book. I also owe Shirley Hobson a huge debt of gratitude for supporting my intention to start the adventure of writing, pushing me to buy a computer to initiate my endeavor, enduring my angry, self-pitying, and often, vile outbursts while I learned to use it. She also bought me a typewriter when I became disgusted with the computer. Mesphin Ambatchew introduced me to people in the Ethiopian community that supported my endeavor by providing information about Ethiopian culture that I found helpful. To the close friend of my marriage, Juanita Brown, I owe the prodding to leave my lethargy behind and to outline the plot. To Louis Brown I owe thanks for being a kind and patient mentor to my learning whatever computermanship skills I have developed. To my brother, Barry I'd like to extend thanks for letting me know what marketing tasks I will face in publication and sale of my book, as well as supporting me emotionally. To my daughters Almeda and Stephanie, as well as my good friends John and Nancy Morcos and Paul Omelsky, I would like to offer thanks for readily offering to proofread. Lastly, I would like to thank the friends of my married life and my job for their support; they are listening to my endless diatribes about this literary venture, as well their reading excerpts from my writings.

I have rearranged dates and altered geography, but I have not altered the outcomes of history. The characters are not real, and no reflection against any real person is intended. I am only intending to express a view of what we have done to each other and what we can do.

# Introduction

In considering man's need to free humanity from cultural bindings that impede formation of natural boundaries, I would like to examine a time period when one nation asserted itself at the expense of other cultures. Though history may be replete with many eras in which this has occurred, I have chosen the time when Spain developed as an empire and a nation. It was a time of the opening up of new ideas and new worlds, but it was also a time of some men manipulating their way to power at the expense of others. Expansion into Africa by way of exploring trade routes to the orient, contacts with nations to the West of Europe, and schisms in the fabric of Christendom all coalesced in a desire to open up a new world and to impose an order on it. For this reason, we couple the discovery of unseen, unheard of vistas with the brutalities of racism, i.e. the Spanish Inquisition.

The rivalry between Christian, Jew, Moslem, Amerindian and Black originated in ancient times. Fear of the Black warrior as a formidable foe date back to fear of Hannibal and Carthage or fear of the Kushite fighter, of Ethiopia. The Romans also recalled the fierce battles for submission of Palestine and Israel. To render the Black warrior less fearful, he was conceptualized as a slave. This transformation reduced the status from threatening rival to harmless commodity. Jews were portrayed as arising out of eastern cultures that violated the Roman need for order. They became equated with magic and deviltry. Europeans regarded the Indian as a noble savage until conversion and diversion of resources were resisted. The stage was set for plunder.

At the outset of Ferdinand's and Isabella's drive for national's unity and establishment of a wealthy, Christian empire, Spain was a veritable crucible of cultural interchange. Jews, who had fled the pogroms of France and England, were welcome. Moors from North Africa also populated her cities. The discovery of Inca and Aztec gold and jewels, the unsettling emergence of Protestantism, and the need for a politico-religious alliance all interacted to convert this melting pot to a seething cauldron of intolerance. The hatred, thus formulated, was exported to the New World and exploited at home.

People that converted to Catholicism and illegally practiced Judaism were incarcerated, made to confess to crimes and sins by torture, and burned at the stake for not giving up their religion. Properties were seized, and monies were paid to secure lesser penalties. This available wealth and that expropriated from the new colonies were poured into the coffers of the governmental and inquisitorial officials alike. Portugal was embarked upon the same journey as Spain and followed the same course. What started out as fellowship and community became a hotbed of fear and hatred that was passed on and has been exploding ever since.

To connect Gideon Retta with these world events and to design him as a prototype for change, I placed him in a minority group that has valiantly fought for its identity for centuries with the ancient warrior, feared by his White rival, who conceptualized him as a commodity to hide his fear and as a practitioner of evil, magical arts. He is a Falasha, a Black Jew, of Ethiopia. Life offers this man perilous choices at four junctures in his lifetime. He learns to save his culture twice by fleeing and to fight for himself twice.

As their history denotes, the Falasha are a proud, isolated, and embattled people. I shall attempt to portray their history to illustrate how their customs are basic to the continuation of the way they have chosen to live. I also intend to show that as beings, which value our individual survival, we can accommodate a change in this fundamental pattern because we create culture; it does not create us.

Before exploring the history of this people, I shall attempt to describe their culture and what has set them apart from Ethiopians and the ancient land of the Hebrews, as well as connected them to it. The religion of the Falashas is one of Mosaism. It is based on the Pentateuch, as is it's Hebraic predecessor, but it is an Ethiopian version of it. The religious language is not Hebrew; it is Geez, the religious language of the Amhara. Their every day language is Amharic. Physically they differ from the Amhara by being darker and more corpulent with shorter faces and smaller eyes. Attire consists of turbans and Roman toga. For everyday dress, they wear short pants or a waistcloth descending to the knee. The head is shaved, and they walk barefoot.

Three classes exist in their society; Nezirim, who appear to be the priest class, Kohanim, who are ordained by the Nezirim and substitute for them in bringing religious customs outside of the Masjid, or synagogue, as we know it. The third class is the debteras, the helpers of the Kohanim.

The practice and symbolism of Judaism is also unique to the culture; many of the Jewish traditions are altered. Falasha do not celebrate Chanukah or Purim, do not wear black hats or long black coats, do not wear zizit (tassels, protruding from an outer garment) or bind their arms and foreheads with tefillen (phylacteries). The Mezuzot is not worn, nor is it on Jewish doorways. The Sabbath is personified as an angel over Sun and Rain that will precede them to Jerusalem when the Messiah comes. On Friday nights all assemble in the Masjid and commence with prayer. Food is brought into the service ahead of time, and all partake after prayer. Fasting on its eve sanctifies the new moon. Fasts include the Day of Atonement, (10th day of month), Michael's Day (12th day), Passover, and Pentecost (15th Day). The second and fifth days of the week are designated as fast days. The commemoration of the destruction of the Temple is also a time of fasting. Cele-brations are Shoferat (New Years), Day of Atonement, Ingathering (People go to mountains, give gifts to the Nezerim, pray and offer sacrifices, and pay tithes to the Kohanim). Tabernacles (People eat matzoh for seven days). In other areas, booths are built. Passover is celebrated by eating a type of bread, called shimberra, as opposed to matzoh. A solar cycle is the basis of the calendar. A month is added every four years to equalize the lunar and solar years.

Women are equal to men in social functioning except in being required to worship in a separate court of the Masjid and in being regarded as unclean during the time of their menses. At this time, they must house themselves separately from the rest of the village. A firstborn male must marry a firstborn female. The surviving male in a marriage must make a vow of chastity after the death of the wife and live as a hermit.

The Falasha do not distinguish between meat and dairy, as other Jews do. However, slaughter is strictly by ritual, and any traces of blood must be removed. Hands are washed, and certain prayers are recited before eating.

Funeral customs are similar to other Judaic rituals. Confession is made to the Nazir before death. Mourners put dust on their heads and cut themselves while the Nazir recites the prayers. The dead are buried at once in graves lined with stones. (This is reminiscent of "Schindler's List".) Grieving occurs for seven days; and offering is made on the third day, or the soul will remain in the valley of death.

The Falasha are Black Jews, whose origin and emigration are explained by several theories and by intermingling with the Agau, a Kushite tribe native to the areas. History has offered three explanations for the origins of the Falasha Jews: one: Solomon united with Sheba, of Ethiopia for purposes of establishing a trade union. This union resulted in a son, Menelik. He could not be a Jew because his maternal line was not Hebraic. Menelik became embittered, stole a Torah from the Temple in Jerusalem, and fled with his retinue to the Tekkaze River Valley, in the Senian mountains, of Ethiopia, the area of their settlement. Some crossed the river. These became Christian. Two: When the Jews left Egypt, some migrated south to Ethiopia. Moses is said to have destroyed a dam to choke off the Nile to avoid pursuit at the Tekkaze River. Foliage and mountain shrubs made the river impassable. Hence, this vale in the Senians became the home of these fleeing Hebrews. To this day, Falasha will not cross a river on the Sabbath due to Moses not crossing. Three: Dan was the black sheep of Jacob's family due to plotting against Joseph. As a tribe, Danites were noted for being warlike and adventurous. They became sailors and carried on trade with Yemen and Ethiopia.

In their travels, contact was established with Yemen, on the Arabian Peninsula. A Jewish population grew in the area. These people flourished as smiths. Moslem and Christian Arabs viewed smithing as sorcery. As in one of the Judeo-Christian-Moslem wars, Jewish captives may have been brought to the Axum-Gondar area, in Ethiopia, where the Falasha now reside. Intermarriage with the Agau people occurred, and the despised trade of smithing came with them.

Having shown the art of smithery as a cause of hatred of Jews, another cause can be attributed to their refusal to submit to the powers that be. This can be summarized as God telling them "The vengeance of the blood of Abel arrived unto me. Therefore, fight against them that fight me." In the tenth century, a hero arose. Her name was Yehudit, or Judith. She was a Falasha queen that rebelled when the Amhara tried to impose Christianity on her people. Much burning of churches and killing of priests occurred during her reign. In the thirteenth century an alliance of Amhara defeated her and ended Falasha rule. A defect in her eye became synonymous with the evil eye as well as a symbol of that evil, smithing Jew. For these reasons, Falashas were portrayed as cannibalistic hyenas, bred in Hell.

The year 1270 marks the beginning of a crusade to destroy Ethiopian Jewry with the reason given as being unreliable in turning back the sword of Islam. Thus began four hundred years of religious wars. In one of these wars, the Falasha abandoned their alliance with the Moslems and allied themselves with the Amhara and Portuguese only to be betrayed. This took place in 1541, a year that was significant to this narrative because it marks the time period of Coronado's expedition to locate the seven cities of Cibola. The Moslems attacked an area inhabited by 10-12 thousand Jews. However, the Falasha joined ranks with the Portuguese with the promise of 115 strong horses, as spoils of war and surprised their foe. After the victory, the Amhara turned on their ally and tried to wipe them out. Because of the unwanted religion, a rebellion arose under the leadership of Redai. A decisive battle was fought at Mashaka, the Hill of the Jews.

The Amhara were not prepared for the cold of the Senian Mountains. The Falasha destroyed the mule paths, threw boulders down on the advancing troops, and burned everything ahead of the advancing army. Unfortunately, the Portuguese supplied cannons to the Amhara, and the tide of the battle turned. Redai was taken prisoner; all Falasha religious literature was destroyed to erase the memory of Falasha Jewry from Ethiopia memory.

Into this world, I have thrust Gideon Retta, a man who believed in his people and loved them. Yet, he found a new surround in which he had to adapt or perish. History books describe this as an age of discovery of new ideas and an age in which a religious tradition was established. This tradition was established by trampling on not only the rights of the peoples in the new lands and the European continent but also among the peoples being manipulated in African and Asian nations that lay along trade and exploration routes which had been embarked upon.

At this apparent juncture of contradictions, I, as a creature of thought, found myself stymied and full of questions. Do our social norms define us? What role do we have in creating these rules of behavior? At what point in our development do we say "This is my call, not my culture's." In every one of us, there is a Gideon Retta, a Mark Enger, or a Kiona Almederson.

This aspect of our culture is reminiscent of the technocracy of the 1920's. Machines were made to make our lives easier; yet, they put people out of work. They seemed to assume a life of their own; Labor unions rose to hold the process in check but not without substituting their own tyranny.

Fear of the unknown, fear of rejection, and fear of standing without support block us from realizing our potential, from tailoring conditions in our surround into useful tools of adaptation, and serve to put us into a mental prison. The Inquisitors, the Spanish conquistadors in Mexico, Peru, and Colorado could have embraced their New World counter parts as fellow brothers and sisters and said: We each have something to learn and something to teach. If Amhara and Falasha could have said we instead of me the emerging bond of Kushitic peoples could have worked to make the desert bloom.

The resulting retreat into confining enclaves of support kept them from ever considering that there might be beauty beyond these supportive walls. The human tendency they followed was to keep their thinking confined to their own cellblocks.

The persistence of an incongruity between learning and clinging blindly to a tradition seems to stem from the doctrine of racism. We do not have to question how we treat other people if we don't look on them as deserving answers to life's needs as worthy as our own. Sadly, if the ill fit remains for every advance made a destructive step will follow.

At some point in our development, we have to realize that we carry the seeds of our own growth or own destruction. If we build walls around ourselves, our capacity to understand how we can harness the tools of the universe becomes impeded. The need to identify causes us to seek out our own kind. This process all too easily can allow our covetousness to take over let us assume feelings of superiority, and a right to hold back, eliminate, or subjugate others. For this reason, France, Germany, England, Spain, and Ethiopia tried to wipe out Jews. Caucasian, European powers enslaved and stole land from those with darker countenances under a falsely derived doctrine of inferiority and evil, i.e. rendering the fierce warrior of Carthage as harmless by dehumanization through slavery.

This conceptualization of a sub-human also impacted upon the European colonizer's view of the Indians. They were noble savages until the Spaniards became covetous of their gold or needed their homes for shelter. Then they thought nothing of expelling the Unchristian thing from its lair. Into this world strode Gideon Retta. Unknowingly he bore the seeds of growth.

The Amer Indian didn't begin the relationship with Europeans under the same conditions of victimization and evisceration; nor were they conceptualized as the source of evil as Blacks and Jews from the East and South were. This native of the West invoked respect for surviving without the benefits of "the civilized world." Yet he represented an obstacle to Europe's taking over this new discovery. The rivalry fostered hatred that equaled the indifference to the Black or the satanic conceptualization of the Jew.

These two strains of thought persisted in the relationship between the Spaniards and the Indians. When the Conquistadors needed shelter and clothing, they were not bothered about depriving the natives of their possessions and homes. Nor did they mind plundering the treasures or raping native women. After all, they reasoned, these people were not Christian. A noble savage was still a savage. Holy Mother Church intervened to make them eligible for slavery and serfdom.

Gideon Retta had witnessed these racist conceptualizations and lived through their expression, but he was to endure the reaction of the persecuted minority to the oppression. This may be translated as outright anger, or perhaps as identification with the aggressor.

The direct anger response is a reciprocation of the dislike received, i.e. reverse prejudice. The Pueblos saw Gideon as a mouthpiece for the White man. Therefore, they did not trust his efforts to be part of their culture. Of course, an equal amount of anger was generated in this emigrated Falasha. How he dealt with it is of evolutionary import. As our internal needs require a new set of relationships for homeostasis, we seek what we need. We are using our culture as a tool to meet our needs, not assuming subservience to cultural imperatives.

# Section I

# Mark Engler

*When I became a man,*
*I knew I would have to walk alone.*

# Chapter 1

September in Iowa was on the wane. School was starting at the University at Ames. Everyone in town was readying for the harvest and the return of the students. Among them was a rather tallish, lanky young man that grinned easily and did not get serious about too much. His hair was sandy and his eyes were a mischievous brown. His name was Marcus Aaron Engler. He had the distinction of being a senior and not knowing what he wanted out of life, college, or his own natural inclination. From the time he was a tyke, he never fitted anyone's image of him. A geometry teacher once told him his construction lines looked as if he drew them with the dirt under his nail instead of a pencil. On a basketball court, his dribbling and shooting rivaled Ichabod Crane. He could read well, but he was bored to tears with Longfellow's *Hiawatha* and looked out the window to watch a dog pee on an old lady's leg, while the class read *Thanatopsis*. This man had no idea what he wanted because everyone planned his life for him.

Once he got to the university he found he had to know why and how the world, his mind, his body, or a horse's body came to be. The quantum theory of mechanics or Wordsworth's poetic dramatization of a field of flowers gave him no answers. Mark had to know what went into developing Hammurabi's code and the conditions under which the people lived to allow such harsh justice.

Mark was not interested in these areas because he liked data or because he saw material gain from the knowledge but he wanted to understand his connection to God and the universe. Perhaps he wanted to know why William Tecumseh Sherman was a hero, and Nat Turner was a villain, or why he was taught not to speak of a Black man disparagingly, but not to sell him his house. In the psychology, anthropology, sociology courses he could formulate opinions that might slake his thirst for answers, but they evaded the enigma of how modes of thought developed.

As a boy Mark was curious about what made people tick and would engage in a conversation about any topic. People smiled at his endless questioning coupled with his gangling awkwardness. Some people saw him as an easy mark. At thirteen, he got off a school bus on a drizzly day. The school hooligan, who brandished a gun and demanded his raincoat, his wallet, and his lunch, greeted him. Mark noticed the gun was a cap pistol and tripped the rascal. He pounced on him. As they tussled, Mark saw bad bruises on his ribs. He let him up and asked from where they came. He held the butt end of the gun toward the boy if he still wanted trouble. The story that emerged was more chilling than the rain. The roughneck's father was an alcoholic, who was laid off from work. He got drunk and beat his son in a rage. Upon hearing this, Mark left the rain coat with one of the sandwiches in the pocket. The boy and Mark became friends. When he died in a shoot-out with police, Mark went in a corner and wept. His parents never knew what happened to the raincoat.

Another incident occurred when Mark was fifteen. A strapping young farm boy, whose father was president of the local Grange, publicly assaulted Mark's family name. He said, "Those damn Englers need to be run out of town. He can't stay home and tend to his farm like any other God-fearing man, but he has to traipse around the country, while his son is nosing around with any riffraff." The usually slumped over young Engler stood up with his face reddened and his lips curled in a snarl. He picked the boy up by the neck, threw him onto the ground, and screamed, keep your mouth off of my family." After that people chuckled at Mark, but his kindness was never mistaken for weakness again. Though not intimidated, Mark accepted people at face value; he was not a wheeler and dealer.

Although this young man had a healthy curiosity about the world and a basic love for those in it, he ignored the fact the he had to prepare to earn his own keep. Needless to say, he was scared. He was the oldest of two boys and looked upon his parents' lectures on thrift and work the way they had looked on Herbert Hoover's answer to the Great Depression as selling apples. Putting his entire thoughts and misgivings aside, Mark began to prepare for registration for classes. He knew he would be tied up most of the day with paying tuition, getting a part-time job and scheduling classes.

On the way to registering, he ran into two old friends; one was Arne Vogel. They studied together, drank together, hunted for women together, and came home frustrated together. They had decided to room together last year, but Arne had changed his mind at the last minute because of some new exchange program abroad. Mark made a mental note to talk to him about it. The second friend was Cheri Fridor; he had met her at a rally protesting Serbian brutality to Bosnian prisoners of war. She was so vociferous in her opinion that he laughed and began to use a pencil as a bandleader's baton to conduct the harmony of her yelling. After this icebreaker, they both laughed. They began to study together, see movies or attend plays, or to have dinner together. They were starting to get affectionate, but neither one wanted a serious relationship. He saw her bend over to pick up a book, but she did not see him. Today he just enjoyed the view. "Oh well, he thought," A nice tush is not a bad way to start the day."

Back to business. He was at the administration building. After he entered the feeling of summer vacation being over set in. He had spent the summer loading trucks for his father's trucking company. There he had met and talked with several different characters. He had learned much about history and culture from them. There was Abe Fromkiss. He was involved with Arnold Rothstein, the gangster, buying and smuggling rum from Canada. Because Elliot Ness and the government were getting too close, he ran away to Europe. Hitler was on the rampage, and Abe was identified as a Jew. He spent the war at Majdanek. The horrors he saw there were worse than any prison. Russell Tiawa was another man with a story to tell. He left the reservation in North Dakota, as a virile, young man in 1938. No work was available if you were not White. He made his way to Duluth and stowed away on a boat to China. The invading Japanese tore apart the town at which he had docked. He was so violently angered at what he saw, that he sought out Claire Chennault, learned to fly an airplane, and became one of the Flying Tigers.

Recovering from his reverie, Mark wallowed in self-pity because he was forced to learn about life from books, not the way his summer companions had. The thought of work brought him back to reality. He went through line and paid his fees. The next task was formidable. He had made out a tentative schedule over the summer. Now he had to haggle over being shut out of classes, reshuffling time frames, and remembered he had to allow himself time to work. After he had spent three hours haranguing, wheedling, and pleading with an old bag of a clerk and an old stuffed shirt of a counselor, the imbecility was finished.

The next plateau was the university employment office. On his way out of the building, the job bulletin board caught his eye. If he found something interesting, he could save himself a trip. About halfway down the page he saw the ad:

Are you interested in studying abroad?
Join our expedition to Yucatan.
We will resurrect Mayan ruins and study this historic culture.
Twenty-five semester credit hours are available.
The trip will be paid by American Historical Society.
If interested contact Professor Maxim Horton.
Rhambo Hall, Office 10

"Very interesting," thought Mark. He copied down the ad and left the building. He also copied two other good possibilities. The first interview was with Dr. Woldman, an economics professor. He needed someone to grade midterms and papers, as well as to Proctor exams. The Doc was impressed with the fact Mark had made a "B" in Macroeconomics and an "A" in Microeconomics. He was also impressed with his understanding of the differential relationship between the supply and demand curves. He did not like the fact that Mark was not an economics or a business major. He also did not like the "C" in calculus. Mark told him that the course name reminded him of the medical term for a kidney stone, and he developed a bladder problem that caused him problems in concentration. Dr. Woldman, burst out laughing and said "I ought to throw you out on your rear, but it took smarts to think of that and guts to tell it." He told Mark to be at a briefing to-

4

morrow evening at 5:30. After that, he went to Diamond's Deli to see if he could get his old job back, working for meals. Bar Kochba Fenzel, the owner, affectionately known as Bartie, liked this lanky farm boy. He made him smile. He would talk to anyone about anything, and they left the conversation feeling they had taught him something valuable. He could use Mark at 11:00 a.m. and at 5:00 p.m. for an hour of waiting tables and bussing. He would eat after that.

Now Mark was resigned to the fact that the summer was over. He drove his impala to the apartment he and Arne shared, at least until he left in two weeks. Mark reached in his shirt pocket and pulled out a piece of paper. It was Professor Horton's ad. He put it on his bulletin board for future reference, in case things did not work with Professor Woldman. His life for nine months would be studying at the library from 7:00 until 11:00, taking a shower, and hitting the sack. On weekends, Cherie would invite him over her apartment if her roommate were gone. Such was the school year. Mark was tired of being a student. He wanted to be about the business of earning a living. After all, he was old enough to do so.

Arne came in and threw himself down on the bed. "Jesus Christ, I am sick to hell of this town, this campus and kissing a professor's behind to make the right professional impression so I can spend the rest of my life brown-nosing another moron to be able to earn my keep. At least in two weeks I'll be in another country showing other people what I've learned about building bridges and learning how they build them over there." Arne liked the idea of learning from others by exchanging ideas. That way people were equals and contributed to whatever process they shared. This quality cemented his and Mark's friendship.

Arne's outburst seemed to have a potentiating effect on Mark's previous thoughts about continuing to be trapped in a kid's life. Over the next few days, he thought about it increasingly. When Cherie and he studied together, she commented about his moodiness. On Saturday night, they went to see the University player's' production of Tennessee Williams' "The Glass Menagerie." Mark really empathized with Tom's last line, which talked about a violently changing world. Cherie sensed his uneasiness and invited him to her apartment. After coaxing him to neck with her on the couch, she asked him what had been eating at him all week. Mark did not want to discuss the matter. She began to cuddle him and to draw him closer to her. She sat on his lap and started to draw him closer to her. She moved her torso against him. Mark began to probe her mouth and to kiss her more seekingly. Suddenly, she stopped his advance and held his hands away, asking what was wrong. Regaining his composure, he took his head in his hands and told her, "I feel as if I'm losing my common sense." He related the conflict within him. The feelings of academia being a suppressor of his need to be a man, the sense of impressing and not controlling or doing, and the general feeling of learning to produce for a prof's gain all poured out of him.

Cherie drew him to her and unbuttoned her blouse. She held him against her breasts and did not stop him as he unhooked her brassiere. He nuzzled her; and she held him tightly. Cherie put her hands around his head and said, "O.K., Big Boy that's as far as we go tonight, you need to be sure of yourself before we can go further."

Groaning, he asked how she expected him to walk home in his condition, they both laughed and he left and drove the impala home. He knew now that Cherie liked him but was not ready for a commitment. Was this because he had the demeanor of a college boy and not a man or did his uncertainty generate uncertainty in her because of fear of her attraction to him? He intended to find out in the next two weeks.

Sunday was a lazy day for Mark. He and Arne went out for brunch at Bartie's. He ate a meal of lox and scrambled eggs. Arne wanted to go play ball with some friends. Mark wanted to be alone to mull over last week's and last night's events.

He had not really established an intimate relationship with Cherie. He liked her enough, and she liked him. He could not assess the depth of her feeling for him. Last night's little tease made him feel she was looking for a stereotype of a man that showed only strength and sure footedness. He grinned and thought she might need a bear or a moose. "Oh well, he thought, we enjoy each other's company, and there will be more opportunities. She feels nice anyway."

The last thought warded off the fear and uncertainty of the ideation he was trying to suppress into his subconscious. However, it would not go away. When he got back to his apartment, a telephone call was on his answering machine. It was Cherie wanting to know if Mark wanted to go for a walk in the brisk autumn weather. He called her number and explained that he had to work out some things that were bothering him. She agreed to meet him for dinner at 5:30, and they would study together. Back came-suppressed feeling of being a man in the world of a kid. Mark yearned for a solution like Arne's. Then it hit him. After class, he resolved to contact Professor Horton. The mountains of Yucatan loomed before his mind's eye. He might have to stay put this semester, but excitement about his potential adventure had replaced his doldrums.

Mark was all excited in class and at work on Monday. It turned out that he had Professor Horton for his Intermediate Archeology course. Instead of calling him, he could discuss arranging an appointment after class. There seemed to be a million people with questions about the lecture or the course or initiation of the brown-nosing process.

Finally, Professor Horton got to Mark. "Yes, young man. How may I help you?" "I saw this ad on the bulletin board, and I'm very interested in participating in the project." Mark went on to describe his interest in knowing what makes people tick. He told the professor how different cultures had fascinated him for years. He related that he had learned Spanish in high school and had supplemented what he had learned by speaking with friends of various Hispanic origins at his summer jobs. He also added that he had corresponded with a couple Indian groups, regarding their sending him language tapes and had begun to try his hand at learning some of the sound nuances of the words.

Needless to say, the teacher was impressed with the earnestness and sincerity of this young man. However, he had just been assaulted by a mass of students, some of which showed the honesty of a counterfeit two-dollar bill. Professor Horton rose to his full height and asked Mark how much he knew about the legend of Quetzalcoatl. Mark knew that he was a Mayan king that had disgraced himself and left his people, vowing to return. The mentor indicated that this student had a novice's knowledge of the legend. He also stated that the purpose of the expedition was to retrieve data about this myth to either corroborate it as historical fact or debunk it as a story. The trip would take place next semester. Professor Horton wanted Mark to learn all he could about the legend and relate what he found out one week from today. This would decide whether he would be going.

# Chapter 2

Mark spent the next week learning about the facts and legend of Quetzalcoatl and the Mayan people. The people were a blend of several warring tribes around the geography of Yucatan. The Toltec and Putun Maya intermingled with each other and their Mexican neighbors in the tenth century. Quetzalcoatl allegedly was traced to Atlantis. He and his followers spread civilization to other people. Another mythology stated he was a Norseman. His name translated to mean feathered serpent. After the collapse of the ruler, Teotihuacan, in the city, Chichen Itza, the Toltecs settled in the city, called Tula. A priest of this city took the name of the feathered snake. He brought many of the trappings of culture to this Toltec civilization, as well as fame and respect. According to the legend, an enemy bewitched him, ruined him, and drove him from Tula. He ended his glory by disappearing from the Mayan culture with a vow to return. To lend credence to his legendary status as a God, various accounts of his demise and resurrection have been offered. He is said to have fled to the East and to have disappeared from the edge of the waters.

Another account describes him casting himself into a great fire. His heart emerged from the flames as Venus, the morning star. In another story, he sailed east on a raft of serpents. Regardless of how he vanished, Quetzalcoatl was thought of as a God. Feathered serpents with a plumed body decorate all the buildings. These same designs decked the altars where human hearts were sacrificed to the serpent God. This may have been evidenced by what appeared to be blood like discoloration around the sternum area of skeletal remains at the religious structure.

Professor Horton seemed impressed that Mark had done some homework. However, he wanted dedicated young men and women to take part in the project. Subsequently he began to dig away at Mark's past and present motivations to build a collage of Mark's persona elements and to ascertain whether or not this symbolic construction could be transplanted to Yucatan. He began to tease away at what made him give away his raincoat or assume such a rapt interest in Abe Fromkiss' and Russel Tiawa's stories, what plans he had with Cherie, what drew him to Arne. The area that seemed of most vital concern was what would Mark's parent's response to the project be.

Because of the grueling questions, Mark felt put on the spot. In an angry, defensive tone, he asked the professor why this program required such intimate inquiry. For a second Professor Horton wanted to dismiss this impertinent lout, but he recalled the response, he had so long ago at his interview for his first teaching position. Therefore, he tempered his anger and explained the hologram he was trying to conceptualize.

Mark explained his need to know how, why, and wherefore of collective thought processes developed in particular areas. He also elucidated upon his endless thirst to understand how he could please those who nurtured him, yet carve a corner of life for himself. Professor Horton found himself mesmerized by this description of a quest that had driven him, as a young man. At the time, the search was equal to Galahad's ordeal to find the Holy Grail. He knew that this man had to unravel the past to weave his future out of the ancient tapestry into a new one. He knew he needed his driving imperative, but he feared for him.

Mark was reared by the generation that had experienced the ravages of the tail end of the depression and the war. His parents were thrifty people with common sense and survival values. They passed their ideas onto their son. However, in their love inspired schemata, they forgot that mark was a person not a possession. The fact that their world had changed was not included in the planning. At this point in time, Mark had to establish that either his parents set his goals, or he did. To sell himself in the prof's eyes, a firm commitment had to be demonstrated. He said to Professor Horton, "I have to sink or swim alone. My parents cannot be in my skin. I need this experience so bad I can taste it. If I have to go to war, so be it."

This young man's dedication and commitment visibly moved Professor Horton. He had also tolerated ostracism from his family until he was able to demonstrate success. "Someday you may hate me for this decision, but welcome to heaven or hell." With this passing of the final test, the two shook hands. The big test would be this weekend when he discussed this exciting event with his father.

He went home to discuss the afternoon events with Arne. His roommate was excited and happy for him. About breaking the news to his parents, Arne seemed to have a plethora of ideas. The first ideas was that Mark had to present himself as a take charge person and not come to his father like a child asking for permission to live his own life. He also felt Mark should show his mother that she had a man-child that had broken the tie of the apron strings. In fact, he raised his beer glass in a toast to the severance of the umbilicus. Arne actually felt a potpourri of responses to his forthcoming departure. He would deeply miss this last remnant of his passing youth. The Friday night beer drinking, the chasing after hot women, the ball games, both as spectators and as participants, the brain pounding study sessions would be relegated to the status of cherished memories. Ahead the road was challenging, potentially fruitful, and ominous. He knew he would miss the acceptance and familiarity of this friendship. He also felt a sense of guilt about leaving Mark to face his last year at school with all its uncertainties alone. Now that he knew that Mark was embarking on a venture similar to his own, he wanted to be as available as a friend could be. He shared the nuances of parental resistance to the former adolescent perceiving himself and herself as creating a place in the sun by his and her own deductive and inductive skills. Arne had to fight tooth and nail for every scrap of respect for his decision made outside of the auspices of parental guidance. He shared the reasoning and methodology that brought him success.

Mark's experience with Cherie assumed a different format. She noticed right away that he seemed to be more self-assured and at peace with himself. There was a mingling of the pique of curiosity and sexual attraction that motivated her to explore what had transpired. She was genuinely happy that Mark had been creative enough to devise the solution of building a life for himself abroad. However, she resented not being available to be a guiding light to him or to share fruition of adaptation to the struggles inherent in learning a new way of life. In her perception, a woman should guide a man where she wants him and let him think it's achieved, as a function of his manly leadership. Due to this duality of motivation Cherie decided to dissuade Mark from his resolve to leave and to test her hold on him.

On the Monday after the decision was made, Cherie first noticed that Mark was no longer at loose ends. He went at his statistics course with a zeal she had not seen before. In fact, this surprised her because he hated the subject. On their study break she slipped her arm through his and snuggled against him while they stepped outside to look at the evening sky. She took him by the hand and led him to the kissing circle.

She told him how proud she was because he did not allow his fears of an uncertain future to deter him from grabbing a piece of identity for himself. With that announcement, she lifted her face up to his and gave him a warm kiss. "What manner of distortion of my lofty educational goals are you plotting," said Mark with a smirk. He took her hand, and they went back into the library to resume their studying. He was already trying to master some of the Mayan dialects that persist in present day Yucatan. This was the assignment in Dr. Horton's class. Cherie was preoccupied with an interior design course in pursuit of an architecture degree. After the library closed, Cherie invited him up to her apartment to watch the news.

She took his hand and led him to the couch, seating herself next to him. She fluffed a pillow behind him and got up to fix him a sandwich. She made sure as she walked by him, that he noticed that she was not wearing any panties under her snug fitting pants. Upon her return she set the plate on the coffee table in front of him and sat on his lap. He could feel himself responding, according to calculations. She began to reach under his polo shirt and was trying to ease it off while kissing him with a growing intensity of passion. Mark was not unaware that this scene was contrived. He could not figure just what Cherie's angle was, but he liked the geometry of getting there. With a growing passion, they began to undress each other. Mark picked her up and found his way to her bedroom feeling like a combination of Rhett Butler and

12

Dumbo, the elephant. They felt like two friends engaging in a mutual adventure. It was an act with much laughter and feelings of camaraderie. After it was over, they both laughed. Cherie smiled as she said, "I can't say I won't do this again. It was fun, but I do not love you. Some woman that catches you will get quite a man. I know this and I'll smile at the memory of this night for the rest of my life." When Mark heard this, he felt relief and expressed it by prancing around the bed naked holding an imaginary cigar in his hand, saying "That's the most ridiculous thing I've ever heard." With the seduction accomplished, they both laughed and fell asleep.

Both of these young people acknowledged to each other that they found each other attractive, but that there was not enough chemistry between them to commit themselves, yet they had regard for each other. However, it developed as a result of trying the culturally appropriate formula for building a relationship. What was right for each of them, and what did they have to go through to find it? Mark felt he was at the point in his life at which he had begun to look.

He surmised that the building blocks for this new life lay to the South in Yucatan. There he could link the patterns of a past civilization with people who are striving to bring forth their impact on the face of the world. Finding the links provided a way for him to discover the application to the search for his own riddle of existence. One answer he had found was that he wanted a companion that was more in tune with him than Cherie. She was fun and made a good friend. Sex with her was good, but any kind of relationship with her bore the price tag of demonstrating mastery of his own life principle. He did not feel this level of competency. Even if he did, he felt a companion should earn the right to share this ability to strive rather than have it bestowed upon her. Then Mark learned from his discussions with Arne that he could expect parental resistance to the project. He spent his last half-hour awake developing counter arguments to potential arguments his parents could contrive. He looked forward to the upcoming weekend when his father and he would get together. Mark planned to have a talk with his parents about Yucatan and possibly involve Professor Horton. He agreed to participate and to speak on behalf of Mark's making the trip.

Jack Engler came from the American Midwest. He believed that a man paved his own way and took care of his own before he embarked on pleasure trips or went traipsing off to God knows where to save mankind. His wife shared the same conceptualization. The only time she was separated from her high school sweetheart and husband, which condition was brought about by the draft board, was when he went to war for his country to rid the world of the Nipponese menace. He sustained a leg wound after climbing the wing of a moving Zero on board the aircraft carrier, Arizona. A kamikaze pilot had landed on the deck and was trying to ram the tower to destroy the carrier. Jack was given The Navy Cross. He did not appreciate non-white peoples after this episode. After the war, he became a trucker and saved his money to start his own firm, his wife, Bertha, was his business manager. They shared the same risks, tribulations, triumphs, and value system. Mark knew he was playing against a stacked deck, and he hoped Professor Horton would even out the odds.

After the game and dinner, the family settled down for an evening of talk and bringing each other up to date. Professor Horton had met the family, and he became a part of the reunion. Mark's parents were all questions about the project.

Jack asked his son how this could be connected to the practical task of learning how to make a living. He went back to the biblical expulsion of Adam and Eve from the Garden of Eden with the dictum of having to earn their bread by the sweat of their brows. Mark tried to give him an answer that would make sense to him. "Dad, I'm not you. You went through the depression to learn what is valuable to your life; you survived a bloody war so we could be here to carry out what you fought for. Our survival is different. No one is setting himself up as the Fuhrer of a master race because we will not allow it due to what your sacrifices taught us. I need to know how to live and let live when we are all covetous, and we have developed weapons that can destroy us all."

At this point, Bertha chimed in. "Your father had the boy hood you're debating about giving up fairly shot out from under him. To-gether, we built a business to shut out the covetousness of others. We built it by knowing what we wanted and making sure that those who were needy due to their own lack of gumption could not take it from us. Historically these gutless people are immigrants to this country and try to take over our country, or they stay in their own impoverished countries and call us selfish Gringos or power lusting white men. Your father went to war against these Rotters and built a solid business. Your education needs to center around pre-paring to take it over and pass it over to our grandchildren."

Reflexly Mark could feel the heat rising to his face. His eyes began to bulge, and his physiognomy started to redden. He shouted, "What the hell did you fight the war for. Did you know that selfishness is not all a virtue? White men did rise to wealth by seizing a country from its native populations, enslaving and using an entire race of people with excuses like you just gave me. In addition, you seem to forget that the very people that came here seeking freedom denied it to others. I want to build something for myself, but I do not want it to be on the backs of others. That is against God's law, the God you taught me to love and respect. Some day I may want to take over management of this business with my brother or manage my own, but I have to know that I am building and creating not stepping on someone because I need to figure out where I have been and where I want to go. I have tried to listen to your advice, but you are my teachers, not my Gods. This is my time to sink or swim by myself."

Jack was beginning to feel that the fundamental concepts that guided him through a nasty, conniving, and grasping world were presented as evil. He did not see the institutional racism in his thinking or the deliberately contrived racist thinking. He thought his son needed some lessons in the hard knocks of life. Therefore, he responded to Mark's challenge, as this was how he received what he had said. "Since you want to build your own dream, I'm going to give you an ample opportunity. You can damn well pay for this irresponsible little jaunt yourself. I will not subsidize it. On your own is what you want. On your own is what you'll be."

Professor Horton thought that this might be an appropriate moment for the intervention Mark sought from him. He said that finding one's self is part of the experience of growing up and of education. He further stated that the depression and the war were the growing fields that he, Jack, and Bertha shared, but they were distorted because, theoretically, the right for everyone to have an even chance had been won by the war and the New Deal, now we had to look at what this means both within and without our previous adjustment patterns. To build a new knowledge base, we, of necessity, need to connect it with the old. If Jack could not see his way clear to help his son with this vital aspect of his maturation, he would do so. He expressed a willingness to explore grants, loans, and scholar-ships, job opportunities.

To this, Jack stated that he did not trust giveaway programs because there always was a hidden agenda. Mark told him that since he would not be footing any bills, he had surrendered any directive capacity.

He also stated emphatically that if his father could not see helping his son grow into his own life. He did not need charity. He would accumulate whatever debt was necessary, but he would also pay it. As of today, Mark Engler was his own man.

Jack was quite taken aback. He was immensely proud of his son, even prouder than he was the day he stood up to that Grange bully. Was he being the same bully in the guise of a loving father?

Regardless of how he perceived the change in their relationship, Mark had cut himself a swath of his own territoriality and would not tolerate gentle manipulative persuasion, threats of being cut off without a cent, or being banned from the family. A ship can only have one captain; now Captain Mark would have to find his own ship.

Jack was amazed to find that the gentle, inquisitive, gangling boy he raised was capable of climbing up the wing of a Jap Zero and shooting a suicidal kamikaze pilot, as his father had been.

Bert was also moved by her son's obstinacy and the sense of being able to appreciate the lessons he had been taught yet to be able to say the time had arrived for him to be his own teacher. Awareness of this side of Mark was not new. She first found out about this quirk when she discovered through one of her son's friends that he gave a perfectly good raincoat to a punk that tried to rob him with a cap gun and lost the fight. This occurred despite the fact that respect for hard-earned property had been ingrained into him. A couple years later, he discreetly isolated himself and cried when the self-fulfilling prophecy took place with the little hoodlum. She remembered her response to this kind of stuff was to carry bricks in her purse and to aim for whatever anatomical target would drive her assailant to consider his own pain before inflicting any more on her. There was no moment of compassion, only relief. Bert envied her son's capacity to love as Christians were supposed to love. What is more he never preached it to another soul, but reserved it for himself to feel. It was like the blind love for home and hearth that impelled her Jack to climb that zero.

The factors that motivated Mark were the same ones that had been tearing at his soul since the days of his youth when he encountered people who were different from each other, and certainly different from him. He saw that their struggles were not to conquer or to fight back, but just to be.

He felt a need, an impulse, to reach beyond the centuries and to filter, siphon out and reconstitute all that man has was to apply the hodgepodge of the remainder to develop a being free of hate, revulsion, and revenge. He felt that he wanted to be free of the almost paranoid state in which most people found themselves. To accomplish this feat, he would have to look into the past and assimilate the data into a pattern that provided a springboard for philosophical amalgamation into a more flexible schema. Was this do able? He wanted to make this trip and see. A utilitarian student of digestion may have captured the essence of Mark's dilemma when he said, "The proof of the pudding is in the eating."

The summation of the weekend was that Mark's parents began to view him with a new respect, but it was not a respect free of cost. The decision to strike out in his own though admirable represented a movement away from the way of thinking that meant survival to his parents. The unspoken communication was "Sorry, Mom and Dad, you're teachings were not good enough for me. It's been good knowing you, I'm going my way now." That was not the way Mark intended the difference to be resolved. He had envisioned Mom and Dad reluctantly but proudly accepting that their son had become a man. In reality, this had happened, but Mark was not ready to have his cake and not eat it. Maturity is not a half-stepping process.

Many have described the process Mark was beginning as the time

of being alone. The comfort of not having to take a stand for one's belief or choice of a life companion or one's life work leaves scars that
either heal or fester in a sore of anger. What happens when we go our
own way? This is a lonely time, a time of unease. It is also a time of
building a time of structuring the Mark Engler who would be pursuing
his own career, raising his own kids, and ultimately facing his maker
for what he did with his life.

# Chapter 3

Now that the tension from the parental confrontation had subsided, Mark had resolved to enjoy his time with Arne and Cherie. He did not know if or when their paths would cross again after this brief interlude. What was so frightening was the unreal feeling that he was interacting with a shade, as Odysseus had done when he had traveled to Hades. Hence, he became more fervent in his attempts to preserve the relationships. All three would go on hikes or ride bikes; study sessions assumed a triumvirate status. At times, this became annoying to each and both of them. The waning sexual interest between Cherie and Mark was at least a contributory factor. Cherie and Mark still studied together, and went to movies and other weekend activities together, but visits to Cherie's seemed to be less frequent. They both felt a little afraid of the directional sensuality that had been released by their night of passion.

Beneath the surface lay the manipulator machinations, which covered a need to preserve the status quo. Cherie discovered that Mark was not putty in her hands, and she felt deflated. Mark saw Cherie's seduction behavior as castrating. He liked Cherie well enough, and he liked sex well enough, but he did not like being used for a person's entertainment and told he was not loved. That women had been abused this way for centuries was inconsequential to him He did not enjoy being a fall guy. He still found her attractive and wanted her friendship.

On the other hand, Mark and Arne clung to their adolescent bond as if they feared the lonely sojourn connected with maturing males. After this year, they would enjoy occasional get together, but their families and careers would be the major preoccupations of their lives. Therefore, the times they spent together were quality times. They saw humor in many mundane tasks. Mutual appeals to the senses were shared to the most minute degree. Acute exaggerations of empathy and over concern for one action effect on the other seemed to dominate their every action. The tide turned when Arne refused to chide Mark for missing a touchdown pass he threw. "For Christ sake, Arne, you're allowed to tell me when I fuck up. "Apples wouldn't grow in Minneapolis if it didn't rain," was all that Mark needed to say. For the rest of Arne's two weeks, their friendship was natural.

They each knew the unknown was in front of them, but they also knew that they negotiated with life to find each other, could continue to do so without each other, and could find each other if need be. As the Good Book said, "When I was a child, I spoke as a child, but when I became a man, I put the stuff of childhood behind me."

Professor Horton added another dimension to the remaining time. Besides learning a whole lot of archeology, customs, languages and dialects of Yucatan, and actual physical features of the land, he had to maintain grades in his other courses. Sexual and romantic fantasies went by the way side; Mark and Cherie became virtual bookworms, but occasionally they would pass a kiss.

Mark began an intensive study of not only the Mayan culture, but also the entire mindset of the Spanish and Portuguese up to the discovery of America. Spain actually had been a cultural crucible; much like America had been for many European groups. The Mediterranean Sea joined parts of Africa, Asia and Europe. The ancient Greeks colonized Sicily. What became of this colony? Julius Caesar fought Visigoths in this land. Where did they originate? Was it from this colony? From whence came the Etruscan civilization? Were they from this colony, or did they represent an intermingling of these early Sicilians with the Visigoths? Moslems settled in Spain. Were they Moors, who wearied of the militancy of spreading Islam by the sword, or were they loyal servants of the sultanate that thought unity of a world under Allah could only be achieved by militancy, Jews also fled to this melting pot when they saw that their necks were the price of their identity. At any rate, Spain began to view unity in the form of a Christian domain as being on the cutting edge of self-aggrandizement.

What's more this innovative view seemed to dominate more than

Spain. The legendary liberality of the enlightened Germany in the nineteenth century, the democratizing verbiage and paternalism abroad of Britain, France, and The United States appear to have had their origins from cultural crossroads, as did Spain. The sources of the political backlashes that denied freedom to others, created minorities, and submerged nationalities stemmed from these roots.

Mark felt he had to go to a culture where these roots began to enmesh for the simple fact that he did not want to raise children learning to hate. Hatred did not seem to be the lesson that any spirituality, about which he cared, taught. If two devastating cataclysms were fought to "make the world safe for democracy" why not practice what so many had died for, instead of hiding it's tenets behind lies and half truths because loopholes were there for the greedy. The search bore an apparent tangle of infinite Machiavellian maneuvers. Mark did not know whether he was scholar enough or man enough to delve into this complex web, but he wanted a better world for his children, as any parent does. He believed the adage: "If you go at the world with what you've got, you'll get what you've gotten."

To get to these quests for truth, Mark also knew he would have to develop skills to be able to look and to interpret what he saw. The archeology course showed him how to correlate what he found in different layers with behavior in varying time eras. Another valuable time measuring tool with which Mark was to gain facility was carbonating. Over times organic materials, which contained carbon, underwent erosive changes due to alterations in the structure of the carbon atom. These chemical modifications resulted in a new element springing from the original carbon molecule. The time in which the carbon atom took to become another element was called the half-life. Thus, the date at which carbon was replaced by another element could determine the date of the artifact. Other useful techniques that became part of Mark's repertoire were counting the number of rings in tree stumps or layers of bark, counting the rings in a cob of corn, looking for evidence of plants or metal or tool usage during characteristic time eras. In short, he was fleshing out his professional knowledge base so that he resembled an archeologist.

Mark also reminded himself that his journey was connected with the mysterious legend of Quetzalcoatl. He was worshiped as a God because he brought knowledge of the arts and sciences, as well principles of a wise jurisprudence. According to the legend, he came from a land to the East and wore a beard. In other literature, he was depicted as a Norseman. He was symbolically represented, as a snake. This puzzled Mark. He could not understand how the purveyor of knowledge was regarded to be evil. It was as if the Mayas knew the parable of the Garden of Eden. This riddle gave Mark cause to reflect on a concept that had subconsciously been teasing his brain for years. The similarity in either mythological or historical explanation brought to mind another parallel in the pantheism of two cultures. The story of the Flood in the Old Testament had a striking similarity to the Gilgamesh legend of the Babylonians. From the extrapolation of this data, Mark developed a concept that would drive his research for years to come.

The belief that we share a commonality and awareness that we share similar explanations of our life patterns across culturally disparate lines suggests that there is more connecting us than dividing us. If these connections can be found, perhaps they can be made to justify the idea that differences, such as who was Ishmael's or Isaac's mother, or whether Ham saw his father indisposed and drunk had nothing to do with defining class distinctions and privilege. It was even within the realm of possibility that men could accept or reject each other based on individual behavior rather than artificially contrived standards culturally defined by segments separated from their common bonding as God's children.

Mark had always felt that something was missing in his relationships with people. The memories of Abe Fromkiss and Russell Tiawa returned and came to haunt Mark. He could not understand how the cataclysms that these men and his father had endured left them only a temporary expanding of their ideas of how men related. He was further puzzled by the return to prejudice and isolated groupings that brought back the messes over which they fought in the first place. Maybe the students could unlock the riddle in Yucatan. He thought of his young friend who had made the choice sordidly that had led him to death. Mark had wept alone because no one would step out of the preconceived notion that taking a risk for someone who had stepped beyond the defined parameters of appropriate behavior was threatening to the status quo. It seemed to Mark's mind's eye that man kind, over the centuries, taught itself not to see the forest for the trees. He feared unless the concept distortion, which started God knows when, was set right that there would be no forests or trees. Something had to be done to show human kind that isolated identification led to self-destruction. The unenviable position in which Mark now found himself was the one of going against established standards. Though flexibility and risk taking held the promise of more fruitful results for all of us, no precedent was available to provide a guarantee. The task with which this journey into the past charged him was to find such a precedent.

The history that Mark knew and the tomes of it that he did not know were filled with man's inflexibility to man, and the collapse of whatever culture was represented. One of the most tragic examples was the civilization of ancient Greece. The beautifully conceived principles of democracy developed by these city states were not to be passed on for a long time because each entity was concerned not with what is good for the whole but what ensured survival to each individual that truth required self knowledge. This could have meant "Be aware of the convenient lies you tell yourself in dealing with others." If the practice of democracy is restricted only to our own kind, what is this democracy? In Revolutionary, France the cry of the day was Liberate, Egalite, and Fraternite. This was followed up by centuries of bullying, usurpation of resources and outright tyranny in Asia, Africa, and parts of North and South America. Part of truth is what we learn about ourselves by listening to others, not drowning them out.

Mark understood his parents were only reacting to having to absorb and or recognize a new component to the truth they had perceived about life. The interfering mechanism was a need to maintain a sense of balance of forces in their lives. Interjection of new concepts was too frightening to them. He also realized that his life was not there, and he knew that he could not live in Jack's shadow. Unfortunately, the needed precedent was not there to guide him. He felt like Kepler or Copernicus, except his discovery was that the old theorems did not work. Where did the new conceptualizations lie? The young student of life could not help but wonder what answers this ancient culture would have for him.

The Mayan and Aztec civilizations have been presented as versions of ancient Greece and Rome. The Mayan culture has been depicted as a loosely connected conglomeration of city-states that could not federate because, like the Hellenic cities of their European counterpart, they could not find the common ground to cement their differences. The quandary was to find a way to help disparate peoples listen to each other, yet respect each other's differences (Present history demonstrates that the enforced conceptualization of a melting pot does not work). On the other hand, the fact that neither culture exists is a testimony to the difficulty of integrating unproven, untried ideas with the thinking that has meant survival. Yet a new culture did emerge from the old, from several old ones; it is Mexico. Where were the ingredients for this amalgamation found? This is the challenge Mark chose to have thrust upon his shoulders. If this Atlas shrugged, the riddle might or might not be as tantalizing to someone else. At any rate, this young idealist would have to stand alone.

# Section II

# Kiona Almederson

*Am I my sister's keeper?*

# Chapter 1

If Kiona liked anything about Akron, it was the beauty of autumn. The trees turned all kinds of breath-taking colors. Cider was always on tap, and Akron University got in gear for football season. Her father was the first Afro-American with a full professorship on campus twenty years ago. He taught philosophy. Her mother, Ruthena Blanchard Almederson was the toughest nursing instructor on Akron's campus. She started out as a nurse's aide, went to school all the way through nurse practitioner, and was immediately hired by Akron upon presentation of her credentials. While she was a young nurse at Akron City hospital, two thugs tried to accost her late at night in the parking lot. She reached for the mace in her purse. She noticed one was White and one was Black. Out of nowhere came a tall dark figure. The next thing she knew, her ears picked up the sound of a cracking elbow. The White boy's arm was hanging. The angry Black man was brandishing a knife. Ruthena threw her Mace can to him, and a face full of mist hit the assailant's eyes. To Ruthena's astonishment, the tall figure speedily handcuffed the would be attackers to each other and called the police by walkie-talkie. While awaiting the arrival of the law, he introduced himself, as Mighty Mouse. She found out his name was Grady Almederson, and he was going to college and working at night, as a security guard. Two days later, she left a can of Mace at his guard post with a note:"My new Mace wants to meet my old Mace can over a cup of coffee in the cafeteria. I eat lunch at 11:30.

At 11:45, in strode Mr. Almederson, carrying a bouquet of violets. Ruthena yelled out, "Yoo Hoo, Mousie, right here." Grady went over to her table with a grin on his face. "How did you find my guard post?" Ruth said she put cheese around at different spots until the right mouse showed up. From then on, they studied together and were never apart until they married.

Kiona was their only child. She grew up as the apple of her Daddy's eye and under the stern protectiveness of her mother. All through school she got better than average grades and was said to work below her full potential. There were always boys around, to be kept at the appropriate distance by Mother and to be scrutinized by Daddy.

The sixties were years of awakening and awareness. Kiona learned to weep for Dr. Martin Luther King II, to anger for Malcolm X, and to march for Civil Rights, and against the Vietnam War; she lived through Watergate The Jackson Five, Motown, Carter Country, and Reaganomics. Then came the preparation for college. The debate started. Kiona wanted to experience and build her own life. Daddy wanted to make sure his little girl got the full benefit of a good old-fashioned education. This could only be achieved at home under his tutelage. Mother wanted Kiona learn to be her own woman, but she didn't want irresponsible young men around her daughter away from her practiced eye. Kiona was readily accepted at Akron. Her father was delighted, but her mother was cooler to the idea and left her apparently maturing daughter the loop hole of possibly transferring to an out of state school in her second year. Kiona had other ideas, but kept them submerged from her parents' discussions. A bargaining point Mom and Dad used was her full scholarship to Akron. However, this bargaining agent had other uses.

Over Christmas break, Kiona had arranged to visit the University of Colorado. She was impressed with the feeling that this area had a past history of multicultural exposure. She was motivated and stimulated by this. She was out of the league of Midwestern practicality and structuring of thought. The head of the history department asked her why she wanted to be a history major. For the first time in her life, Kiona coalesced several thoughts and feelings that had been submerged in her ego for more years than she realized.

As results, doors that many Black people had learned to tolerate being shut were opened. Kiona expressed an anger towards America for recognizing that a back drop of the great Roman culture excused Mafia killings, or Dutch Schultz was ignored, and the courage of the Jews at Masada was remembered. However, when an Afro-American was guilty of misbehavior, the heritage of Hannibal was not remembered, nor was the establishment of a trading center at Timbuktu by the Mali civilization even considered. What jogged the memory cells of the average American was that the poor devil came here from a backward culture as a slave. The origin is even branded in terms of a curse that was inflicted because Noah was indiscreet. The young lady went on to clarify that her culture was maligned.

As a history student Kiona hoped to show the White man, as well as the Black man, that many Black civilizations comprised the African heritage, and that inclusion of these cultures is part of allowing a realistic assimilation into this culture. In her rage, she practically screamed that she was tired of being thought of as a daughter of Ham.

Kiona went on to describe her adjustment at Akron as one of being viewed as a bright version of a second class group of people. If her parents were not attached to the faculty at the University, she most probably would have been treated as if her sense of rhythm was the only contribution she could make to Akron's social community. Kiona also mentioned that she had a full tuition scholarship to Akron University and that she had to stifle her feelings about recognition of the greatness of the contribution of Blacks to America due to their integration of a multiplicity of African and other cultures into the fabric of their makeup. The reason she felt a need to silence her views was fear of embarrassing the social position for which her mother and father had worked so hard.

The result of this little talk was a conference between Grady and Ruthena Almederson and the admission committee, along with the director of the history department. Kiona was granted a full scholarship to the University of Colorado. The University also agreed to pay moving expenses for Kiona and free access of research facilities to either parent.

That night in their motel room Grady and Ruth were snuggling in bed, when Ruthena said to her man, "Mousie, I never understood how a man that is so sweet to Kiona and me could disarm and disable two men in less than ten minutes like you did." Grady smiled at her and said, "Shucks, any hero has to know how to fight, otherwise the bad guys win. "She playfully socked him on his biceps and asked him about the scars on his legs. He asked her if she wanted to hear a grisly story. After she assented, he seemed to look in the distance. His voice became low.

"In Texas is a town called Cut and Shoot. My momma, three brothers, my daddy and me, share cropped a farm there. There was no money, so Daddy, went to work in a factory that made manure for the crops. To keep costs down, the factory owner hired sharecroppers, who were looking for a way out, and paid miserable wages. We were in the South of the '50's. A White man could get away with paying Blacks and poor Whites slave money because he provided jobs for the town.

A union organizer came down from New York. Daddy and some of the other workers listened to him. My father tried to organize a meeting. That night hooded men came with torches, burned a cross in front of our house, and burned down our home. It was not easy for them because Daddy made Momma, David, and me go down in the cellar while he stood them off with a shotgun, a hatchet and a bullwhip. I was the oldest one left at home. I would not stay in the basement. I fought with my father. He was killed in the fire, along with the rest of the family. I was fourteen and the merciful town's folk put me in foster homes and a home for emotionally disturbed children. Daddy taught me the value of an education. As a result, I stayed until I finished school and leaned toward learning the arts of self-defense. In response to Ruthena's question of how he survived the fire, he replied that his father realized that the fight was lost and forced Grady to let him wrap him in a tarpaulin. He then threw the tarp outside the house. The Klansmen caught him and cut his legs with a razor. He did recognize one voice. After he finished high school, Grady joined the merchant Marines. Before he left he learned the habits and hangouts of the man, whom he had identified, approached him when he was drunk, wearing a mask and white gloves. He also rehearsed the drawl of the typical Cut and shoot Texan for his speech to the Klansmen. He took him behind an alley, made him strip naked, and put catnip all over him. Grady then tied him to a gutter and turned loose a bag of five cats on him. That was the last time he saw Cut and Shoot Texas. The loneliness at sea helped Grady do his grieving and put his hatred of Whites into perspective. However, he could never socialize with Whites on any other than a superficial basis. To free himself from the prison of hatred and to help others avoid it, he resolved to help others learn how to think correctly. He chose to become a philosophy instructor. He did not want his wife and child, or children, to know the same hatred he did. At one point in his lifetime Grady wanted to reunite with his two brothers, who had left home. They were all he had left of his family of origin.

Grady fell in love with Ruthena on sight. When he saw those two young punks plotting to accost her, he developed a counter plan that would burst their bubble. He immediately put it into motion when they crossed his path. After they had married and had Kiona, Grady vowed nothing would ever hurt his two ladies or make them feel the hatred he did. He sincerely hoped he could put it out of his system.

Ruth was overcome with love for this kind, intelligent man, who had borne so much with only the silent sea to hear his cry of hurt and loss. She took his face in her hands and kissed him tenderly then said "After twenty years of being married to you, I found out you have a mean bone in your body. I have had reason to hate Whites, but not near as much as you. When I was a young nurse at Akron City Hospital, all the White College boys would always try to feel on me while I examined them. The worst thing happened while I was on the surgical unit. I assisted with a White resident on surgery. The patient was an older Black, lady with a Berry Aneurysm, (that is an aneurysm on the blood vessels to the brain.) I remember, after surgery, he was, so attentive to her that I was moved by it. I thought, here is a loving man. I let myself become attracted to him. We started taking coffee breaks together and learning about each other from conversation. After a while we started walking each other home. It took about two months before we slept with each other. Two months later, I found out he was married, and his wife was pregnant. My view became that all men are dogs, and all White men use Black women. When I grew up, I took responsibility for my own horniness, but I was wary of Whites." With this mutual cleansing of their secret sins of the past, Ruthena laid her head on her man's chest and took his hand in hers. They went to sleep feeling much tenderness and love. This never changed, but their daughter would give the strength of this bond plenty of room for stress.

From the cementing and solidifying of a life that has been built, our thoughts now move to a young lady who is in the process of choosing and directing the patterning her blossoming adult life will assume. Kiona just made a significant break with her parents. She used the weaponry allowed by her position as Daddy's little girl to manipulate herself into a position in which she could free herself from the control of others. However, the converse is expressed as a corollary. When one frees oneself of control, one stands or falls alone. The discomfort, which the position of solitude generates, is similar to taking a chance on the unknown. The richness of the reward is beyond one's expectations, but the punishment is at least envisioned as, further than the lowest rung of our own personal hell. However, not quite to this point, Kiona had begun the process of making her own decisions and divesting herself of both encumbrances and support. Her management of this issue is the core of the riddle does our culture determine us, or de we determine our culture.

Fortuitously, Kiona had not done this without forethought.

She truly believed that the only way she could stand up for herself and her people was to stand alone and not carry the burden of speaking tongue in cheek because of fear of hurting her parent's social position. Therefore, Daddy's and Mommy's pet had to walk on the wild side if she wanted to learn to walk on her own feet. She also had to know and appreciate the depth of the risk she was taking. Kiona was not born yesterday. She knew that her father would give her the moon and that her mother would go along with it if she felt it was safe. What she needed to know was how do you connect back to earth from the moon.

After her session with the chairman of the history department, her parents were full of questions about why she wanted to leave home. Everything was safe there, she had plenty of friends, and she was respected. Kiona tried to explain that the source of her respect was not her, but her parents. She had to make her bones to earn people's belief in what she stood for. In Akron, she felt that all of the faculty would turn out to hear what Grady's and Ruthie's daughter had to say about an issue; but if she got too loud or too committed to a stance, to which the school was opposed, the sufferers would be her mother and father.

Loss of tenure could be explained away in other ways than "We do not like your daughters anti-university opinion nor her displaying it public". However, that would be the cause. Grady assured his daughter that she meant more to him than any job. Kiona did not see the sense of sacrificing one career for another. Ruthena brought up the mother and daughter bugaboo of slick boys having their way with Kiona. As with any daughter trying to leave adolescence behind her, this woman reacted in full-blown rage. "Damn it, Momma, how did you learn what to look for in a man? Did you not make some mistakes? To find someone, with whom I can live, I have to find with whom I cannot live. You are a nurse; do you think every time you told Daddy about the White patients that tried to get in your pants that I did not hear it? On the other hand, maybe I was not supposed to have sufficient cerebral capacity to understand it. Mother, I will always love and respect you, but the man I choose has to be my choice based on whatever mental equipment I have developed to be able to make a choice."

Ruthena was flabbergasted. "Everything we've ever done or planned to do was for you. How can you be such an ingrate? Do you have any inkling of the horrors your father and I endured to see to it that you have the chance for an abundant life? I cannot tolerate the fact that in your impulsive hurry to be an adult you'll squander all the common sense we taught you."

Kiona sighed with impatience and frustration. Her emotional entropy was at a standstill. She deeply loved this tough, good woman, but she could no longer endure the concept of being thought of as the fruit of her maternal loins and not a person in her own right. With an effort at control that must have rivaled the power that held Vesuvius in check, she approached Ruthena with the facts that she appreciated her parents' struggles and would always cherish the lessons about life they had taught her. However, what she had learned would have to be demonstrated in the laboratory of life. She also reiterated that her mother did not permit her own mother to choose her life's companion, and neither would Kiona.

Thus ended the historic debate that all mothers have had with their progeny of the same gender from time immemorial. There might be a few new wrinkles added to this version.

# Chapter 2

Kiona was nervous about moving to Boulder, Colorado, but here she was. She had moved into women's dorm, Desmond Hall. Her roommates were Amy Fenstermacher a journalism major, from Teaneck, New Jersey, and Rachel Tekle an Ethiopian girl from the village of Gondar in Ethiopia. Both were Jewish. Amy was a reformed Jew with all the material accouterments, liberal philosophical viewpoints, and spoiled behavior that was stereotypically projected upon middle class, Jewish females. Paradoxically, she could be a loving friend, a loyal supporter of what proved credible to her, and a steel-cold avenging angel if she felt cheated or misused. Rachel was quiet, just as much of a loving friend, but more cautious in extending and sharing of herself. She was a Falasha Jew and came from a sincere, pious family. Her village was not wealthy, and physicians were in dire need. Therefore, she declared her major pre-med. Rachel was also tremendously proud of her heritage, which she traced back to Menelik, the son of Solomon and the Queen of Sheba. The Falasha were recently recognized as Jews by Israel after along struggle. They were accepted as Black Jews, descended from the tribe of Dan.

Over the course of studying together, meeting each other's families, double and triple dating, becoming aware of snobbishness and silliness of sororities and fraternities, the three young ladies became fast friends. From Rachel, Kiona learned about the ancient respect for the Black warrior, she became acutely aware of the Hannibal that almost brought Rome to its knees, or about the center for trade, established at Timbuktu by the Mali civilization during the Middle Ages. She became flooded with knowledge about the Kush fighters and of the wars between the Amhara and the Falasha that were as brutal as the pogroms of the Czar in Russia or the Spanish Inquisition. The Nubian civilization of the Sudan and the culture of Zimbabwe, to the South, were all brought into her ken. What she did not learn in the classroom, Rachel supplemented.

From Amy, both girls learned how to get the last laugh in a relationship. Rachel met a young man to whom she became openly and obviously attracted. They had a couple dates, and he took advantage of her feelings for him. He then proceeded to brag to all his Fraternity Brothers about how loose African women were and about how they could not wait to make it with an American. The young lady was crushed.

She became afraid to mingle with White or Black American males. She sat at home and avoided mutual friends. Kiona found out about this from Amy's boy friend, Ron, who was also a pre-med and class-mate of Rachel's. That night while Rachel was out studying, Kiona told Amy what had happened. Amy hit the roof. A gleam came into her eyes. She called Ron up and asked him to come over. Once he had ar-rived, in her sweetest voice, Amy asked him if the boy who had dropped out of his anatomy class still had his spot in the lab undis-turbed. Ron acknowledged that the spot was intact. Employing her fe-minine wiles, Amy asked him if he could sneak the cat cadaver he had been dissecting out of the lab. When Ron asked why, Amy related how the young man had cruelly treated Rachel. Amy then included Ron and Kiona in her plot of vengeance. The plot was for Amy to attend this fellow's fraternity Halloween party with a gift-wrapped package, the dead cat. She would be wearing a conspicuous costume and mask, se-duce the boy in question to his room, present the gift and exit through the window, he always kept open. Amy and Kiona were to convince Rachel to attend the party as Ron's date to keep suspicion off her. The caper was executed that Saturday. Kiona had to go to convince Rachel to attend. Kiona was garbed as a Jane-in-the box. She punched out the bottom of a cardboard carton, attached suspenders to it, and slipped it over her. Amy punched holes for legs in a plastic trash bag and wore a hollowed out pumpkin for a mask. The fool let his huge, macho ego lead himself right into the trap. In later, years when their youths were behind them, they laughed uproariously over this escapade. They even referred to Amy as Ma trash.

A shameful incident took place on campus that polarized the students. A Black historian, who was well liked by the faculty and students alike, was refused a research grant to study the activities during the Civil War of a family that had settled in Boulder after the War. They had been a slave holding family. The professor's family had also settled in the community after the Civil War. The man had run to Canada via the Underground Railroad and returned to fight in one of the Black regiments in the Union. According to the Homestead Act of 1862, he was allowed to settle a homestead, as a war veteran. However, the homestead he sought was denied. The man was not to be denied. He started a blacksmith business, and he later built his own home from his own savings. The mechanics of the denial involved some historical peculiarities. Because President Lincoln must have foreseen that land would be difficult for impoverished veterans to procure and because much of the great Plains land was difficult to farm, the land was given to whomever would live on it for five years. Transportation hardships discouraged settlement. Therefore, the railroads, building out to the Pacific became the distributor. They elected to sell the land.

The professor unearthed information that linked the emigrated Southern family to the railroad. What's more, they felt that an upstart that was an inferior Son of Ham was trying to step out of place and get free land to which his former master was entitled. Hence, by an unsavory bribe to the railroad, a deserving veteran was cheated out of land, for which he had fought. The University faculty felt that the unearthing of this information would harm innocent progeny of the criminals and not the perpetrators of the crime; therefore, they suppressed the research. Many faculty and students saw this as money talks. They felt the prof's family was entitled to remuneration for this heinous racist act. Their opponents felt that innocent family members were being told to rectify what they had not done. One of these was the head of the history department.

Kiona, as well as her two roommates, was in the faction, arguing for the injustice to the professor being made right. The quandary before her was: Do I jeopardize my parents' privileges here by changing my major, or do I follow my own mind? Wrestling with this concept brought back the old conflict that caused her to leave home. Any conclusion she reached would have to be based upon what she felt was just and fair to Black people and all people, in general, including her. Kiona was a 4.0 student, in history; she thoroughly enjoyed it, but she felt her people had suffered enough injustice at the hands of the White man. In talking with her advisor, she got a reiteration of the Department Head's opinion. Kiona's already synthesized stance was that if a prominent family could not look at themselves enough to right their injustices, they were not worth much as human beings. If a history department felt it was better to keep the slime of the town under the rug rather than to pursue the truth to prevent repetition of the heinous act, then it was not serving any purpose of history that motivated her to study it. Her advisor was very sympathetic to her anger. She felt that Kiona was going through a kind of battle fatigue. It was analogous to what priests go through when they see all the senseless pain in the world and lose their faith in God, she suggested that Kiona find a way to take some sort of sabbatical and get her head together. She showed her sensitive, perceptive student Professor Horton's ad, which had been sent to several schools around the country.

Kiona's initial reaction was one of anger. What business did this snooty, academic in her ivory tower have to tell her she was punched out. To be polite, she looked at the ad. In reality going abroad and learning how, to gain the skills to unearth the evidence of past great civilizations of Black peoples could be the very weapons she needed to disprove the stupid legend of the curse of Ham. Before considering the proposal, Kiona felt she had to vent her longstanding rage.

"Professor, Do you expect me to still the rage at the indifference that allowed so many lynching, murders, deliberate denials of economic opportunities or even the right to live like every other American or any one else who came to these shores? I feel that the History Department is saying that continuing to suffer injustice is better than hurting the feelings of a great White Family, who at one time caused a grave injustice and need to atone for it. I also refuse to accept diagnosis for my anger as exhaustion, emotional illness, or some variation of P.T.S.D."

Years of advising students had prepared the advisor for this outburst. Besides, she full well realized the value of Kiona's potential to the University and to American society, as a whole. Therefore, the educator understood she would have to choose her words carefully. "Kiona, if I may call you that, your fight is a worthy one. If you fight when you are in an uproar and as a student with no power, the forces that believe that the honor of a family is more important than decency or justice will crush you. If, on the other hand, you separate yourself from your emotions, you can assess your enemy's and your own strengths and weaknesses. Professor Owens did not seek student support because he realizes that it will be student sacrifice. However, even he, the one who suffered, is not in retreat; he has chosen to regroup and marshal his forces. The final example I can give you is out of Roman history, Spartacus was a slave and a gladiator. He thoroughly hated Rome and the corruption with which they debased the worth of a person. He arose against them, but only after he had amassed an army by taking the time to learn the hearts of men. This army did not defeat Rome, but it kept it trembling in fear for four years. I am not begging you to stay with us though I realize your value as a student. I am asking you to decide how much you want to commit yourself to your people, and to take the time to develop a winning strategy."

The last interchange with her adviser provided Kiona with some food for thought.

She still seethed with anger, but she had to admit that taking time to develop a game plan did make some sense. Kiona decided to discuss her dilemma with her roommates. When she got home, all she heard in response to her summons was an echo. No one was home. After her call, she heard them on the stairs and ran down to intercept them so they could go out and discuss the problem.

The three friends got in their car and drove to a relaxing Italian restaurant a little north of campus. Kiona relayed her advisor's offer and her opinion. Amy expressed her anger at the advisor for taking the administration stance on the issue. "You'd think that at a university, the so-called center of learning, enlightenment, ideals, and truth would have some value." On the other hand, Rachel who had come from a minority, struggling for recognition, raised a more strategic concern. Do you remember what she said about Spartacus? My people had a similar struggle getting recognized by Israel and getting the Ethiopian government to allow us freedom to leave. Every step we took required careful planning and timing. It took patience, perseverance, and having the chutzpah to wait and time it right because we had a firm commitment. Maybe this is God's way of telling you to take the time to shore up your strength because the battlefield you will enter will give no quarter."

All three laughed at Rachel's use of the word, "chutzpah". Kiona chided her for going back to Yiddish when she could have used a soul word like "Heart". Amy said, "You can take the Jew out of Israel, but you can't take Israel out of the Jew."

Kiona now knew that the ball was in her court. She knew that her friends would stand by her, regardless what her decision was. However, another dimension of pain just got added to the decision. Kiona realized the beauty of the relationship she shared with these girls. Where could she find this in Yucatan? As if reading her mind, Amy said, "You know, dear, we both love you very much, and we know you feel the same way about us. The decision with which you are wrestling is one with which we also struggle. The form may be different, or the issue may vary, but we all have to cut our apron strings. This means we will be going our own way. It doesn't mean we'll forget one another or that we won't need each other, but our lives and needs are going to change."

Kiona thought about her values and her new conflict all weekend. Her aims at leaving home, the realities to which Amy and Rachel had exposed her, the arguments, and the memories of her parents, all interacted. Was her advisor being sincere, or was she trying to convince Kiona to keep the University out of a sticky situation? The uncertainty of this problem caused her to seek out Professor Owens. The next school day, she made an appointment to see him. Professor Owens told her that the last thing he wanted was for her to be a sacrificial lamb. Next, he asked her if changing her major from History to Black Studies would further her experiences or assist Black people in their struggle. Furthermore, he asked how it would affect her impact on her own life so that she could get the attention of the White man. He reminded her Dr. King stood up to the White power structure with loving and reflected back to the Caucasian, who he was, while Malcolm X stood up and let him know that hatred generated hatred. Both weapons were powerful; each had to be applied with appropriate sensitivity and appropriate empathy. His final word was "If you change your major, or do not change it, the knowledge base will be the same. If you opt to change, in effect you are saying, I have retreated from telling the White man we both occupy this world together. You are saying you only want to know about the Black world. It is a hard choice, but whatever choice you make, you have to live with it. This, theoretically, is what you came here to learn how to do."

That evening Kiona wanted to retreat from missions and high-minded purposes. She, Ra and Amy went out drinking and dancing. They began their evening joking about Profs they knew or characters they knew from class or the dorm. Out of the corner of her eye, Kiona noticed a tall, plumb black, young man eyeing her. After a while, she got up to get a pizza for her and the girls. She passed by his table as the band announced a line dance. The young man excused himself and asked her if she would teach him to line dance because he was tired of being awkward at parties. Kiona apologetically explained why she got up. She said at the next line dance she would dance with him. Back at the table, Amy thought his eyes looked warm and gentle like a doe's. Rachel thought she saw a calculating look in his stares at her.

When the next line dance came up, the young man was back. He introduced himself, as Reed Hymer. He seemed a little shy and self-conscious at first, but caught on rapidly. The band played a few cha-racteristic fast numbers, and the couple enjoyed these numbers.

Kiona could not help but notice Reed's perfect, white teeth when he smiled or the carefree merriment of his laugh. She invited him back to their table to meet her friends. They found out he was a third year medical student with the goal of opening up a clinic in an inner city neighborhood. His father was a well-known Gynecologist in Denver. He verbalized that Black people should not turn their backs on each other, but that they should remember that the right set of circumstances can place a Black man into poverty. Kiona was almost brought to tears by the apparent beauty of this statement, along with Amy. Rachel alone remained suspicious.

During the next couple of weeks, Kiona and Reed saw as much of each other as they could. They studied together, when he was off his clinical rotation. At that time, he was on pediatrics. He enjoyed work-ing with kids, who were so honest and open. However, he wished he could tolerate their pain enough to cure them. This remark touched off a wave of tenderness in Kiona. She knew she was falling in love with Reed.

She decided to confide in him about the conflict inside her. The war to be her own person, the injustice to Professor Owens, the stance of the History Department, and the choice before her all came spilling out of her. Reed listened to what she had to say and told her that switching majors had no effect on how Black she was or in fighting her battle that all people had to fight in America. He added that the trip afforded her the chance to cool off and to develop the skills she wanted to put flesh on how this battle could be fought. She felt a flood of relief for the first time in weeks. Kiona had never made the first move in a relationship. She asked Reed if he would miss her while she was in Yucatan. He said that he would, but he was engaged to a girl back home. Kiona's heart was crushed.

"How could you lead me on as you have? Didn't you see that I was falling in love with you? Maybe you damn doctors think we women live to satisfy you in the sack. Could it be possible that I might want to be a woman and not just someone to meet your need to vent your con-flicts about children."

Reed answered with as much control as he could muster. He told her that he found her attractive that first night and that he was afraid of falling in love with her or vice versa. He stated that he saw this com-ing. He also stated that he thought they had a rich friendship, and that he wanted to continue it. He replied in a calm voice, but the pain showed in his eyes and face. Kiona was hurt, but she saw that Reed Hymer was not scheming or malicious, just lonely for a friend. She agreed to accept this arrangement.

Kiona realized that the time to get off the fence was now. She con-tacted her advisor and set up an appointment. This student, who seemed to have garnered support from students and faculty alike, was stepping out of her shell. With baited breath, the history department advisor awaited her response. Feeling like a quarterback trying to throw a final touchdown pass, she told her advisor that she now understood that her battle had would not change with a change in her major. She admitted that she had to learn generalship. The temporary leave was an ideal adjustment because it would impart the knowledge of how to go about restoring the great Black civilizations of the past to destroy once and for all and point out that the curse of Ham was so much bologna.

Having made this choice, Kiona only had to tell her parents and to adjust to the changes in her friendships. Amy and Rachel were an endless source of camaraderie, support, and mutual growth. The pain on leaving the nest of their community of sharing was immense. The parental break would have its drawbacks and complaints, but it had essentially had been made. Kiona had dropped sufficient hints to them to let her mother and father understand that the trip was an imminent potential. They voiced their fears about their only daughter going to a foreign country that was not always friendly to America. They recounted the problems with the Sandinistas in Nicaragua and the murder of three nuns in El Salvador. Kiona did not know how to reassure them, but she did tell her parents that she loved them both. However, the potential skills that she could learn outweighed the risk. Ruthena and Grady refused to be consoled. They felt no growth was worth risking her life. To this Kiona asked if Martin Luther King and Malcolm X had died in vain. Her parents stated their deaths were a severe loss, whether in vain or for a worthy purpose. The issue was left at a stalemate. Kiona suppressed it, but an element of uncertainty and fear would follow her to Yucatan.

Rachel, Amy, and Reed seemed to weave a protective circle around Kiona. There were many weekend outings to canoe or to ride bikes. There were study sessions followed by many head sessions.

They often talked about the opportunity that Kiona would have to learn how to trace the presence of a culture and to have a skill that most people could not begin to know how to use. They also made her aware that she would be assuming a vanguard position akin to the one Alex Haley had in writing Roots. A toll was in the process of being developed that could impact on the several roots of people that had been labeled as having one. Africa was not a homogeneous source of

Black people. Nor was the source of Black culture in America a function of Ham's seeing Noah at an indiscreet moment. Kiona's mission
was defined not only by White injustices, such as, the land swindle to
the Owens family, but also by Blacks that bought into the definition
that lumped all people of color as Africans and all Africans as inferior.
The different thought patterns of Mandingo, Kikuyu, Sudanese, Ethiopian, Mali, Bantu, were not considered nor were the Aborigines, of
Australia or the Maoris, of Polynesia thought about. With such an ex-
tensive culture of progenitors, how could the White man dare to label
an entire race emerging from this blend? Worse, yet how could Black
men and women be a party to their own dishonor?

Kiona's friends wove the importance of her commitment into the
fabric of her being. What they neglected to add was that part of her
responsibility was to reach into the psyche of the American Black and
to incorporate what she found into it in a positive way. She did not
know if she had the right or the strength to be her sister's keeper.
Hence, her sojourn was not only a time to build skills, but also a mora-
torium to explore the thin line between how to live for her people and
herself.

# Section III

# The Meeting

# Chapter 1

When we lean over a globe of the earth and look closely at the landmasses, often times they appear to assume the shapes pictured by our imaginations. The other day I tried this looking at Mexico from a north/south direction or upside down. This mass gave the appearance of a long-necked dinosaur; the neck seemed to widen South of Texas. At the other end, the head portion went into the Gulf of Mexico. The head of our imaginary beast is Yucatan. Of course, the Continental Airways pilot was not at a sufficient height to enable passengers to view these imaginary configurations. People who are experiencing flight for the first times are wont to give vent to their creative or artistic bents, as they are exposed to the world of the sky. Others create pictures in the sky.

Kiona sat on the seat adjacent to the left wing of the plane. She vividly recalled her visit back to Akron a week before she left. Grady and Ruth were near tears because they feared they would never see their daughter again. As insurance, she brought Amy and Rachel home with her. Reed had also come along, and out of respect for the Almedersons, he stayed at a nearby motel. Since Amy was the most forward of the three, she stepped into the vanguard position. She spoke about how proud of Kiona the whole campus was. Rachel related that the discoveries made by archeologists were a large portion of bringing her people from the abyss of obscurity and incredibility to recognition as a national group. Reed added that forever laying to rest the racist myth of the son of Ham would help turn around how the White man looked at some of this own motivations and actions and how the Black man viewed himself. By gaining the skills to unearth the truth Kiona could be the very force precipitant in the healing of Black anger in response to White greed and fear of reprisal for the wrongs done in its name.

These arguments appealed to the philosopher and logician in Grady. He could identify with the cold hatred he had to purge from his soul by a lonely and harsh sea. How beautiful it might be if Whites and Blacks could sit down together, free of hatred and work together to make the Earth livable for all.

Ruth could also see that Kiona was not a frivolous little, college girl champing at the bit. She was a mature woman that had learned to discern people and to develop realistic and challenging goals for herself. She felt that she could now sit back and let her daughter manage her own life. The aspect of this was sad, but it was pride filling.

Through Kiona's head swam the images of the three great friends that helped transform their despair to parental pride. The farewells at Boulder's airport were characterized by a lot of hugging and choked back tears. There were the usual promises to write and vows to never forget each other. This young lady, all at once, began to wonder what relationships would develop once she touched the soil of this new land.

The plane landed at O'Hare, in Chicago, to exchange passengers. Kiona observed the new people getting on the plane. One lanky, tall White boy got on the plane. He was engrossed in conversation with a professorial appearing gentleman, who seemed half his size and about twice his age. The discussion looked like a heated and animated one. That lanky fellow seemed to have a good deal of jaw work attached to his conversation. His mandibles seemed to assume a force of motion of their own accord. As they got closer, she heard them discussing the Mayans and the Aztecs, as transplants of the ancient city-states of Greece and the militarism of Rome. The elder gentleman was positing the development of a research project looking for a connection between these civilizations and their European analogues. The legend of Quetzalcoatl was suggested as a possible source of a linkage.

When they sat down in front of her and continued their conversation, oblivious to her presence, she made an entry into the discussion by announcing that she could not help but overhear a discussion pertaining to the history of Yucatan, to where she was traveling. She asked if they were headed the same way. The lanky one replied that he was. He said he was part of a study of the verification of the legend of a Mayan king, Quetzalcoatl. Kiona smiled and stated with pride," I am also going there to study the legend. I am from the University of Colorado. My name is Kiona Almederson."

The young man introduced himself as Mark Engler and his companion as Professor Horton, both from the University of Iowa. After a round of handshaking and the tedium of small talk that begins a friendship, Mark brashly grinned and candidly retorted that he saw Kiona paying rapt attention to their conversation, not just being unable to help but overhear it.

Kiona was shocked and taken aback by Mark's perceptiveness, but his grin was infectious. Furthermore, his next remark caused her to burst out laughing. He said, "Most people notice how I move my jaws when I talk because I am tall and thin and look like a praying mantis." With that said, Mark then invited her to partake of their conversation.

The beginning of the chiming in started when Kiona stated that she heard that Quetzalcoatl was said to have escaped from Atlantis before it sank to the bottom of the sea. No one knew the origin of the Atlanteans, if there were any. They could have been Europeans, tribes of Amer Indians, who left the continent, or slaves, who escaped the slave ships.

"What a brilliant conceptualization", interrupted Professor Horton," I could easily lose myself pondering that idea. Do you realize the implications of the theory you are suggesting? Not only was the New World a source of civilizations, but African cultures also were."

Kiona rhetorically replied that Africa was the source of a multiplicity of civilizations. "We are of the Mali, from the world trade center, Timbuktu, of the ancient Kish fighters, of Ethiopia, of Zimbabwe, of the Nubians of the Carthaginians, feared by Rome. I wouldn't soil the dignity of my soul by thinking I came from the disgrace of Ham, viewing the depravity of his father, Noah, in a drunken state." To this she added," I want to unearth these past glories so that White and Black men understand that we have brought an enormous blend of cultures to this Land and contributed no small amount to its development. If, in learning about Quetzalcoatl, I can learn the skills that will aid me in unearthing my people's past, I will feel gratified."

Mark's only response to this was; "You've taken on a helluva job.

All I want to do is find out how other people fit in a world together so I can find my own place in it. I am really tired of people thinking I'm a nice guy and trying to make me over in their image. I may only be a virtual image, but virtual or real, what I find will be me." Then he began to sing "No, they can't take that away from me." He then began to bow to everyone on the plane. An older gentleman commented that he had a tenor voice the quality of Jeremiah, the bullfrog. Three passengers agreed with him; a group of musicians gagged, while a precocious six-year-old held his nose. The child's mother smacked him. Not to be beaten into submission, he gave his mother a loud raspberry.

Mark laughed at this, unabashedly. Professor Horton tried not to smirk, and Kiona tried to hide behind a pillow. However, she had a large smile beneath her blush.

Some of the other archeology students had already preceded this group. They had basically traveled the same route as the others. They had flown on either American Airlines, Continental, or Aero Mexico to Quintano Roo, the airport in the southern most state in the province of Yucatan. From there they rented a car and drove to a site outside of Chichen Itza, where they pitched a camp.

The camp consisted of series of tents around a central building that served as a meeting place, mess hall, and a quartermaster supply. Around the tents was a ring of huts where guides and their families lived. The archeology students were from several cultural backgrounds. The guides and their families served as a means of learning the language and dialects and enculturations. Sama Kutrah was from Goa, an Old Portuguese colony in India. Amund Svolba was from Norway. Henri Bordeque from Port au Prince, Haiti. Helga Seredensky was from Kiev, Ukraine. Ahmed Zotar was from Morocco. These people would be companions in learning and in trusting each other.

Into this cultural mix were thrown Mark, Kiona, and the Professor. There were classes in archeology, language and cultural exchanges, and outings at which ideas and innovations were developed by brainstorming and calling upon each other's cooperation and individual ingenuities. For example, a problem was presented to the entire group: A city was unearthed that was in an area where an active volcano spewed forth lava, also war like cultures surrounded the city. The city was of-

47

ten victimized by attacks. Two different layers were uncovered, in which destruction was evident. The group was charged with discovering a way to distinguish damage from the volcano from the ravages of war and to hypothesize a potential location for this civilization.

As Professor Horton had hoped, each student researched areas of the problem where interest or ability predominated and shared, argued, and /or compromised their conceptualizations, configurations, and personal and cultural viewpoints to reach workable conclusions. Sama brought knowledge of a volcano that had erupted in Bali in 1963 after six centuries of silence. This was part of Indonesia, which had a large Hindu population. The people were angry with the priests for botching the ceremony. He suggested that looking for dike like rock formations, · due to the mudslide hardening into rock might provide a clue. Amund related how Icelanders derived heat from a volcano, and that Vikings may have been attacked by Britons and other seafarer nations. Ahmed suggested that the Aegean Sea was the site of intercultural military adventures including three Peloponnesian Wars. In 1620 B.C. a series of volcanic explosions sank an Aegean island, called Santorin. According to Greek legends, this island was Atlantis. The Atlanteans appreciated the works of art and huge palaces the way the Mayans did. Henri also reminded the group that, according to one legend, Quetzalcoatl came from Atlantis.

Kiona and Mark gravitated toward how to distinguish military destruction from damage by the volcano. Their pooling of data came up with three types of lava flow which resulted in three different terrain's and different residual products: Slow flowing lava hardens with a broken, rough surface; obsidian, or volcanic glass is an after product. To the contrary, runny, fast flowing lava has a smooth skin covering over it. It wrinkles to form ropes of rock. By products of this type of flow are basalts. What is known as pillow lava erupts where the flow oozes through cracks in the ocean floor. It is seen on dry land that was once part of the ocean bottom. Plugs, dikes and sills are formed from this type of flow. Granite is left behind. Gases rise to the surface with the flowing lava. When the movement is slow and sticky, gases build up and explode violently. The result is clouds of hard bits of rocks with a porous appearance, called pumice. Ash is blown over crops and kills them. Finding bits of pumice or barren areas around vegetation cold indicate volcanic activity. Military activity would be indicated by blackened areas on bones or bizarre positioning of remains or jagged edges to bones.

After putting together their perceptions with the benefit of several skull sessions, the collection of students, which was now a team presented their joint thesis: The excavation took place either in the Aegean or around Sicily due to activity of a military nature taking place due to cultural interchange. Both sites also had active volcanoes. The professor acknowledged the industry and the thoroughness of the students. He responded that there was no actual site because he was interested in building a team of people that shared, trusted and relied on each other rather that fact collectors. This way they could teach each other what they had to know.

They admitted to themselves that a valuable lesson was taught. However, they also felt they had one to teach: Do not use me to teach me. We are people, not objects. They were unified in the performance of a work task, but they had learned to care for one another and to have their efforts directed to a purpose. The skull sessions continued. The reconstituted purpose was to let the Professor know he was part of the team, not above it. After a week of digging, all eight, acting very excited, asked Professor Horton to meet them at the dig because they had discovered an artifact that would revolutionize how the history of World War II will be taught in school. He was to meet the group at the dig at two a.m. to feel the full impact of their discovery. What he saw was a straw dummy in army dress with a note on it that said, "I am an atheist in a fox hole." From out of the trench, where the make believe soldier sat, emerged the octet with a huge sign that said, "We are all a team, and we all sink or swim together."

# Chapter 2

As the Maya tribes fought and as economic areas rose or diminished however, cities changed their names and names of Gods became different Hence, the feathered serpent god changed from
Quetzlcoatl to Kukulcan. This indicates that power had changed hands
from the Toltec to the Itzas. At the site of the Pyramid of Kulkulcan,
the legend began in the period when non-Mayan cultures infiltrated the
Quiche. The time frame was 900-1500. During this time a mysterious
White God appeared. He is said to have brought new political ideas,
military tactics, religious practices, and a new type of artistry. He was
represented as a Plumed Serpent. This emblem was a decoration on all
major buildings.

According to what had been crammed into their heads a few short
weeks ago, the temple of Kukulcan was located in the center of town.
At the site, parts of a squarish building could be distinguished in the
jungle brush. Huge thick trees and thorny, tangled shrubs concealed
this artifact. Mark discovered that putting a tarry or resinous substance
on the plant had the effect of smothering it and making the main stems
stand out. This helped him hack and cut with greater results. As a concerned team member, he shared his information with the others. As a
result the building was exposed in about a half day. It was Amund,
who discovered the serpent design on the steps. Now the archeologists
knew two things: They had located the center of town. They had found
the Temple of Kukulcan.

Dating was done by applying the principles discussed earlier about
radiocarbon dating and by extracting maize cobs, since it was a food
common to the area. Age was estimated by counting the rings at the
cob's edge. When analyzing stone objects, carbon dating could be
used, or rock formation could be measured against estimated periods

of volcanic eruptions. Thus, as their knowledge of archeology and geology of the terrain increased, their efficacy increased. The work was hard, and the headwork was demanding. The young people had tremendous respect for Professor Horton because of his knowledge and because he had learned the lesson, they taught him at the first trench. He believed that if he walked with two men, one of them was his teacher. Another method of discovering the development of this civilization was to study the chemical remains of the waste products. From these coprolites, the diets could be ascertained. How the vegetables began to vary between rural and urban communities, what kinds of meats were being eaten.

As more and more of the Maya way of life became exposed, Mark began to feel a restlessness that seemed to consume more and more of his being. At first, he could not put his finger on what it was. However, as he began to ask questions in class and to put them together outside of class, Mark began to realize that he was not learning what he needed to know about people and civilization: How men thought and related to one another. He found himself pondering how the tools, eating utensils foods, remains could be integrated to build a picture of this. There appeared to be some kind of key he was missing. His conversations began to become replete with his unrequited thirst for the link that would unlock thought patterns, which either united or divided human beings from each other.

Up to this point, the group had pieced together that the Mayan culture was a literate one, but it was also a theocracy. Mark reasoned that any reflected thought would be found in the religious writings. In other words, there had to be a library in the temple. Mark knew that he would need assistance in locating the tomes and the libraries that housed them. He decided to present his thesis to the group. Henri had bridged his thoughts when he brought up the topic of decoding the phonetic symbols that they had found on some of the friezes they found beneath the gables of the temple. Amund was for expanding their efforts to locate other structures that might have these phonetic symbols to coordinate with the pictures on the columns, steps, and friezes they had been exposing. Helga proposed an idea that showed some similarity to what Mark was thinking when she brought up the subject of secret panels, that were like the ones that hid Anne Frank and her family. Ahmed felt knowledge would be of benefit to all and would be shared publicly the way the ancient Greeks did. Before Mark could respond, Kiona stepped in with "We are talking about a theocracy. Priests saw themselves as distilling knowledge for the public before exposing them to it."

Mark took up these last two arguments. He synthesized a concept based on Kiona's and Helga's ideas: The Inca in Peru hid objects of value in, not secret panels, but in rooms connected by tunnels, possibly underground. Locating and excavating these tunnels might prove to be a formidable task. Professor Horton added an input; "We seem to be divided.

Why don't we split into two groups: Those, who want to excavate other sites to find similar phonetic symbols to decode and put them together into a language, and those, who want to find sources of literature at one site to locate more of the symbols, etc.

Needless to say, the group was enthusiastic with the suggestion. They divided into two sub-groups. Mark, Kiona and Helga constituted the set that would look into the temple to find a library. Ahmed, Amund, Henri, Sama, became the segment that chose to excavate other sites to find more writings. The prof said he would be available to the first party, since they were shorthanded.

The next day they went to work. It was a balmy Monday. The wind was blowing in gusts. To be out in this weather was either foolhardy or intrepid. The wind blew Kiona's skirt around, and Mark happened to catch a healthy glimpse of her legs. She was thoroughly embarrassed and felt herself turn beet red, but she could not help but smile at his self conscious, almost shy, but definitely wanting look. She hardly noticed the thickened branch-like structure moving toward her, as if the wind were blowing it onto her. It seemed to have a bud at the end. It was almost in her face when she saw the slits at the sides of the bud that were its eyes. Before awareness had fully hit her, a hand darted out behind the bud and snapped it off.

"My God, Mark, you just saved me from that snake. Where did you get reflexes like that?" In response Mark told her that the reflex came from covering up for seeing what he wasn't supposed to be looking at, which were not supposed to be displayed. At this point Helga, who had heard and seen all, and the three of them laughed.

With the ice breaking done, the trio began to chop and scrape away at the brush. Helga was sitting on a sturdy clump of vines hacking away at the growth above and behind her when they gave way beneath her. She yelled for help, and Mark and Kiona came to her rescue before she fell. Helga and Kiona blocked Mark's path and kissed his cheek. Then they simultaneously said, "That's for saving our lives." Mark responded, "Why, I've never seen such brazen behavior. As a gentleman of breeding, I'll just have turn the other cheek." He then turned his face in the opposite direction for them to kiss again. Instead, they threw dirt on him.

The fact that they had found a hollow space led them to the inescapable reality that it led somewhere. The first step was to burn away the broken vines through which Helga had almost fallen. After this, they hung kerosene lanterns from holders they found in the descending walls. They were on an increasing slope and continued digging until they reached a point where they felt level ground beneath their feet. They were doggedly tired. Their workday went from dawn to dusk, but the excitement of discovery put an energy within them that propelled the climb to the surface with the momentum of jet propulsion.

March is the time of the vernal equinox. It also marks the time of a spring fiesta. Parades or posada had preceded the fiesta. The streets of Chichen Itza were teeming with families and children at play. No one wanted to sit in a stuffy meeting. Everyone wanted to partake of the festivities. As soon as the group stepped out on the boulevard, they were pummeled with eggshells filled with confetti. Dancers in gala costumes, moving to lively Latino rhythms were followed by a solemn line of the holy carrying candles and wearing white gowns to remind mankind that God brings us the beauty of spring. The evening was capped off with a display for fireworks. Restaurateurs had booths on the streets with tasty maize dishes, all sorts of seafood varieties, tortillas, and wild duck.

Helga appeared to be preoccupied with Henri, and Amund, Sama, and Ahmed seemed to be wrapped up in the festivities around the games and food. Mark and Kiona found themselves alone with each other. They were distracted by some kids trying to break open a piñata to get the prizes out. The laughter reminded them about past holidays at home, and both cried and smiled a little. Kiona talked about her war for independence, her love for her people and her anger at the injustice to Professor Owens, in particular and Black people generally and her conflict about self expression in relation to her parents' careers. She told him about Amy, Rachel, and Reed. Mark related his desire to know what made men tick so he could figure out how he ticked without every Tom, Dick, and Harry forcing his formula for successful adaptation to life on him. He told her of his war with his parents and about Arne and Cherie (He left out the sexcapade part). When they got to her tent, he hung his head and looked sad. Kiona, anticipating a story about a fiancé at home, asked what was wrong. He said, "Dunno," and kissed her. Trying to sound affronted, Kiona asked tartly "What did you do that for?" Mark answered, "The snake didn't get a chance to, and I felt sorry for him. Besides, I liked it." Kiona smiled and laughed for fifteen minutes after he left.

The work became intense and work tactics had to change. For instance, as the trio dug further, they found the walls getting steeper. As a result they made ladders and placed them at the first point of the slope's leveling off. Much of the excavation was tedious and just plain backbreaking, time consuming work. In other words, the hours were long and hard. They had to use night-lights more. After three months of hacking and sawing under growth, shoveling hard packed earth that accumulated over the centuries, a passage was found. Apparently, the temple had been built over a dried up riverbed. Caverns were formed by the flow of the waters. Eventually the surface crust collapsed, and a well was developed to allow access to the river at the surface. After the drying up of the waterway, an underground chamber was left. This passage may have been connected to the temple, or the temple might have been built around it. Whatever the structural engineering, the three of them found themselves in a huge room, full of artifacts and archives.

At the meetings, the others related they were finding artifacts and other samples of writing to match up with the picture symbols they had collected from other excavations. The neo-archeologists believed in as much self-sufficiency as possible. Consequently, they constructed a rudimentary facsimile of the regional language. The scripts, found by the trio appeared to be of a technical nature, and more precise assistance would be required for effective translation. Professor Horton suggested that the Language Department at the University of Guadalajara or a closer school be contacted. Kiona discovered some papers detailing the architectural plan of an arena and like structure and rules for playing a sport that involved a ring and a small ball. Helga had found some primitive books made of folded bark. However, the contents were anything but primitive. A system of days, weeks, months, and years was elaborated in relation to movement of the planets, the sun, and the moon. More of a skill than what they could glean on their own was needed in the linguistic area.

At the meeting, Mark's burning curiosity about thought patterning that led to defining a place in the world seemed to infect every one else.

Professor Horton reminded the group that their charge was to verify the veracity of the legend of Quetzalcoatl, not to bring about a New World understanding of Mayan thought. Everyone clamored around him. They were shouting that they could not test any truth unless they understood how the people expressed what they believed and what they knew to be fact. Besides, the purpose of studying legends is to learn something about the people. Otherwise, we could all get through life writing fairy tales. "Oh well, a child shall lead them," Kiona replied just as sardonically. "I am not a child." "Either am I," said Helga as she hugged Kiona. "Either am I," said Mark, as he hugged Kiona from the other side. "You just want a hug," giggled Kiona. "Damn right," teased Mark. Helga and Kiona both socked him on the arm.

Though all their spirits were high, the workweek had been exhausting. Mark asked Kiona if she wanted to go to dinner and a movie if they could find one in Chichen Itza. The restaurant displayed its wares on a table outside the restaurant. Arranged in the most appealing presentation were fish, sautéed in garlic, conch, one of the staples of the area, levich, a delectable fish marinated with lime sauce, onions, and a host of spices. Last but not least, was pato, the wild game of the day. On this day, it was wild duck. Once inside, they were seated by the window because Kiona liked to see what people did as they ambled by. The lady ordered first: pilyl (chicken in banana leaves), black beans and a tomato with guacamole on it. Mark ordered the wild duck with a tortilla and the same tomato with guacamole. To drink, they both had Mexican beer. A strolling band of musicians came by and asked for requests. Mark asked for "Snoopy and the Red Baron" while Kiona almost choked stifling a laugh. In a serious tone, he then asked the gentleman to play his version of "La Paloma." The most beautiful melody was emitted from the guitars, while the sweetest contralto either had ever heard sang the words. Many patrons of the restaurant were in tears, including Kiona. Then they played "Snoopy and the Red Baron." Kiona and Mark sang along and taught the other customers the words. In fact, Mark danced an older lady around the room. After dinner neither felt like a movie, so they walked the streets and stopped and talked to kids, old folks, teens, anyone, who had something to say that could communicate in some comprehensible form.

Dark was approaching, and they realized they would have to be heading back to camp. They caught the last bus back. The peace and friendliness everywhere impressed them greatly.

Mark would probably try some of his antics in Brooklyn or Sheboygin and would either get away with it or give a damn good fight, but Kiona knew she'd have to choose her words and conversants with caution and carry, at least, a can of mace. The couple was discussing these matters when a loud pop was heard. The bus had a flat tire. The driver told the passengers that the repairman would be along in an hour. Mark and Kiona felt they could be back at camp by that time. The night was nice and balmy; they decided on a nice walk to give them a chance to get to know each other.

Mark and Kiona began a leisurely stroll. They saw two boys fighting. Mark seemed to smile wistfully and looked sad. Kiona noticed the change to a pensive mood and asked what brought it on. Groping for words, Mark told her about the time he was attacked at the bus stop and befriended the boy, only to see him die. He also told her about Abe Fromkiss and Russell Tiawa. All of a sudden, Kiona said, "I bet you like cowboy music or ballads about strong, lonely men that think they can fight the world alone. "Mark admitted he was partial to this kind of music, but he also liked Muddy Waters and Beatles because they seemed to show patterns of feeling that many people felt pent up inside of them. Kiona thought about this, but she could not see pent up feelings in the Beatles. He asked if she thought "Let It Be" and "Jude" did not have pent up religious tones to them. She agreed that they did, but not like Kris Kristofferson's "Why Me" or any Black gospel that she heard in church. She then told him about how the cheery songs, so full of hope, and belief saddened and angered her because her father had to take his grief and pain to a harsh and unfeeling sea, because Professor Owens had to choose to be a stoic in the face of racist behavior. When Kiona saw Mark looking sad, as she spoke her heart, she knew he was a loving man beneath his silliness and gangly appearance.

Without thinking, Kiona took his arm as they approached camp. She had never done this with Reed. The only other man whom she showed any affection in this manner was her father. That she had such a response startled her. She was even more startled when they reached her tent. For, in the moonlight, she drew him to her and kissed him softly and seekingly. Mark was just as startled. However, he held himself back at first then also began to seek. They both recognized their passion, but they did not want to be so vulnerable from the start.

# Chapter 3

Kiona and Mark could see that they were beginning the struggles of a strong attraction for each other. Yet, this felt different. Kiona had taken a step forward with Reed but had never made forward moves. She had never wanted to kiss a man the way she had done with Mark. Mark, on the other hand, could not understand why he had cast caution to the winds, on the one hand, and was reticent about getting involved too quickly, on the other. The other complicating factor was that they both worked together. The tendency to want to take snatches of time together at work to be alone with each other began to reach aggravating proportions. On weekends, hiking, picnics, bullfights all provided them time to be together. Kiona learned about Mark's parents' racist ideas and their small town provincialism, while she told him about the White students and doctors that had so hurt Ruth. She also told Mark about the Klan in Cut and Shoot, Texas. She also reiterated how Grady had to manage his grief. Neither felt their parents would be receptive to the relationship. Yet neither one wanted to let go of the other.

Neither could stand the conflict within themselves; as a solution, they decided to ask their friends for advice. Mark wrote Arne and explained his dilemma. Kiona did the same with Rachel and Amy. Both sets of friends were glad to hear from each of them, but they were not much help. The responses were that they did not know the new person enough to make a rational decision and that each had to look into him/her self and weigh what was important to his/her life.

This mental wrestling match was temporarily forgotten about due to the arrival of a language consultant from the University of Guadalajara. He attended the meeting and stated that the script they had pieced together was skillfully done, but some factors had to be taken into account. There were different time periods represented by different layers. Artifacts could be used to date different eras. The number of rings around tree stumps, corn cob ends, radioactive carbon dating the use of metal implements, etc. He also added that the period of Quetzalcoatl was a period when the latest conquerors of the Chichen Itza area the Quiche, were mingling with non Mayan Tribes of the area, so that language and other cultural traits were blending into the Mexican culture. This would be reflected in the picture/word correspondence.

These neo-archeologists were now exposed to a concept in the art of translation. The consultant linguist very carefully explained the concept of cultural utilitarianism. He explained how the artifactual tools came to their patterns of construction because they were used to carry out functions that the culture wanted to be performed. These were defined as attributes of the artifacts. This schema could also be applied to language. Sounds combined into words according to functional rules agreed upon by the particular society. The social group also set up functional rules for how these words were combined into thoughts. Deciphering what lay behind the ways in which implements they found were designed to be used provided clues as to how the language was put together. This was also offered an explanation for the success of correlating pictures with words.

Each one felt the electricity of discovery coursing through his/her nervous system. The digging and delving into the literary artifacts seemed to reach obsessive proportions. Comprehensive data was retrieved about an athletic event following an event of historical significance. Mark was curious about this event and decided to research it further with the description of ring ball game found by Kiona as a starting point.

With the driving forces of youth and zeal from learning a new concept, they tore into the art of exploration. They even began to work at each other's digs. Helga and Kiona not only worked with Mark to formulate some sense of the rules by which ring ball, as they called the game, was played and tried to assist in building the words and thoughts from the sounds they teased out from pictures, but they joined Mark and the other young men in excavating a new site the guides thought was the sports arena.

They also read, or deciphered, about the celebrated sporting event.

From what could be decoded, a weeklong celebration took place after a victory over the Putans. The culmination of the celebration was to be a game between the conquerors and the vanquished. Whoever won or gave the best accounting of himself was to be honored by offering up his heart to Kukulcan. While Mark was helping the others Helga and Kiona busied themselves with the literature in the library. They were working on the ritual of sacrifices to Kukulcan. A piece was found that described this August event. The chosen victim did not see him/her self as a victim, but an honored gift to the God that could serve him by giving his/her most precious asset, life. By sacrificing youths that were a valuable asset to the community, the geographic unit showed its worthiness in the eyes of the God and would be given the favorable boon of prosperity or weather, favorable to the crops.

Another artifact that was brought out of obscurity was a description of a great and ferocious battle between the Quiche and the Putans. A young warrior distinguished himself in battle. He was a Putan. In pictures in the bark books, he was depicted with many bodies with serpent-liked designs on their uniforms, helmets, and shields around him. Other friezes on the walls represented him as leading a ring ball team to victory. Still other pictures showed him on the altar with a bearded man with different facial features than the other men around the altar. This figure had a feathered snake about him.

Over the next week, Mark, Kiona, and Helga dug and scraped with the feeling that their arms were being torn from their sockets. They were not sure what they were looking for. A passage was found leading from the library. It ended by some stairs. These led back to the outside to what appeared to be a field with raised platforms as high as walls. The field was about the size of a tennis court. There were small rings in each wall. Ahmed and Kiona were delving into the codices, as the bark books were called; they found a description of a game that had implications for the type of justice practiced by the Quiche Maya. The face of a God was placed in the center of the field. This was the face of Quetzalcoatl, the God of good. However, movement away from the center was movement toward the God of evil. Symbols of good and evil were placed along north-south and east-west lines passing through Quetzalcoatl's face. Priests talked with the accused, their families, witnesses, suers, etc. Hurdles were placed on the symbols, and the accused was given an assigned number of rubber balls and given a position on the line. He/She had to face other accused ones and move toward the center by putting the balls, allotted in accord with the accusation, through holes in the hurdles. The balls had to be propelled by knee, hip, or any body part except arms and hands. Finishing in the center was synonymous with achieving good. Distance was synonymous with movement toward evil and regarded as worthy of punishment. Hence, the presence of temples with sacrificial altars near the ball courts or the nearness of wells for drowning.

Although the evidence found by this duo was an attractive explanation of why so many remains, such as skeletons were at religious sites, it did not explain the same person being at a battle field, an athletic contest, and a sacrificial victim. Mark decided to pursue another line of logic. His line of attack was to find out just who this person was and what role he played in the battle and the game. In 987, Quetzalcoatl is said to have come to Chichen Itza. According to legend, Quetzalcoatl was a priest and a ruler before he assumed the role of a God. He ruled in Tula for twenty-two years. He brought prosperity and a renaissance in art, astronomy, politics, and religion to Tula. Then he was said to have been bewitched by an enemy, Tezcatipoca. He went to the East and disappeared. History tells a different story. In the year earlier mentioned, a civil war took place in Tula. The Toltec faction was driven out, and the army, headed by Quetzalcoatl, appeared at Chichen Itza and took it over from the tribe that already inhabited the area; this transplanted Toltec civilization was to be the site of Mexicanization that came from attacks from the Quiche from the North and the Putun from the South.

Mark reasoned that in the games, as well as on the battlefield, enemies were identified as enemies of the good (Quetzalcoatl) or proponents of the bad (Tezcatipoca). Hence, a threat on the battlefield or on the ball court had to be eliminated. The obvious method was sacrifice. This was justifiable murder.

In keeping with the logical schema he explained why temples and their sacrificial altars were within the temple he, Kiona and Helga chose to excavate. Connections were also maintained with a large sacrificial well, or cenote. In her readings, Kiona discovered the Popul Vuh, or book of counseling. This described the customs and beliefs of the Quiche Maya. The principles of sacrifice were described.

Mark and Kiona began to decipher the Popul Vuh together and to systematically incorporate ideas, the others had found in their explorations to begin to assemble an organized body of knowledge. Three methods of sacrifice were used: The subjects were thrown into the sacrificial cenote and drowned. Another way was to lie the chosen candidate down on the altar and dissect open the thoracic cavity. After this the heart was torn out, torn into pieces, and offered to the Gods in a cup called Choc Mool. The last of these grisly methods was decapitation. This may have been reserved for prisoners of war.

The next task on the agenda was to find the identity of the person in the friezes depicting this warrior and athlete. The Popul Vuh was vague enough to allow interpretation of events it described. Mark and Kiona debated, conjured up explanations, formulated hypotheses and sometimes argued subtle and basic points until they felt satisfied with their conclusions. Then they presented them to the other members of the team.

The team theorized that the mysterious stranger was a ranking officer who was worthy of respect for his fighting prowess because of the large number of bodies around him. However, a victor in battle would not want anyone around his or her community that could inspire rebellion. Hence, he could have the dignity of a fighter in leading a team in an athletic event and rendered harmless as a prisoner. However, if he led his teammates to victory, he had to be disposed of. The most acceptable way was to offer him up to their God, Kukulcan, as Quetzalcoatl was known by the Quiche Mayans.

The theorization was arrived at through an almost elegant conceptualization. However, what were needed were facts. This meant that Mark would have to come up with physical evidence that the events he described so eloquently actually took place. As a result, he began to look around at the ball court, the altar, and other ball courts that had been excavated and other altars. Kiona and the others tried to help him in this project because of the energy that went into his obsession and because he was an integral part of the group. While working at the back surface of the altar, mark had discovered a hinge. After prying it open with a crowbar, three skeletons, were found inside the structure. One wore what at one time were regarded as religious accouterments of dress. A tarnished golden helmet and bracelets adorned one, while a second one wore a wreath on his head. The area near the sternal border was darkly stained. The helmeted figure carried a dagger in his neck. The third figure had no head. The ultimate consequences were obvious to deduce, but unraveling the circumstances around them was a formidable task.

None the less, Mark undertook the search for corroborating evidence with the zeal of Clarence Darrow. He felt he had stumbled onto a powerful concept: The means by which power structures maintained themselves. He needed more data from delving the available mythological and historical materials they had gleaned thus far.

The research involved not only reading the materials in the library of Kukulcan's Temple but also from the other ball courts and temples that were excavated. Everyone sat down with each other and put together their common translations. The story they constructed was not unlike the sensational publications at the supermarkets.

During one of the Quiche invasions, a fierce and fiery leader of a platoon, or the Quiche equivalent was captured. He was a charismatic individual. The Toltecs reasoned that he had to be destroyed, or he would incite a revolt. The stratagem designed was to invite him to lead his team in a game of Pok A Tok, a game that used a rubber ball and the two rings on the walls that may have been a progenitor of basketball. For this, he and his team would be greatly honored. The honor was to throw team into the cenote to drown, to tear out the captain's heart, and to offer it to Kukulcan. However, one clever lieutenant caught on to the subterfuge at the last minute and lagged behind the others. He hid behind the altar and buried his knife in the priest's throat. In the melee that followed, he was decapitated. Ritual murder was part of the psyche of the Maya because a great deal of effort was put into mind conditioning the same way it was done in inquisition Spain and Nazi Germany.

A small minority of people in a society seeks control of the larger population. Their rationale is that they provide a bulwark against disorder and mob rule. Emotional states are created by publicizing their positive and negative images in terms that appeal to the emotions of the larger mass about which an apparently logical system is built. Such an elitist group feels that they have the right and responsibility to plan and think for everyone else because they have developed the skills of propagandizing and brainwashing. They learned to use emotional, suggestive appeals at the right times. Such shenanigans were not beyond Mark's awareness or acuity, but he was astounded and depressed at the ease with which people could be moved to either accept killing or carry it on. Just who was this Quetzalcoatl and Kukulcan? He brought art and culture, on the one hand, and senseless, ritual slaughter, on the other.

At this point, in Mark's philosophizing, Kiona walked by with Helga and Henri. She beckoned him over as if she wanted him to be part of an adventure. "Hey, Long and Lanky, how'd you like to camp out this weekend." He noticed that she wore a pale green halter and turquoise shorts that brought out the tawny tones of her skin and the onyx like qualities of hair and eyes. This breath-takingly-beautiful portrait of a woman stunned Mark, but he did not want her to know it. Therefore, he said, "Goshes and gollies, yes. But what will we use for tents and how do we get there? Ride an alligator." Excitedly, Kiona explained that Henri and Helga had been saving their checks and bought a cheap little car. The prof was willing to loan them two tents for the occasion.

# Chapter 4

Traveling through a land that had the exotic past commingling with a vibrant modern nationhood carried with it an appeal to anyone who that had a feel for history and an appreciation for the pristine beauty of lush jungles of greenery. They drove about 98 miles southwest to Belize, where the campsite was. Once there, the tents were pitched with as much hastiness as their inexperience could allow. They were restless from being cooped up in the car for better than an hour and decided to go for a hike along the riverbank. The bird life was magnificent. Right at the shore were several hues of flamingos, toucans in the trees, chalachs, held in reverence by the Mayas, and plumed quetzals, protected by government interventions. The natural beauty was breath taking.

Dinner was by self-efficacy. Henri and Helga stayed behind to start a fire, while Mark and Kiona grabbed two fishing poles and spears to bring home the bacon, (if bacon swam). After a couple hours, they had landed about ten good-sized salmon, a rare breed of which spawned in the Cancun area of Mexico. Mark was reeling his last catch when Kiona decided to call it a day. All of a sudden she heard a loud shout and saw Mark pull something off his line. She ran over to him to see what it was. With a flourish he said, "For my little lady's pleasure", and gave her a beautiful purple and white piece of coral. At first, it almost took Kiona's breath away; to give herself time to regain her composure, she said, "I'm not so little." She found a loop in the curvature of the shell and put it on her necklace. Kiona smiled to herself because she knew Mark was waiting for her to kiss him. She inwardly chuckled and thought he was a spoiled brat. Without thinking, she slipped her arm through his as they walked back to the camp.

When the two of them got back to the site, Helga and Henri had a cheery fire going. Each helped scale the fish and remove the bones.

They fried nicely. Helga and Henri had prepared a salad from various herbs they found in the area. All seemed to enjoy their home made repast. Henri, as a pleasant surprise, pulled out a guitar, and the group sang folk songs together until the fire died out. The issue of who occupied what tent was settled by Helga taking Henri's arm and steering him to their tent.

Once inside their new domain, Kiona tenderly kissed Mark and thanked him for the beautiful coral. He was hesitant about returning her kiss and then gave in to his impulse. They began to seek each other and to press closer. Mark murmured that her lips were like the soft beauty of a delicately designed silken scarf. He began to kiss the softness around her eyes and ears and told her that her senses were all beautiful because they led to her soul. For a short moment, they looked at each other breathlessly. Kiona removed her halter and stepped out of her shorts. Mark was frozen for a moment because the beauty of Kiona's body astounded him.

Then he nuzzled her breasts and the cleavage between them, remarking that they were like the golden apples that Jason, Sinbad, Odysseus, and Sir Galahad had sought after to show what beauty meant. His mouth sought her nipple, and he felt it harden. Kiona began to softly moan. Mark told her that her nipples were like the grapes of spring and put his mouth around them once more. She let her hands wander over him gently and lovingly. Without thought or any premonition, she reached for him, loosened his trousers, and dropped to the floor. He continued to woo her with kisses and words. He told her that her navel was the well of life and that her flat belly was as beautiful as the Nile Valley. Kiona reached for Mark and felt him growing. "Take me", pleaded and commanded Kiona. Mark entered her feeling that he was entering a temple; a holy place that he never wanted to leave. They both began to rock and to almost scream together. Their love seemed like the crest of a never-ending omnipotent wave, but it did end; they slept in each other's arms. Neither the eruption of Mt. Vesuvious, nor the flooding of the Euphrates River, or the dropping of the Atomic Bomb could equal the sensations elicited by these two young people. For their power unleashed, was the power of love.

Kiona awoke before Mark. She stood pensively at the front of the tent. She jumped with a start as he squeezed her bottom and kissed her cheek. She turned to face him and kissed him. "You bad boy, do you think you are supposed to have your way with me whenever you want it." Mark began touching and stroking her skin very gently and said, "Yup." Kiona smiled at him took his hand in hers, and told him she had a secret she wanted to share with him. She told Mark that she had vacationed here as a little girl with her parents and found a beautiful place she wanted to show him. Mark's response was "Damn it, that means we have to get dressed."

After they were dressed and Kiona had packed a knapsack, she took his hand and led him to a path down by the lake. The two of them walked hand in hand through sylvan woodland punctuated by the green of a pristine, lush jungle and the songs of birds. At length, the terrain gave way to gently sloping hills. They stopped where a waterfall ran down a mountain on the opposite shore. Kiona shed her clothing and began to undress Mark. He, not too reluctantly, helped her in the process. Kiona said in a little girl's voice, "Gosh, Alfie, let's race to the falls." When they reached their objective, the water was shallow enough so that they could both stand. Kiona produced a bar of soap, which she had taken from her knapsack, unbeknownst to Mark. The pair began to wash and touch beneath the waterfalls. Their kisses felt like the morning dew, and they never wanted this time to end. They made beautiful, passionate love standing together on God's green Earth. Then they swam back to their clothes and the real world. Before they dressed each other, Kiona drew Mark to her and said, " I felt like Adam and Eve in the Garden of Eden. I hope all our days will be like this." Mark said nothing, but he picked some leaves from a tree and presented them to Kiona, saying, " For Madame's evening attire." Then they kissed and each felt the tear in the other's eye in appreciation of the beauty they had just shared. They strode back to camp arm in arm. This time they started the fire and sent Helga and Henri out to fish.

They came back with a string of fish that resembled black bass. However, neither one could identify the species, so they scaled them, filleted them, cooked them with onions and tomatoes, and ate them with a great deal of gusto without socially or scientifically defining the specific locus of Linnaeus' and Darwin's social register. This proved the edifying hypothesis that we do not have to understand all of God's creatures to eat them. The quartet played charades until Henri pushed Mark in the lake because he could not catch the clue he was acting out. Mark picked up the guitar and began to sing "La Paloma." The others were taken aback by Mark's fine tenor voice, and they joined in to create an effective harmony. They all joined hands and sang songs they all grew up with. Each split into their respective pairings and retired. Mark and Kiona sated themselves with lovemaking and lay snuggled in each other's arms. While stroking his chest, Kiona asked her man, "Hey, Lanky, what about our folks?" Mark paused for a minute and thought before he answered. He felt that they should be told and that they should try to share their love. If they refused, the door should be kept open. They decided to write their parents and let them know where matters stood.

Before they fell asleep, snuggled together, Kiona whispered in Mark's ear, "How about one more time before we have to face work. Mark answered, "Just what is it you want to do one more time. " She bit him and needless to say, no holds were barred. Neither was any sleep gotten. With their new relationship defined, a sense of peace prevailed during the ride home.

All was in a hubbub when they got back to camp. Fierce arguments were breaking out between factions of the guides that culminated in violent attacks between individuals and families. The core issue was whether or not Quetzalcoatl was a God or a man or whether he even existed. This went straight to the heart of Mayan culture. After all, the heritage that made an identity for a group that did not enjoy economic privilege or preferential treatment under extant social stratification patterns was threatened by questioning a foundation of past glories. A strong impetus to complete their task of verification was laid before the team.

Work began in earnest. The Popol Vuh was poured over; more studying was done at the libraries in Chichen Itza and neighboring cities. The universities of the area were frequented on weekends and evenings. Meetings and brainstorming sessions became more frequent. In the ensuing skull sessions, Kiona raised a sensitive issue: In ancient

Near Eastern civilizations, why did people unquestionably follow their leaders with blind faith? Numerous explanations were offered, but the core of the theories lay in the leaders either being viewed as Gods or having some communication with them. When asked what she was driving at, Kiona boldly stated that she felt Quetzalcoatl was a real man. He came from culture and brought it with him. She deduced that being away from his culture group resulted in a combination of loneliness and delusional thought patterns that may have led to need to rule others so that he could rebuild the grandeur he had left behind him, for whatever reason. In other words, he passed himself off as a God. From whence he came, this pseudo God brought with him intelligence and knowledge, but he also brought a liking for power that did not mind human beings sacrificed to him.

A corollary, which spun off this hypothesis, was to wonder what kind of ego injury could elicit such a lust for power.

Of the several explanations which were offered, the most plausible one was that this man was forcibly taken from his home and escaped to enter Mayan life at Tula, was on the losing end of a power struggle, fled with his army, and reappeared at Chichen Itza in 987. In his 22 years at Tula, he most probably learned that those who were revered as Gods held an absolute power. By virtue of this power, he could restructure the society around him to fit his comfort zone. His previous examples, unfortunately, were many in number. Not all tyrants did all badly. Mark added that they were not always self made either. Tyrants arise because the people want them to arise. Their wanting this kind of leadership may have several sources of thought.

He delineated that perhaps economic or social conditions sometimes paved the way for a strong man to take over. In response to the puzzled looks he got, Mark said, "Propagandists gauge the public's mood and tell them what they want to hear. They also use emotional appeals to link the perceptions of the people with their own." He added that he thought Quetzalcoatl showed evidence of being such a propagandist. The artistic architecture, militancy, using sacrifices as a tool to wipe out potential rivals and to establish the imprint that he was a God all appeared to Mark to indicate some central planning.

The others thought heavily about both of these formulations. Reported literature had described Quetzalcoatl as a Norseman and as a survivor of the destruction of Atlantis. Legend also stated that Atlantis, (if it existed), was an island in the Aegean Sea. Several historians compared the Mayan City states to the too loosely federated cities of Greece. If he were indeed captured by Norsemen, he would appear to be prone to seek a warmer climate for an escape. The possibility of him being a runaway from a slave ship also had to be considered. As to his motivations and psyche, he would not have been the first man to be wrested from his homeland, nor the first to seek revenge by seeking control over men's hearts and souls. Lenin did it, Hitler did it. There may have been a historical precedent set or followed by this feathered serpent, as his name was translated.

At any rate, the violence had to be stopped. Helga proposed a beautiful solution. This was the land of the Maya. Those, who were their descendants, were fighting. Should not their perceptions of the fact and legend be heard and presented before a legend was defined and taught by others, who were outsiders? To do otherwise seemed to be like America and the European states walking into China and dividing it up for themselves, ignoring the people, who were there for centuries before the Westerners. From this discussion, came a decision to include as many of the guides and/or their families as wanted to participate in the skull sessions. All had something to learn; all had something to teach.

Professor Horton thought that the group was expanding the parameters of the program too far. For the first time, Mark spoke in anger. He said, "Dr. Horton, do you remember what Kiona's goal in seeking knowledge about archeology was?" The teacher responded that it was to vindicate her people from the false impression created by the story of Hamm. Mark gritted his teeth and turned beet red as he said, "That story was passed from one generation to the next without finding out from the people who lived in the area what their perception of how they got there was. It became a justification for apartheid and racial supremacy doctrines that spread to Germany and led to a world war. Our generation is bringing children into this world, not yours. I do not want my kids to be taught the same racist horse crap, I was." They all caught the tear of gratitude and love in Kiona's eye.

Helga's plan was more easily proposed than implemented. The guides and their families were not easily assembled. They did not like outsiders coming in and imposing their ideas upon them; nor did they like young people, whom, they assumed, never did a lick of work, giving them instructions as to how they should lead their lives. One man, in particular, seemed to be a focal point for a significant portion of the feeling of nonverbal expressed hostility. After about three sessions of dodging opportunities to state their opinions, he piped up in anger, "I know that you White college students think that you came to uplift us savages to your superior way of life, but most of what you have, we had centuries ago without unreliable machines to produce the goods. As far as the superiority of your Christian religion that called us barbaric because we held sacrifice rites let me ask you how many people did you torture and slaughter? I know this is true because I went to your universities to better myself. The funny thing is that I discovered that I bettered myself by coming home and living the life of my people and by worshiping the God of my choice, not yours."

Kiona rather heatedly responded, "We may all be students, but we are not all White by coloration or by viewpoint. I, for one, do not care a damn what you believe. All we want to do is to find out how you think so that we can work together instead of blowing each other up. If that does not suit you, none of us is afraid to fight. I think such a fight is stupid, but if that is what you want, come and get it." With that said, she sat down just as heatedly as she stood up.

Everyone, including Mark smiled at Kiona's show of bravado except the gentleman whom she had addressed. He apologized for his anger, directed to a lady, but he would not back down from his stance. To disarm the situation, Mark began directing questions to the man. His name was Jimenez Bartomas. He asked if Quetzalcoatl was regarded as a man or as a God. Jimenez answered that as Jesus was regarded as a God figure because of bringing God's word to man, similarly, Quetzalcoatl brought teachings that enriched Maya life; this was equally worthy of Godliness. The tortures brought by Spanish missionaries destroyed Mayan and Aztec life. He could not see the logic of rejecting Mayan Pantheism and accepting a Christian God that preached love and practiced arrogance and cruelty. To this response,

71

Mark said that he only wanted to understand what Jimenez believed, not to judge it. The act of judgment was the prerogative of God. He said, "The only way I judge a man is if he hurts me or mine."

Because he was impressed with Mark's honesty, Jimenez stated he felt some confusion as to just what is a God and what is a man. He had heard of kings declaring themselves as Gods, yet they conducted themselves as men; they coveted property, they manipulated men and women, they died, never to be heard from again except in the legends of a people.

Mark's answer to this was that many Christians, including himself, shared this confusion. For this reason, he felt this is an issue that people needed to learn from each other instead of fighting for supremacy of their belief systems. The way of the supreme doctrine and dogmatically forcing it on others has created too much destruction. He added that he was interested in learning truth, not preaching it because he did not know enough to be preaching.

When Jimenez and the others heard what Mark and Kiona had to say, there was still skepticism, but not hostility and mistrust. The guides were exempt from participating in the studying and research, but their ideas were heard and their opinions along with everyone else's. The development of games based on justice was presented as evidence of his having God-like wisdom. The contrasting viewpoint was presented as Hammurabi, Solomon, and Justinian were harbingers of a just code of laws, but no one said they were Gods. The ancient pharaoh of Egypt said they were Gods, but they bled like anyone else. The Mayans asked why was Jesus a God if he bled and died. The answer that was presented was that Jesus is the way of God, not God. God sent him to man to teach His word. Throughout history, many men carried this message in different forms. Men, such as Gautama (Buddha), Mohammed. These men all carried God's message, but were not necessarily, God. Hence, the students got the idea across that they were interested in figuring out what status Quetzalcoatl occupied. Was he a man or a God? Jimenez did state that the status of Godliness depended on what people believed.

Mark acknowledged that Jimenez's statement had some truth in it, but that people had many reasons for their beliefs. He further averred that ordinary people telling the selected population that they were Gods had duped many people. Kukulcan, or Quetzalcoatl, appeared to indicate some tendencies to incite the public for his own reasons; interpreting the Popul Vuh discovered this data. The researchers had committed themselves to finding out the truth. If their interpretations were in error, they wanted to know about it. For this reason, they would greatly appreciate the help of the folks, who were the Maya, in the discovery of the truth.

The resulting information was distilled by study, data gathering, and the intellectual fermentation of argument. Sometimes the arguments became so heated that the windows had to be closed. Through this, process two cultures, often at odds with each other, were beginning to blend because their task seemed to have more worth than their rivalry. If nothing more came out of the mutual conference, they learned that men can work together when they want to do so.

Though the project was progressing by leaps and bounds, other areas of life were also coming into bloom. Of the potential in-laws, Kiona's parents showed the most receptiveness. Ruthena recounted the bitter experiences and treachery she and Grady had experienced at the hands of Whites. Mark's parents, on the other hand, re-affirmed their stance to let Mark make his own bed. Grady and Ruthena, at least, agreed to keep the door open to meeting Mark. This was saddening but expected. However, Mark was hopeful that time would make the difference.

The newly defined couple was beginning to realize the old adage that when you try to build a life together, all you have is each other. They were in the process of formulating a plan to take a job together and to try to set up housekeeping under one roof. From that point, they would let nature take its course. The next item in this plan of organization was to find an appropriate archeological site. Professor Horton was making inquiries, and Kiona had written both the History Department and Professor Owens at the University of Colorado. All was shared with Reed, Amy Rachel, and Arne. Cherie had been contacted, but seemed to have other interests since another female had come into the picture. The correspondence between the parties referred to nebulous plans for a reunion after graduation and future plans for their pending engagements, marriages, etc., were firmly established.

Even though they knew that defining themselves as an entity meant that they had to cling together against the whole world, a world that defined their parameters of clinging together, but showed them no way to do this. The only educational tool was to offer rejection or acceptance. The hope behind this mechanism was that the pair would provide sufficient motivation to stay within the fold, whatever that meant. The obvious alternative was for Kiona and Mark to define their own parameters and let the fold either expand over time to include them or be shed like the molted skin of a snake. In other words, the decision was to take a job together, see if they wanted to weather life together, and do so if this was what the experience showed them.

With their personal dilemma defined before them, they and the reconstituted research team returned to the task of evaluating the form and/or reality of the mysterious figure that was the object of their endeavor. His picture was in the frieze of the battle and of the sacrifice after the ring game. Was there an actual representation of a person, or was it the pictorial drawing of the God that is ever present? Factionalism caused this body politic to become just that. Why would a God show up at Chichen Itza leading an army in 987? How did he get to Tula twenty-two years before that? Where did the style of architecture he introduced originate? These questions dominated the arguments and logical presentations of all concerned. Again, the windows had to be closed so that the public would not have to be subjected to the linguistic delicacies that were transpiring.

The construct that the team, including the newest additions from the country itself, presented was that of a man, who might have been a Norseman or one of their captives. Apparently, he wanted to bring what had been comfortable to him to his new home. This was home because magical powers were attributed to him. These powers, in all probability came from a culture that had skills that the progenitors of the Mayans did not. The theories of Erich Daniken, described in "Chariots of the Gods" could not be excluded, but particularly the native segment of the team did not believe them. The condoning of sacrificial offerings suggested a figure that derived a sense of subordination of others to himself or, perhaps, some racist feelings. Quetzalcoatl, or

Kukulcan or whatever name other peoples called him had been a real physical presence and had brought a sense of glory to the present descendants of the Mayas. They carry the memory of this in their hearts today and have a right to this pride because they advanced mankind, as much as any group did; one presence was there to introduce these advances. He was Quetzalcoatl.

# Chapter 5

Before leaving the enchanting interlude that had transformed their lives and created a guiding purpose, these people began the processes of preparing for the realities ahead. Helga, Henri, Kiona, and Mark had found each other, but they did not know if their new relationships would be of any duration. Sama, Amund, and Ahmed remained unencumbered by an attachment or a direction. The group was caught in the web of clinging together superimposed upon going their separate ways. Kiona and Mark seemed to be caught in an experience of Déjà vu. They both tried to retreat to their old friendships but found they were not the same. Then they recalled they had each other with their parental supports knocked out from under them. While awaiting the replies to their job inquiries, both the groups, including the guides and their families, all had picnics and get-togethers before the final departures. Jimenez told Mark that he would never forget any of them because of the honest and sincere effort to discover the truth and to involve the people in the search for it.

Mark and Kiona also took advantage of the time to be alone. They hiked, swam, rode bikes, jogged, and went sight seeing by themselves. There was also time for quiet lovemaking and deep and private talks. They shared mutual feelings about leaving good friends and an aspect of their youths, but they had experienced this before. A new feeling was added to this. It was the leaving of a home that they had built together in the space of almost a year. They did not know what would be done with the knowledge they had meticulously and painstakingly derived. Underneath this was an uncertainty. Was this discovery accurate, and would it have an impact on how human beings related to one another? Only time and what the researchers did with the information would tell the difference. The feeling was not unlike a child being transported out of a foster home, where he/she has done well, to be reunited with the biological family not knowing if the family has grown to match his/her growth. The interim between leaving Yucatan and returning home to graduate and depart for their final destinations seemed like the waiting period between leaving a foster home and returning to the family of origin.

Kiona was likewise in a state of limbo. She was concerned that her dream was slipping away from her. She shared this apprehension with Mark. He reassured Kiona that he would be as supportive as he could and would participate in achieving this goal as much as he feasibly could. He even suggested that if no job offer came through that, perhaps, they could find a project that would disprove the story of Hamm and its racist innuendo. They might even embark on a dig to uncover knowledge about one of the African civilizations to begin at destroying this myth. Upon hearing this, Kiona threw her arms around Mark and kissed him. He warned her not to get him started. They both laughed at their silliness. Then he said getting him started might not be such a bad idea, after all.

Professor Horton sensed the anxiety in all the group members, but he was acutely aware of Kiona and Mark's newly found love and Mark's need to get started on his own life. He had been present when the umbilical cord was cut. He had given them both excellent recommendations to the Archeological Department at the Universities of Colorado and Iowa. He had also recommended them to archeological societies in several states. As a result, he also had acquired his own set of anxieties. They were not those of a foster child awaiting transition, but of a father wanting his children to implement the goal, they have chosen. He was also reminded of his own past. The struggles to compromise their own individual plans to arrive at a mutual one, the problems in rearing children to a healthy adulthood while continuing to work on their dreams, and finally the untimely death of his wife all interacted to make him shudder for these two young people. They had so much to give each other and to humanity. How would they channel their goals? How would they compromise them into a workable whole? There was so much he wanted to tell them, but he also understood that life and themselves had to be their teachers.

Kiona had come to Mark's tent and sat nestled on his lap, while the stew they were cooking for dinner was cooking in the pot on the fire. She said, "Lanky, what happens to all our dreams when we leave Yucatan and Quetzalcoatl behind us?" Mark answer that all that he could predict was that he knew he needed Kiona to feel complete as a person. That the story of Hamm was a great injustice to Black people all over the world was obvious. Mark pledged to join her in disproving this poppycock, whether as a life's work or as a way of life outside their careers. If Kiona would be busy uncovering data via uncovering the contributions to mankind made by ancient African Black civilizations, Mark could extrapolate on how George Washington Carver saved the South from economic ruin and had the foresight to educate himself under insurmountable odds or how Langston Hughes, W.E. Duboise, or Booker T. Washington had accomplished equally powerful goals under duress and oppression. One did not have to go back to ancient times to acknowledge the meaningful contributions Blacks had made to American and world culture; only an imbecile or an extremely vestedly interested lunatic could go back to the story of Hamm after learning about these many achievements.

Kiona was very touched that Mark shared her goal and stroked his face. She feared but understood and shared the feeling of his next words. "What we're doing is frightening to our families. We have to believe in who we are to stand alone and cling to each other through our doubts, fears, anger, and even our selfishness'. That will be scary. Our families will probably pounce on any sign of doubt, mistrust or fear. We have to talk and work them out by ourselves with no going to either parent, brother, sister, aunt, uncle, cousin, or friend. Otherwise, we are leaving ourselves open to have their values imposed on us rather than to develop our own. This will take a tremendous will to work together."

By now, Kiona had gotten up and closed the tent flap. Her next words, "Last one to take the other's clothes off is the south end of a north bound skunk." The race was fruitful. Afterwards, as she lay in the crook of Mark's arm, she wondered if they would find the strength to withstand the pressure of the forces that could drive them apart. She also could not help but wonder if anything they had learned would help them stick together.

The next day proved to be a memorable one for this young lady. As she was walking to her tent in the morning, she tripped over what appeared to be a stone. It was shiny. Kiona dug it out of the earth. It was a gemstone mounted in what appeared to be silver. There was writing on the back. The team went to work on matching the pictures with words. The translation was "Welcome to the city of Chichen Itza, under the mighty powers of Kukulcan may this be the token of your good fortune and the love of our God. Fare you well." This was Kiona's omen that she and Mark would stay together. Over the years, she and her choice of a man had stepped forward in righteousness God's word.

The writing also moved Mark on the gemstone back. Some other ideas were also preoccupying his mind. He was reading "The Covenant", by James Michener; he was bothered by the concept of the Afrikaners belief that they felt that they were preserving civilization by subjecting the native populations to second class citizenship in their own country, as well as barbarism and brutality. Their defense was the statement that cursed Hamm for seeing Noah indisposed and drunk, by stating that he would remain in Africa and sire an inferior race of people. Michener pointed out that just as dangerous as forgetting history and having to repeat it, was being obsessed by it and poisoned in thought. Such were the Afrikaners, and such was Kukulcan. Maintaining a civilization used as an excuse to disguise covetousness and killing people to maintain an image as a God because having power over others felt good has occurred a multiplicity of times throughout the ages. The concept becomes an obsession because human beings pound it into their heads as being righteous to hide from the wrongs they are doing to others to advance their own needs.

Mark was excited for discovering a truth in studying the Mayas that related to the evil doctrine Kiona was trying to debunk. He was so excited that he ran to look for her, and when he found her, he did not see her circumstances. She was engrossed in a conversation with a young man from the guide staff. As Mark approached he heard the man say, "I know that you are sleeping with that White boy. What is the matter, aren't I good enough for you?" With that, he pulled out a knife. Mark did not think. He picked up a nearby log and charged the man. The log hit with such impact that it knocked the knife from his hand. Another guide picked up the weapon. The assailant picked up the log and began to charge Mark. Mark saw a blowtorch lying nearby, instantaneously lit it, and began walking toward the man. He wanted him to make the choice to burn or to drop the log and stop the fight. When he saw that Mark meant business, the attacker dropped the log. The other guides rushed him and held him for the police. Mark went to Kiona and held her while she finally let herself weep. Later after a walk and a soothing dinner and an evening with friends, Mark and she talked about his discovery and the relationship to her concept.

From there, Kiona developed the idea to throw back the dirt on the Afrikaners that they threw on her People. She mentioned that she liked Mark's idea of going back to the individuals who accomplished for Blacks and humanity along with presenting evidence of powerful and cultured Black civilizations throughout history. She was also preoccupied about history repeating itself via Mark's present action. She told him about the circumstances under which her parents met. She also told him about her mother calling her father, Mousie, the way Kiona called him, Lanky.

She said, "I guess we are meant to be together, after all." Mark followed this up with, "What did you say, shorty?" Then he ran, as she chased him.

The difference between not forgetting history and being poisoned by obsession was not lost on Kiona. This kind of thinking obscured the concept of dealing with another human being, which had sensibilities and feelings. The effect of this type of thought process is to reduce personhood to an object that is secondary to an ideal. This ideal often times is a cover for an unsavory desire to advance at the expense of another. Hence, many if not all empires were built on noble sounding ideals that covered a treacherous need to walk on somebody else. To do this successfully, this high stepper must convince him/her self that the other party does not matter. The propaganda machine is created to justify the ideal that covers the ugliness of covetousness.

Kiona reasoned that this twisted thinking was created and passed on at all fronts and had to be attacked on all fronts. For this reason, an opportunity to learn more skills would be needed. One of the jobs, for which they had applied offered a chance at learning some of the skills their redeveloped task entailed.

The creative flow in them that felt as if the juices could not be stopped drove the pair to ache for any chance to be used productively in this field, which seemed to beckon to them. Letters arrived either wanting to know about them or rejecting their applications in the kindest language imaginable. Finally, a letter came that told of a job in the Mesa Verde area of Colorado. It described a dig going on at an area that had been populated by a tribe of Pueblo Indians from the thirteenth to the seventeenth centuries. A flurry of activity seemed to be occurring around a cave that had been newly discovered. The potential seemed to stimulate them both. The added plus was for Kiona to return to the area in which she had enjoyed the friendships that helped her grow from an adolescent to a woman. She knew that conditions would not be the same but she felt excitement at returning to the site where she took a vow to right a grave wrong done to her people. Adding to the surge was the fact that her newly found partner in life wanted to join her in this battle.

Mark saw this excavation as a way to unearth another truth in man's development and to possibly connect the truths he had learned in Yucatan with what he was about to learn. He also liked the idea of sharing and pooling knowledge with someone about whom he cared. He also was excited about being part of her quest. For this quest smacked, in part of his search for knowledge of Man, and in part in the search for a righteous justice and morality. The seemingly senseless way that humanity tore at itself really got to him. Mark did not realize that he was looking for a spiritual connection, a connection between Man and God. He also wanted both he and Kiona to find such a connection through a connection with each other.

The discussion these two had did not require any deep discussion or any skillful strategies to convince the other. Since the decision had been made, all that needed to be done was to accept the positions and get a starting date. Out of courtesy to their families and friends, they did let them know their plans and opened the door for further contacts; they did not expect acceptance or rejection but would build their love for each other with or without their support.

# Section IV

# The Dig

# Chapter 1

Mark and Kiona had agreed to attend each other's graduations and to meet the significant others. The first was in Iowa. The reason was obvious because they were moving to Durango, in Colorado to start their jobs. To Mark a sense of strangeness engulfed him. It was eerie. He was anticipating a feeling of discomfort when meeting his parents, but the feeling of emptiness made him feel as if he no longer belonged to this world. Jack and Bert tried to be aloof with Kiona, but the charm of her little girlish ways made them smile in spite of themselves. Of course, they had too much of a sense of arrogant pride to even consider that their view was in error.

Mark spotted this vulnerability and knew that they would yield in time. He took Kiona with him to explore some of his former haunts and to pick up Arne at the airport. After they got him, they all went to Barties. Bar Kochba Fenzel was so happy to see Mark and Arne and so delighted with Mark's lady friend, that he cooked one of his special omelets with corned beef, pastrami, bell peppers, tomatoes, and onions. He grabbed three waitresses, formed a circle around the table, and started dancing the hora. Arne began to accompany them on a harmonica. When Mark asked how he got it, Arne related the story about a kid trying to pick his pocket with the harmonica sticking out of his own pocket. While he picked Arne's pocket, Arne picked his. Arne followed him and negotiated a trade then bought the harmonica. One of his fellow engineers taught him how to play it. The four of them told stories and laughed until about ten o'clock that night. On the way out, they met Cherie and her fiancée. He was a graduate student in physics with a thesis studying the tensile strengths of metals to be used for pipes in zoos to carry the fecal matter from various animals. Kiona politely stifled a laugh; Mark and Arne chuckled and said to each other, out of Cherie's earshot, that it sounded like a shitty project. Kiona heard the tail end of this after the couple had passed. There was no more stifling.

At graduation, Kiona sat with Mark's parents. If they felt discomfort, they did not show it. After the ceremonies, they, Professor Horton, Arne, and his folks went to dinner. Mark was given a $2,000.00 bond for a present. Jack and Bert were sad about the short time together and said they would be in Colorado to visit them. Mark said that before they came to see them, he wanted his parents to meet Kiona's. When they protested, Mark said, "You put me on my own. My decision is that you have to accept me as a man. Part of that acceptance is accepting my woman. Another part of that is knowing from where she came. If your intent is to rebuild our relationship, it has to be based on knowing the entire world in which I function. You may not agree with my way, but it is part of me and has to be respected as that." Jack did not talk about learning about the hard knocks in life, but warned Mark and Kiona that they could not lead their lives for them, but they had to understand that their pain had to be their own. Mark agreed and added that the beauty did too. However, the door was open on his and Kiona's side, but Jack and Bert had to want to walk through it.

Bert and Jack had learned a new respect for this man, known to them as their son. He was not hostile to them, but he displayed a brazen cast off of the protections they had designed for themselves and him. They did not know if they could cast off the philosophical base that protected them. They asked themselves and him whether or not he had the right to ask them to disrupt the homeostasis they had contracted over the years, and did he provide any homeostatic mechanism that would protect them. The crux of the decision was it to be Mark and Kiona's struggle for their own identity, or would it be part of theirs.

Arne had made up his mind that the academic world may have its attractions, but it prolonged a state of youth and dependency that he found demeaning. He was starting a job working as a troubleshooter for foreign engineering projects under the auspices of UNESCO. He had to leave for New York in three days.

Kiona's graduation was not for another week. The couple decided to visit with Arne in the Big Apple for a few days. They took in the Statue of Liberty, and the play, Saigon. Arne told them about his adventures in Kabul, Afghanistan. The project was to fortify flimsy bridges built into the face of crumbling cliffs over narrow, bottomless chasms. The work was back breaking because the heavy rocks had to be moved almost one at a time. The Afghans would not use steel substructures, due to the fact that iron was not available as a resource and they did not want to rely on the United States or Russia for trade. After about a year there, one of the young ladies of the tribe took an interest in Arne. The feeling was not mutual. Her father did not appreciate Arne's rebuff, and he let it be known that he was coming after him. Arne hid in a basket of sheepskins to be traded with another village. The basket was transported in a camel caravan over the mountain pass via a bridge that he had just finished fortifying. Arne was also allergic to wool. Every time he sneezed, the trader would stop the caravan and see what was wrong with the camel. Arne threw him off by making grunting noises. Stopping in the middle of a bridge, upon which he was not sure the cement hardened was also nerve racking to this engineer. When he got to the new village, he did not have to worry about any other chieftain's daughter because he smelled like a sheep. In fact some of them looked at him funny.

Arne wished them well and said he would write. Kiona felt as if he were an old friend and kissed him good bye on his cheek. Arne replied, "I've never seen such behavior, I'll just have to turn the other cheek." Kiona told him he better change his line because she heard that one, and all it accomplished was to get Mark a dirty face. With that, they had one last laugh until they met again.

When their plane landed at Boulder, Kiona was like a little girl. She was exuberant at the aspect of seeing Rachel, Amy, and Reed again. Reed brought his new wife, Michelle with him. The two girls exchanged hugs. Amy and Ron had become engaged. Rachel was not there yet, but would arrive the next day. She had been accepted at Case Western Reserve University Medical School for the next year, in Cleveland, Ohio. She was visiting friends there. Ron would also be starting there. Reed was in the process of starting a pediatric residency and assuming an externship at a neighborhood clinic in Boulder. His wife was a pediatric nurse. Their plan was to take over this clinic once Reed had completed his residency. His father had offered to loan Reed the money, but Reed had some of Mark's need to be independent of parental beneficence because he thought it meant parental control.

Rachel had experienced her own set of adventures, together with Amy and Ron. These involved the young man, against whom Amy had sought revenge. He had proved to be more than an egotist. He had shown a severe character disorder that was unleashed by Amy's Halloween present. He was essentially a bright young man, but an undisciplined one. He did not like being bested by a female and did the detective work to find out Amy was the culprit behind the scheme with the cat. The form of his vengeance was to stalk Amy and Rachel. The ladies, in turn, went to Ron and Reed for help. The first step was for the girls to file a complaint with the police department. These young men knew it would not be acted upon. They reassured the girls that the rest of their plan would take a while, but they would not let anything happen to them. They followed him during his stalking with a camera and took pictures of his attempts to scare these women. The evidence had to show both him and, at least one girl in an unquestionably fear-evoking situation. With this accomplished, the enterprising fellows decided to let him see what a little terror felt like. They followed him on what proved to be his last stalking episode. They both wore identical trench coats and gloves and masks to look like college boys out on a spree. Reed wore a Barbara Streisand mask while Ron wore a Goofy mask. Each got on one side of him and picked him up. They blindfolded him in an alley and took his clothes except for his shorts, which he was wearing, and put him in a waiting car. They drove him out of town and brought him back thoroughly frightened. They stopped the car, took him out of it, and made him put his legs through an open cylinder with handles, to which his hands were tied. A necklace was placed around his neck with what felt like an envelope attached to it. In the morning, the police found a blindfolded young man on their steps wearing a hollowed out garbage can and a necklace with an envelope attached to it. The envelope contained the girls' complaint, pictures of various stalking that left no doubt of the intent to evoke terror, and a note, written on common notebook paper that stated, "If you would've done your job, I would not have had to." It was signed Poetic Justice. The police did not pursue the culprit because to do so would be an admission of dereliction of duty. The young man was found guilty of harassment and sentenced to follow up on harassment complaints to the Telephone Company for two years. In addition, he had to spend weekends in jail for two years.

Of course, Kiona and Mark exchanged anecdotes with Amy, Rachel, and the Hymers. The Almedersons showed up about the time Rachel had begun describing the adventure. They laughed uproariously at Reed's note to the police. But the descriptions of Mark's antics on the plane and in the restaurant, coupled with Kiona's obvious enthrallment made them smile from ear to ear. They were equally touched by Mark's decisive action in dealing with the snake and the angry, young man. Yet they kept to their predetermined reserve because they did not really know him, because the relationship was in the beginning phases, and because of what their relationship to White folk had been. As his parents had done, Mark sat with them to see Kiona graduate.

Kiona could see that her parents liked Mark, but she surmised that they would play their stodgy game. Subsequently, she saw Mark's wisdom in letting the acceptance be gradual.

As a result, she told them she wanted them to meet Mark's family before they visited them, not just her. Amy, Rachel, and Ron agreed to visit from Cleveland, and Kiona and Mark said they would try to make it east to see them. The Hymers, Mark, and Kiona promised to keep in contact. The distance between Boulder and Durango was not that great. That night, as they lay snuggled together, they voiced that they felt everything would work with their families if it worked out with them.

# Chapter 2

The Mesa Verde area was first settled by the Anasazis. Their progenitors had migrated from Asia via the land bridge in what is now the Bering Strait. The migrations apparently occurred during and after the Ice Age, as Asian hunters and their families followed the herds of mastodons, these groups moved into the Yukon area and, subsequently, along ice-free routes until they reached the Rockies. The first human beings in the area arrived about between 10-12 thousand years ago. Around 550 AD the Anasazi Indians settled around the Mesa Verde area, of Colorado. They, at first built mesa top homes on the cliffs and altered this pattern to dwellings under rock overhangs. This evolved into multi storied cliff dwellings with the pattern of a large central plaza surrounded by apartments, which led to subterranean rooms. These were known as pueblos. A system of multi storied apartments with underground apartments was developed with inter connections evolved as a defense against outside invaders. The cliff dwelling tribes eventually moved to the New Mexico area. The cliff dwellers were the Zuni, Tewas, Hopi. Other tribes in the vicinity attacked the Pueblos. They allied themselves with European and American groups as they showed interest in the geographic site. These tribes were the Shoshones, Utes, from the mountains, the plains dwellers (Cheyenne, Comanche, Arapaho, Kiowa), and various nomadic tribes (Pawnee, Sioux Navajo, Blackfoot, Crow, and Bands of Apache). Spanish and French explorers exhibited a sense of rivalry and allied with these tribes both to subdue the Pueblos and to counter the other European competitor during the seventeenth century, but the alliance under Napoleon and the growing rivalry with Britain tended to obscure the competition between them. The fact that a desert led to Colorado and a steep mountain range led from it, caused interest to wain in colonizing the area. The main reason for attracting Europeans was the potential for gold, gems, etc. When discovery and extraction efforts proved fruitless and Napoleon's war chest needed bolstering, the Louisiana Purchase took place and the territory became American.

The nineteenth century saw Colorado as a refuge for people who were sick of the burgeoning monstrosity, known as civilization. These were the restless explorer scouts, and mountain men. Soldiers with fading careers or incorrect political behavior were relegated to this locale to fight Indian Wars or man a fort alone in the desert. A gold rush occurred in 1859, but the mineral proved hard to extract and find. Immigrant groups migrated there and rediscovered the irrigation farming that the Anasazi had used centuries before. However, a lucrative silver mining industry was built up in the latter quarter of the nineteenth century.

After World War II, Denver brought attention to the West because of opposition to cheap public housing, and because a conservative business attitude was against labor unions. The mountains created a growing interest in winter sports. With the growing attraction came an interest in history and culture. Into this awakening walked Mark and Kiona.

Durango is about 60 miles Northeast of Mesa Verde National Park. The discovery of silver in the Rockies, after a short and rather lack luster gold rush, led to the building of a railroad in 1882. This goes from Durango to Silverton, where a large mine existed. This railroad is a major tourist attraction of the area. Around 1881 souvenirs of the Pueblo culture were being pilfered. As a result, a society grew to preserve the history of this culture; the resultant move to respect the past provided an impetus to create Mesa Verde National Park, along with several others. Included in this movement was the area within Durango and other sites in the perimeter of the old mining area. The name, Durango, seems to carry a mystique of its own. Old time westerns on the television always seemed to have an incompletely developed character known as the Durango Kid. Kiona and Mark chose this site as their home because it was close to Mesa Verde.

The discovery of the cave appeared to arouse curiosity of the archeology community because it appeared to be an anomaly to the Pueblos connected to the top of the mesa. The structure was spacious enough to allow a family or a similar grouping to live there, yet it was barren. There were some signs that the cave may have been fortified. The question that this possibility raised was against what or whom was it fortified. Furthermore, it was located on a ledge strategically, as if the site was picked for a specific purpose and dug out of the cliff. Another mystery was evidence that some kind of building apparently stood in front of the entrance to the cave, this was demonstrated by remnants of a hearth and adobe remains of what looked like a foundation. The room for Hypothesization and potential to unlock yet another hidden facet of Man's development held a sufficient enough attraction for Mark and Kiona to pursue participation in the project.

The head archeologist was Aaron Donleavy, a graduate of Princeton school of Archeology with fifteen years experience digging in the Mediterranean area. He assumed a competency in his staff and pretty much gave them a free hand in how they laid out their work. Three other archeologists were part of the team. They all had at least three years experience at digs. One was from the USSR, Jonos Tevrisz; the second, Mattani Bmgai, was from South Africa and a very strong-minded religious young lady. The third, Qamar B'aatyn, was from Oman, an emirate of the Arabian Peninsula.

A lot of rivalry seemed to be present between staff members because their positions were for pay, and because they were exposed to professional greed and the sequellae of being stabbed in the back that has become part of the work a day world. They had all striven for validation of the theses for which they had been hired, and addressed their employers as the archeologist, instead of a team working together to discover a common truth. At any rate, the spirit that was there in Yucatan was not present with this group. Their long exposure to the world of work had jaundiced these professionals.

Kiona and Mark would reinstate the feeling of teamwork, but a great deal of trust building would have to be expended. Added to this would be the time period to adjust by building respect for their competence as archeologists. Therefore, they dug into whatever material was available from the university library on the Pueblo culture. Perhaps knowing how to wield these professionals into a team was linked to understanding them as Coloradans.

This depth meant going back in time to the Pueblo dwellers: Anasazis, Zunis, Hopis.

They were individuals, who had difficulties with other tribes because they believed there was a special symbiosis between them and their land. Simply stated it was: We were created on this land. Our lives are centered about it. If our thoughts are harmonious to this spiritual connection with the land, the land will be good to us. This feeling for the land was carried by the miners, who hunted for gold and silver in her riverbeds and mountains, farmers, who diverted streams for her truck farms, furriers, who sought her game. As late as the fuel crisis in the 1970;s, Coloradans were conflicted about merging oil companies to fight Opec's control of oil flow through prices so that the United States could avoid dictatorial control. Coloradans did not want outsiders, who did not appreciate the beauty of their land controlling the mining of their oil. Yet they also and not want Americans to be subservient to foreign overlords.

Mark and Kiona decided to see how much Coloradan individuality had permeated the thinking of these archeologists. What they found was that three people were separated from their cultural roots and were desperately attempting to bond to their new home. Therefore, the two new comers had to demonstrate that they were not interlopers, but a vanguard of more efficient archeological function. The first plateau to efficiently working the mesa was Aaron Donleavy. Their line of attack was to present the accolades from Professor Horton about the project in Yucatan. They explained that the concept of cooperation encouraged a development of a pool of knowledge that enabled the deciphering of a language none of them knew; the people about whom the students were hypothesizing, added knowledge because their efforts helped the body of knowledge grow. In short, teamwork led to a greater output that could be shared by all. Aaron seemed to go along with their arguments, but he threw responsibility for selling this team concept to his staff to the new pair.

At the first meeting, after the concept of teamwork was presented, a heavy silence greeted Mark and Kiona. Jonos was the first critic to verbalize his mistrust: "Why should I trust you? My people trusted yours as allies during the war only to have to protect themselves from your capitalist greed and intrigues."

Kiona's response to this was, "If you do not trust me for what my forefathers did, you are creating and recreating enmity. Was not one of your earliest postwar acts to agitate among my people, not for respecting us, but for propagandizing us to let you be our masters. Your Comintern hollered about lynching down South, but you did nothing to stop it. Black Americans were not treated with any more respect by North Koreans than by South Koreans. The testimonies of returned prisoners of war, as well as returned GI's verify that. Do I need to go on?"

Mark added, "If you base your mistrust on what my father did, you are saying my actions have no meaning. If I present behavior and ideas from which we can all gain, it will be for nothing because your judgment will have been made. Do you look at a book's cover and decide to throw it out or read it, or do you at least look inside to see if some of the content is worth your while? If you do not want to be judged, do not judge me."

To this, Aaron added the accomplishments of the team in Yucatan. He also related that a working team was structured by their action and their feelings for the task, as well each other. He left a manuscript of the results of the Mayan Expedition for them to read before they made up their minds about the proposal before them.

That night Mark and Kiona worried about whether had gotten over with the group, but they also tried to formulate a way to work on Kiona's concern about debunking the story of Hamm. Mark had already decided to research George Washington Carver and Garret Morgan in terms of disqualifying this myth. He chose these two examples because they showed a curiosity about the world in which they lived. They also worked out how much they would compromise their plan if it were rejected. The next morning could be a heavy one for them. It could mean having found a roost or going back to not knowing where they had prepared themselves to fit.

The eloquence of Kiona in attacking use of the past as a defense against facing the present, and Mark's anger at being judged by someone else's actions combined to motivate this professional staff to question the merits of their rigid solutions. They were at least willing to try to alter their stance against mutual sharing to build a broader, more compromised and reasoned out base of knowledge. The converse corollary also was in force: If the results would be a disappointment, this state would induce a strong and opinionated rejection of the concept of sharing and mutual idea building. Thus, at least tentatively, some flexibility was elicited.

As a group, they entered the cave. It appeared to be a huge room that may have had some common group function, such as a meeting hall or religious structure. Window like apertures appeared at either end. Gun mounts or equivalent defensive structures were placed on either side of each opening. The arch of the doorway seemed to be an arrangement of curves that a shovel would make rather than the smooth surface that a river or other waterway might erode over time. Furthermore, these gun mount like structures also seemed to reappear in the middle of the room. They also seemed to point upwards. A stalactite like structure rose above the gun mount structure. The upward growing growth was about the width of a man at its base and much wider at the top. One of these scientists had the idea of tapping the structure and discovered it was hollow. Shining a light on the base revealed a hinged plate at the bottom that might be a door. Jonos noticed that the stalactite was embedded in a wall and not in the middle of the cave as a normal one was.

Kiona got an idea at he same time as Mattani; the two smallest members should get in and climb to wherever the tube led. The two, who were elected, were Qamar and Kiona. A crowbar was produced, and the duo got in and began their assent. They soon discovered that the opening widened into a tunnel that could hold all of them. They hollered down to the others to join them. After they did so and all reached what appeared to be the end, there was a drop into a large room. Looking around they discovered two things: There were many rooms with a large room in the center. They also found that they were in a building of more than one story. Making their way to the outside, they were atop the plateau that was called Mesa Verde.

The time had come for the team to digest what they had learned. Kiona and Mark welcomed the return to skull sessions. The first conclusion arrived at was that the cave was a man made opening. The scalloped edges of the arch precluded natural erosion as a cause. The tunnel that was traversed was apparently some sort of escape hatch. The gun placements indicated a defensive function, which also indicated military activity. A puzzle was presenting itself. Preparations seemed to be on line for a battle, yet there were no weapons or signs of destruction, save the evidence that a building had stood in front of the cave and had been torn down. The enigma could unfold only with further excavation and pooling of resources.

With the opening up of the definition of their task, Mark decided to follow up on his commitment to Kiona's sworn task. He began reading up on George Washington Carver and Garret Morgan. George Washington Carver exhibited an intense desire to learn in an atmosphere that was anything but conducive to self-improvement of Blacks. He excelled as a botanist, an artist, and a humanitarian. If he were wont to stop with his won pleasure and achievement, he would have stopped there. However, he went on to become an agriculturist at Tuskegee Institute, to aid the Black share cropping farmer while he also aided the economy of Southern agriculture with his research into soils, plant hybridization, and plant foraging. He tried to encourage White and Black farmers alike to rotate their growing toward more marketable produce than cotton, which was depleting the soil.

Garret Morgan also grew up with an inquisitive mind. He was always interested in learning why, how, and wherefore of any mechanical device. By the time he was fourteen, he was so discouraged with the lack of opportunity that the South offered him to develop a sense of actualization that he asked his parents for permission to leave home and find a way to make a life for himself. He came to Cleveland, Ohio where he started out working at a factory and was put in charge of seeing that the machines were in operable condition. He grew tired of the headaches of working for someone else and started his own repair shop. He was concerned for the safety of others. To prevent the danger of smoke inhalation he invented a gas mask that was used by the American Expeditionary Force in World War I. He was not given credit for this invention. Yet, after witnessing an accident, he invented the traffic light. The city of Cleveland would not recognize it or let him operate it. He had to go to Willoughby, Ohio to get it recognized. GE bought it for $40,000.00, but he was not given credit for this until forty years later. He died four years after this while trying to find help from a hospital.

These two men had talent and knew they had it. Yet, they tried to benefit humanity with their skills. These choices were made knowing that the White dominated society would not accept their genius or their love of man. Perhaps they had intuitively grasped Martin Luther King's message that love expressed in the face of hate would show to the White man what he was acting like. The inferior race of Hamm's issue would not possess the intellectual equipment to synthesize such a powerful weapon. Maybe this explanation of origin was a lot of hogwash. Maybe it was developed as having the authority of gospel because its designer(s) may have had a streak of greed to hide.

Mark incorporated his data and his analysis of the conclusions and effects on people and their reasons. He also believed that a propagandizing schema lay at the root of such thinking. He referred back to two giants, in their own right, who had every right to play the race game on Whites and use them to be victims of their own greed. To the contrary, they saw themselves as bearers of God given talent to be used for the betterment of mankind. The fathers of segregation and apartheid saw their mission as preserving civilization by denying people that they deemed as inferior a right to receive benefit. The difference in focus had its roots in the orientation and distortion of fact. The fact motivating the inventors was that if all men would establish a higher level of attainment there would be less envy, friction, and attempts to hold back rival populations. The segregationists, on the other hand, created a mythology to justify appropriating another's property or entitlement of it for the sake of their own greed. In their eyes, stealing from someone else did not matter because they were not as worthy as the thief in the thief's perception. The percept was a distortion that gave the thief his excuse to steal without jeopardizing his/her soul. The outcry was not to right the injustice, but to create the opportunity for man to be what he is supposed to be.

In keeping with what he had just learned about mankind, Mark proposed to hold up the mirror to man the same way the reflection did by adding the results of his research on people to whatever Kiona was able to glean from her efforts. Hopefully, the integration of their efforts would shake the foundations of the inhumanity of the sects and their limitation of what God had meant for all.

Having begun to embark on their new journey and initiated a blending of their goals, Mark and Kiona began to explore the Durango geography. The town grew up around the 1870's when Colorado was in the heart of its silver boom. The railroad bypassed Animas City, and its residents formed their own town to the south. A railroad was built to connect the miners with the big mine at Silverton. Today it carries tourists. The population is 12,500. The summer and spring seasons are the time of the tourist. Motor Homes, trucks, trailers and whatever vehicles that can be adapted for summer travel swelter the numbers in the town. Here is a veritable tourist Mecca.

In keeping with this image, a host of activities and attractions have been brought into play for the historically and culturally inclined. Museums, culture centers abound in the area, as well as state and national parks that preserve the flora and fauna of nature and some of the Native American culture patterns indigenous to Colorado, such as Pueblo (Zunis, Hopis, Anaszis), Utes, Arapaho are readily available. For the more robust hiking trails, rafting sites and kayaking are seen along the valley of the Animus River. Salmon, trout, pike, and walleye abound in this and other rivers in the area. Mountain climbing and mountain biking take up a lot of the outdoors peoples' time and energies. In the winter cross-country and mountain skiing keep the hunger for the great out doors alive in the hearts of the winter athletes. Shopping malls and a fine array both of restaurants and country western entertainers are also plentiful in and around Durango. This was, indeed, a city for a burgeoning American youth, and a youthful couple had found it.

However robust and hardy this couple was, there was a plentitude of work to be done. The great mystery of where the Pueblos had gone and why preparation for what appeared to be a fortified structure was found with weapon mounts, but no weapons begged to be solved. The ingenious design of a multi-storied building connected by tunnels and leading to an escape tunnel via a man made cave offered several attractive hypotheses that were in need of exploration. A new excavation was about to begin.

# Chapter 3

Mark and Kiona started their new adventure by buying a small used Honda Acura and attaching bike racks to the trunk. They rented two mountain bikes and drove to Mesa Verde Park. Because of their obsessive curiosity, they rode the bicycles up the mountain and stopped at the kivas, the two-storied dwelling to which they had tunneled previously. The knapsacks they carried had some digging tools. The kiva was a towered structure, and guided tours were given throughout the day. Once upon the tour, they learned that the Anasazi had abandoned this area in the thirteenth century, but Zunis and Hopis occupied it after them. These Pueblo tribes were in the area in the 1500's when the Spaniards were on the prowl for gold. Two wars between these indigenous and invading combatants occurred. The Pueblos won the first round, but, unfortunately, they lost the second. Much had occurred to provoke these wars, and it involved cruel treatment, expropriation of native villagers' property, and the rape of some Pueblo women. Also involved was the greed for wealth and the refusal to accept the validity of non-Christian religions and give human respect to their practitioners. The pair also discovered that relationship difficulties occurred between the Pueblos and the various Plains and Nomadic tribes of the area. This affected the alliances with the Whites and Indians for centuries to come. One more bit of data was gleaned from the mini-expedition: The kiva was linked to other dwellings by underground tunnels. All this material was shared at the next meeting.

Left unexplained were the remains of a building that had stood before the cave almost flush against it. Upon further exploration, charred stones were found on the ground surrounding the putative structure. The two of them wanted to start digging after the tour, but they had learned sufficient Colorado history to know that the populace of this state was jealous of their resources, and that they no longer had the freedom as students to rove about the countryside in search of knowledge with impunity. Consequently, they held back on their curiosity to bring up their findings at the meeting on Monday.

That Monday night the meeting was held. Restlessness seemed to pervade everyone. They wanted to get about the business of unraveling the mystery at hand. Aaron wanted each to learn skills from the others so that an understanding and sense of teamwork would evolve. He also wanted each to learn the entire project. Hence, he reasoned that if the task could be broken down into different sub areas worked by different people, who rotated between different phases of the dig, they could not help but develop an understanding of the whole project. This would be enhanced by the integrating mechanism of the meeting.

Subsequently, Mark and Jonos would dig in the area in front of the cave where remains of an apparent building stood. Kiona and Mattani would work in the cave, itself; Aaron and Qamar would work in the multi-story building, or kiva. After two weeks, the team would reorganize and switch sites. For the moment, this plan seemed feasible.

Mark and Jonos began their work the next day. At about three feet down, they found a large room. Shelving, or the remains of it, appeared to line what was left of the walls. A series of steps led down to the floor, apparently from the outside. Several dish and bowl-like vessels were extricated from the shelves, as the digging proceeded. Further digging revealed rings, necklaces, etc. Mark even modeled a mildewed shirt with a frilly front, worn by a Dandy of the era. Jonos threw weeds at him in mock admiration of his stylish affect. What really intrigued them was a skeleton they found in a back passage they had excavated. It wore a breastplate and conquistador helmet. An arrow was lodged in the soldier's neck. A musket lay next to these remains. The back appeared to be a storage area and both sides of it converged to a central passage leading out toward the cave entrance. The artifacts that had been found seemed to be in a state of disarray. Each archeologist was beginning to wonder what cataclysm took place here.

Kiona and Mattani found that the cave might have served as a storage site for munitions, foodstuffs, as the eating artifact frequency seemed to indicate. Besides, the number of corncobs in the area was an indicator of the consumption of maize or corn products. Several were collected for testing by counting rings or carbon dating. The direction of the earth seemed to be towards the periphery from the central tunnel through which the group had ascended to the kiva. Munitions storage was indicated by powder marks and the remains of crates. The gun placements without rifles remained a tantalizing mystery from the other day's visit. An attractive concept that was formulating in the minds of the young ladies was that either someone hostile was coming, or people were fleeing from an attack.

Aaron and Qamar were up in the kiva. The dig revealed skeletons in bizarre positions with jagged bones and weapons scattered in many directions. Dark stains were seen at the jagged edges of extremities and sternal borders, and numerous powder burns were in the area. Arrows and spears lay about. Anything but a peaceful family get together was suggested.

The most obvious conclusion that could be reached by putting together their observations was that some kind of war took place and that Spaniards were involved. Kiona enlightened the group that in the fourteenth century Spain was out to extend both it's and Mother Church's dominions in Europe and in the Americas. Part of this extension was a greed for gold and other forms of natural wealth. Concrete reinforcers for the money lust were the successful wrestling of jewels, gold, and silver from the Aztecs (who were later descendants of the Maya) and the Incas by Cortez and Pizarro. The desire to seek favor with Ferdinand and Isabella coupled with this exploitative wanting led Francisco Coronado to engage in a futile adventure to find seven cities of wealth in the area inhabited by the Pueblo dwellers. The results were ruthless exploitation, outward projection of a self-rage at letting himself be duped, and several wars to expel the greedy, power hungry colonial minded Spaniards. She suggested that Mesa Verde might be the site of, at least, one of these battles.

Mark and Jonos built on this interpretation by relating the finding of conquistador's skeleton in the structure before the cave. From the artifactual extractions, they deduced that the building served the functions of a store or center of business. They were not able to figure out its connection to the cave. A connection between the vertical tunnel, the cave, and the kiva was there. This tunnel served dual functions. If the enemy forced its way into the kiva, the tunnel could serve either as a retreat vehicle or as a ground to launch a counter attack. Hence, the purpose of the gun placements became apparent. What was not apparent was the dearth of Spanish skeletons in the cave and the absence of guns in the placements.

Likewise, Aaron and Qamar figured out the link between the tunnel, the cave, and the kiva. They also expounded the theory that the store acted as a front for the cave because the cave entrance seemed serrated, as if cut out of the mountain, and because only three borders were distinct to the foundation. During peacetime, the cave may have served as a storeroom. As it was beginning to unfold, history was defining the Pueblos as aggressive, cagey fighters. What role Mesa Verde played in the militarism of the era and the ultimate congruency of these constructions to the outcome of history appeared to exert a teasing effect on their psyches.

When Kiona commented on this teasing effect to Mark, his retort was that the resultant release of a need to be relieved of such tantalization could only cause any red blooded man to seek his woman. Then he began to chase her around the room. She laughed and led him to the sink after which she poured a pot of cold water on him. Mark stated he needed a cold shower anyway and proceeded to take one. However, he did not protest when she pulled the curtain aside and got in there with him. Afterward Kiona asked, "Is my gallant sailor through with being teased by the siren of archeology?" Mark said, "Nope." In fact, Mark was into the fighting back phase of the Siren's tease. His curiosity about what went on here all those centuries ago was whetted to a sharp edge.

In pursuit of this knowledge, they went to the library in the community and looked up the historical basis and Coronado's motivation in seeking the Seven Cities of Cibola, as well as his response to the Pueblos. Spain was in the mood to extract riches from the New World to continue to finance its inquisition. According to legend, seven bishops had erected seven cities on an island in the Atlantic. These cities supposedly, had towers. An embarkation to Florida led to the capsizing of the boat in a storm. Apparently, the survivors did not want to look foolish and wished to cover the fact that the expedition was a waste that incurred the loss of life. Therefore, they aggrandized their experience, telling tales of a wealthy kingdom in the north of the Mexican territory. A priest was dispatched to verify the story. This cleric sent a scouting party, under the auspices of a Moorish aide. This aide foolishly wore a gourd that was an emblem of a tribe that was an enemy to the Zunis who lived in the village he happened upon. Needless to say, he was received with hostility and slain as a spy. His followers told the priest that they had indeed found the first of the Seven Cities of Cibola. The news was relayed to the viceroy of Mexico. The result was Coronado's expedition.

The reportage was given by non-Spaniards, who served in a servant capacity and feared the wrath of their masters. They also knew about the greed and gullibility of these White men. Hence, they fed them fictions that would avoid their ire and distract them from criticism for the clumsy manner in which they had handled their responsibilities. As was to be seen Coronado also shared this duality of dysfunction: pride to cover half thought out endeavors and greed that blinded the common sense to question data put before them. News of Spanish exploitation (as well as that of White men, in general) had been dispersed among many tribes, but the deeds of Pizarro and Cortez were widely known. Consequently, a chief in the area lured the greedy fool away from the Pueblos to Kansas with a tale of wealth. Coronado was so enraged that he imprisoned this chief through the winter before he killed him. History knows him, as the Turk.

Vindictiveness displayed itself in other ways in Coronado's soul. Finding an ordinary village instead of gold and jewels angered him. By dint of the superior firepower of his force, he disregarded the dominion over their homes and property, to which these indigenous people had a right, and confiscated homes, food, blankets, horses, and whatever resources were available. A rape of a woman also took place in at least one village. These Indians were sub human because they were not Christian and did not matter. If the mood struck to punish them for not being the harbingers of wealth Coronado wanted, taking out violent tantrums on them was all right. These Native Americans did not perceive unwarranted expropriation of what was theirs by a stranger that displayed neither courtesy, respect, nor brains as all right. In fact, several wars took place to expel him and his kind. One was finally successful for the first part of the century. After this Spain proved might was right and reclaimed what was wrongfully, and never intended by God, to be theirs.

This was what Mark and Kiona had gleaned from a weekend of study. It helped put their observations into a schematic, and they shared their knowledge and adjusted thoughts with their colleagues, as they were becoming bonded to be. A team was beginning to emerge. As all relationships evolve from a state of strangerhood to acquaintanceship, to colleagues, to friendship, so would these relationships grow. Now a scene of warfare was in the process of being reconstructed by this newly emerging team of professionals.

Mark put what he had learned in Yucatan into the new profile of humanity he was deducing from these observations. Once people had digested the propaganda and were brainwashed into the acceptable belief system, they exported their learning. For this reason, the Spaniards brought with them the condescending attitude that they were dealing with lesser beings because these people were not redeemed in the holy teachings of Jesus. Hence, their dominion was not asked for in courtesy, but demanded as the right of a superior being. To be treated in such an offensive manner evoked violent feelings on the part of the indigenous population. What better provocation could there be for war. The aggressor, in order to avoid questioning his own motivation, addressed the negative response as further evidence of the native savagery and inferiority. More recalcitrant entrenchment in their propaganda -synthesized beliefs resulted in more savage warfare to stamp out this effrontery to their lord. To Mark the mass production of attitudes and their rapid exportation was frightening. It also brought a horrifying insight into the human psyche; once convinced of a truth; men followed it to the extent that it assumed a power beyond them. It became an end in its own right. However, this could be taken a step further into the realm of defense mechanisms. A moral proposition, such as winning conversion of heathen masses to the arms of Christianity, could be a cover for coveting resources from a people. To avoid facing their more dastardly motivations, the holy dictum becomes substituted for the greed and becomes the dominant thought every time the guilt for the real motivating factor surfaces. Thus, an obsession is born, the thought that poisons the way we learn history.

The obsession with the origin of the obsession drew Mark back to the commitment he had made to research great American Blacks lives to disprove the myth of Hamm. In the course of his study, he discovered some of the writings of Martin Luther King Jr. Dr. King had dissected the structure of White racism and traced it back to the legend of Hamm. He stated that racism stemmed from a rationalization of assuming power over another's domain because of a belief of superiority. Institutions of society were called upon to justify the brutality of treating a person like a thing that belonged to another person. As a result, the Bible and the concept of religion were distorted. Noah cursed the children of Hamm when this son saw him naked and drunk. St. Paul is said to have said, "Servants, obey your masters." These dictums were the cover for the abnormal excuse for a White man collaring a human being and saying since God states I am better than you, I have a right to use you for my own gain.

The results of this kind of thinking were not only that the White supremacist had his excuse for not looking at himself, but that the Black man thought of himself as a nobody, and his color was a constant reminder of it. In a moment of maudlin reverie, Mark wished he could share Dr. King's perceptions and deductions with his parents; he knew that they would only reach these conclusions if they opened their souls. Instead, he shared them with Kiona.

When Mark went back to their apartment, he found her attired in night clothing getting ready for bed. He explained that he had been doing research and showed her his work. She threw her arms around him and asked, "Why do you always bring me this type of subject matter at bedtime?" His reply was to look like a pitiful puppy then to say, "Because I want to get in your pants." Kiona smacked him and laughed. But she did not resist his touching her and kissing her. Afterwards while they lay snuggled together, she said "Lanky, what happens if I get pregnant?" Mark looked at her for a second and fondled her belly lovingly, so lovingly that it showed in his eyes. Then he said, "If it is a boy, we will name him Quetzalcoatl; if we have a girl, we will call her

Stinky." Kiona, as usual stifled her laugh and said with mock anger, "I am not raising a girl named Stinky." After this Mark said, "I want a baby, but I want us to be married a while first. Our commitment to each other has to be on solid ground first. More than our feelings are involved." With that she kissed him and hugged him. That was how they were when they fell asleep.

Their love was growing along with a blending of their separate ideological beliefs. One could reconcile needing to know where he/she stood in the world and analyze the thought processes by which the standing evolved with the righting of an ancient wrong that led to needless pain. Both of them were about to learn how strong the ground they chose to walk upon would or could be.

# Chapter 4

Mark found himself more and more intrigued with some of the Black writers and philosophers on their views of the origins, responses, and answers to doctrines of racism and White supremacy. He found this both helpful to Kiona and her thesis and to his understanding of how people ticked, and how he could plug into it as a human being. Therefore, he began to study Dr. King, James Baldwin more intensely than he had before. His conclusions were that the story of Hamm was a fabrication that was designed by the White man with a duality of purpose. The first aim was to assuage his conscience for treating a fellow human being as a thing whose need for dignity, integrity of a basic family structure, pride in ownership or achievement did not matter because it was secondary to his own. The second function this theoretical conceptualization held was to brainwash a competitor for limited resources into removing him-/her-self from the market. These dogmas were built into the Church and other institutions to the extent that Black slaves in the South fought for the Confederacy in the Civil War. Reaction to this caused many to be bitter about achieving the hoped for and promised freedom, as well as anger at themselves. The freedom that was publicly granted after the war's end and privately withheld also fanned the resultant anger, frustration, and self and oppressors hate. The only solutions to this dilemma were based on changing the status of the Black American from a second class citizen to a force that had to be reckoned with because the said minority had as much right to the freedoms granted by virtue of spending his/her own blood to get it.

These giants among men chose to fight back by not fighting, but by loving the Whites by holding a mirror up to them. This was meant to heal the festering sore of racism by allowing us all to assume our prerogative as fellow human beings. Of course, other solutions were proposed by other leaders, but the ability to research, analyze, theorize and hypothesize any solution cannot be the product of an inferior being from an inferior progeny. Mark reasoned that if the legend, indeed, had any credibility, then Noah should have kept his shorts on instead of spouting off a curse that reflected his sense of guilt at immoral behavior and allowed an entire race of people to be trampled on.

Mark also tied in the feelings between the Spaniards and the Pueblos to these concepts. A stranger that comes to your home and helps hinder your life by appropriating your house, food, and companion at will is not very welcome, to say the least. This stranger would have to be relieved of his grubbiness, if not the hands that are so grasping. Showing by love and reflection would not be the first option that crosses one's mind. In no way can this person be construed as a host, even though the previous example was a bizarre, if nonexistent, stretching or construction of this social definition.

Making this connection between the American Black's and the Pueblos' response to White racism brought Mark back to the issue at hand. A war had been postulated, Mark could not figure out why a structure like the tunnel would have been conceived if not to be able to trap and shoot large numbers of the enemy attempting to get through it. The fact that gun placements were in the cave gave testimony to using this type of strategy. Yet, if this strategy was in the minds of the defenders, where were the guns? Perhaps more digging in the cave would give some more answers.

The rotation had changed, and Jonos and Mark were now in the cave. In one corner of the first chamber, a stalagmite and a stalactite grew together, and behind it a peculiar rock formation projected from a wall of the cave. There were shrubs on the top of this mini plateau formation. They seemed to form a ring around a central portion. Mark climbed the mesa-like protuberance and started to observe. With his pick and sledgehammer he broke the rock around one of the plants and used a crowbar to pry it loose. He then sawed the main trunk of the plant so that the rings of the trunk were exposed. By a simple counting of rings, the age of the plant could be guesstimated. The approximate age of the shrub was computed to be about 450 years. This would mean that the shrubs were planted in the 1500's. Climbing up after Mark, Jonos observed a fissure in the rock behind the shrubs. He began to use the crowbar and sledge to probe the rock. At one end, he found a hinge. This appeared to be a sort of door. Dark was approaching and the conundrum as to where it led would have to wait until morning.

Mark brought Jonos home to dinner that night. They ordered a large deluxe pizza to be delivered. Kiona had made Swedish meatballs and noodles to go with it. They washed this down with Guiness' Stout. For dessert, Kiona had baked a cherry cobbler that melted in their mouths. They began to talk about how a concept of what was going on in their lives was relating to what they were starting to uncover. It seemed strange that four individuals from such a diversity of backgrounds could learn the processes in working together while studying two cultures that were in the process of tearing each other apart because they did not know how to break the oppressor/oppressed code of behavior. They theorized that the difference in the two situations could be related to the fact that the coming together of different cultures without awareness of each other created an upset in each party's comfort zone. The easiest course to take was to reduce the challenge to feeling discomfort by rebuilding the familiarity at the other party's expense. However, the offended party did not appreciate having an outsider come to them and ignore the comfort pattern that he had built. Was the difference between the diverse group of archeologists learning to live together and the Spaniards trying to force their ways on the Pueblos solely due to the unawareness of each other due to isolation, or were there other factors that operated in deciding whether different factions of humanity moved toward recognizing each other or trying to blot each other out? Was their role to be the vanguard of education and show that civility and decency evolve by establishing communication that breaks down the barriers between culture, race, and nation? Perhaps the answer to this riddle lay somewhere in this cave.

That night Mark had his first night of troubled sleep. He dreamt God came before him and said, "My son, why are you tampering with my decree to man. Did I not warn Adam and Eve in the Garden not to eat of the tree of knowledge, and did thou not defy me by so eating?

He screamed his rebuttal:" Was I not created in your image, so that I may come to know you?"

What I seek is for the good of man. God's answer was " you are created in my image, but you are not me." " Is it your plan that we destroy each other to find you?" To this, God replied, " I took you unto me to have as your God, not to know me."

The noise of his tossing and turning woke Kiona. She, at first, was stunned by what appeared to be bizarre posturing. She snapped out of it after a few seconds. The she shook him awake. As Mark came out of his trance he threw his arms around Kiona and began to cry. "That is what the Garden of Eden is all about. I have the fear that I am violating protections that God granted us."

Kiona put her arms around him and cuddled him against her. She then, for the first time in her life, shared her womanly wisdom of how the world is put together. "We are so used to responding to an authoritarian concept of God and are afraid to have trust in a loving God. In human affairs, we talk out of both sides of our neck. We speak of love and exercise power alternatives that bespeak anything but love in our daily affairs with our fellow man. As a result, we do not believe in a loving man, so how could there be a loving God? There is evidence that man has distorted some of God's work for his own ends, but there is also evidence that God's love comes through. When we read the Twenty -Third Psalm, we learn that God is our comforter, not only through death, but also through the parts of life we do not know or of which we are afraid. If He did not want you to probe or delve into his territory, He would stop you. Right now, He is helping you walk through a shadowy valley of life. Do not be afraid because I love you, and I am also walking with you."

For about a minute Mark was frozen in a reverie like state, but he was not in a trance; he was only absorbing the wisdom of what Kiona was saying and extrapolating on what the dream was really trying to tell him. He threw his arms around her and kissed her. With a sense of relief and new awareness he said, "Sweetheart, I think you tuned me into the idea that God is making his will known to me. He is telling me that our dreams are intertwined into one dream. That by debunking this racist perversion of his word, we can learn how we tick as organisms. We also stand a chance to lower the barrier between God and us. This is scary, but God will be beside us, as if the unknown were like the death we, all face: With this spoken between them, they fell asleep in each other's arms.

# Chapter 5

The next day found Jonos and Mark back in the cave. They climbed the projecting ledge with crowbars attached to their belts. When they reached the top, they began prying the fissure on the side opposite the location of the hinge. Inside the door that they pried open, lay another structure, a long narrow box. After they climbed down into the chamber, their suspicions were confirmed. It was a coffin. Neither Jonos nor Mark thought of themselves as desecraters of graves. This realm of life belonged to men, called Renfield or hunchbacks, called Igor. For a moment, each felt an eerie dread but it passed because a new feeling replaced it; this was a penetrating curiosity about life. Vesalius and Da Vinci had this thirst to learn when they traced nerves and blood vessels on cadavers to teach the world anatomy. Every medical student experiences this mixture of dread of violating a norm of society coupled with an almost obsessive need to learn and know. An archeologist is also a scientist, and his/her quest for knowledge transcends what is ugly or morbid.

Before the great unveiling, both decided to share their discovery with their colleagues. Besides, six people rather than two could lift the casket out of its tomb easier than two. Once the discovery was announced, a plan had to be devised to raise the sepulcher. Crowbars were used to raise the coffin, while several long lengths of tough leather thongs were placed on the under surface. Once the thongs had passed under the coffin, they were knotted on either side so that they came together in a central knot on either side from which a lengthy strand emerged. The strands on either side were thrown over the edge of the tomb opening and inserted into a system of grooved desk wheels with their stems inverted and pounded into the earth of the cave floor. In other words, a system of pulleys was built on either side of the sarcophagus to hoist it out of its mesa-like tomb. The thong lengths were sufficient enough to lower the box to the floor once it was out of its container.

The others wrestled with the conflict that had at first beset Jonos and Mark. They both were curious about who was buried in the unusual memorial structure in the cave and felt that they were violating a sacred rite and the peaceful repose of the dead.

As with their predecessors, these scientists let sense of professionality win out so that they were steeled enough to look at the dead. The next move was to pry open the lid and view the body. What they saw held them spellbound.

Before them lay the well-preserved body of a Black man, who appeared to be about 6'4". He had a long, tapering nose and was wearing an outfit that resembled a toga that the ancient Romans wore. Upon his head was a turban. Next to his cadaver lay a scroll. His head was shaven, and he was barefoot. The scroll was in a language that seemed like Arabic, but it was not quite like it. The body size and apparent rigor of the musculature indicated that in life he was a strong man. The absence of dirt under nails indicated that he was a clean man. Upon removal of the clothing, they found scar tissue in several places, but concentrated on his back. They also found evidence of circumcision, which denoted either a Semitic origin or connection with Semitic peoples. Obviously there was an odd collection of data to organize and fit into a pattern.

All were astounded and excited by the possibilities that the discovery unleashed. Their coordination of the data they had found had to be begun. Clothing samples were taken and sent to the Anthropology lab at the University, copies of the scroll were made and sent to the language lab. Professionals were at work; the self-sufficiency that was so painstakingly taught in Yucatan here deemed unnecessary when a university was available and just a few hours away. Mark and Kiona volunteered to take the trip to Boulder to get the information analyzed. This would give them a chance to visit with the Hymers. That night Kiona telephoned them and confirmed the plans. Michelle seemed, as if she were too happy to hear from Kiona. Maybe she was jealous, or maybe Kiona was paranoid, but the contact would further define where the issue stood.

That night Kiona asked Mark what was the difference in the space of time that had changed them from archeology students in Yucatan to archeologists in Mesa Verde. Mark smiled and said there were no water falls in Mesa Verde and started to lead her to the shower. She smiled gently and said she was serious. Mark could see she was troubled and asked what was wrong. She took his hand and led him to the couch. For a minute, Mark was haunted by the memory of Cherie using a similar tactic to gain control of him However, Kiona was not Cherie, and Mark decided to give her the benefit of the doubt.

Kiona's next words dispelled Mark's misgivings. She said, "We never would have just sent that material to be analyzed without trying to figure it out ourselves first. Does being a professional make you feel too good to dig out information yourself? "Mark stated that doing scut work does not necessarily make you a better professional. He then asked her what was really troubling her. Kiona then related her wondering at her perception of Michele's response to the call. Mark explained that Michelle is a new bride and would be frightened by the friendly overtures of an attractive woman out of the past. When she asked him how he surmised this, Mark said that he harbored such neurotic fears about Reed.

When she asked how he knew that they were neurotic fears and not realistic fears, he asked her to step in the shower and find out. She laughed and jumped in. He splashed her. She put soap in his eye. Somehow they wound up in each other's arms. The fears were not realistic. That weekend the couple took their car to Boulder. They had their mountain bikes with them, as they did not think the weather was cold enough for skiing. The drive took about three hours, and they were famished when they got there. Reed and Michelle took them to a bar and grill, Your Mother's Moustache. Here they all enjoyed themselves thoroughly and showed their sense of fellowship by their laughter. After an evening of this, Reed suggested that the newly befriended couple stay in their extra room Michelle went along with the plan, but Mark sensed some hesitation on her part.

Kiona had a hard time sleeping. Maybe the cause was being in a strange house; maybe she felt unwelcome. At any rate, she went down to the kitchen and heard someone weeping. Upon entering the room, she saw Michelle sitting alone and crying. Being a concerned person, she asked, "What is wrong." Michelle told her that she was unhappy because she was alone a lot due to Reed's long hours even though she had long hours, but they were at different times. Now an old girl friend was coming back into his life. She was afraid of losing him to his pediatric practice, and now an attractive woman out of the past was occupying his mind. It was just as Kiona had feared.

Kiona took both of Michelle's hands in hers and very clearly and tenderly said, "Your husband is a very attractive Black man, and when I first met him, I fell in love with the gentle, compassionate doctor, the Black doctor I saw in front of me. For two reasons I stepped no further. The first was that he loved you too much to hurt you, and the second is that I fell in love with an image without getting to the man. There is a third reason: I love Mark. Now can we stop this bullshit and be friends, or do you want me to leave. I do not stay where I am not wanted." With that they hugged and it was over. Kiona went back to bed, answering her previous uncertainty with a confident thrust of her head onto the pillow. There would be no break in the friendship between the girls for the rest of their lives.

Saturday was spent on a trip to the health museum where Reed was asked to speak to children about any concerns they had with their growing bodies. Kiona warned Mark about any shenanigans. By the twinkling in his eye, she knew her warning was needed, and she smiled to think of what bizarre episodes she would have to endure today. While they were at the display of internal workings of the eye, Mark asked Reed whether a Cyclops had to be fitted for a contact lens and if two twins had double vision could they be treated for quadruple vision. During this interrogation, Reed tried to keep a straight face when he gave the answers that a Cyclops would need monocle and that quadruple vision could not exist because all four eyes were not connected. The girls laughed, but Kiona put a Band-Aid on Mark's mouth.

One thing that came through was that Reed really liked kids. He answered their questions sincerely and as clearly as he could. He even picked up a little girl and placed her on his shoulders so that she could see something in the tooth display she did not understand so that she was able to see the subject of her question. That he would be an excellent pediatrician was obvious. For a second between talks Reed was alone. He sought out Michelle and took her hand. By the look in her and his eyes, there was no longer any doubt of the love between them, if there ever had been any.

At lunch Mark told Reed and Michelle about the body they had found and about the scroll that appeared to be written in a Semitic language. They both seemed interested in knowing their analyses of all the data they had put together. Mark and Kiona told them that they apparently had uncovered a war between the Spanish conquistadors and one of the Pueblo tribes, and that the team's guesstimate was that it took place between 1500 and 1600. The appearance of a Semitic language in the middle of all this did not make much sense. They would have to learn about it by translating the scroll. At this point, Reed offered the suggestion that Rachel might be able to offer some assistance since she was from that part of the world. Both agreed that this might be a good plan.

In celebration of their find, Reed rented "The Mummy's Curse." They laughed uproariously at Bela Lugosi's antics in the film. The curse reminded Mark of his dream the other night, but his memory of Kiona's intervention sustained him so that the fear was well defended against.

The idea of asking Rachel to be a translator actually had not occurred to either of them, but the utility of such a suggestion had to be considered. Of course, her busy life as a medical student would probably preclude any involvement in the translation of the document. However, that a possibility was there for some help could not be bypassed or ignored. Each made a mental note to contact her.

Since their talk, the awkwardness between Michelle and Kiona disappeared. A kind of feeling of sisterhood seemed to prevail. Basking in this, they decided to go shopping and to leave the boys to themselves. Reed challenged Mark to a racquetball game. Neither had played for a time, and this theoretically was supposed to even out their game. Reed demonstrated facility for the game and easily defeated Mark, who had become used to using different set of muscles. After the first game, Mark had built up a sweat. This combined with the usual sense of frustration Mark felt at defeat combined to motivate him to fight like hell to avenge being beaten. He fought like a demon. This motivated Reed to fight harder and they were battling point for point. Finally Reed got a lucky two in a row by the ball caroming from one wall to the one perpendicular to it after winning a point then gaining the opportunity to score another, thus winning the game by two points. They retired to the showers to get ready to meet the girls.

Back at Reed's and Michelle's apartment, Kiona seemed all excited. She could not wait to show Mark what she had bought. It was an extremely short, red negligee. Mark turned as red as the undergarment and said "If you wear that around me, you won't wear it long." Reed and Michelle laughed amusedly at the couple's apparent naïveté. Kiona also smiled and added, "My, my, did I cause all that reaction?" She also showed Mark what she had bought for him, a coon skin cap with a raccoon tail and a yo-yo with rhinestones in the center.

That night, after both couples had retired, Michelle said to Reed, "Kiona told me how you two became friends because we were engaged, and you wanted me for your wife. Well, you got it, buddy." Then she kissed him. Reed was very grateful because he had sensed something was bothering Michelle and could not put his finger on it.

Sunday's leave taking after a breakfast of sausage, bacon, and eggs with waffles and three kinds of juices was sad and coupled with Reed and Michelle's promise to return the visit. They had also agreed to explore the possibility of Rachel helping with the translation.

# Chapter 6

While waiting for the information from the university, work was at a standstill. Mark and Kiona decided to devote some time to her project. Mark concentrated on some of the Black movements that advocated Black Separatism. In concert with this direction, he decided to explore some of the thinking of Booker T. Washington, W.E.B. Dubious, Marcus Garvey, and Malcolm X. Kiona took up the focus of looking into the motives of some of the translators of the Bible.

Mark started his study with Booker T. Washington. He was born into slavery. He sat up at night to educate himself. He saw for himself the lack of caring and skills teaching to the Black man was liberation from one form of slavery to another he felt the Black people should develop their own sense of vocational independence and their own businesses, but he also realized that he lived in a country that saw itself as White and would not acknowledge the contribution. Blacks had made this nation too. He was concerned that his people be able to take care of themselves where their backs were broken, their blood spilled, and the best that the White man could do was to count a Black as 3/5 of a person. Booker Washington became a teacher and with federal help founded Tuskegee Institute, which taught vocational skills and agricultural innovations to Black and White farmers. In fact, he hired one of the country's most capable geniuses of plant biology, Dr. George Washington Carver, to do this. Because he built an institution for Blacks in White America, he had to collaborate with Whites and was labeled as an "Uncle Tom."

W.E.B. Dubois was a severe critic of Booker T. Washington. He was the first Black Ph.D. From Harvard. He greatly resented the vocation only educational contribution of Tuskegee; he felt that a talented tenth could be a vanguard for advancing Blacks and that they should be an educated vanguard. He also believed that Booker T. Washington was so in league with Whites to give Blacks their charity that he turned his back on Black civil and political rights. He believed in organization for these rights and started the NAACP from the Niagra Movement. He was an outspoken critic of White colonialism in Africa. During World War I he was an advocate of peace through socialism and harassed as a foreign agent until he turned to communism and became a citizen of Ghana, where he died.

Marcus Garvey was born into poverty in Jamaica and became involved in African independence, as did his predecessor, W.E.B. Dubois. He wanted to unite the Black peoples of the world and began a massive Black Nationalist movement. It was comprised of a Black Factories Corporation, a Black Eagles Flying Corporation, a Black Cross Nursing Association, and the Black Star Steamship Line. He was chosen to be the president of a Black republic. In Liberia by the Harlem Convention 1920. However, Britain and France put pressure on the U.S.A. to stop this activity because it interfered with their colonial policies. Since these alliances with Whites apparently were more important, to American political strategy than was protecting the freedom of Blacks from their own country, as well as others, the Government silenced Marcus Garvey with a prison sentence for mail fraud after The Black Star Line went bust. The threat to our holy alliances was over, but the building of Black Nationalism was not.

Malcolm X, born Malcolm Little, suffered the murder of his father due to support for Marcus Garvey, White racism and the mental breakdown of his mother in the wake of these events. He found, in the hellhole of prison, that Black people did not have to try to get along with their persecutor. They could separate from the White Devil into their own society and build their own nation. By means of discipline and sensible rules could be developed a society for men and women to govern themselves and develop strong family ties that the White man discouraged. However, he discovered that the disciplined society he sought could be corrupted. He also discovered that some White people wanted a world where White and Black could live side by side with mutual respect. Unfortunately, he was killed before this could be explored.

These four men could not be connected with inferior origins. They lived with repression and became angry and fought against their oppression, not with the yeomanry that guided Robin Hood, but with an unorganized thought out plan and philosophy. The only rationale for labeling their progenitor culture as inferior would be to cover the abnormal base of thought that led one group to use another. As Rome feared the skilled attack of Hannibal and the retaliation of Spartacus for their own feeling of inferiority in battle and confrontation for man's injustice to man by God, so feared the American and the Afrikaner who attempted to defy nature by defining inferior and superior characteristics where they did not exist. The remnants of Egyptian, Nubian, Ethiopic, Zimbabwean, Mali, and Songhi cultures would demonstrate that no one is defined by a monolith that someone invents for the convenience of not facing himself.

As Mark undertook part of this huge task to share the burden with Kiona, she had to lay some of her own groundwork. She took unto herself the task of pointing out that Man has tampered with the written word for his own ends. This created the opportunity to hold one group in check while another group built on its back. As an explanation, perhaps, some motives of humankind needed scrutinizing.

During the Middle Ages, the Church was the guardian of the light of knowledge. Monks received the written word in the languages of the ancients. These were the Hebraic (Torah and Pentateuch), Latin Vulgate), and Greek (Septuagint). The monks of several orders devoted themselves to distilling the knowledge that came from these holy works derived from our cultural progenitors. Of course, these men were all blameless and unbiased in their baptismal distillation. There were no Papal wars, no false representations as Messiahs, no picking up of useless junk and selling it as a holy relic, no pardoning of sins by charlatans, whose transgressions made Beelzebub look like Little Red Riding Hood. People got sick and tired of these incongruent preaching and practices.

People, such as Martin Luther, John Huss, John Calvin started questioning the sincerity and ability to decipher God's message to all peoples' ears. They felt that each person should have access to his/her Bible in his/her own language. Thus, the Protestant Reformation was launched.

Kiona had gleaned much from her educational experience, as a history student. She understood that humans with human motives were involved in some of the translations. Nationalistic feelings were nurtured by equating them with truth. In the "Battle Hymn of the Republic" George Washington was sifting out the worthiness of men from a judgment seat the Way God did. Being in favor with God meant supporting the rebellion against Britain. The problems of oppression and/or industrialization were translated in whatever way supported the status quo. What verification is there that St. Paul said, "Slaves, arise not against your masters", and not an industrialist translator that wanted to maintain free labor. Some of the English translations appear to reflect omissions of materials of "lesser importance." Revisions of translations appeared after the translator's death. Servile classes were not allowed to read the Bible that was meant for each person. With all these opportunities to twist The Scripture of God into the idolatry of Man, how could the statement of Noah's curse be acceptable without question?

Now that this groundwork had been laid by both of them, their thoughts and action were returned to the ancient corpse in front of them. The University stated that the language was Semitic 1. It showed similarities to Aramaic and Amharic, a language of Ethiopia. The raiment dated back to approximately 1500-1550. They would continue to attempt to decipher and to geographically typify it.

The team was disgusted with the fact that the school could not pinpoint the language. But their need was to be met by other means. Reed was true to his word. Rachel was on an extended vacation due to a combination of events. She was on a temporary leave due to an illness of unknown etiology striking one of her key professors in the research section of her biochemistry course. There was also some bad weather, which made transportation untenable in Cleveland. Therefore, she would be available to offer assistance with the translation of the language. At least there were two potential sources of finding out the how body got there.

Another peculiarity began to absorb Mark's thinking. He had heard that bodies were preserved for thousands of years by the mummification process, practiced by the ancient Egyptians. He could not grasp how the post funereal preservation skills got out of Egypt. Was this man, indeed, an Egyptian or from an offshoot of this Coptic civilization? The lab results showed that the empty body had been filled with sawdust and linen pads, immersed in a substance, known as Natron, or sodium carbonate. This method of preservation went back to the ancients of Egypt, but the connection over the span of approximately four thousand years had Mark totally nonplussed. He decided to do a little research in this area.

Delving in to this ancient cultural patterning left Mark more frustrated than he was before. He found that during a period in their history, the Egyptians had an obsession with religious concern and had become missionary to neighbors to the south and west of them. Some of these peoples had contact with the Hebrews, on their exodus from Egypt. The Agau, of Ethiopia, were among these people. They converted to Judaism. A community was formed from this intermingling and located on the Nile, to the south of Egypt. It was known as Elephantine. Could these evacuees have learned the secrets of preserving a body from their former masters and passed it onto the Agau? Was this man an offspring from this blending of peoples? The endless permutations of possibilities was driving him crazy. He felt like he needed some answers to put the whole series of facts into a comprehensible perspective. He was beginning to feel like Indiana Jones chasing after the Ark of the Covenant.

Mark went home to share his frustration with Kiona, who had invited the others to lunch. She took his hand excitedly and directed him to the kitchen. No one was in the room, but the table was cluttered with sandwiches and hors d'oeuvres. All of a sudden, everyone came out and shouted, "Surprise". Reed and Michelle, Amy and Ron and Rachel were there. When Mark asked what the occasion was, everyone shouted at once. "It's National Body Discovery Day, you dumb bell." Someone brought out an old record, and the next thing that happened was that everyone began to sing and dance to The Monster Mash. After a few hours, the doorbell rang; Arne was out there dressed with a minister's collar and a Groucho Marx mustache, nose, and glasses. He said he was Brother Finibar, and he came to view the body after the exhumation ceremony. He then pulled a violin out from behind him and began to play "Fascination." The party lasted until 2:00 a.m. Kiona had calculated correctly; Mark's depression vanished. He was ready to go back to work. So were the others. Rachel was included in the work force.

# Section V

# Gideon Retta

# Chapter 1

The party was over. The time to get down to brass tacks had arrived. In keeping with the ribald merriment of their getting together, the next day they went to the cave for the exhumation ceremony. All were amazed at how alive the corpse looked, even after 400 years. Immediately, Rachel approached the coffin and began to look for the scroll. After she took it out and started reading it, she gasped, "This is Geez, the religious language of my people. This man was a Falasha, just as I am." She went on to explain that European Jews learned Yiddish, and North African and Western Asiatic Jews learned Ladino as every day speech, but reserved Hebrew as the language of scripture until the modern nation of Israel came into being. This resulted in Ashkenazic and Sephardic divisions of Jewry populating Israel. The root languages were German for Yiddish and Spanish for Ladino. In the synagogue, schul, or temple these were rejected because they represented the Diaspora, the time of exile and adaptation to the cultures that dominated, or tried to dominate Jews. Because the Jews of Ethiopia were isolated from other Jews and wanted their independence from a Christian group, obsessed with uniformity, they too developed a need to communicate with people about commonalties, but to communicate with their God alone. Hence, they spoke Amharic in the street, but Geez in the Masjid. This was at least one explanation of why the translators ran into difficulty with the translation. An Ethiopian could have easily done the translation because the tradition of one language for the laity and one for the church was passed from to the Disciples to Rome and onto the African church. In other words, The combination of Geez and Amharic also are used by Ethiopic Christians.

Over the next two days, Rachel read the scroll and translated it onto a computer. She acquired a feel for Gideon Retta and a sense that he played a role in Mark's and Kiona's lives, a role from beyond the grave and beyond the centuries. She could not help but wonder if some form of repetition of God passing His commandments to Moses was being re-enacted for the benefit of her two very close friends. Perhaps a message for all of mankind lay in this intertwining of life and death and the old with the new. As Rachel read the document, she saw elements of her friends in the tales of the odyssey that this man made from one corner of the world to the next. In his travels, he fought a plethora of physical and emotional battles.

All these mental gymnastics ran through her as she processed the ancient scripture and translated it into an understandable form on the computer. Throughout the narrative was the suppression of individuality and the courage to do battle for one's sense of pride in himself/herself.

After the weekend, the translation was done, and the computer printouts were projected onto an overhead screen for the group to read together. The unfolding of the life of a person from a world so far away seemed to show how small the world really is. As Mark and Kiona were forging their own pathway, so did this courageous individual carve his way through a sea of enemies and Mark managed to keep himself from being his worst one. Here stood Gideon Retta.

Rachel transcribed her translation onto a computer. "This is the story that Mark and Kiona has presented to them. "To whoever has opened my tomb: Gideon Retta is my name. I was born in a land far away from this New World, as it is called. Yet, some of the aims of people are not so far apart. The need to control one that is different and to use the differences as an excuse for exploitation seems to be common amongst all races or nations. Let me start at the beginning." He stated he was from a minority in Ethiopia: The Falasha, or Black Jews. This minority was said to be of the Tribe of Dan. Gideon was of the class, Kohanim, those that teach the Falasha ways to the laity. His father worked as a smith, an occupation despised as being magical in nature and being said to be in league with the devil. He was the eldest of three brothers and engaged to the eldest of A Kohane daughter, as was deemed appropriate by Falasha norms. A militant sense of anger seemed to pervade his personality structure. He grew up witnessing the victimization of his father because of being part of a stubborn group that refused to subject themselves to the control of the loving arms of Christianity and because he practiced a black magic art. Another source of Gideon's militant stance was a boyhood incident. He was bringing some jewelry, fashioned by his father, to market when he was accosted by three Amhara youths. They tried to goad him into attacking by cursing his father's trade of smithery, the practice of devil magic. They also called him Buda, a term which referred to the deformed eye of Judith, a warrior queen of the Falasha, who, two centuries previously, had terrorized Amhara priests in one of the many wars between them. Further humiliation came when they pulled him from the wagon, tore off his clothes, and threw him in the mud. To this audacity was added the confiscation of his wagon of trade goods. He was left to walk home naked and covered with mud. His rage and thirst for vengeance was so great, that the next time he came innocently appearing driving a wagonload of straw.

When the bullies approached, he let them get very close to his cart, and then threw clay containers of hot lye, which shattered on them. He then grabbed a pitchfork and stood ready for any impending assault. He decided to abandon the life as a holy teacher and to become a soldier. His father objected strenuously to his decision citing the Falasha prayer, "Blessed be God, the lord of Israel, who gave me a mouth, a heart, thoughts, and intelligence."

Gideon responded with another prayer, "The vengeance of the blood of Abel arrived unto me. Therefore, fight against them that fight against me." His father slapped him across the face and shouted in his rage, "Go from my house and show me your face no more." Amidst his mother and brothers' tears, he left, never to see them alive again, for they became victims of the war between Amhara and Falasha, as well as Christian and Jew. For this part of the world became a part of a wave of a need to have unified Christian empire, an empire that felt the world had to be purged of the infidel cultures of Islam and Judaism.

As Moses was said to rule the desert for forty years and as Odysseus wandered for ten years before he found his home, Gideon Retta roamed the Falasha enclaves of Ethiopia looking for Redai, the Falasha commander in hiding from the Amhara. For five years this sojourn continued in an isolated valley. Gideon survived by finding work for shelter and food, as he needed it. It is an isolated valley, where the Tekkaze River cut a gorge though the Senian Mountains. The now fifteen-year-old stripling stopped at an inn and asked about the whereabouts of Redai. The innkeeper looked toward two huge men wearing the armor of soldiers, who were already moving toward them, having over heard the inquiry. Both of them strode over to Gideon, picked him up, and slammed him down on a table. "Why do you seek Redai? Who are you? What is your business with us?"

In the most defiant tone of voice he could muster and with the most bravado that would cover his fear, this toughened youth retorted, "I seek Redai to join him in his fight against the haters of Moses and Aaron, who cannot let us be unless we wear the yoke they have chosen for themselves and for us." The soldiers laughed both in relief and in admiration of such spunk in one so young. The laughter was short lived, for Gideon drew his knife and slashed the warrior's hand. "Never approach me in violence again. If you do, one of us must die." The flames that seemed to shoot out of his eyes bespoke more than spunk, it was a symbol of unrequited rage.

Maybe it represented a memory of the good-bye slap and maternal and fraternal tears that turned him from a child to a man. Maybe he thought the bullying of the Amhara youth should be returned in kind. At any rate, today, a fighter was born.

The two men of war told Gideon that they would take him to Redai, but he had to be blindfolded until they knew they could trust him. He let them do this. Subsequently, they pulled him on a cart and drove into the hills to a cave carved out of the face of the mountain. Redai was a tall thin man, whose body was sinewy and hard like the tail end of a whip. He had an air of tension about him as if he were a coiled spring ready to snap into action at the slightest provocation.

When he looked at Gideon, he smirked when a mere youth, which probably had not experienced sex yet, but was ready to try battle, stood before him. After witnessing what appeared to be innocent expressions of an adolescent craving to wear the armor of a man. Redai gently nudged this youngster out of his way. The battle-hardened veteran of many skirmishes was taken aback when this man-child was at his throat with a dagger within as instant. Snatching the wrist of the knife hand and bending back, Redai made Gideon drop the knife. The warrior to be was undaunted; he kicked the seasoned fighter in the shins and kneed his face when he bent down from the kicks. Both soldiers had to pull the lad off the leader. Slapping him across the mouth, he menacing said, "In my army, violence is purposeful." Only an undisciplined moron fights his own men. You have much to learn. When you raise a dagger, know how to use it, use it quickly and exactly. I could have killed you with my hands before you raised your foot. You will need that rage for Sarsa Dengel, not me. We will teach you to direct your feelings where they will do you some good. Do you want to learn to fight or to have tantrums?"

Now that Redai had got his attention, Gideon was ready to give his wounded ego the disciplinary workout needed to transport him from an injured boy to a finely, honed weapon, a fighting soldier. With several other young recruits, he practiced hand-to-hand combat, physical fitness exercises, and rudiments of operation of weaponry. They marched and learned to respond to the officer's disciplines in a reflex manner. In the space of six months, he did not recognize the scrappy, but uncontrolled gutter fighter he was when he came to join the army.

He would not let his emotions lead him nor deter him from what had to be done; if a point had to be taken, and the obstacle to taking it was young or elderly or a close friend, the compassion became secondary to the objective of battle. When it came to war, Gideon Retta scrubbed the boyhood from his soul and replaced it with the armor of a fighting machine. The next year tested the flexibility and tensile strength of this mechanical monster, while the ensuing years tested its toleration of emotional and physical pain.

The wars between Christian, Moslem, and Jewish factions had been going on since 1270. However, a new twist was added when the Christian nations in Europe became greedy for empire, particularly Spain and Portugal. The Spaniards concentrated on finding routes to the Orient through the West, while the Portuguese chose to go around Africa at first then to plunder the peoples there for their resources, as the Spaniards did the peoples in the lands that lay to the West. One of many strategies used was to play upon the theory of divide and conquer. To maintain a power balance, the Falasha would ally themselves with the Moslems against the Christians Amhara. The Portuguese convinced the Falasha to break with their traditional ally and join with the Amhara, only to be betrayed by them. The interplay of these events had an effect on the emerging manhood of Gideon Retta.

Within the heart of this stripling sat an unhealthy conflict. He was no longer his parent's child. He was without home and a base for his growing ego. He was outraged by the unjust manner in which Christian majority was trying to force him into the fold they had created for him. He thought he found a new parent figure in his people, and Redai and the rudiments of soldiering personified this. He was later discovered that rage was not a substitute for love.

The wars between the three religious factions had interludes of toleration during the fourteenth century; the Falasha tipped the balance of power between the three factions. The Jewish and Christian factions seemed to grow closer because the Moslems were threatening them in anger for some of Judith's excesses. In retaliation, the Falasha, induced by the Portuguese promise of booty, led these Europeans to the Moslem force and took them by surprise. The Amhara turned on the Jews, who would not accept authority, and the hatred and war raged on.

The Amhara were trapped in the Senian Mountains by a combination of being unable to sustain themselves in the cold, a scorched earth strategy, and Falasha destruction of the paths the mules followed, while they hurled boulders down on the confused army attempting to advance. The Portuguese turned the tide of battle by supplying firearms to the Amhara. The Falasha, rather than be captured, killed themselves. Gideon experienced the defeat. He saw Sarsa Dengel, the Amhara leader, take his new father figure prisoner, then burn all the Falasha literature that was the model under which he knew security, peace, and love.

The final straw the broke the soldiers back, was a return to his village. Moslems, who had lived in this village, sought revenge for the Falasha alliance with the Amhara. They sought out the home of the

Jew, the Smith to create a target for their hate. Hanging in what was the main room of the fighter's home, were the lifeless forms of his father holding his mother . His two brothers' heads were between them. The door was intact, and Gideon hid behind it when he heard the noise of someone entering. He saw a soldier figure holding a lance. Circling behind him with his dagger, Gideon slit his throat. He then lifted the corpse onto the door and drove the lance through it. Now he knew that he could not stay. He crossed the Tekkaze River and advanced north to the Blue Nile. He felt he no longer had a home in Ethiopia, the Gondar area, or anywhere else. He was ready to bid a bitter farewell to his heritage of Menelik, Saul, Sheba, Moses. In his brief wandering in the area, he came upon the ancient colony of Elephantine, populated by Jews who came from Yemen. They feared a pogrom by the Amhara and were preparing to flee the area.

A Portuguese trader had happened into this geographic sector, looking for trading opportunities when he learned about the unfortunate tidings of the Jews. He had an idea what would be happening, as a consequence of knowing Sarsa Dengel through trade. This trader was a deceptively gentle man. He would accept people at face value, but if he felt betrayed or deceived, he accepted no part of the person again; any one, who even appeared to betray his trust, was no longer regarded as human. He also learned to substitute money for his misplaced trust. If anyone wanted to escape the area, all he had to do was make the sailor's wallet fat enough. His name was Ericio DePelunis.

The escaping Falasha all made a point of seeking out Senor DePelunis's ship, "Enigma of the East."

It was a light fast moving craft similar to the style of the British privateers, such as Sir Francis Drake. He took on a load of passengers that would sufficiently enrich his coffers. Three days later they set sail with an army of Amhara after them. DePelunis ordered his cannoneers to fire on the soldiers. He called Gideon over to him and showed him how to fire a harpoon gun. Then he gave him a torch and a pile of oily rags. The man of the sea put these all in a pouch that the young fighter could strap to his shoulder and bade him to climb the mast to the ship's crow's nest, wrap an oily rag around the harpoon to be fired, light it, and aim for the horse's rump. He did so, and the resulting conflagration wiped out the Amhara army. For the time first since he saw he re-mains of his family hanging, Gideon wept and screamed out his hostile farewell: "Goodbye, you bastards. When I return, it will be to burn the rest of you."

The "Enigma of the East" sailed up the Nile out of Africa and turned west. At the Barbary Coast where Tripoli, Tunisia and Algeria intermingled, they ran into pirates. Two corsairs surrounded the Portu-guese vessel. Captain DePelunis turned his ship about and began to move toward shore. He told his gunners to take theirs places and to fire when he gave the word. Gideon was placed in the crow's nest with the harpoon gun and oily rags and torch. His orders were to shoot when the others did. Both corsairs gave swift chase. One was faster than the other and was gaining momentum. Just before the shore line was a line of sharp rocks, jagged remains of an under water mountain range. At the point at which the lead corsair's momentum could not be reversed, DePelunis suddenly turned to the opposite direction, causing the pursuing ship to follow its momentum and careen on the rocks. The other corsair had also gained on them. He turned his cannons and Gideon's flaming harpoons on this second ship. The result was devas-tating and barred from Barbary history because this was an obvious loss of face, as well as less public portions of the anatomy.

After a week of travel, the Falasha were transferred to another ship at Gibraltar and taken to Lisbon, where they docked at night and were met by the Marranos population of Lisbon. They learned that law for-bade the practice of Judaism and that the only reason they were al-lowed to live was that they were converted to Christianity. At the risk of their freedom and lives, they practiced their own faith. This was the age of the Inquisition.

# Chapter 2

Spain and Portugal were rivals in trade and in establishing colonies. However, they were both Catholic nations, and they were neighbors. In order to maintain peaceful borders, Portugal, the smaller country, would go the same way as its powerful neighbor unless its basic survival was threatened. Thus, when Spain instituted an inquisition to purge itself of non-Christian peoples, two things happened: 1) Jews fled to Portugal to avoid tortures, confiscation of property, or Auto Da-Fe (burning at the stake). 2) The Portuguese, who did not want Jews any more than Spaniards did, developed their own inquisition. Marranos were Jews that had chosen baptism and conversion instead of extermination. Some of them secretly practiced Judaism and true converts continued to maintain relationships with these secret Jews. The result was suspicion and mistrust of the Marranos. The church court was empowered to ferret out the secret Jews, which it carried out via a spy system, and by seeking confessions to actual or manufactured crimes. Witch hunting also became a common practice, by which people greedy for others' property accused them of being "Secret Jews." Tortures took place in subterranean dungeons. The accused were beaten with canes, had skin peeled off, and had their heels scorched. The object to these sadistic practices was to wring confessions out of people. Sentencing varied from public confiscation of property, to exile, to temporary or lifelong incarceration, to death by burning at the stake. Along with this flourished an entrepreneurial industry; the seized property went to the king. This was contingent upon the number of verdicts. Also a part of this "piously obtained lucre; went to maintain the tribunal, as well as the Inquisitor. Into this world walked Gideon Retta, follower of the God of his people turned fierce and unrelenting fighter.

The new immigrants moved into the Marrano/Jewish section of the city. They did not mingle comfortably with the Jews in the community because their Judaism was different in part due to differences in exposure and due to racist feelings of some of the Jews from other European countries that did not want to acknowledge a connection with Blackness. Hence, they clung to each other and found a spot to which to erect a Masjid and to organize their religious and social lives into a community based on what they had left in Ethiopia.

An Ethiopian Fallash, named Elijah Tanndela had been living with Portuguese very uncomfortably for about a year and welcomed companionship with people of his own country. He helped this group to their community. Something about him was familiar to Gideon. He rememberd Gideon from Redai's training camp because he was the innkeeper to whom he addressed his inquiry, as to the whereabouts to Redai. He was especially helpful in assisting Gideon in getting a curio shop set up. In three months, their community was flourishing. The Nezirim, Kohanim, and Debteras all knew their functions and connections to the community. The hut of women in childbirth was organized to isolate women in labor or in their menses. Elijah educated the newcomers as to how to go about paying and avoiding the tax collector, who was and who was not a spy and how to hide their Judaic activities from the Portuguese. They were able to forget the bitterness of their experiences in the several wars that terrorized their villages and the feelings of being unwanted in the land they inhabited that was characteristic of the Diaspora.

Gideon began to be preoccupied with feeling he could not explain. He was industrious by nature, and his shop prospered. He did not feel uncomfortable in the community of his people, yet he did not feel uncomfortable in the community of his people, yet he did not feel a sense of belonging. The piety he learned at home seemed to dissipate from his soul. He did not attend Friday night services as the other Falasha did. He clung to his anger to fill the void created by being cast from his father's house, the sense of never being left alone to develop into an individual person because of the constant threat of the Amhara, and the demands of his own people for conformity to Falasha ideals, his training as a fighter, the humiliation following Redai's defeat, and witnessing the debasing destruction of his family. The ex-soldier felt the God, whom he was taught to love had no love for him. He felt that spiritual love was an exercise in futility. For him, love became what would gratify his senses.

Since he began to perceive himself as a man with sensual needs and did not want the community where he once had faith to witness what he viewed as his degeneration, he began to wander away from this community in Diaspora to satisfy his physical needs. This brought two new events into his life: The first was Guintera, a dancer at the Turtle's Shell, an inn he frequented. She saw him isolated and alone with an unending sorrow and a fiery rage in his eyes. A sailor grabbed her, and this lonely figure rose to his full height and told him to leave the lady alone. The man of the sea summoned two friends to silence this busy body of a stranger.

Gideon hit one with the edge of his hand and broke his collarbone. The original sailor advanced with a dagger, only to have an olla of hot soup thrown on his genitals and a heavy pewter beer stein hit his eye. The third ran off as Gideon chased him, brandishing the second gentleman's knife. Guintera asked him to escort her home. This was the beginning of a silent relationship, in which she knew not whence he came or who he was, but that he had an insatiable, driving need for sex. The second event had more harrowing results to his community. He saw the familiar friend of his people, Elijah Tanndela, talking with government-like and church-like appearing officials. This veteran of man's treachery to man, saw Tanndela reach out his hand and count money. Suddenly an insight hit Gideon. He did not know this man from Redai's but from his own village. He was part of the Muslim family that lived in his town, part of the family that murdered Gideon's family. Stepping into the shadows where he could not be seen, he threw the sailor's dagger through the spy's neck. Unfortunately, this did not end, but began the final pogrom that Gideon Retta was to endure on Old World soil.

Gideon fled into an alley before the government and church prelates realized what had happened. Once safe, he proceeded on to his evening debauchery. Guintera hugged him to her and took her clothes off. She stroked his skin as she undressed Gideon for she felt special about him tonight. He responded as he usually did, with lust and desire. However, afterward, he wept. He said only that his people were in danger, and he had to get to them. Guintera held him against her and also wept. She joined him in weeping because he was a strong man that was not used to expressing himself. She also saw the scars on his body and knew he could deliver violence, as well as receive it. She also knew he was a Jew by the suffering in his eyes and a fighter by how he handled the three sailors. She wanted to hold him and ease his pain.

However, his deep rage frightened her though he never hit her. Stilling his fire was like cooling a blast furnace, and that would not be invented for two centuries; this exotic enchanter knew that she could not hold back the flames that were simmering, but she could make this night memorable. That is what she did.

In the morning, Gideon arose and walked back to the ghetto where the Jews lived. He saw his people being rounded up like cattle, the way Ferdinand and Isabella wanted, the way the Egyptian pharaoh and Nebuchadnezzar wanted it before them, and the way Hitler wanted it after them. As Moses may have asked Ramses, "Why do you do this to my people," so asked Gideon Retta.

He was told, "Jews are a murdering lot. They have killed one of their Jewels that sincerely took unto himself the ways of the Lord, an honest Marrano. He was unlike them who drink good Christian's blood at their Seder."

Gideon shouted, "Stay your hand. They did not slay your spy, I did. He not only was not Christian but also not even a Jew. He was a Moslem that was part of a family that murdered my family while I was away fighting a war. It was I that slew him for the lying swine he was. Take me to your dungeon, but let them be. They are innocent of the crime of which you accuse them." With this confession, Gideon was arrested, but the other arrests continued. Moreover, the Falasha community did not view him as a hero but as the villain, which had brought this pogrom on their heads. Their mentation was not that different from this father's. He laughed hollowly, as he heard that slap all the way to the dungeon. Coupled with this he heard the jeers of those for whom he had done battle to preserve an identity. These would be the memories he took to the stake with him.

Gideon was taken in chains to the dungeons of Lisbon. He occupied a cell with two other men fated to die. One had stolen a jewel out of the eyes of a figurine of the Virgin. The other had raped and sodomized a nun. The words of the jailer, as he led Gideon into the cell were, "here is a Jew to befoul your eternity for your damnable sin." Before the door was shut, one of them swung the shackle of his chain, which had been opened to allow him to eat. He hit the fighter in the forehead, knocking Gideon to the ground. They both kicked at his head, laughing insanely. The jailer joined the unfrenzied merriment until the Ethiopian lay senseless at their feet. The keeper revived him with a bucket of tepid, dirty water and chained him to the wall. His parting words were, "Tomorrow you will meet John De Mello." These words echoed in the Falasha's ears, as the keeper of the keys strode out of the cell and down the labyrinthine corridor. He knew of De Mello, for he was the Inquisitor of Portugal. In his power, lay the fate of Portugal's religious prisoners?

Dawn had not yet broken, when a tall, robed figure entered Gideon Retta's chamber of living entombment. He patiently waited for the prisoner to awake. He held documents in front of him and stated; "In the name of Holy Mother Church, my son, you are charged with the inhuman act of murder. You have taken away the life of a person, who came to see the true light. What say you to these charges?"

"I say I am not your son. What you consider an inhuman act was retaliation for what the lying dog and his family of curs did to my family and my people behind my back while I was away fighting a war of the honor of my people's right to live as they believe, without your kind imposing what you falsely call Christian love. It is not love you pass on, but subjugation. If this were your concept of love, offer it not to me. I have had a bellyful of this kind of love. You brought me here to take my life for what you see as crime: Take it and be done with it."

"We are all God's children, my son. Your act forfeited your life, but how you spend eternity will depend upon how you choose to reach God. If you choose the way of Our Lord, Jesus Christ, surely, your soul will know the blessedness of heaven. My place is to help you free that soul for heaven and keep you from sending it to burn for eternity."

In a rage, the soldier screamed, "Just what claims does a mass murderer like you have on souls? Mine is soiled by killing, but I killed in war, and I killed quickly. I did not hang a person on a wall and cane him, or scorch his skin to get a confession to an invented crime, and then present myself as God's servant, who saved a soul. Your hypocrisy will earn you a rung next to mine in hell." With this outburst, De Mello slapped Gideon and ordered the torturer to begin his ministrations.

During the period of his incarceration, Gideon had two visitors: The Nazir from the Masjid and Guintera. The Nazir told him that in the eyes of the Falasha community, he was guilty of bringing a pogrom to the Marrano community, and their attitude was one of anger. The fighter responded with sadness at this rejection. He looked at the religious leader and said, "I fought because I loved my people, and I could not bear the violence to which we were exposed because we want to worship our own God in our own way not be shunned and violated because we are not a model of someone else's expectation. I did not like us turning on our Moslem allies, but I felt that my family did not have to be murdered by Elijah Tanndela and his family, as he calls himself. He knew I recognized him somewhere, and he made up that story about knowing me in the camp of Redai. I remembered where I knew him when I saw him talking with Church and government officials, apparently planning the pogrom of which you accuse me of bringing to our people. I am aware that I must die because I took a life, but it was not for bringing pogrom. The Christians here are no different than the Amhara.

They want to eliminate us either by slaughter or by absorption of our souls. If you wish to believe that you will get along better with our persecutor or by selling out your own, so be it. But do not come to me with their lie on your lips." To this Nazir said, "I will convey what you have said, though I doubt they will believe me."

To Guintera, he presented another facet of himself. She knew of the rages that drove him and that sex was the vehicle by which he expressed them. Yet, he had stood up as a man to protect her. She reasoned that underneath his fire, there lay a good man. She wanted to address this good man before he died and tell him of her love for him.

When she saw the burn marks and skin peeled from his legs and feet, she shuddered inwardly and wanted to heal his pain. Gideon sensed her feeling for him. He said, "I wish I would have met you at an earlier juncture in my life so that I might have appreciated you more than I did, please be careful of whom you bestow the treasure upon that is you. For you are a treasure; who else could give of themselves in the face of my moodiness and in the face of my coming to you as a defeated and embittered soldier. You had no part of my pain, and there was no need to impose it on you. I know not know whether or not I am to love, but I feel tenderness for you. For your sake and for my memory of you, please find a good man that is worthy of the precious love you have to give. I have not been so worthy, nor would I have been were I to live." Guintera wept for the love that might have been, but the substantial part of her, that loved life, knew that Gideon was right. She vowed to herself that she would follow this advice.

In this way, Gideon Retta prepared for his departure from this Earth. He felt both God and his people had deserted him because he had chosen the way of war. God's house was supposed to be built on love, not hate, and savagery, but where was this love; it did not reside in the followers of Jesus, the Nazarene. They preached it, and practiced wanton bigotry and murder if one believed differently than they did. Yet his fellow Jews were divided over White and Black and would rather turn on one of their own rather than challenge the oppressor. He saw no point to staying in a world where fighting for identity had no point; it was so much shadow boxing. He scrupulously avoided using another person. Although he was honest, he denied to himself that he was beginning to feel love for Guintera; he chose to push her to realistically deal with her grief at his leaving this life. Whatever lay ahead in the afterlife, he felt a sense of acceptance that he was not leaving a wake of pain behind him.

Because man is an image of God, he is imperfect in his thought processes. The disillusioned soldier was not able to comprehend that the plan of the Father of his people had singled him out for another plan. He learned from other prisoners that a vast new world was discovered across the sea, and that Spain and its ally, Portugal, were planting their flags there to exploit this world for themselves. Many prisoners were being pressed into service to absorb the dangers of the trip or to be annihilated by the journey to the end of the world. These were the guinea pigs of the theories that spoke of a round world. After all why should God fearing men have their souls put at risk when their dungeons were do full of the unworthy? Thus, was this perceivably unworthy soldier against the righteous army of the Lord chosen by the purchase power of a greedy Spanish entrepreneur to continue his earthy life? A visitor came to Gideon Retta's cell. His name was Escobar. He presented himself as the son of a man, who survived a curious accident at sea. The accident had occurred on an expedition to Florida to find the legendary Seven Cities of Cibola; cities built by seven bishops on an island, called Antilla. These cities, according to the legend, were paved with gold and had many palaces with jeweled structures in them. While searching for this mythical island, the searchers encountered a shipwreck and attacks by Indians. There were four survivors. One of them was Escobar's uncle.

Gideon was not impressed with the idea if chasing after an idiotic legend to further enrich his persecutors. To this point, he found that greed or power lusts were the prime motivators of White men. Therefore, he told Escobar to go on his merry chase without him. He further stated that the treachery of Man sickened him, and he wanted to be done with this life. Escobar entreated the soldier, stating that his geographic ability to learn about terrain and the fighting skills he mastered at war could be of use to the ally of Portugal. Gideon openly sneered and said, "You persuaded my people to turn on an ally of generations, then turned on us to complete your dream of a Christian or a White Christian empire. Now you come to use me as your instrumentation to subject another person to your rule. I am not stupid. I expect hellfire because I killed apart from war and because I brought my people from one hellhole to another. I will not use you to cling to a life, in which I no longer believe."

The next day, Gideon had three visitors. Two were in chains, Guintera and the Nazir of the Falasha community. The third was John De Mello. Gideon emitted a gutteral growl and snarled.

Undaunted, De Mello stated, "As you can plainly see, your compadres have been beaten.

Because we want to rid our shores of your kind of criminal element, and because we found a trace of you children of Satan in this woman, their fates will mirror yours. If you choose to leave with Escobar, they will leave with you on the same vessel. They will go as far as Majorca and be dropped off to live a life of their own choosing. If not our Lord will have three souls at your burning." With that, he spun around and left the cell.

Three days later, the three of them boarded ship. Gideon was in chains. When John De Mello came aboard to bless the ship, Gideon spat one his foot. This time he did not slap the grizzled warrior because he was in public, not in the privacy of a torture cell. Escobar explained to Gideon that he was an infidel and follower of the religion that rejected his Lord: and he could not permit him the freedom of a Christian. Gideon laughed and said, "You are not free, you are slaves to your own greed," Gideon maintained a stern uncompromising stance toward Escobar that was meant to invoke a feeling of guilt for interfering with his decision to exit from this human existence. He spoke to his fellow captives, discovering the Nazir was named Nahum, of Gondar. He had enlisted in Redai's army to end the constant strife against the Falasha, who wanted nothing more than the decency of respecting their right to be different. This break with tradition had hurt him in two ways; His family declared him dead, and he was so horrified at the wholesale slaughter around him that he vowed never to stray from his prescribed life again. This vow had almost cost him his life. He stated that he envied Gideon's courage and was grateful that this comrade in arms had the compassion to not drag him before the stake with himself. Guintera, he discovered, had no Jewish blood, but she was made to confess to this for reasons of state. For this outrage, Gideon vowed a vengeance murder of De Mello if her ever saw him again. The night before the landing at Majorca, Guintera gave herself to Gideon, chains and all. Their union was not fierce but gentle and tender expressing gratitude and the love that might have been.

Escobar had explained that the error in the planning to the journey was in turning south, instead of North, where the Pueblos had originally lived before some of them had migrated in the southerly direction. Therefore, the ship docked at a Mexican port, and the journey became

139

a land trek to what is now Mesa Verde, Colorado. Consequently, they crossed barren desert, rivers, and mountains.

They passed through the domains of hostile and curious natives, baking heat, herds of buffalo, and mournful sounds of coyotes, bitter mountain cold, huge grizzlies, and predatory mountain lions. They learned that water was stored in the cactus. Gideon also believed that the plant contained something that made Spaniards crazier than they were. The words, mescaline and peyote, would be soon added to many language groups although natives knew them as ways to negotiate the desert by creating a hallucinogenic world. At a later date, Gideon was to use this information.

At last, Escobar and his band reached cliffs that seemed to have a system of houses carved out of them. As they drew closer, Gideon saw Spanish soldiers cavorting about on horseback behaving arrogantly and boisterously. They seemed to advertise an attitude of "I am better than you because I have come to the true word." Therefore, even though your way of life has been here for centuries, my needs have superseded it. The thought of this conceit brought back the memory of a proud young boy being made to walk home naked and caked with mud. If these Indians, as they were called, were anything like that stripling of so long ago, these conquistadors were in for a lot of trouble. The smoke of battle in his nostrils seemed to clear the air. Perhaps there was a reason to go on living.

Upon entering the village, Gideon could not help but notice the first person to cross his line of vision. Her hair was jet black and hung to her waist. Her eyes were expressive and took all around her into their perspective. They were the warm brown of a gentle doe. Her skin was of a coppery hue, and her corporeal features were athletic and statuesque appearing. She took his breath away. He was to find out her name Dark Waters. He knew that he must keep his distance from her because he was a stranger and because he had a mission, never to let Spain and Portugal forget what their inquisition would cost them.

# Chapter 3

Rachel was lost in thought from her translation. She did not hear Mark and Kiona come up behind her. They noticed the tears in her eyes. In mock severity, Mark said, "Why weepest thou, my lady?" Rachel played the translation for them and asked why people cannot let others alone to determine their own destinies. She thought it was extremely stupid to build an ego structure with its base being the branding of a different ego as inferior. She also voiced a fear that the intolerance of the world had been defined centuries ago, and the Mark and Kiona were fighting too much of this cultural imperative to survive. She voiced sadness for their struggle. Gideon's struggle to be independent, yet to continue to love his people seemed indicative of the futility of this struggle, as he appeared to be misunderstood from both ends: the Falasha and the Portuguese. Does crossing cultural lines result in either side pulling the stray into their own bailiwick and hating the one who resists the pull from each side?

Kiona took Rachel's hand and took Mark's hand with her other hand. She said that about a month ago, Mark was troubled by a nightmare about questioning God in his own pursuit of life's answers. In helping him deal with it, she referred him to the Twenty-third Psalm. It described, "Walking through the Valley of the Shadow of Death" with God as a guide. From this, we can conclude that when we feel hated or misunderstood, God will be there, if we have enough faith to look for Him to show us where our path lies. Even through his bitter, raging veneer, Gideon Retta found his path. To cap off her conceptualization, Kiona added that she and Mark knew that their lives had been bound together by a force beyond their awareness. She showed Rachel the gemstone she had found in Chichen Itza. Teasingly, Rachel asked Mark if he had a symbol of a force that bound them. He said, "Yep, I'll go get it." He came back with the red nightie Kiona had bought with Michelle. The two women chased him out of the house and made him bang on the door for a half-hour before they let him back in.

When he was more serious, Mark told Rachel that he and Kiona had grown with each other, as they found the many ways that Man had come to accept that he was a child of God. When he became arrogant and saw himself as the center of the universe, man aggrandized himself and gathered propaganda that rationalized this assumption.

The result was that God's children learned to create pockets of hate based upon a faulty system of logic. He and Kiona were learning to look for the signs of God's love by what they learned about how Man grew from one era to the next.

Kiona hugged Mark and said, "My, my how Lanky has grown. I'm really impressed." Her pride came out so blatantly that she kissed him. Of course, she knew what to expect immediately after she did this. For Mark whooped up and down and shouted gaily, "Yeah, tonight I score." Both girls smiled and put him out of the house again. However, that night he did score, and they both laughed themselves to sleep in a warm cuddle afterwards.

Rachel also began to see that life was a blend isolating and blending. The catalysts that brought about the mixture of separation from others and bonding to each other were faith in self that there was something to give and to receive, faith that the balance of giving and receiving was appropriate, and faith in God that the couple could sustain each other. Could Mark and Kiona or, for that matter, Amy and Ron, Reed and Michelle balance these forces to achieve this balance could be helpful to all of them.

Rachel was lost in thought from her translation. She did not hear Mark and Kiona come up behind her. They noticed the tears in her eyes. In mock severity, Mark said, "Why weepest thou my lady." Rachel played the translation for them and asked why people can not let others alone to determine their own destinies. She thought it was extremely stupid to build an ego structure with its base being the branding of a different ego as inferior. She also voiced a fear that the intolerance of the world had been defined centuries ago, and that Mark and Kiona were fighting too much this cultural imperative to survive. She voiced sadness for their struggle. Gideon's struggle to be independent, yet to continue to love his people seemed indicative of the futility of this struggle, as he appeared to be misunderstood from both ends: the Falasha and the Portuguese. Does crossing cultural lines result in either side pulling the stray into their own bailiwick and hating the one who resists the pull from each side?

Kiona took Rachel's hand and took Mark's hand with her other hand. She said that about a month ago, Mark was troubled by a nightmare about questioning God in his own pursuit of life's answers. In helping him deal with it, she referred him to the twenty-third Psalm. It described "Walking through the Valley of the Shadow of Death" with God as a guide. From this, we can conclude that when we feel hated or misunderstood, God will be there if we have enough faith to look for Him to show us where our path lies. Even through his bitter, raging veneer, Gideon Retta found his path. To cap off her conceptualization, Kiona added that she and Mark knew that their lives had been bound together by a force beyond their awareness. She showed Rachel the gemstone she had found in Chichen Itza. Teasingly, Rachel asked Mark if he had a symbol of a force that bound them. He said, "Yep, I'll go get it." He came back with the red nightie Kiona had bought with Michelle. The two women chased him out of the house and made him bang on the door for a half-hour before they let him back in.

When he was more serious, Mark told Rachel that he and Kiona had grown with each other, as they found the many ways that Man had come to accept that he was a child of God. When he became arrogant and saw himself as the center of the universe, man aggrandized himself and gathered propaganda that rationalized this assumption. The result was that God's children learned to create pockets of hate based upon a faulty system of logic. He and Kiona were learning to look for the signs of God's love by what they learned about how Man grew from one era to the next.

Kiona hugged Mark and said, "My, my how my Lanky has grown. I'm really impressed." Her pride came out so blatantly that she kissed him. Of course, she knew what to expect immediately after she did this. For Mark whooped up and down and shouted gaily, Yay, tonight I score." Both girls smiled and put him out of the house again. However, that night he did score, and they both laughed themselves to sleep in a warm cuddle afterwards.

Rachel also began to see that life was a blend between isolating and blending. The catalysts that brought about the mixture of separation from others and bonding to each other were faith in self that there was something to give and to receive, faith that the balance of giving and receiving was appropriate, and faith in God that the couple could sustain each other. Could Mark and Kiona or, for that matter, Amy and Ron, Reed and Michelle balance these forces to achieve a satisfactory relationship? Perhaps learning how Gideon Retta achieved his balance could be helpful to all of them.

# Chapter 4

The pattern that Escobar had established was based on fear of reprisal for wrongs; these wrongs were the wrongs that came from making someone else's home your own. This practice had begun with Francisco Coronado, who felt that these savages owed him the wealth for which he had come, and started the precedent of disregarding the humanity of the Pueblo people who had lived for centuries in the territory he had invaded. For the sin of leading the Spaniards away from the Pueblo area, a man was imprisoned in the winter and strangled. This outlander took over an entire pueblo in the village of Tiwa. He actually ordered people to leave their own homes so he could quarter his own men there. Blankets and warm clothing were confiscated. To further the outrage, a Spanish soldier raped a Tiwa woman. Gideon Retta was in the middle of this, as a prisoner in chains.

A prison is only one if we make it so in our head. Gideon was well aware of this concept via his recent incarceration. He sensed the fear of the retaliation by a just and loving God, if not his victims', which lay beneath the repression. He also saw that a political union between him and the people of the many-roomed houses could defeat these arrogant colonists. The first step was to get and keep the chains off. That the Conquistadors were gullible fools, led by their lust for wealth, was obvious to the soldier. Subsequently, he approached Escobar with " Pardon me Senor, if I were free to get the feel of the village, with my military skill about terrain and the strategies that invaded peoples use to hoard their wealth, I might be able to help you locate the wealth you seek: The chains were removed the same day.

The next step was to learn about the people. This took more skill and craft. He knew that he had to establish rapport via finding some common ground. The common ground was hatred of the oppressor. All had seen his chains. As a result, he was not perceived as the friendly ambassador to Spain. His dark pigmentation addressed the fact that racial and cultural differences existed. The Amerindians identified with this and also identified with their having the culture of the Spaniards foisted upon them. The final attempt at rapport came by evoking smiles from the villagers. Gideon began to show a fun loving side by joining small children in their fun and child-like games. Thus, he began to be perceived as a victim of the oppressor that liked to smile and laugh as they did. They began to share their food with him and to smile at his antics and friendly overtures. They began to try to communicate with him and teach him their language. He began to teach them his language. As there seemed to be a sense of openness developing, a feeling of friendship grew with it.

Now Gideon was playing a dual role. He had done this before as a Marrano in Portugal. As he had once feigned loyalty to Christian ideals to be able to live to practice Falasha Judaism, so did he build a warm and genuine friendship with the Tiwa villagers and pretend to be the grateful recipient of Spanish mercy for saving his life. He talked about where the Spaniards cached their weaponry with instruction on how to use them, while, on the other hand, he kept feeding the greedy and stupid Escobar tales about getting closer to the secret of the Pueblo treasure. At night, while their captors slept, the Tiwans began to steal munitions and weapons in small amounts and to train themselves in the proficiency in their use under the tutelage of this fighter.

However, there was one fly in the ointment. Gideon knew that in order to build the alliance needed, he must avoid liaisons with women folk. This would be offensive to his potential allies, who would perceive him as just another exploiter. The beautiful maiden, Dark Waters caused him a problem. He could neither admit his attraction to her or himself. To make matters worse, her father, Watering Ground, was a religious leader, center of community respect, and a focus for organizing the rebellion in waiting. This was quite a dilemma. Gideon had gone patiently over the workings of the rifle so that the villagers knew every part and its function well enough to be able to dismantle or assemble a rifle. The next lesson was in marksmanship. While going through this training, Gideon had a brainstorm. The rifles from Europe were of the blunderbuss variety the kind fired one shot at a time then had to be reloaded. He reasoned that if several of these could be tied together and a pliable rod could be put through the trigger mechanisms, one could fire several shots at once. The result would be an ability to shoot at more than one man. Gideon and Watering Ground went into the desert to test out this new field piece. Dark Waters went with them. This was extremely distracting to the drill instructor. Every time she knelt or bent over, Gideon's attention was diverted. At one point, he almost shot off his hand. When Watering Ground ask him what was preoccupying is mind, the warrior answered that was reminded of a battle where this new weapon could have saved many lives. He feared that his interest in Dark Waters would offend the shaman and destroy the ability to launch an effective war.

Effective or ineffective, a war was being launched in the hearts and minds of the Pueblos. The Kivas or dwellings were joined by tunnels to allow escape from an invader. If the tunnels could be coalesced to a big tunnel, and the enemy, who had appropriated the Tiwa Kiva, could be attacked from without, the colonial invader could be shot down as they emerged from their escape hatch by a force waiting for them with Gideon's new weapon. The Black man, as he was referred by the inhabitants of the village, had even invented a cover story. He told Escobar that the Pueblos were ready to show him their treasure, only a cave had to be dug into the cliff. A further embroidery of this fairy tale was that he had tricked them into building a tunnel from that Kiva to allow escape from the Gods once man had been discovered making off with what belonged to them.

Watering Ground could sense the feeling that he had for his daughter. He was growing to like Gideon, but he did not approve of a relationship between the two of them because Gideon was an outsider, and there was no certainty of his sense of honor. He was relieved for the good sense that the soldier showed. The source of his fear was that Dark Waters not only sensed his attraction but also had one of her own to provide reciprocity for his. Once a conquistador approached Dark Waters in Gideon's presence, and Watering Ground saw the fighter snarl like an angered bear. He grabbed his daughter by the hand and took her from the scene. She was also flattered by it. He started to call her aside and tell her about the dangers of a liaison with a man about whom she knew little, but he remembered that she was an adult and would not let him reach her, as she did when she was a child. He decided, as a loving father, to not step in unless he was asked.

Gideon, on the other hand, was in a constant state of internal conflict. This woman was not only not Kohan, but she was not even a Jew. In fact, she was not even Black. What could she offer him, or what could his hate filled soul offer her? He reasoned that nothing good could come from such a relationship like this. They would both be better off if nothing took place. He got into the habit of taking long walks and keeping to himself to avoid the visibility of his violent persona. He had wandered out in the desert following a coyote after he had heard the song of its mournful cry. Never had Gideon given himself time to grieve for his losses. He had figured out, about a seemingly million years ago, that his path was to fight, not to mourn. He was pondering his resemblance to the lone coyote, when hew saw a beautiful maiden cut open a cactus catching the juice in a bucket. He asked in the language that Watering Ground had taught him what she was doing. She stated that the area was dry and that centuries ago the Pueblos had to divert the mountain rivers to them, the water was always in short supply; consequently, they had also learned how to increase the water available by getting it from the plants. He helped her carry the bucket home, but he was careful to hand it back to her at the outskirts of the village. After this they began to meet at the cactus plant every day. They shared their cultural and several other experiences with each other and got to know each other well.

Gideon tried to curb his attraction because he sensed a reticence to accept it on the part of her father and a fear of offending her father, on her part. Therefore, he plunged his efforts into preparation for the oncoming war. He explained his invention to Watering Ground. In a month's time, enough rifles had been stolen to begin assembly. Green branches were used to fire the triggers because of their pliability and elastic strength. Teams were organized to fire and load and drilled to do it by rote repetition until it became an automatic reflex. Gideon also taught them the policy of burning the earth behind them and to obscure trails and fire on the enemy while the confusion occurred. Another tactic he used was to raid the Spaniards' camp at night, set fires, and steal horses, weapons, armor, and ammunition. There were constant drills and war games in these tactics. The practice of tying warriors to their horses was to be used to confound the enemy to arouse the superstitious fear that they were invincible because they could not be killed due to staying on their horses. Alliances were sought and made with outside tribes, and secret meetings took place at site outside the village to cement these relationships. Although the effort was made to deny a growing attraction between two people, despite the motivation, an army of power was being forged.

Threats of war were occurring because the insults the Spaniards heaped upon these people were assuming intolerable proportions. In response to commandeering the winter clothing of twelve villages and the rape of a woman, the Pueblos attacked the horse herd to weaken the invader. However, this invader had the advantage of an organized army and superiority of arms. The Tiwas tried to run to the mountains and resisted this behemoth for fifty days, but the cost was 200 dead and burning of captives at the stake. Training continued under Gideon. After troops with religious clerics ordered the town of Onate evacuated for Spanish troops, and Acoma was blasted in retaliation for stealing a turkey and treating a woman rudely when she protested this, the embattled villagers began to defend their ground. Four hundred colonists and twenty-one missionaries were killed. The rest of the army fled back to Mexico. Such strategies were used as leading a large band of Spanish soldiers into the cave they had dug then turning Gideon's new weapons on them, while other troops came down the tunnels from behind them through the Kiva and attacked them with atalatl (spear throwing shafts). Another rout occurred when a stolen cannon was turned on the Spaniards' military camp in the late hours of the night after the munitions and weapons had been confiscated while the soldiers slept and burned in the center of the camp. Furthermore, the few native soldiers that were killed were an inspiration to fear. They were tied to their horses creating the impression of not being able to be killed. This representative of the power that was Ferdinand's and Isabella's turned their tails and ran.

The hour of celebration was at hand. The hero of the hour was

Gideon Retta. He was asked to join in their dances, partake of their food, and participate in their games. In the seeming delirium of victory over their oppressors, the difference between Gideon and the others seemed to disappear until Dark Waters appeared to show him some attention, as an attractive man. Watering Ground recognized the change and said, "My brothers, this man knew of the differences between us when we had to learn to fight the White men. We did not question his difference then. It is not right to question it now." The men glowered, but they did not question the shaman, at least not to his face.

Now that the war was over, and the stress of their hatred was gone, the Pueblos turned on Gideon, Watering Ground wrestled with himself, and Dark Waters began to turn to Gideon as if to her man. He tried to resist her, but more and more, he felt that to go with her feeling was in keeping with Nature's law, if not Falasha law. He was still bitter due, in part, to the rejection for bringing down the wrath of the Portuguese, which he had only exposed. In part, he was reflecting the need for adaptation of his life to what was there for him. He knew that he would never see the Falasha again, but right now, he was experiencing fair weather friendship. In spite of this, he very much wanted a relationship with Dark Waters. This was about to be tested with the proof of fire.

Their next meeting at the cactus was to be an eventful moment in their lives. Gideon began their communication.

He told his narrative: The humiliation by the Amharic youth, his father's tyrannical demand for passivity to anti-Semitism, his expulsion form home, his identification with Redai and witnessing the humiliation of his defeat, and his exposure to what Christian love really meant to one outside of its embrace. The evidence was on his feet and legs. Dark Waters drew him to her as he said, "I am an evil man. For I cried out against the sin against Abel and became the Cain that slew him."

Dark Waters took his battle gnarled hand in hers and said, "I know not of whom you speak, but I saw a man who knew he was different from my people respect that difference, and, at the same time teach them how to feel their self respect by casting off the indignities heaped on them by a mean, mad coyote. That makes a good man, not an evil one. For this, if for nothing else, I shall always love you." With that, she took him behind the cactus, embraced him, undressed herself, and begged him to take her. He was awe struck at her beauty. Her breasts were like the golden goblets of Solomon. Her thighs were power of Moses, as he parted the waters of the Red Sea. Entering her renewed his place in the world of man. He hated himself no more.

# Chapter 5

Watering Ground sensed something different in his daughter and in the stranger. He said, "I have long known that you love my daughter and that she loves you. I cannot condone this because I know my people do not like this, and will shun both of you. I also saw you show enough caring for us, despite what seemed to be an anger at all men, to help us throw off evil men. For this, you and my daughter will not stand-alone. I shall stand with you, though we all three stand alone." Gideon gave him a manly hug.

Within the space of a few weeks, the council of Elders approached Watering Ground and Dark Waters. They stated that they did not welcome The Black Man into the society of their tribe. She could not believe this since he had helped them drive away their oppressor. Their answer was that he was not one of their people and could not be one of them. No one could predict when or where he would betray them. The tribe was moving to new hunting grounds. If the Black man was with them, they could not join them. Refusing to believe such cruelty from people, he had known his entire life, Watering Ground asked how they were supposed to survive; they were told it was their problem. After they told Gideon this, he urged the father and daughter to join their tribe. Both refused. They would take their stand together. A door was put on the cave and made to look like part of the cliff wall. With the cliff as a back wall, a house was built facing frontward. Travelers over the mountains or across the desert would need food, water, and supplies. With gunpowder, Gideon blasted a stream from the Mountain River to provide water for trade and irrigation. Tomatoes, potatoes, squash; corn and lettuce were grown. Dark Waters preserved fruits and vegetables and made thick, warming soups. Spanish, French, German, Dutch, and even Russian explorers made their ways to Gideon's Dark

Watering Ground, as it came to be called. They became famous for bear stew, pureed mountain goat, loganberry pie, squash-potato-barley soup. They made and sold otter boots, bearskin coats and traded with Utes Paiutes, Kiowas, Arapahos, and other tribes in the area. The language, in which the threesome spoke was an amalgam of Amharic, Pueblo and various other tribal dialects. A religious aura of gratitude for their deliverance seemed to grip them. Their belief system was also a blend. A stern Mosaic concept that personified the Sabbath as an angel and included Gods of weather conditions came to be the voice of their beliefs. They worshipped their God(s) by loving each other. Between two of them, this love was punctuated with a lot of sex. Gideon's Dark Watering Ground had made a name for itself in the region. Once in a while one of Watering Ground's old fellow tribesmen came through. Politeness was always there, but friendship and camaraderie, which permeated this last stop before the mountains, was not to be found.

Gideon had not known love for a long time. When he found it, he cherished it. What's more, he would never let anything or anybody hurt Dark Waters or Watering Ground. Sex that was once an expression of violence became the vehicle of demonstrating warm passion and caring. In fact, he seemed to care an awful lot. The happiest moment of this new relationship came when Dark Waters told him she was pregnant. He fussed over her and would not let her do any heavy work. Every night he listened for new sounds from her swelling belly. They laughed together at the discovery of the new sounds and other signs that the birth was getting nearer. Gideon also felt pain when she did. Once she had to forget about her own pain and nurse him. They both laughed about it. Watering Ground brought a midwife whose origin was never mentioned. If Gideon would have known she came from the village where the rejection had occurred, he probably would have sent her running from retaliation by the sixteenth century equivalent of a shotgun. Although violence was recognized as part of his angry, lonely past, when Gideon thought his family was imperiled he would re awaken it instantly. On one occasion, a drunken trapper made an advance toward his wife. A split second had elapsed when he was kneeling outside the store door holding a broken arm and facing atlatl, or throwing spear at this throat. Spanish explorers were tolerated as long as there was no arrogance brought in the door.

In this setting, there was no cultural referent. The only mores that had any consequence were the ones that pointed to survival and protection. As a result Gideon's Dark Watering Ground became a haven for social gatherings, political discussion, and bringing people together as equals interchanging ideas and experiences. No culture tried to define itself at the expense of another, but whatever cultural pattern that appeared in the doorway picked up innovations that were tried on for size at home. This development may have been responsible for movements to clean up corrupt religious practices or break away from old, stodgy ways of thought. For no old ideas are challenged unless new ideas are brought in as a basis for comparison. Such new ideas never evolve unless something creates a necessity for a change in adaptation. Gideon Retta had come from a culture battling for its right to exist as individuals among a massive opposition. Rather that lock antlers like two angry stags, mightn't a breakaway to another clime by the author of change and individual expression allow that expression to become visible and allow opponents to either weed out or accept this anomaly before them?

Amidst the clamor for new ideas, one day, a great cry was heard. Watering Ground recognized this sound and ran for the midwife. Seven hours later Dark Waters gave birth to an eight and a half-pound boy, twenty-one inches long. Gideon was beaming from ear to ear. He told his woman she did a good job. He and Watering Ground hugged each other and danced in circles. After Dark Waters was recovered, they decided to name him Fiery Water, in recognition of the temper he was beginning to show. He was immediately the apple of his father's eye. Gideon visualized teaching him to spear fish with the atlatl, to hunt, to build his house, to fight, and to know when to lay down his arms. The strangest thought came into his mind. He wanted to take his son to Ethiopia, to enter the Masjid and sit down with the Nezir and say, "God loves us all, my brother." Yet, he knew the way of the world.

And the way of the world was this: Moses, the representative to God of his people, the Falasha, was chided by his mother and sister for marrying with a Black Woman; Ham had seen his father, Noah naked and was said to have sodomized him when he was drunk. For this, Noah cursed him to be the progenitor of an inferior Black race. This inferior Black race had been the cradle of many African civilizations. The origin of these ways of looking at people had to start with Man not God. The Christian Bible talked of the love of God and slaughtered anyone that deviated from his or her view of the world. Right then and there Gideon Retta took a vow. Fiery Water would know that violence existed, but he would not be trapped into making it into the mode of his life. He would, at least look for beauty and acknowledge it before turning to the cult of killing as a mode of life, as his father had done.

For all the violence that had created Gideon, the soldier, his family never even knew him to raise his voice. He taught his son the ways of nature and came to accept the God of the universe as God of nature that was a consequence of natural occurrences. Gideon found his old religious documents, which he had hidden from the Portuguese and taught Fiery Waters to read from them when he was old enough.

He also took him for walks in the desert or to the mountains where they studied plant and animal life, habits of animal herds or prides, wind directions, and any other way he could find to bring him into harmony with the world around him.

From his mother, Fiery Water learned to put himself in other people's shoes. She taught him to not use or abuse other people or animals. She told him what the Spaniards did to the Pueblos and the memories his father had of them. She also explained why his father was not friendly to the Pueblos that occasionally came through the trading post. She too wanted her son to know as many different cultures as possible. She urged the scouts, trappers, and hunters to leave books and literature so that her son could learn something of their languages. Fiery Water was also interested. He also interested in learning what made the world around him operate. He had learned from the reoriented soldier to seek a harmony in nature. He wanted to take what he learned about family life from observing a pride of mountain lions and see if it was applicable to the lives of people around him. He learned to communicate with the trappers, hunters, and explorers despite language barriers. Once he got past these blocks, it was easier to learn bits and pieces of their languages from the materials they left at his mother's urging. His parents were also anxious to learn, and an almost university-like respect for knowledge about different cultures seemed to prevail at the trading post. The time for manhood rites was approaching, and Fiery was to have a strong test that would bypass all that the normal tests that prepare a youth for the Trans migration into manhood.

The test consisted of the experience of saving a life and enduring the demise of a beloved family member. During Fiery Water's thirteenth summer, a French fur trapper happened into the area of New Spain north of the Rio Grande River. He kept going until he came to the country known for its red earth, in Spanish, Colorado. He trekked through the desert to an area that preceded a mountain range of towering peaks. His name was Joaquim La Rouxe. His wanderings took him to an apparently deserted network of cliff dwellings. He did notice a trading post in the area. The first rule was to establish human contact, in case an emergency should arise. Without further adieu, he went inside to do business as an introduction. Once beyond the door, he beheld an Indian woman of breathtaking beauty, an adolescent lad that may have been a racial mixture, as denoted by flashing, dark eyes and an almost beautiful olive caste to his skin. Beside him stood a very tall, very wiry Black man that looked as he could go into killing mode instantly, if set off. They communicated mostly by sign language and the common grunts all human beings have in common. Joaquim made his needs known and found that both parents wanted their son to be able to communicate in his language. He agreed to teach Fiery Water some of the rudiments of French when he was in their vicinity. The crux of the arrangement was that he would be supplied as needed in return for one quarter of his pelts and the French lessons. Their arrangement went on for about six months, and all of a sudden Joaquim stopped coming and stopped taking Fiery Water back to his camp. This occurred in early January. Joaquim usually ran out of supplies around this time, but he was about a half week behind schedule in making an appearance at the trading post. Fiery Water decided to go to his camp and make sure all was well. He got on his horse, packed food and water, took medical supplies, in case they were needed, and headed for the mountains, where the camp was located. Joaquim's cabin showed no signs of human habitation. Fiery Water followed over to the stream that flowed by his cabin. As it rose up the mountain, it widened into a river that turned into a system of rapids, as it ran over rocks. A loud, fearful call for help could be heard. Fiery Water turned to the noise. He saw Joaquim gurgling in water adjacent to a raft. He attached one end of a rope to a horse and swam out to Joaquim with the other end. He tied the end around the Frenchman and pulled him to shore. The raft went over the rapids. The reason the trapper did not swim for land was that he had been trapping for otter and stepped into one of his traps while it was on the raft and fell into the water. The youth, who lived by his wits, pried loose the trap and bound the wound until they could get back to the trading post. "God bless you, Mon Ami", stammered the man of the mountain. Neither of them ever forgot the incident.

The rescue of Joachim was gratifying and showed that Fiery Water cared about his fellow man, but now he was to endure the deep pain of grief. Watering Ground was an honored member of the Pueblo tribe for a long time before the war. He sincerely loved Gideon, Dark Waters, and Fiery Water, but something went out of him after the exile. The many friends of his formative years dwindled via the aging process and deaths. He cherished those that survived with him. When they cast him off, the pain was unbearable to him. Something snapped inside of him. He would undergo bouts of melancholy and have memory lapses. At times, he would wander away. The rest of the family would have to go search for him until he was found. Part of the cause was a severe pain that recurred. A Spaniard's musket ball had penetrated his ear and he suffered periodic disorientation, loss of balance, and excruciating pain after each attack. During these episodes coupled with bouts of depression, he would wander off to God know where. Although he was loved and cared for at home, he would stay away for days and eat whatever scraps of food he could find. Watering Ground wandered off to the mountains and was missing for three days. After this length of time, Gideon and Fiery Water went looking for him. They found him by a stream with half-eaten a piece of moldy, half-eaten bread in his hand. A half-eaten piece of fish also lay next to him. Evidently, he had fallen asleep eating. They shook him, but, for some reason, he would not come awake. Gideon felt for a pulse and listened for a heartbeat.

Nothing was felt or heard. He was cleaned up, put in a canoe, and secured inside it while Gideon prayed in Geez and made offerings as Dark Waters and Fiery Water chanted prayers over him. The canoe was set adrift on the river with much sadness and feelings of loss. The family knew the emptiness of losing a very loved and loving presence in their lives. Fiery had to contemplate this while he underwent his manhood rites alone in the mountains. He had to learn to make his clothing, hunt and prepare his own food, and endure the pain of circumcision, along with grieving for his grandfather. At the end of a week, he had completed his program and his man's name: Gabriel Fiery Water Retta.

Although he continued to be called Fiery Water by his family, his full name was presented to outsiders. The outsiders increased in a number as word spread about Dark Water's cooking, Gideon's fair dealings, and Fiery Water's helpfulness. Many Ute's, Paiutes, Arapaho, and even, Apache came to trade with this family. Of course, languages were shared between tribes, as were cultural and political ideas. When Spanish explorers, trappers, hunters, came around Gideon was always cold and aloof, as he also was to any Pueblos that came around. At these times, Fiery Water would remind him, "If you save one life, you save humanity."

When Gideon heard these words, a tear came to his eye. He thought of his father and remembered him for the kind man that he was. He was also the man who sent him into his manhood with a slap. A slap that propelled him into battle on land and sea and in the foreign land of a treacherous, greedy race of people.

Until he met Dark Waters, he had doubts about whether one life or humanity was worth saving. The beauty that she and this innocent, yet wise boy brought to him seemed to transfer Gideon Retta from a fixed fighting machine back into a human being. His judgment of humanity seemed to mellow a little until he started to notice that Spaniards were in the area. He could not allow himself to trust them. He did not like the mistrust that seemed to dominate his thoughts every time he saw a Spaniard or Portuguese. He thought of Erico De Pelunis, who may have been motivated by greed, but also gave him a chance to prove himself as a man of mettle, and worthy of respect. Maybe humankind did have some redeeming qualities? He was attracted and frightened by this aspect because he wanted to believe in the innate goodness of Man but had seen so much evil. At least he knew that his son, wife, and father-in-law qualified as good, caring people. Perhaps a new base line could be drawn. He had also come into contact with Spanish explorers and hunters that reflected no bias toward him if he bore them none. He witnessed this through the eyes of his son and wife, who bore no person a grudge, unless that person blasted hostility by his/her behavior. Although this made for truer friendships, it also created real sincere states of enmity.

Gideon felt some of his previously conceived wrath melting away. Yet, he was too mistrusting to give it all up. He was connected to what had meant survival to his people and to himself, but he saw his son and wife reach out to others and to prosper from taking a risk in their fundamental views of life by investing into others, rather than by exploiting them. He felt that the physical results he was seeing were restoring his faith in humankind and in God behind him. This is not to say that there were not bitter moments when he rejected God because of an endless appearing stream of frustrating events. Thus despite the examples of his wife and son, the angry flames still could ignite his soul because this response was all that he had to fight an insane world for a good many years. He did discover that if he really worked at it, he could exert a great deal over his impulses to retaliate.

Gideon began to wonder from where this capacity to love originated. Was it from the same site as the Falasha proverb his son often quoted to him? How did such diverse populations arrive at the same conclusions? Is there, indeed, a plan that the creator has for man? Maybe Moses was able to communicate with God, and maybe each and every one of us could stretch our ability to conceptualize what God is trying to tell us. The stretching is the secret because we are an image of God, which means that part of God is in us. This part puts us in contact with the part of Him that is beyond us to the extent that we see enough to appreciate what he wants used to bring us closer to Him. As our trust in ourselves increases so does, our knowledge and trust in Him increase. The state of awareness is brought about by observing where natural occurrences lead, not by devoting ourselves to blind obeisance to miraculous phenomena we cannot sense or otherwise visualize. The testimony to faith in the God of our fathers comes, not from our fathers' dogmatic pounding of it in our heads, but from being sensitive enough to perceive the Word, as the natural world God created shows it to us. Until he had a family, he was his father's son, not his son's father. Gideon was on the brink of creating a new pattern in his life, but he wondered where Dark Waters had developed the wellspring that she had given to Gabriel Fiery Waters Retta and now to him.

The healing that came over Gideon involved two basic mechanisms: accepting the fact that the world we live in may not be perfect, but it is the only world we have; we cannot change the world into Plato's Utopia, but we can exercise some control over what comes into and out of it. This, in turn, is possible if we realize we can not have our cake and eat it too. He had come to realize that he could not inspire fear and have someone want to protect him from the fear if this some-one was afraid of him. Therefore, he found that if rather than one person taking and asserting control over another, enduring relationship could be built. This meant that two people chose each other, despite what a society dictated. If a change arose and was strong enough to endure, the society around it either incorporated the alteration because it was essential to survival of a New World, or they shut it out. In this case, either the society would extinct itself by refusal to adapt to the inevitable or the change was not strong enough o persist and died out, As Gideon had tried to teach Fiery Water that changing states occurred in nature and only had to be observed. This was God's law. Humans could use their faculties to alter the outcomes, but each alteration had its price. To bring about a change, one had to examine the outcomes and determine whether the price exceeded the benefit or vice versa. Hence, cultural patterns are a tool of humankind, not an immutable law. Through the bitter experience of clinging to themselves, Gideon saw the Falasha almost destroy themselves via the destructive forces of rigidity. By altering their pursuit of their way of life and standing alone, his people had achieved a measure of survival. To survive further, more adaptive processes would have to be developed.

Once again Gideon had to admire his wife and the Pueblos for gleaning these secrets from the works of nature. In comparison to their former oppressor, seeing who was civilized was easy to observe. Where the difficulty lay was how Dark Waters had maintained such a loving attitude with so much anger, hatred festering around her.

# Chapter 6

Gideon set Dark Waters up as a paragon of virtue because he felt he had none. His memories were of having to still the outrage within him because he was raised in the tradition of turning the other cheek. When his anger boiled over, he demanded justice measure for measure. He forgot that God metes out punishments or reward. Although man administers and devises laws and consequences, the ultimate answer must be made by God. In his blind rage at the frustration of never being allowed to express his inner being, Gideon became the warrior. He could not even remember the name of the Muslim he slew, but he saw him as a visualization of the loss of his family and the failure of his people's right to be considered as individual human beings. A further source of frustration was his people's preferring to live under tyranny, and make him a villain for making their freedom his fight. He had to accept the correct fact that he had the same virtue as Dark Water, but he had endured frustration beyond his limit due to not learning how to manage the anger he felt.

Raising a son to keep close to natural realities and sharing a life with someone, who had beauty by living close to life helped Gideon learn the art of putting his wrath in perspective. However, there was a reflex that got touched off when he saw the conquistadorial garb of a Spanish explorer, settler, or someone that resembled one of the pueblo villagers whom he had taught to fight the Spaniards. Rather than give in to the violent impulses, Gideon would remind himself of the bungling greed of the Conquistadors or the blind shortsightedness of the Pueblos, who did not realize what profits they could have reaped by staying where they were and opening up a trading post, as he did.

Even though hatred and anger had to be given up, being on guard and cautious was always an order of the day. It was also an order of the day to not underestimate the strength of a gentleman. Joaquim had a younger brother, who came to live with him. He did not have the same respect for Fiery Water that his brother had. He saw him as being one of the weak because he saw only concern for the animals of the forest or not wanting to hurt other people. Gideon saw that the brother saw his son with the myopic eye of the covetous for he was pale and thin looking. He also seemed to demonstrate a tendency to prosper by manipulating relationships. Gideon chose to watch what happened and let his son learn this valuable lesson in life himself. Unfortunately, this particular lesson would strain the father's patience to the degree of almost learning control to the utmost of his ability. The brother was in the store alone with Dark Water. He was also bewitched by her beauty and put his hand on her thigh while supposedly helping her ascend a ladder. Fiery Water heard his mother scream and ran into the store. He saw at a glance what was going on. The Frenchman saw that he was not alone. He saw Fiery Water had entered the room. "Well, well if it isn't our little forest nymph. It would do you better if you went out to play with your birdies." The youth picked up an empty musket and hit the brother so hard in his chest that he fell to the floor. Once on the ground Fiery Water pounced on him and began to beat his face with the rifle butt until he saw blood and continued until Gideon came through the door and pulled his son off him.

His words to the scrawny Frenchman were "I saw and heard everything. My first instinct was to kill you, but I wanted you to see that kindness is not a weakness. Now I am going to make you live with my unkindness." He then gave his son a loaded musket and instructed him to hold the gun on the man. He stripped off the brother's trousers and shoes and spread honey all over his posterior and legs. He then threw him out the door where a chained bear was waiting. As the man ran, Gideon unchained the bear. He then suppressed a laugh and said to his son with mock severity, "If you save one life, you save humanity." In the spring, Joaquim's brother left the area.

Gradually Gideon learned to forgive his violent feelings of past years. He would look upon Dark Waters feeding the baby or watch her at her chores. Together all three of them hiked, swam, fished, hunted; life was good. One day, Gideon came upon his wife bathing in a mountain stream. Stealthily, he swam behind her, picked her up, and dunked her. She began splashing him, and she caught his hand. He held it against him, and she gently caressed him. They swam to shore to a wooded area. Gideon picked her up, and carried her under a spreading fir tree. They touched each other and kissed tenderly. She could feel his throbbing and reached for him. He felt as if he were penetrating a Mountain Brook. Their union reached a crescendo that was like the waterfalls beating on the rocks below them. Afterward they clung to each other and vowed that Eden could not have been more beautiful. Yet, no violence was involved.

Gideon had to know where people who understood every aspect of loving one another originated, all that Dark Water could tell him was that stories had been passed on from one generation to the next. Long ago they lived in another land.

An enemy came in the night, rounded up all the tribes, and scattered them through the realm of Asia. Some of them made their way to the sea. Some went North to steeps and snows; others negotiated the Urals, Arals, and Himalayas. In their Diaspora, they wandered, settled down, and got involved with planting, hunting, warring, and intermingling that peoples do. Some of them always were restless and wandered onto whatever quests they had. Some, however, had to move on. In whatever processes they engaged they either left a mark upon history or were obliterated by it.

Dark Waters was unable to give a rote account of her people's growth and development, but she knew that they had borne a lot of joys and sorrows to get where they had. A certain amount of perspective and balance evolved over their wandering until they had stopped at Mesa Verde. The arrival coincided with the time that early Christians were struggling for their existence with Rome. These arrivals from afar came to believe that the land gave birth to them, and that if they took care of the land, it would take care of them. In other words, a belief system evolved based on respecting what they saw in nature.

Across the Atlantic, a counter movement was occurring to the breaking away from Roman Christianity into Protestant religions. Militant reformers, such as Ignatius Loyola hunted out heretics and meted out punishments, but they also cleaned up the acts of the Church. In addition the might and right of Spain were being brought into question. The Belgians and Dutch were challenging their stranglehold on Europe along with the British. Jews began to fight and not walk into their own funeral pyres. They joined the Netherlanders in their war. Among the Jews, a remarkable thinker arose. His name was Baruch Spinoza. He struggled to develop a pantheism based on blending nature with God. He criticized the logic of the Pentateuch, and by so doing, he was ex-communicated from the Jewish religion. He was condemned to an existence of isolation for trying to develop a religion more in tune with the real world, as it was observed. Over six thousand miles away, Gideon Retta was learning to free himself of unrealistic symbols and to communicate with the world around him. His wife and her people had known this freedom for centuries.

Despite the counter reformations in the church, there was some wisdom in the assumption that a leopard does not change his spots. In keeping with this philosophy, a missionary one-day came into the trading post. His name was Father Benedetto. Physically, he resembled Friar Tuck. He appeared full of fun and the earthiness of the Saxon peasant that followed Robin Hood. When he announced himself as loyal subject of Ferdinand and Isabella, who wanted to bring the love of the True God to this savage land. Gideon thought of the love that expressed itself by tearing his skin off his extremities to the knee. For a split second, he snarled inwardly and reached for his knife. An inward force intervened and stopped the potential murder. A thought wended its way to the surface of his brain. This man carries the memory of the act of the dog that tortured me, but he does not have to be that dog. It would be better if I gave him a chance to show me what he is about. He seemed too robust a soul to carry evil.

To the contrary, Father Benedetto represented the thinking of an empire to restore itself after it has fallen or to prevent an inevitable decline. He was schooled in the events of the war, in which Escobar was ejected from Mesa Verde and in Gideon's role in it. In the guise of using his position as the bearer of God's word to restore a righteous Christian nation to power, he was to gain information about troop strength, weaponry alliances. Of course, he fed the information to the viceroy of Mexico. None of the tribes in the area were fooled by his

"Friar Tuck" pose. Although he tried to give him the benefit of the doubt, Gideon soon found out he was a phony. Both he and several individuals from some of the tribes in the area (Arapaho, Kiowa, Utes, and Cheyenne) decided on a plan to get rid of him by destroying his credibility. The plan of attack was to act secretively over scribbling on a piece of bark in his presence and to accidentally leave it where he could find it. They would leave "accidental" bits of conversation that hinted about a new weapon that was being designed in fragmented stages on similar pieces of bark stashed at various sites which would happen to be mentioned while the good Father was in earshot. Benedetto would dutifully send the bits of bark to a mission in the nearby mountains where the new weapon was assembled as each new section of bark was sent. The plans were producing, apparently, a catapult like weapon that was driven by water pressure. The water was placed in a container with an opening at one end that was attached to a channel through which water flowed. The water flowed to turbines on the inside walls of the channel, increased its momentum, and directed the water to a lever behind a spring that would release it.

The projectile would sit in the spring and be hurled into space as the water pressure released the lever. The inside of the structure was lined with manure from the desert and mountain animals of the area. This served an insulator function, as it did in their buildings. The insulation was essential to keep the water from freezing. A rope was connected to a trap door and a cork that stopped up the opening into the channel. When the operator pulled this rope simultaneously, the stopper and trap door opened, enabling easy observation of the working of the machine.

This was the plan the Father had translated. He prided himself on mastering the languages of the area. He memorized the instructions to the most minute detail and passed them on to the workmen. Father Benedetto kept himself apprised of the progress on the weapon. He kept hearing the strangest report that this armament was assuming the shape of a huge buttocks with a diameter of five feet and a depth of four feet. This man of God could not for the life of him understand the logic behind designing a weapon in the shape of a buttocks. He reasoned that it must be part of a pagan fertility rite. After all, who could conceive what these poor misguided savages could put in their primitive heads? Regardless of the ridiculous geometry of the catapult, the Father could not wait to demonstrate the new weapon to the government and church prelates. No doubt, a bishopric would be waiting for him after this mission for God and Christianity.

The Retta family watched the missionary's antics of ego boosting with much amusement. They did not have to choke back their rage because being looked down upon by such an obvious fool was not an insult. At the forefront. He strutted about the trading post area, trying to hide his disdain for these savages by strutting about like a preening rooster.

As the project grew closer to its completion date, this ambitious cleric began to grow more demanding of the workmen to finish and of the Church and government officials for a presentation date. The date was set for two weeks after the receipt of the communication from Mexico. The family served as guides to return to Mexico City. The Viceroy, the Cardinal of all of New Spain were to witness this glorious display of the arsenal of God. Gideon had traded for three sets of spyglasses so that he and his family could observe the festivities from a bluff overlooking the ceremony. What they saw was the catapult brought in all painted and polished. Bearers brought it to the center of a clearing between newly fertilized fields. The catapult was placed on a scaffold beneath, which stood an official, who would pull the string. He was dressed in highly polished armor, and his pride, at being chosen for the auspicious occasion was obvious. Even before he pulled the rope, Gideon smiled. For he knew the outcome. He did not tell his family because he wanted them to enjoy the surprise.

The rope was attached to the trap door and the stopper in the water tank so that both opened simultaneously when it was yanked. Only the water immediately dissolved the manure lining, and the feces poured throughout he trapdoor onto the proud conquistador. Dark Water and Fiery Water laughed uproariously. The audiences below were not so amused. Soldiers seized Father Benedetto upon the orders of the Cardinal, whose face was as red as his robe. The weapon was also pulled across a newly fertilized field by a mule and Father Benedetto was tied to it. The catapult was burned in the fireplace in the Viceroy's home.

On the road home, Dark Water took her man's arm and stated "When I first met you, I knew you needed a little love to bring out the gentle man that you are, but I never, in all my life, realized that all those volatile feelings could be turned to make you laugh, my man." He replied that all the fiery anger of his youth made his stomach hurt so he had to learn to laugh. Dark Water whispered in his ear about a special cactus plant waiting for them at home. By the smile she evoked in him, she knew she better run, but she smiled while she trotted.

They laughed and enjoyed each other all the way home. Yet, Gideon felt a sense of airiness, as if he had a premonition of things to come. Only they were not things; they were Spaniards and other White men hiding their egos beneath the doctrine of enlightening the noble savage with the teachings of Jesus as a cover for their unbridled greed for wealth and power. In his bones, he knew they would be back.

Gideon was not jesting about the Spaniards coming back. The humbling of their overgrown ego by a non-White population was something that stuck in their craw. The smashing of the mighty armada in the Irish Sea, the raids of privateers, such as Sir Frances Drake and Captain John Hawkins preyed upon their shipping, the rivalry with France in the Colorado area all reduced money in the Spanish coffers. Yes indeed, Spain was coming back; they were not stupid. They had learned about the terrain where they had planted colonies successfully or unsuccessfully. They had studied men like Gideon Retta, who had shown leadership to learn their skills, weaknesses, and strengths, alliances of tribes, vulnerabilities and strengths of some of the trappers and mountain men. Spain wanted it's dream of hidden and real treasure, it's security of being the top power in the sea, and the surety that it was really advocating the morally superior way to an eternal life. Otherwise they might have to acknowledge that, underneath all the pious bologna cast about; they were paving their own road to Hell. Imperial Spain or any aspiring nation, for that matter, had no choice but to return or to learn another way of negotiating besides self-lying and exploitation.

From his reflexes of the past, Gideon wanted to warn the Pueblos, but another reflex had been conditioned into the system. He remembered that he and his wife and father-in-law had been left to starve. His son sensed the conflict inside him and threw the quotation back at him to save a life is to save humanity. To this Gideon replied that starvation because of a different racial or social heritage was not a human act and not worth saving. Fiery Water chided his father, only to be thrown a look that meant, "You did not teach people to defend themselves only to see their gracious return to you in rejection and a death sentence of sink or swim by yourself, I did." Fiery Water knew that on certain subjects there was a wall between him and his father. He did say that some people follow majority rule because it is the only way to survive that they know. Gideon's answer was to let the Spaniards be their teachers. Yet when he saw a family that had been involved in their exile, he tried to indirectly warn them that he guessed that the conquistadors would be back with new methodologies and old vengeance's, and he warned them to protect themselves. Needless to say, Fiery Water and Dark Waters both noticed this behavior. They knew him to be a good and decent man despite his mouthing.

This colonial power, motivated by the greed and power lust that stems from enjoying the fruits of misusing others and wanting that power over others restored once it's taken away, prepared itself for a new war. The preparations entailed learning what opportunism or ideals motivated alliances or treachery among the native populations, what adjustments had to be made in armaments and weaponry, clothing, organization of the camp, strategies of deployment. As greedy and Machiavellian as this imperial nation was, it was also willing to critically look at its functioning and apply industry to restore its former ego state.

The adventure with Father Benedetto sensitized Gideon that the colonizer was coming back. His wife and son put pressure on him to warn the other Pueblos, and, he agreed to journey to their new land with him. After swallowing his feelings of being betrayed and unwanted, he was amazed and enraged that he was regarded as a foreigner and unworthy of their trust. He railed at them "I trained you to defend yourselves so you could let me and mine starve. Now you ignorant swine have the nerve to doubt my veracity. If not for my wife and son, I would have let you descend to Hell and fry in your own pig grease and putrefaction." With that, he turned on his heel to walk

169

away, when a young warrior jumped on his back and tried to plunge a knife into him. Gideon flung him to the ground, bent the wrist of the knife hand until he heard the bone crack. He then wished him God speed on his journey to Hell for which he would have plenty of room, since it was only half full. He also said that there would be no more warnings and the lot of them was not worth the backside of a hippopotamus. To his wife and son, he said he did not hate the way he used to do, but some are not ready to cast off their protective armor. These people will always achieve a certain margin of safety, but they confine themselves to a mental prison and will not prepare for famine during the years of plenty. No one from their numbers would accurately assess new dangers because relying on stereotype was easier and more convenient. Yet he made several trips to the mountain and tried to share the knowledge from his this reconnaissance's with the Pueblo, but they scoffed at him. A young fighter that became known as Crooked Wrist led the scorn.

# Chapter 7

Despite the failure to use their survival instinct, Gideon made diagrams, maps, charts, and artillery for anyone that had the sense to use them. As he had previously said, "Hell was only half full." He also began to try to organize the traders, trappers, and mountain men into an army. The peaceful years had bred a complacency and a belief that Spain had become a second rate power. And so no angry fighting force had emerged, despite the warnings of the old fighter. Thus, Gideon came to realize that he was responsible for defending his own home in the event of an invasion. He began to refortify the cave and trading post the way it was before and in keeping with the new knowledge he was able to gain from his reconnaissance, which he felt was scanty. The information he had gotten would have to be supplemented by information that was gotten from within, but the former man of war was at a loss to find a spy of sufficient prowess and innocence. The man was now walking into the trading post, Joaquim La Rouxe.

Gideon quickly explained what he needed from Joaquim. He was to present himself as he was at the Spanish mission at the foot of the mountain, where the Rettas had observed Father Bennedetto's comedy of errors. His overt purpose was to establish a trading arrangement with the Spanish government, but he was to throw hints that he would be available to provide information about tribal alliances, plans to fortify the trading post and any troop movements of nations that were rivals of Spain. Of course, any information he gave them would be information that he and Gideon had fabricated. Each month a different Apache would wander into the area allegedly to buy provisions. The mountain man was to provide him with whatever information he had received; this in turn was conveyed to Gideon. The Apache were chosen as couriers because they were nomadic. A different one came each month to avoid identification. The system of planned intrigue apparently seemed to be successful. However, in the eighth month Joaquim was caught.

He was enamored with a dancing girl in a cantina and felt an increasing need to express his attraction to her. She sensed this and began to give him meaningful looks and sidle up to him. Joaquim was an isolate, and subsequently not used to the attentions of women. He became flustered and left the map of troop movements he had just stolen from the commandant's office on the table in plain view of two conquistadors. He was arrested and sentenced to hang in three days. The Apache courier got back to Gideon by a miracle that same day and brought him the news. Fiery Water and Gideon went down alone for the rescue mission. They also arrived at the mountain the next night. A length of fusing was laid around the perimeter of the guard camp, and a generous supply of oil was distributed while the soldiers slept. A cannon, powder, and shot were stolen from the camp and placed in front of the jail that held Joaquim. Fiery Water was waiting in a second wagon behind the jail, wearing a monk's cowl. Gideon lit the fuse at camp starting a conflagration and a panic within. Then he raced to the jail and lit the cannon aimed at the jailhouse door. After the constable and deputies ran out to find out the cause of the explosion, Gideon sneaked into the jail, opened Joaquim's cell door with the key that was left behind in the excitement, and hustled him into the second wagon. They were over the mountain before the Spaniards realized what had happened. Joaquim never left the mountains again. Having whetted his appetite, he did begin to take an interest in women.

The information that was brought back to Gideon indicated that something had begun to change in the Spanish psyche. The church was just as powerful, but stringently moralistic in its stance toward all Indian tribes under its domain. Some of the excesses taken by other colonists against these indigenous peoples were exposed. However, the motives did not change, just the openness with which they were viewed.

This son of Redai was only concerned with preserving the freedom for which he had so fiercely engaged himself in the past and which had cost him so much. He taught his son, his wife, all the mountain men, and the tribes that were willing to ally themselves with him the ways of battle he had learned so many years ago. He traded for and stole weapons to rebuild the fortress of long ago. He cleaned out the tunnels that functioned as escape and attack routes. He felt as if a handful of men were withstanding the onslaught of the hordes. Yet, he felt that this handful made the difference between living a natural life that made appropriate use of what the good Lord provided and living a stilted life based upon greed and disregard of other human beings.

He shuddered inside when he thought of that cell back in Lisbon only to discover that the world these colonizers were creating was just a big cell. There always had to be someone to hate, someone to punish, someone to brand as an enemy, and to hold back. It was not the work of God that spoke for these people, but their inability to see others as sharing the world with them. At this point in time, Gideon remembered his encounters with John De Mello, the Nazir, Guintera, and Escobar. A tear trickled down the side of his face for the time he had wasted as a creature of hate and vengeance. He longed for the day when he could hang up his hatred, suspicion, and live without these defenses. However, he knew that to be so idealistic was to be naïve. Gideon did allow himself to be amazed by his growth in feelings. Before he had met Dark Water, violence and killing were his life. Now that he had something for which to fight, he entered the battle that was relish to him with reluctance. He also knew that he and the handful would be fighting the hordes the way Leonidas fought the Persians at Thermopylae.

In order to strengthen the handful, Gideon tried to ally himself with as many of the tribes between Mesa Verde and Mexico as he could. He also tried to develop a universal code of communication between them. He met with mixed success in this area because he did not find the link that would connect the various languages. However, in an entirely different area he had remarkable rate of luck. He was able to arrange that an independent privateer would harass Spanish coastal ports on the Pacific as well as the Atlantic sides so that a bandit was able to smuggle arms onto the ship in trade for furs and food stuffs. The privateer was Ericio De Pelunis.

The old warrior began his training. He trained his son and Joaquim as lieutenants, and together they went out and distributed arms and knowledge acquired by discipline to any tribes willing to join in the fight. Surprisingly, many of the trappers and hunters in the mountains joined the fledgling army. They also had bad memories of the Spanish territoriality over what was not theirs, particularly since they demanded tribute for hunting within the territory of New Spain. To a trapper or hunter, who came to eke out his own living and to get away from the bossiness and disrespect for the worth of an individual in the settled areas, a demand for tribute was a fight looking for a place to happen.

Fury was the motivating force behind these isolates. In order to build a unified army, the mountain men met at the trading post to learn of each other's diversities and how they could be used and blended for purposes of engaging in battle. The trading post also served as an intercultural exchange medium. The tribes also gathered with the mountain men. The two, or multicultural fighters learned how they could break down language barriers and attempt to understand each other's culture. These divergent and sometimes hostile to each other groups were learning that the beginning of an army was the spirit of singularity of purpose that is put together by compromise.

Fury may have been the motivator for establishing unity, but an army needed knowledge and supplies. Arguments occurred over how to camouflage themselves and whatever weapons that could be procured, the virtue of night raids versus early daytime raids, knowledge that was learned about Spanish military organization. Spanish spies and provocateurs were also in their midst. A cause of disagreement arose about how to manage them. One school wanted to execute them; another wanted to feed them misinformation to take back to their leaders. A representative of the execution approach was Joachim La Rouxe. He was grateful for Gideon's intervention on his behalf, but he wanted these wanna be conquerors to feel the fear of death he had. Gideon reminded him that dislike for what Imperial Spain brought to them motivated all these people to unite and fight; were they doing so to repeat their misbehavior, or were they trying to build a world where human life was valued. This was more than a moot point. More than an understanding, but a rallying point that was also needed to establish a commitment to do battle.

The Spanish colonies were organized into three classes: The Nobles, who were Spanish émigrés, Mestizos, who were mixtures of Spanish and Indians, and Peons, who were the Indian laborers. Members of the alliance of tribes, including Apaches were able to infiltrate Mexico and learn about troop movements, steal weapons, and bring back information about strategies to this liberation army.

No one knew when the Spaniards would invade again, but all knew that they were coming. Developing a sense of unity was difficult, but it was possible with a little discipline. In this army, because of differing cultural bases, people had to work at the art of compromise. That people had strong feelings about was their differences brought out in a public forum.

At first there was much scoffing at the process, but, as it was put into effect, even though feelings were strong, and the air rang with many curse words in different tongues, feelings of mutual bonding were beginning to emerge, this principle works because each contributed something, each had works of value; each view point was measured by its merits and flaws. The unity was forged on the anvil of weighing on advantages against disadvantages as each one saw it.

The disadvantage was that this was an army of reason, not one of iron discipline. A country, such as Spain was able to separate out emotional issues from the virtue of winning because they had owned, whether rightly or wrongly and want the resources and prestige back because their lives were better with them. Ideals were not of concern to them; wealth was. They also did not like being beaten back by those that they regarded as inferior. This colonial power went over its past errors and developed new arsenals to correct their shortcomings. They knew that Gideon Retta was no fool. They kept their weapons development and military strategies secret from him and his agents by doing the brunt of their building and planning from Spain and European strongholds. They developed an armed wagon with a cannon at each end to prevent being boxed in by two armies coming from opposite directions and were able to mount additional guns in between if needed. Harpoon guns were used to scale heights and to cause fires with burning rags attached. To carry arms and other goods across the desert wheels were attached to sailing vessels. These developed high speeds in windy weather and also had the advantage of multiple guns. They could be set afire and used as incendiary devices. The sources were thinkers of the day, such as Leonardo Da Vinci.

Facing a formidable foe was not new to Gideon, but this time he felt as if he were facing the Philistines with the jawbone of an ass. His army had spirit and fellowship, motivation, and alliance that held together. Would their battle for human dignity be another Thermopylae or Masada? He knew that these "embattled farmers" did not want their shots heard around the world, They wanted a bully to know that picking on me will mean you will have to bleed as a price for disrespecting me.

# Chapter 8

Kiona was reaching up to put a dish back on the shelf, when she came down on her heels with a startled squeak. Mark had sneaked up behind her and encircled her waist with his arms. She turned and kissed him. He, in turn, began to encircle her bottom. "No, no, Big Boy, Mama has work to do." Groaning, Mark said, "I do not think that I can make that lonely walk upstairs." Laughing, Kiona replied, "There's a nice shower in the bathroom down here, and it has plenty of cold water."

"What'd you guys do today?" Kiona asked interestedly. She knew that the group was trying to coordinate the work they performed with what they learned about the history of the period throughout heir studies and Gideon Retta's narrative. Mark answered that Gideon's perseverance in trying not to hate but to protect what exposure to love had brought him was commendable, but it was also difficult to understand. In the mountains, in what appeared to be a dried up riverbed, a large piece of wood was found with a faded inscription on it that said "Enigma" on it. They would have to dig further before they could guess the significance of it. Kiona made a mental note to call Rachel and go over the translation with her.

That night they made passionate love, and afterward Kiona was pensive, as she ran her fingers through Mark's hair. He knew she was about to speak her mind and was waiting to hear it. "Lanky, I want to have a baby." They had had these discussions before. Gritting his teeth, Mark replied, "Kiona, baby, I want a child, but we both have chosen such huge battles to fight, and parenting would take so much time and demand. Besides, I want a warm, supportive environment for our son or daughter. Our parents have not made move one to establish a friendship. How can we raise a child in isolation from his/her grandparents?

Kiona became just as impassioned as when she argued with Jonos about trusting her at the time of their coming to Mesa Verde. The heat of her reply could be seen in the tension of her jaw and the flames in her eyes. She went back to Gideon Retta: "Dark Waters, Watering Ground and Gideon were isolated from the Pueblos and believed enough in life to bring a baby into the world that would know the value of human love. The love they felt was not based on a culture accepting them, but on their accepting each other. It may even be why God led us to each other. Furthermore, my father was a lot like Gideon. No one could have had more hate in him when he left Cut and Shoot, Texas. I know how Gideon scrubbed the hatred from his soul. A war ripped it out of him by showing death and gore, as its consequence. In my father's case, he had it scrubbed of him at sea fighting the loneliness and storms that shook the foundations of his life. Both were ready for a good, strong woman that could understand them and love them for what they were. Neither found this good woman because they lived in a cocoon of love, but because they had the self-destruct mechanism of hate and turned elsewhere. I haven't had hate as a companion, but I have a deep love for you because you believe in me and my cause and helping me reach it. Damn it, I want you and me to live on into the next century."

Mark was calculating. He wanted the freedom to grow with a woman and for her to grow with him. He wanted to travel the world, to see what Man has done to Man, to develop a scheme to clean it up: was the best scheme to step out and live life the way Gideon and Grady had done it? He didn't know, but neither did they. Fiery Water and Kiona didn't turn out so bad. While Mark was ruminating, for the first time in their relationship, tension brewed. They only had polite remarks to make to each other. At the end of two weeks of this wall, Mark brought home a huge rubber tree plant and a card that read "Anyone knows that an ant can't move a rubber tree plant, but he had high hopes, high hopes, high-apple pie-in the-sky hopes." Beneath this, he wrote, "You better make me a boy, so I can blow cigar smoke at the barber shop, pull on my suspenders, and say that's my boy." Smiling for the first time in tow weeks, Kiona took his hand and led him upstairs In mock protest, he said he thought he needed a cold shower because Mama had work to do. With a smile she said, "All work and no play make Mark a dull boy." Afterwards Kiona asked her man how he felt, and he said he felt as if he were embarking on a new adventure.

Ironically, the next day they received a letter from their parents that they had indeed made contact and that a friendship was developing between the two couples. They were both facing retirement and wanted to develop a joint business venture. They wanted input from Kiona and Mark and would be out to visit them in a month. Kiona and Mark were all excited and couldn't wait to tell them the news. Both knew that there would be pressure to marry and they were not sure how they would respond to it. They knew they loved each other, but they understood the track record of marriages in America. They also perceived that they had chosen a way of life during which the chances of their being apart much of the time were good. The terrains, in which they would work, also afforded a fair amount of risk. Was the concept of marriage a yielding to pressures of decorum or an expression of mutual love? Grady, Ruth, Jack, and Bert had this mutuality, but so did Gideon and Dark Water. No marriage ceremony united this couple. Yet, the life they shared together was as beautiful as either of these couples because, in all three cases, there was a caring and an honest attempt to understand the other.

Kiona and Mark wrote their parents the next day so that they would have time to process the pregnancy before the visit. This also gave them time to process their response. After both sets of parents arrived, they were full of questions, confrontations, and opinions. Instead of playing into a hostile armed camp, they had arranged that they all look at Rachel's translation and discuss how Gideon Retta had been forced to answer the questions they were asking. The message that came across was that if beauty is in the eye of the beholder, then that beauty should be beheld, as it is perceived. Each pointed out that in the framework of a depression, a devastating war, racial violence and thought distortion, these parents carved their own disciplines and their own lives. Their children had the same rights and opportunities to behold in their own individual manners and perceive with the mind's eye that beheld it. The discipline and the lives carved were up to the perceiver, as well as the consequences of misperception. Two beholders perceived their own beauty and wanted to share it with those they loved. The translation, which was about to be viewed, was a testimony to the beauty that can evolve for a person if she/he allows the evolution to take place in her/his soul. With that said, and with the dissenting issues efficiently disposed of, the computer was turned on. Rachel narrated it.

Jack, Bert, and Ruthena were amazed at the structuring of such a significant chunk of history and geography, but Grady, the philosopher, was astounded by the grass roots and ecologically sound system of thought that this family had created from the barbarity of being left to starve. They had a right and a responsibility to themselves to create a culture of their own. The rightness of the position his daughter and son took permeated his soul. "Wait a minute," his mind's eye told him, did he just refer to Mark as his son. By God, these two were slick." Everyone in the room felt this sense of kindred. They were all smiling, as was he. The journey into the past helped these young adults to find themselves.

The next item on the agenda was what kind of business venture could unite the Almedersons and the Englers. Mark suggested they could be shepherds, and they all threw popcorn and orange peels at him. The citric acid must have gotten to him because an idea germinated. The plan would involve taking on another partner, Professor Horton. Groups of retiring or near retiring business men could sign up for archeological expeditions and be brought to an old destroyer rescued from graveyard for old ships by the company purchased by Jack's truck line. The ship would be the site where Professor Horton and Professor Owens, if he were interested, taught principles of relevant archeology and history. Jack and Grady, who went around the country locating sites within the confines of America and abroad, provided a selection of digs. A boat line provided transportation to the dig. Equipment would be leased from the ship. The capital would be provided from the retirement funds. Investors and small business loans from the government. The shipping could offer reduced rates for groups of senior citizens and, perhaps, qualify for tax deductions. Jack said to his son, "I never knew you had such a business head." Mark said, "Neither did I."

That night the two parent couples spoke about how good Mark and Kiona were for each other, no matter at what level they chose to keep their relationship. The fact that they were willing to take the risk of bringing a child into the world without the guarantee of legally binding contract bespoke a lot of love and a lot of courage. After all, they found a meaningful set of careers in their own ways responsibly. They had also made a creative effort to unite the two families to the extent of suggesting contacting acquaintances out of the past. The couples agreed that these two had really grown up. At least one element of their binding cement seemed to come from out of the years of history in the person of Gideon Retta, the stone hearted warrior that found how to love as a man and to put that love before his hate. Jack remembered how he charged that Japanese Zero with coldness, menace in his heart, and was able to return to the good woman that waited for his return with the love and caring they shared. Grady never forgot the cold hatred in his heart when he left that klanner in the alley. It was so hard that he had to go to sea to have the storminess and the solitude scrub it off. The savage violence returned when he saw Ruthena, whom he had admired from afar, being attacked. They could not help but wonder from where the capacity to replace the hard, originated, sometimes, fiery hate with love of humankind that could be just as hard came. Jack's and Grady's came from knowing and sharing their lives with good women that drew this capacity out of them. What was it about Dark Waters that caused Gideon and her to cross cultural barriers to seek each other out? Perhaps, a journey into their past might provide some answers.

# Section VI

# Dark Waters

# Chapter 1

I came into this world, perhaps on the wings of history, perhaps as a sequel to a legend of a people. At any rate, it is I that am here, and I'll make my own mark, for, I believe that this is what God wants, however we see Him.

A huge land mass called Asia separates the Mediterranean Sea and the entrance point into North America and a large ocean called Pacific. However, a narrowing point exists at the Bering Strait. At one point in history there was not a land/water separation, and mammoth and mastodon hunters were able to follow herds from dry desert areas through the lush grasses of the steppes in what is now the Kirgiz area of Kazakhstan through the icy mountains of Mongolia or across the barren, frozen plains of the tundra to a frozen Bering Strait or the remnant of a land bridge that was once there. In this way did migrants from Asia make their way across. "What migrants?" History or legend has to tell us.

Dark Waters was unable to tell Gideon from whence she came because she honestly did not know. The migration had occurred centuries before through areas where Bedouin tribes populated the desert, through areas where the liberated Hebrews made their trek to the Promised Land. They came into contact with what were to become tribes of Armenians, Moslems of Azerbaijan, Uzbekistan, and Kazakistan. Fierce tribes of Turks, Taters watched their movements. Sometimes they had to do battles with these denizens. Sometimes a fight could be avoided by paying tribute. Families of the migrants would settle in an area. Others had to move on led by whatever impelled them. Some even became involved with sea-faring people and left. The movement took several centuries until the part of them that became Dark waters' progenitors came to Colorado. Was there a beginning?

Where was it? The Amerindian is said to be descended from the lost tribes of Israel. To test the veracity of this claim, we must start in the city of Ur, follow the ancient Hebrews through their Exodus from Egypt, and understand the meaning of the division of the Israelites into twelve tribes.

The Hebraic history presumably had its start with Abraham. His wife, Sara was barren into her old age. God spoke to him and told him he would have a son, but it was not until after his wife sent him to her handmaiden to start a family through this servant. A son was born from her, Ishmael. His wife conceived Isaac. He, in turn, received the covenant from Abraham. Isaac had two sons by Rebekka, Jacob, and Esau. Rebekka favored Jacob and tricked Esau into selling his birthright to him, although Isaac favored Esau. Esau went away, and there was bitterness between the two brothers. Esau, now king of the Edomites, arranged an uneasy peace between them. Not trusting Esau's motives, Jacob fled. At Bethel, Jacob wrestled with a stranger whom he could not defeat and could not defeat him. This stranger was God. He told Jacob that his name would now be Israel because he had fought God and man and had prevailed. Israel had twelve sons and a daughter from two concubines, his first wife, Leah, his second wife; Rachel, came Joseph and Benjamin. From the two concubines, Bilhah and Zilpah came Dan, Napthtali, Gad, and Asher. Rachel died after Joseph and Benjamin was born. The older brothers were jealous of Joseph and threw him in a hole, telling Israel wolves killed his son. They presented the coat of many colors that Jacob had given to him, spattered with blood. After extracting himself from the pit, Joseph was taken prisoner by the Egyptians and worked his way through the prison system to become a governor. He invited his family, now in Canaan to join him in Egypt. This was only the beginning of the Hebrews role in history. For these twelve sons plus Ephraim and Manasseh, Joseph's sons became incorporated into the twelve tribes of Israel. How did they get from Egypt to Israel?

The Hebrews, according to scripture, were enslaved for four hundred years and led to their freedom by Moses, a Hebrew raised as an Egyptian. He was made aware of what he was and of the plight of his people through a contact with his God, was led to murder an overseer, and fled to the desert. Having heard his God, he returned to Egypt with the demand that his people be released. What followed was a war between Hebrew monotheism and the Egyptian pantheism by which plagues were visited upon the Egyptians until the pharaohs released them, God had parted the waters of the Red Sea, and their forty year sojourn to the Holy Land began.

The currents of history, as studied by man, the cultural inputs of various ages, and the legends have coupled together to show the linkages of truth and discrepancies in data and logic that raise questions in the chronology and the reality of this pantheon. Yet, evidence also seems to cry out about its veracity. During this era, a Pharaoh, named Akhnaten, had introduced monotheism into Egypt. He had passed on, and the following Pharaoh, Horemhotep, was not a fan of this religion, nor were many other Egyptians. Monotheists were persecuted. Some believed that the Hebrews were this persecuted sect. Others believe that a foreign culture called Hittites had been considered an undesirable and was these Hebrews. Whatever the origin, this undesirable sect was cast from Egypt. They were also said to be part of an alliance of sea peoples attacking the Egyptian mainland. Much of the genealogy bears a resemblance to a legendary war between the Egyptian Gods, Horus, and set with Osiris, as the partiarch and Isis, as the matriarch. Horus represents Jacob and sometimes Isaac; whereas Ishmael, Abraham's first son, and Esau are represented by Set. Osiris represents Abraham; Rebekka's counterpart is Isis. Moses was said to be a priest of Osiris, who became a monotheist. He is said to have become a worshiper of Aten, the God of Akhnaten. Yet there are unexplained phenomena that are related to the settling of North America that lend credence to the genealogy, an Indian tribe in the Andes that worshiped a God with a name that sounds like Yahweh, a phylactery, or pair of cases containing scriptures worn on the head and connected by thongs (to the head and arms), found at an Indian grave site in Vera Cruz, Mexico, dated between 100-300 A.D., Roman coins found in Amerindian burial mounds, and the finding of a stone in a burial mound in Bat Creek, Tennessee with Hebrew inscription dated 100 A.D. all testify to a Hebrew presence in America in ancient times in native American cultures. To connect these events with what developed Dark Waters' ability to be loving, in the face o hate and pass it on to her man will necessitate delving further into the history of people that were her pro- genitors.

After wandering in the desert for forty years and battling at Jeri- cho, Mount Tabor, etc., the Jews arrived in the Promised Land. Two lands were created. The ten northern tribes formed Israel, or Samaria as it has been called, and the two tribes from Joseph's sons: Manasseh and Ephraim formed a nation to the South, Judah. A war-like civiliza- tion was thriving and raising havoc in the Fertile Crescent: the Assy- rians and their emperor, Ashurbanipal. In 722 BC the ten northern tri- bes were invaded and taken to God knows where. Some may have died as Assyrian prisoners. Some became seafarers; some moved on and eventually settled. Some became the hordes that terrorized Asia and Europe; some became the tribes that settled in Colorado.

Micah and his sister, Brynna lived in the area populated by the tribe Naphtali. They were basically people of the earth, who were hap- py to be able to provide for themselves. They loved the smell of the crops ripening to grow into their own food in their own land, blessed by their own God. The dawn of the day the Assyrians hit them felt the way that the plagues struck Pharaoh. Fourteen of the Naphtali tribes- men were chained neck to neck and marched from their newly found homeland to only God knew where their captors were taking them. From the lush green hills through desert, they marched to the crack of a whip while the huge bearded son of Ashurbanipal laughed his growl that seemed to emanate from Satan's furnace. At night when he felt the need for a woman, he would unchain the neck collars briefly and select his companion for the night. The night the brute selected Brynna, Mi- cah rose to her defense before he could put the collar back on. He threw sand in the Assyrians face and tried to beat him about the eyes with a rock he had found. What happened next frightened Brynna and every one else amongst these prisoners. The huge robot of war un- hafted his broadsword and ran it through Micah. Brynna stood frozen in horror as the life giving blood of God drained out of her brother. He chained the others and took her by the hand without even letting her look back.

Brynna was numb to his ministrations and did not dare to weep for the loss of her brother. He drank compulsively; taking huge gulps like a hippopotamus at a lake and passed out with a hideous leer on his face. He was not cautious enough in his drunken state and did not retrieve his sword from the desert shrub against which he had propped it, nor did he bind Brynna. With the tension of the fear gone, the sense of loss and outrage overwhelmed her. She made her way to the sword and brought it over to where the sleeping beast lay with the grin that he would carry to eternity on his face. She raised the blade with both hands and severed the head from its neck.. "For my poor, gallant brother!" She screamed and fell asleep weeping with the bloody instrument of death in her grip.

In the morning, Brynna awoke and untied the sash holding the key to the neck collars. She made her way to the prisoners. To their astonishment, they awoke to find her returned to them alive. She unfastened the lock that held the common lock of their neck yoke and said "Now we are all free, but I cannot remain here with the memory of my brother's murder on my head. I can no longer even be Brynna and will have no name until I find who I want to be. May the one above go with you." With that, she spun on her heel and left.

The lady of no name left without knowing what direction she would take or where she would go. All she had were the clothes on her back and the sword in her hand. With no sense of her direction, she turned to the north and east leaving the Fertile Crescent, sleeping in shrubs, under crags and precipices, or caves where she could find them. She learned to hunt and skin her own game also to make her own clothes out of their hides. Her trek had led her to the Caucasus Mountains. She learned to follow herds of deer and goats to find water and food. She learned how close she could get to wolf packs and still get some of their kill for herself. She discovered that men rode on horses and raided villages from which they took women captives. Her hand tightened on her sword with the memory this evoked, but a certain loneliness seized her also. The former Brynna was beginning to feel some longings for connection. Years and geography drifted by, as the lady of no name moved further east and north. She came unto a vast barren land that became a frozen wasteland in winter. Later on, men would call this Siberia. With the drift in time, memories faded, and Brynna and Micah seemed like visions of a distant world. One day when rubbing stones to build a fire to keep away wolves, she saw a herd of riders approaching. They saw her fire and split into two columns, each of which swooped down on her and surrounded her. A tall muscular man motioned her to climb onto his horse. When she refused, he climbed down bent down, picked her up by her ankles, stood up, slung her over his shoulder, and tied her down to his steed.

# Chapter 2

The riders took her over a great distance to an encampment of tents. She could smell meat cooking. The tall one carried her to a table in the center of all the tents. Men were gathered around this table. Some were ogling her already. One reached for her, and the tall one reached for a firebrand and burned his hand. He then drew a dagger out of its sheath and circled around for all to see his intent. Next he strode to the table, cut a chunk of meat, and offered it to her. Hungrily, she devoured the nutriment put before her. For now, there would be peace between them. This was not a brute of which she had a dim memory. He did not have to tie her to go to his tent with him. Once inside, they sat by the fire, and he offered her a bowl of warm water to wash herself and a thick blanket to sit on and to sleep in. he rose to his full height and took his helmet off and to change into a nightshirt. It was then she saw his long blonde hair and his muscular and deeply scarred torso. He said, "My name is Tamakar. I am a soldier of Tatary." The unnamed lady shrugged because she did not understand. Over the course of the next few weeks, she roe with the d, showing them that she could wield a knife, a spear, or a sword. Tamakar taught her more and more and more of the language. She began to communicate the vague memories she had of her suffering. She also had one clear memory; she would not take a name until she found who she wanted to be.

Tamakar never touched her sexually, but he let it be known that no one else would either. She was able to contrast the gentleness he showed her in his tent with the ferocity he showed as a fighter. Bodies and the treasures of battle were always heaped around him after every skirmish. He was always covered with blood and scars. He never availed himself of the booty of war. One day she could stand the silence no more. She asked him why he was this way. Looking away, he said, "When I was a small child, we were raided by Mongols. My family was captured. I escaped and was seeking the opportunity to rescue them. From behind a rock, I saw them laid down on a scaffold and beheaded. I vowed revenge and made myself the most formidable fighter in Tatary for when I would meet the Mongols in battle." She did not say a word, only took his hand and put it to her breast and drew herself to him. That night they made love. In the morning she said to him, "I will now take a name. I do not know in what language it is, but to me, it will mean light of your life because that is what I intend to be. My name will be Lavinia.

From that day forward, she never left his side on the battlefield. She felt a God had given her responsibility for his life. She assumed the womanly tasks that went with being in a couple's relationship. Lavinia was sparked to release her anger at her brother's murder without being consciously aware of it through Tamakar's story. She loved waging battle as much as he did, and the material rewards had the same meaning to her. She kept from pregnancy because she did not want to give up being by her man's side. They began to feel an emptiness in their lives. Finally after two years they had a child. It was a boy. His name was Itor. Itor was tall and powerful like his father, and he enjoyed the roughhouse games of boys. An incident frightened him badly; his father came home from a war with a blood soaked bandage around his chest and a torn up face. His feeling for battle was never the same. He kept this feeling private from the other boys in the village, whom he feared would ostracize him, and he kept it from his parents because battle seemed to mean so much to them. At fourteen, he went through the customary puberty rites of the village. He was now eligible to accompany his parents to battle.

The battle to which his parents proudly brought him was against a Mongol stronghold that had raided their own village in the past and wreaked much havoc. In the middle of the skirmish, a spear was cast at his mother. Itor spurred his stallion onward and leaped into the air to catch the shaft in its trajectory. Another shaft struck and killed his horse. He became separated from his parents while on foot and sustained a spear wound to the thigh. Itor made for a snow-embanked ridge to tend his wound. The spear was well lodged in his femoral muscle, and it caused him much pain. He also felt febrile. He passed out.

When the darkness came the battle had ended. Numerous dead bodies lay in the mountain passes soaking the snow with their blood. Lavinia and Tamakar sadly realized that their son was not with them or with the bodies that had been recovered. They had witnessed the heroic leap of their son and found his dead horse. With broken hearts they went home and prepared funeral rites. For the rest of their lives, he would be their lost hero.

For two days, Itor lay in a stupor. A Mongolian widower found him and summoned his daughter to help him carry him back to their modest farm. They put him to bed in warm blankets to prevent shock and forced warm liquids down his throat. In addition, they pried the shaft from his leg and dressed the wound with poultice and herbs they kept on hand. They fed him warm soups until they heard him groan back into the conscious world. These neighbors lived close enough to each other to have some facility with their languages. The man's name was Ulan Cator. He was a mountain farmer, who had lost his wife two years ago when she had kicked a mountain yak that would not pull a plow, and the enraged animal bit her; as a result she contracted a fever and died. He lived with his sixteen-year-old daughter, Atun. They ate a humble but nutritious supper, played some games, and retired early. Late at night, Itor was awakened by a scuffle. He heard Ulan saying to his daughter, "You are my chattel. Your mother is not here. I need you to warm my bed. This was followed by a loud cracking noise like a slap. This angered Itor because he did not like bullying. However, he resolved to stay out of people's business, especially since they had saved his life. The next day, he feigned sleep until Ulan was gone. He saw Atun sitting in a corner weeping. Her face was red and swollen. He asked what was wrong even though he knew. She said, "My father treated my mother and me like beasts of burden. I believe she wanted to kick him instead of the yak. If I do not give him sex upon demand, he beats me. I believe I am with child because of him. I want to leave this God forsaken life while I may still find a man to love me.

For a long moment, Itor looked at Atun. He had a family that cherished him though they did not understand his revulsion to violence.

His death as a hero would probably be better accepted than his repugnance to battle. He gave a two-word answer: "Let's go!" Their journey took them through the mountains, through the Gobi desert to the eastern coast of what is now Russia. They endured packs of wolves, the heat of the desert alternated with the frozen mountain climate, and Atun's morning sickness. They skirted The Sea of Okhotsk, past Sakhalin and the Kurile Islands. En route Atun gave birth to a little girl. Her name was Kurilia. Atun looked at Itor with shame and tears brimming in her eye. Without waiting for her to say what she felt, Itor put a finger to her mouth and said, "She will be my child. Blood is thicker than water, but it is not thicker than love. We will also have more." They settled in a fishing village near the Bering Sea. The village was isolated and quiet. Its name was Vitoskva. Itor became a skillful fisherman and learned that the best way to build a business was to mind your own. Kurilia was a quiet, unobtrusive child because she perceived that was the way her parents wanted her to be. However, she had a secret self, an artistic self that was able to portray the beauty of nature to God and man. Her two younger brothers, Tragor and Petron were tall and strong. They also loved her deeply and protected her. She was never able to get beyond this protection, and it sometimes annoyed her. She looked for someone with whom she could share thoughts among the generation of her age in this isolated little corner of the world. Any time she found someone that seemed to match her need to be able to discuss her sensitivity, her brothers were there to protect her from that gossipy girl of no worthwhile repute or that aggressive young man, who did not have any steady work habits.

Itor and Atun were happy with their quiet life away from the wars that senselessly tore people and lives apart. They knew that their children were intelligent and adaptable. They also knew that Vitoskva was not the seat of intellectual ferment. They watched Kurilia grow through adolescence and to adulthood with something festering inside her that could not be satisfied by the small town by the sea. Tragor and Petron had found suitable wives and were starting families. During this time, a killer whale was terrorizing the village. The creature had tasted human flesh and wanted more. Not only was this denizen of the deep a threat at sea, but it would also plague the shoreline. A town meeting was called to develop a strategy to deal with the killer. One suggestion was to approach other villages and form a loose federation that would cooperate with one another to eliminate the menace. In a meeting of the new federation, which surprisingly took place in Vitoskva, a plan was suggested.

The whale was cyclic in its attacks on the land. It only came to the shore on the fourth week of the month, as if this were hormonally controlled. Prayers and offerings to the Gods of the sea did not seem to do any good. Kurilia stepped forward with a plan. The whale had a predilection for a certain type of fish that all the fishermen sought and kept well stocked because it sold well. Several boats would go out with a string of this fish on their bow. They would lure the beast to an island central to the location of the sites of the locales in the federation. There would be waiting, a host of men and women from all the villages with firebrands and flaming spears to destroy the behemoth, once and for all.

Some of the stodgy fishers laughed at the ignorance of a woman. After all, if the Gods of the sea did not see fit to intervene, how could mere humans control this monster? Out of nowhere, came a bellowing quality to Kurilia's voice. 'Did not God part the Red Sea so that his flock could depart Egypt. God does not turn away from His people when they seek him. Yet, the world is of Man's habitation, and it falls to man to figure out how to do this."

The elders from several communities challenged her. What Red Sea? Where or what is Egypt? There are many Gods of the sea and land! Who is this one God of whom you speak? Kurilia could only answer "I don't know." She was shunned as a mad woman. The next fortnight her parents and brothers were killed on a fishing expedition. The whale had appeared and demolished the boat they were on. The villagers sought her to hang her as a witch, or sorcerer, to use their word. She hid in a boat and avoided capture.

The boat in which Kurilia chose to hide belonged to a fisherman who went out in someone else's ship. This person was killed on the last fishing trip. Therefore, it was a safe hideout. The next news she procured was not so pleasant. On her third night of her seclusion, she heard what sounded like crying. Thinking it was probably a cat; she went to sleep and dismissed it. The next night she heard the same noise. Her curiosity was piqued. She went out to discover the cause. She saw a small boy sitting on the dock crying. She asked the cause of his weeping. His mother and father had been on the boat destroyed by the whale. All of a sudden, he drew away from her in horror. "You are the witch woman that everyone is looking for. You killed my parents." He began to beat on her. She caught his arms in mid blow and said, "I did no evil magic; I only tried to give them a new idea to which they were afraid to listen. I did not want my family to be killed. I loved them as you did yours." Some of what she said seemed to sink in. Suddenly she threw her arms around him and also cried. After they both had wept, they decided they needed each other. The boy's name was Kamchatka, after the peninsula where he lived. They decided to leave this horrible place of death and ignorance. Kamchatka was only five, and consequently had accumulated no property. They both got into the boat, set sail, and headed due east.

They fished for their own food since all the equipment was available for their use. The water assumed a purer blue than what they had seen from the Vitoskva harbor. They also began to enjoy each other's company. Kurilia laughed more in these few days than she had for most of her life. She was amazed by the fact that a little boy could bring her more enjoyment than a village full of people her own age or older. Something seemed to create an ominous shadow ahead of them. In the distance, Kurilia, could see a school of whales. One was apart from the others and seemed to be heading toward their craft. Kurilia had been prepared for this event. She brought out the spears, harpoons, oily rags, and lantern oil. She explained to Kamchatka what was ahead of them. She also told him to go below deck and tie himself down to whatever he could find. The youngster stood his ground. "My family was killed too. If we need each other, we need each other in a fight too." Impressed with his courage, she showed him how to dip the spears in lantern oil and light them with the lantern wick. She also cautioned him that he had to throw when he was close to the whale and to aim for the eyes or central pore in it's head through which it sprayed water.

When the beast attacked, they were ready. The pain from the searing spears maddened the whale, and it attacked with more rage and no caution. Hence, the eyes and pore were more vulnerable. Both Kurilia and Kamchatka concentrated their battle efforts there. The monster was weakening. The tide of battle was beginning to turn. In a blind fury, the creature threw itself at the boat. Because it had been burned blind, it missed its target and died right in the water. Kurilia and Kamchatka both hugged each other and gave thanks to the God that helped them save themselves. Another ship had pulled alongside her. The captain had signaled her to allow her to board. He was one the residents of Vitoskva.

She gave the captain the whale for the village as payment for the ship she had stolen and said that this settled her debt to the scourging little dot on the shore. Her family was gone, and she felt she would not go back to a town that labeled her as a witch because she thought with her own brain instead of hiding her fear in a superstition. She stated she hoped that the fact that a woman and a small boy could do what they could've done themselves should make them think of the lives that were wasted because they were too stupid or too afraid to act. "If you value what I did, she said, then tell them what I said to you now. I am finished with such small mindedness and will live my life elsewhere, free from idiocy, good-bye." With that she ushered him off of her ship and was on her way.

Kamchatka and his newly found mother figure passed by islands and let nature make its choice for their new home by running the boat aground on the Alaskan shore. Perhaps God meant this to happen. Perhaps it was part of the cause of the symbiosis between Man and the land that the later Pueblos started here. Maybe the teaching that passed between Gideon Retta and Fiery Water about following God and Nature together started with this landing by being grounded on the rocks. Maybe giving to a boy that had lost everyone, taught Kurilia what love was about. Maybe the kind of love that flowed from Dark Waters to Gideon and softened his hate had its start here.

In the area, which later came to be known as Alaska, Kurilia and Kamchaka made their new home. There was abundant fruit, streams with a plenitude of salmon and other fish, as well abundant game. Here they settled. Kamchatka loved his new mother deeply. He saw the brazen courage with which she defeated the designee of the deep. He admired the plain moxie of her stance against the village that labeled her as a witch because she dared to show that a woman had a mind equal to a man's when she wanted to use it and was capable of rendering the world controllable as was a man also. Standing up to this prejudice showed him what was meant by God's love: God loves Man. Part of this love is standing back and letting this creation in His image learn which way to go to reach Him. Kamchatka learned a lesson in life to pass on: Live and let live.

Over the years, the two of them learned to appreciate the spawning cycle of the salmon and established a fishery of sorts that carried on a flourishing trade with the inland tribes. The principles of commerce were based on an old adage. During the years of feast, prepare for the years of famine. The springs were abundant, but the winters were like blasts from the North Pole. They also lived according to the salmon cycle because huge numbers of parr had to be hatched and grown to be released to make the long journeys of their cycle and brought back to release a new spawn, or mass of eggs. Constant stock pilings had to be made and constant river routes had to be mapped. Fast friendships were formed with many of the islanders.

One day a ship docked at their fishery. A prosperous appearing man asked for the owners of the establishment. Kamchatka was away mapping salmon routes. Hence, Kurilia greeted the man. Something about him was familiar. He spoke of being from across the straits. Looking more closely at the man, she recognized the sailor to whom she had bequeathed the corpse of the whale as her reparation for theft and as a symbol of her outrage. He said he always thought of her with compassion and with respect for her courage. He told her of her enrichments as a holy and brave figure in the history of Vitovska. A tear came to her eye and she hugged him. He said his name was Adolphus Ventov. Over the years he had thought of her because she was the first person in the village that had questioned the mental stagnation that made him think of schools of fish each time he returned home from a fishing trip. He wanted something in his life that demonstrated that he could innovate, create, or do anything beside her and feel like a child of some God and not an enlarged gill flap. Kurilia laughed and said half humorously, "Is that a proposal?" Adolphus said he thought it was, and they both laughed.

With the launching of this new relationship, a restlessness began to consume Kamchatka. He had grown to manhood during these years and desired to learn something of the world about him and to have a companion of his own. His mother sensed this feeling in him. One day they climbed the mountain nearest the village that was growing around their fishery. Taking her hand, he said, "My mother, we have shared the adventure of creating a life out of nothing. If I am to regard myself as other than a large berry or moose, I have to create some thing myself. I don't even know what that some thing is, but I can not bask in your achievement as if it were mine and boast of a connection with a God or Gods. I love you, but I must step away from here and find what my contribution to life is." Kurilia hugged him to her and said, go forth, my son I know the fires of curiosity that sear your soul. For the same flame burned mine, there will always be a warm hearth for you here or wherever I am. Your time with me is past. I can no longer hold you." With that, she slipped down the mountain back to her own life.

Kamchatka had long since forgiven his mother for her alleged practice of witchcraft, but there was one piece of it he did not understand. The story he had heard was that she had spoken in an alien voice and said that God had parted the Red Sea. She had also had spoken of a mysterious land, called Egypt. During his youth, Kamchatka had tried to question her about this event. To his chagrin, his mother had no memory of this oration. She was told she said it, but she had no recall about it. As he had encountered certain members of the many inland tribes with whom he had had contact, that communicated with the Gods, had one God communicated with his mother? This solitary young man couldn't help but wonder. In his wanderings, this question was always at the back of his head.

Kamchatka did not stay in the area. He did not even leave the mountains for several years. His beard and hair grew to a tremendous length. He resembled the link between ape and man. He learned to follow herds to find food and shelter. He wore skins to keep off the cold. Oft times he had to outfight lions or bears to see who would occupy a cave. He even learned to communicate with wild life in a form of grunting. He would go sometimes for months without hearing the sound of a human voice. One day he came upon a large body of water. There Kamchatka saw beaver and deer, an abundance of salmon and other fish, and a woman. She came there to bathe and to swim. He made his camp in an old hollow tree and silently watched her for a week. On the morning of the eighth day, he followed her to a village where there were houses and vegetables, as well as goats and pigs. Spurred by his curiosity, he observed the life of the village. He had not experienced communal life since his biological parents' death. He saw people sharing the food that they grew and cutting pieces of game that they cooked on a spit in a fire at the center of camp. A part of him wanted to join the laughter and to feel the warmth of the fire. Another part of him sensed that his guttural sounds would frighten them, as well as his hirsute appearance. The next day, Kamchatka beat the maiden to the water. He washed himself thoroughly. A sharp rock served as a shaving device so that he could feel almost human. He was done by the time she made her appearance. He happened to see a movement in the grass behind her. The woman also heard the noise and turned to see a huge panther leap toward her. She did not see the figure swimming toward this scene of the hunt. Kamchatka arrived as the cat leapt into the air. They faced each other snarling. The panther bit and clawed at Kamchatka while the man tried to get its throat either with his hands or with the rock he had used for shaving. Kamchatka could feel himself bleeding where part of his ear had been bitten off. His hands were slippery from his own blood. He had already cut the panther below the eye and was trying to balance his weight for a thrust to the throat of the feline at the same time the beast was springing into a leap for the neck of the man. The combatants collided, and the force knocked the rock from Kamchatka's hand. Throwing himself into the panther, the hunter found himself on the belly side of the cat while it viciously slashed, clawed, and bit at him. Only one way existed to end the battle. In an act of desperation, he lunged into the beast and bit deeply and firmly of its throat. He yanked his head and heard the flesh rip. The cat yelped once and died. Kamchatka stood away from the panther, gasped and fainted.

Several days had passed without Kamchatka knowing it because he was delirious and in and out of consciousness. He awoke to the pleasant smells of female nurse and the aromatic herbs of healing. The remains of the loser of the hunt had nourished him. He was made an honorary member of the tribe and was given the name, Panther Slayer.

His rescuer could not help but notice how his body had been torn and ravaged from years of exposure to the elements, aside from what the huge cat had done. After the first few days of being fed hot fluid and having healing salves and pastes from pulverized herbs smeared on him, Kamchatka began to get too restless to lie around a sickbed. His nurse, the maiden for whom he engaged the panther in primal war, entreated him to stay and be one of hem. He noticed the pale green of her eyes and the fiery auburn of her hair. He had learned some words in the tribe's language by listening while he convalesced. The woman told him that the entire tribe respected what he had done, that they needed men of his mettle because neighboring tribes wouldn't let them grow their crops and fish in peace. She told him of the name he had been given. He eyes shown with unshed tears, as she told her name was Green Fawn. She said she knew that someone had been watching her for about a week. She had been bursting with wanting to know who it was. She stated frankly that now she knew him by sign, she wanted to be his and for him to be hers. With that she threw her arms around him and kissed him.

Kamchatka felt overwhelmed. For years, he bore only a name. There was no mark on the earth to give evidence that he was there except one that may have been just as easily made by a bear or wolf. He wanted roots. Yes! He would stay. At first, when he was addressed as Panther Slayer, he would look around to see to whom the party in front of him was speaking. As time passed, Kamchatka became a memory of the past, and Panther Slayer began to feel like who he was. His energies could go toward taking care of his family or taking part in a hunt to get food for the whole tribe. Their well being became the seed of his roots. Yet, a part of him wondered how his mother and Adolphus were getting along. He was particularly stirred by the memory of her address to the federation. He could not help but wonder whether or not his mother had communicated with a God. Perhaps only one God existed. He had heard rumors of a mountain tribe far to the south that worshiped one God. His name was Yah weh. Panther Slayer did not know what meaning this name had.

One day a long boat pulled into the Bay of their large outlet to the sea. After going through the docking procedures, the captain strode ashore. He was none other than Adolphus Ventov. Behind was a petite lady. The woman was small and dressed in dresses she had artfully decorated with seashells. Mother, cried Panther Slayer. Kurilia ran to embrace him, with her arms outstretched.

They hadn't seen each other in years and had lots of bringing up to date to do. Adolphus and she were tired of the long, bleak winters that caused them to have encounters with joint pain and respiratory ailments. Their son told them of his new name and how he got it. He also brought them to his home and introduced them to his beautiful, green-eyed wife. Adolphus had traveled far in his long boat, and Kurilia was always his traveling companion. They had many adventures to relate. One such tale was of a journey to a sea where three landmasses were separated from one another (Europe, Asia, and Africa). Adolphus had traveled to the area to establish a trade agreement with the Phoenicians, a nation of sea farers. These people communicated by making marks on paper. They showed both of them how to use what they called their language.

At this point Kurilia's eyes widened with astonishment that had remained from the episode she was about to relate. A people had been slaves for four hundred years. One of their members asked the king to free his people. When the king refused, this man prayed to the one God over his people. The result was that plagues were rained down upon the king's people. The king let the people go. This took place where a sea separated two landmasses. The sea was the Red Sea, and the land of the departure was Egypt. Their God parted the waters so that the people could cross. They both recalled that day of the federation meeting. The only conclusion the former Kamchatka and his mother could reach was that the God of these people spoke to Kurilia that day. As a corollary to this, they also concluded that somehow Kurilia was connected to these people.

Panther Slayer was basically absorbed in this tale. However, he had settled down to a life with roots of his own. He did not want to give them up. That night Green Fawn told him she was pregnant with their first child. His conflict was ended. Yet, he did have a part to play in his mother's saga.

Adolphus had learned the language of the Phoenicians in greater depth than Kurilia had. He was able to write. In fact, he had started a narrative of the Exodus. Panther Slayer and Green Fawn wanted them to stay and see their grand child grow up. They could see that they were both preoccupied with tracing the history of their connection to this people. Panther Slayer's role was to receive the documentation periodically from Adolphus and to pass it on to following generations. Slayer was lonesome for his mother but he could see how much connecting with her past meant to her. Suddenly the land began to tremble. Fissures began to appear in the earth around them. Huge boulders began to fall from the mountains. Adolphus' long ship sank to the bottom of the sea. No choice remained but for them to stay with their son, at least until a replacement for the long boat could be rebuilt. Was this another example of the work of this mysterious God about whom they all were learning?

The trembling and splitting of the earth lasted two days; then just as suddenly as it came, it stopped. It had left damage in its wake. Houses were torn apart, boats were damaged, animals were terrified and had run to the forest, only to find trees uprooted and limbs broken. The tribe had its work cut out for them. Within six months, the village was rebuilt, and the ship was about halfway reconstructed. By a conservative estimate, it would be completed by fall. This would coincide with the birth of the baby. During this time, Kurilia and Green Fawn became like mother and daughter. This was developing into an intricate relationship. The elder woman was teaching her new daughter the Phoenician alphabet as she had learned it and the rudiments of writing, as she had learned them. The mother figure's reasoning was that her family might have a connection to history, and she wanted word of them to be passed on. The script was etched onto pieces of bark with a sharp instrument. The scroll-like documents were to be kept in a large tubular case, not unlike the pouch, in which arrows were held. This was to be stored in a safe, dry place and taken with them if and/or when they moved. Thus, a tribal scribe was developing. Kurilia and

Adolphus left after Green Fawn gave birth.

The time to begin recording history was an opportune one. Two events would initiate the "quiver that held history" being filled for a few years. The first was the birth of Panther Slayer's children. For Green Fawn gave birth to twins, a boy and a girl. The next event was an unusual war that was prosectured with a skill that Panther Slayer learned in his long period of isolation in the mountains. The birthing began innocently. Green Fawn was bathing in the river where Panther Slayer had exercised his voyeurism that led to their meeting. Being a creature of habit, he repeated his peeking. His wife heard rustling in the shoreline grasses and laughed and said, "Your eyes are never satisfied. Do you enjoy looking at my huge belly filled with your child?" the answer that came was, "No one here but us bulrushes." With a smile on her face, Green Fawn bent over to pick up a rock out of the water and throw it. She felt her water break and shouted "Get the midwife." The fierce hunter of yore banged his foot on a rock and had to hop to the midwife's house. Unfortunately, she had to run behind him with all her birthing equipment, while he hopped. Green Fawn saw the tail end of this steeplechase and laughed uproariously despite the pain of labor. After thirteen hours of pain and Panther Slayer's foot throbbing and hopping, she delivered a 23-inch long and eight-pound boy, named Long Branch, and a pretty, perky, dark-eyed girl 16 inches long and 7 ½ pounds. She was named Fawn Eyes. The next recordable event was not quite so pleasant. The area around the body of water (Later to be called Puget Sound) was fertile. Those tribes that stayed in the mountains were forced to become hunters and predators. Panther Slayer knew this; when he heard they were massing to attack, he launched one of his own. The wizened fighter communicated with the fauna with whom he had hunted and against whom he had fought for shelter. The result was that prides of lions and wolf packs attacked from the rear, and bears threw down tree limbs and huge boulders from the same directions, while a rim of burning woods and brush faced the predators in front of them. Behind the burning ring lay the warriors of the Sound with flaming and poisoned arrows ready. Though the mountain tribes sang of Panther Slayer for many years, the documents recorded and hidden in the quiver preserved his prowess in battle and in siring twins for history.

Long Branch grew to be a tall man with a gentle nature, but if any-one hurt his family, he could turn the ferocity his father did on the panther, onto them. He was, on several occasions, put into precarious situations because of this. For his sister used those flashing, doe-like eyes to her advantage. Every male in the tribe was attracted to her, and for the years of her youth; at least, the spring season seemed to be like the mating time of stags or rams. Those that were spurned brought back their rage. Panther Slayer was beginning to show his years. He had provided hearth and home. Now he wanted to be alone with his wife and his campfire. Thus, the protective arm fell to Long Branch. He had to deal with medicine men's sons, chief's sons, males of other tribes, who were interested, and brothers, who became adversaries over Fawn Eyes. In desperation, he implored his sister, "Find someone to share your life with. I spend so much time protecting your honor, that I can't live whatever life the Gods have planned for me."

Fawn Eyes' acceptance of a suitor coincided with her acceptance of her mother's role of scribe and historian. On a blustery autumn day, she found herself feeling restless for no explicable reason. She went for a walk into the forest that sloped up to the mountains from where her father had come so long ago. She had wandered a goodly distance from the village when she heard the cry of a man in pain, or maybe it was an animal. She drew closer and saw and heard the wails of a man in pain. He was caught in a bear trap. On his head and arm, he wore a small leather case attached to leather thongs wound about his forehead and left arm. She freed his leg from the trap, used sturdy branches to splint the limb, and tore strips from her clothing to tie the branches. She left him sitting under a tree and brought back a stretcher with two bearers, one of which was her brother.

In his recovery, the stranger revealed an attraction for Fawn Eyes. Long Branch began to strategize about how to defend his sister's and family's honor. However, the stranger had a strange tale to unfold. This tale turned to have a link to the tribe that made the stranger Fawn Eyes' last man. His name was Elk Horn. He was not tall and wiry, as Long Branch was, but he was barrel chested, with broad shoulders and powerful arms and legs. He replied to their unsaid questions that he came from far away from an ocean shore where the mountains were smaller and more rounded than the ones he been recently seeing. Once a trader came to his people in a long canoe with many oars. He was olive in color and had a pointed beard and dark, shifty eyes. He wore the accoutrements that Fawn Eyes had seen Elk Horn wearing. The trader told Elk Horn that he came from a land that had the sea on one side and mountains and desert on the other. He said that his people came from another land. Invaders came and disbursed this population over many lands. One of these lands was called Phoenicia. This was the land from which the trader came. His people believed in only one God. The leather cases contained small pieces of parchment with the laws of their God inscribed on them. The case was a reminder to any of these people that their God would always be with them and that they were responsible for keeping His laws. The trader stayed with the tribe for many years. He took a wife, and that wife was Elk Horn's mother. A neighboring tribe invade and decimated Elk Horn's family in the ensuing war. Elk Horn fled and took his father's leather cases with him to remember his trader-father. Green Fawn was holding the cases and opened one. She saw the same characters as the parchment in the quiver contained. She was even able to read a few of the faded words.

Green Fawn found a large piece of bark and entered this recitation of events. She seemed to know, as women generally seem to know, when another has found her Mr. Right. Therefore, she began to teach Fawn Eyes how to read and write the Phoenician alphabet, as her mother-in-law had taught her. She then showed her where the quiver was hidden. A new scribe had made her debut into history.

A long boat was sited making for the harbor. It was Adolphus and Kurilia. They hadn't been back for around ten years. Gifts were exchanged. Kurilia brought back colored glass and beautiful stones from the orient. She also brought news of mysterious people. The people, who were slaves in a land called Egypt, were known as Hebrews were liberated from bondage by one of their people, who grew up as an Egyptian. He came to know the one God, Yahweh, whom they could only address as Elohim. These Hebrews went to a land promised to them by their God. The newly liberated slaves formed two states and divided the land among twelve tribes. They prospered and subdued many of the outlying tribes. A time came when one of these states became corrupt. A mysterious enemy attacked and disbursed the tribes to many lands. Green Fawn and her new scribes entered the new information into the quiver and related the news they had added, including Elk Horn's addition.

Long Branch was impressed with Elk Horn, and he knew that this man had lived with enough pain so that he would not inflict it on others unnecessarily. Although there was little physical resemblance between Panther Slayer and Elk Horn, there was a personality similarity. Both were extremely close to their families and valued their connections to them deeply. There would have to be a certainty that an outside person intended harm before the anger was unleashed, and when it was established, the explosion that came forth was extinguishable only by death or an equally devastating retaliation. With Fawn Eyes in good hands, Long Branch was planning to leave his home and determine his own destiny. This was both finalized and hastened by the sadness that comes to all families. Adolphus and Kurilia died together in their sleep. They had loved and enjoyed each other intensely and had shared what they had gleaned from life with each other. They had died connected to each other and had begun a search that might connect all human beings. They were set adrift in their longboat for their soul to find what their God or Gods wanted them to see.

Long Branch did not make up his mind to leave immediately. The feeling had been building in him gradually. Elk Horn's appearance and his grandparent's deaths only served as a concretization device that brought his dreams into the realm of consciousness. Secretly he had been building a longboat of his own. His head began to become filled with ideas of new worlds to conquer new lands to explore. When he could tolerate the emptiness of being unfulfilled as a dreamer no more he spoke his piece to his loved ones, got in his boat, and left for parts unknown. He went north and spent several months in the islands between Alaska and Canada, taking note of the seals and sea lions. The climate was too cold for his liking. Hence, he turned to the south. Surprisingly, he did feel some pangs of loneliness. As he passed the sound, but he knew his time there was finished. The time had come for

Fawn Eyes and the others to build their own lives without him. He had memories of love and good times, but nothing to indicate that he had lived on this earth.

Long Branch was to travel much and to see much to the extent that he would reach a point in his life that he craved to settle down. The initiation came when he emerged from a respite to replenish his supply of fish off a south pacific coral reef. He was surrounded by two sampans with weaponry poised to fire. The two ships were pirates. They could call no land their own because they ravaged and pillaged from all. His boat and his catch were confiscated; the choices left to him were to join them or die. The pirates were always on the run. They were pursued by Egyptians, Phoenician, Greeks, Roman, Chinese, Japanese, Indian, and any other nation that dared to cast its ships upon the sea. To say the least, the crew was motley. It was composed of brigands from Japan, china, India, Ceylon, the city-states of Hellas, the Peninsula of Korea. Only the language of money, blood lust, and rapine united them. Their empire of plunder ranged from the Pacific to the Mediterranean. For ten years, Long Branch sailed with them, hating what he had become.

In the end, the pirates fell to a Roman galley in the Mediterranean. The battle was short lived. Both sampans were shot out of the water. The survivors were fished out of the water and taken back to Rome to be crucified for having the effrontery to attack a Roman vessel. Long Branch tried to evade capture by hiding under a piece of wood broken off one of the sampans. He had almost drifted out of sight, but a sharp-eyed legionnaire saw his foot. He too was fished out of the water and bound in chains. Long Branch met a man who was to be beheaded in Rome. His name was Saul. He had been a tentmaker in Tarsus. Long Branch learned from him that the Hebrews had made their way back to their Promised Land. They had withstood many invaders, but the might of the Roman military machine was too much for them. Despite this, many revolts against Rome occurred. A leader emerged who did not offer to do battle with Rome, but spoke to masses of the poor and lame. He spoke of love for one another and preparing to live with their God in a world after life. The Romans were conditioned by fear for their own power to fear this man and executed him. The sect of Jews

(The Hebrews became known as the Jews) who followed this man were called Christians because they believed he was the Son of God Christ, sent to earth to redeem Man for his sins. This Saul of Tarsus was a follower of this Son of God.

Life was rigid to Long Branch, as it was for many people, but he had never encountered such strictness about adherence to what they called laws, many of which were designed to cover their inhumanity to each other. Contact with the Romans was Long Branch's first contact with White people. He and the other pirates were kept in a dungeon until their execution date. From other prisoners he learned about the Roman Circus where men killed each other for the sport of others. He also learned of one of these fighters who led a slave revolt against Rome. He had stood off this mighty empire for four years and was defeated and crucified, as Long Branch was about to be. However, an opportunity was about to be organized for this thin fighter.

One of the pirate crew was taller, even than Long Branch. He was also tremendously obese. However, he became increasingly anxious about his fate. He could not eat, and the weight dribbled off him rapidly. A lot of people were awaiting execution, a time lapse did occur. The prisoner's clothes actually became several sizes too large for him, large enough for another person to fit in them with him. They had sharpened their eating utensils into weapons. The night before the heavy pirate's execution date, Long Branch got into his clothes with him as per custom only his hands were bound with ropes. While still in the corridor Long Branch cut the ropes loose from his comrade. He was able to slip out of the clothing in the dark and slit the hindmost guard's throat while his partner did the same to the forward guard. Then they put on the uniforms and walked into the open air and ran. Long Branch made it to the docks, where he hid in a boat bound for China via the Mollucca Straits. The ship docked at an island to the south of China. There the wiry warrior stole a sampan similar to the one in which had been kidnapped. He made his way to the island where his replenishment of foodstuffs was so rudely interrupted ten years before.

# Chapter 3

Now that Long Branch was at the start of his new life again, he felt a need to return to his family and help update their chronicle. He made his way to the settlement at the inlet to land. He saw several changes. His mother, Green Fawn had died, and Panther Slayer could not stand the world alone. He had gone back to the mountains. No one had heard anything about him. Fawn Eyes and Elk horn had raised three strapping sons: Little Elk, Rain Catcher, and He-Who-Makes Smiles. The time was one of famine. Long Branch felt he had to do right by his family before he left them. He went into the forest on the periphery of the mountain to find game. Winter was turning into spring; the snows were melting. He saw the frozen body of a man thawing out and recognized it as the remains of his father. He brought the corpse back to the village for burial. Since Long Branch had not been in this area for ten years some of the geography had lapsed from his memory. He took a wrong turn and ended up on the border of a large plain. He startled a huge furry horned creature that resembled a bull of some sorts. The animal charged him and gored him viciously. He leapt upon its back and plunged a spear between its shoulder blades. The buffalo, as he later learned the new denizen was called, collapsed dead. Now he had to figure out a way to get his father's body and this creature back home to the village. He used two tree limbs and placed two other limbs across them, tying them together in a rectangle. He then put cross logs in between had tied them in place. He attached the rectangle to his horse and placed his father's body and the buffalo carcass on this makeshift sleigh with the hope that it would be strong enough to bear the weight and that the snow was not sufficiently melted to make sliding difficult. He found his bearings and started back to the village.

After three days of this uncertainty, Long Branch arrived at the village. He was greeted with much anticipation because his long absence was beginning to make people believe that he had befallen harm. They were about to organize a search. Long Branch presented the buffalo and Panther Slayer's remains rather impatiently. He had struggled for his accolades alone and was not used to this attention. His inner timer was telling him the time to move on was approaching. A clean, but empty cave at the foot of the mountains was chosen to intern his father. All joined hands at the beir and extolled Panther Slayer's virtues as a protector of his family and his prowess as warrior. Long horn called aside Fawn Eyes afterward and recited the experiences that were pertinent to her chronicle so that she could record it in her Phoenician script.

The time to depart had arrived. Long Branch had missed his family and tribe over his long absence, but he had difficulty managing the hovering and clinging that came with his return. He stayed long enough to build up a supply of game, fish, and herbs. Then he turned his Sampan to the Pacific, bid those connected to his past adieu, and sailed into whatever fate had in store for him. Before he got too far out to sea, he noticed a small boat moving toward him. It appeared to be following him. He put in for the nearest shore, and the small craft followed him. He anchored the sampan into bay, left the boat, and hid behind a pillar of rocks so that he could surprise whoever his pursuer was. To his surprise, he saw a pretty young maiden emerge from the canoe. He circled around behind her and kicked her ankle out from under her. He caught her as she fell so that she would not get hurt by the fall. "Who are you, and why are you following me?" he demanded.

The young lady introduced herself as Falling Leaf. She had come from a nomadic tribe and had been traded for eighteen horses, three tents, and a crop of hybrid corn to an older man that had the appearance and aroma of a moose. Her tribe had settled near a river that led to the sea. Since she could not endure her fate, she had decided to rearrange it by stealing a canoe and going out to sea to discover what lay ahead for her. She began to follow Long Branch because he had a larger ship than hers. She reasoned that this sort of acquisition carried with it some ability to navigate and some skill in building a life for one's self. Therefore, she followed him. Their discourse was interrupted by a loud noise followed by the smell of something burning. Their ships were afire. A band of pirates had seen the docked boats and torched them to prevent escape from what they believed to be their stronghold. Long Branch and Falling Leaf hid behind the rocks and took a path that led into the foliage of a jungle. They saw an army of the indigenous population of the island, stealthily on the march to dispel the invading pirates. Hiding behind the trees the pair watched as the army marched to the edge of the forest and took positions. Suddenly Long Beach seized Falling Leaf's hand and ran for the shore. Before anyone knew what had transpired, the two had boarded the pirate craft hauled the anchor up, and turned about, heading out to sea. The pirates and natives were left to do battle with each other.

Even for a sailor as experienced as Long Branch going into uncharted waters carried risks. After being becalmed for several days, a ferocious storm hit them. The mast was hit by lightning and split. Long Branch and Falling Leaf had to abandon ship and make for shore in the canoe. Once on shore, they pitched the tent which was part of the goods the older gentleman had given for Falling Leaf's hand. A mountain range lay in front of them. Falling Leaf had made a fire and had cooked a fish that had been caught. They sat in an exhausted silence. Suddenly Falling Leaf broke the silence. "Long Branch, I have seen you to be a powerful man and a cunning warrior, who knows when to run and when to fight. You have not lusted after me the way other men would have. Do you not have need of a woman?"

Long Branch thought of the years during which he had been Fawn Eyes' protector and the years he was at sea. He reflected on the animal lust he saw every time he and his compadres pillaged a port and about how he had once approached a young female captive and could not follow through because of the terror in her eyes. He also remembered how Roman guards used women among their Christian prisoners. The image was distasteful and made him feel that such acts were bestial. He was about to try to explain his feelings to her when she silenced him with a finger to his lips. She drew towards him and pulled his head down to her. Then she kissed him very gently and with a growing seekingness. They fell to the earth beneath them and seemed to merge with it. She drew him to her breast, and he marveled at its beauty murmuring that the God of life must have drunk nectar from this vessel. They undressed each other slowly, and Long Branch entered her body, feeling as if he were entering a temple.

In the aftermath of their lovemaking, Long Branch held Falling leaf in the crook of his arm and told her how he had viewed sex, adding that he had no idea it could be so beautiful. Before this, he felt his role in life was to be alone. To protect but not to ever need protection, to answer the need to covet by taking, yet not to enjoy what was taken or the act of taking. However, when taking and giving are interwoven, a feeling of communion with the world and nature ensues, a communication with God. Without this communication sense, we are but empty shells. Falling Leaf took his hand, and they knew that, no matter what befell them, this communication would be the bottom line of their life.

The truth Long Branch and Falling Leaf learned that night was a truth that Dark Waters was later to teach Gideon Retta, or that Ruthena was to teach Grady Almederson or that Kiona taught Mark. It is a universal truth, uttered by the Christ preceding his death march to Calvary: "Love one another as I have loved you." By loving one another is meant reach beyond the barriers between you and another person. To reach God, we must reach ourselves and find its complement in another to see what we have reached. Perhaps the communion between Man and God is not by building visible shrines, such as ethnic or religious cleansing, or impressive churches, or even unified sincere religious denominations. Maybe we reach the pattern we seek by finding our way back to the Garden of Eden by creating our own garden where we are.

# Chapter 4

Long Branch and Falling Leaf reached for each other to find their direction in life. Unfortunately, it lay over a steep and treacherous mountain range in the change from winter to spring. Ice was melting causing rivers to flood their banks, boulders to fall from their frozen moorings and landslide, and to create a sloppy, sluggish terrain. They took whatever food and water they could carry weapons with which to hunt, and minimal fishing gear. They left the dower tent because they planned to use whatever nature provided for shelter. They had encountered a wounded wolf cub with its paw in a trap. Falling Leaf freed the creature while Long Branch looked for wood for a splint and herbs for a poultice. They nourished the animal back to health and shared their food and the warmth of their fire with it. The trap had to indicate the presence of man or men. Long Branch scouted the area and found no evidence of human habitation. After a week, they decided the wolf was sufficiently recovered to find his way back to his pack. Surprisingly, there was a twinge of regret because they had begun to develop nurturing feelings for the cub. They found an abandoned cave and started to unpack. They hurried through this process because they wanted to nurture each other, when three burly, armed men appeared. They demanded food. The couple didn't mind sharing their food, but one of the strangers got a glint in his eye and grabbed for Falling Leaf. Long Branch went for his spear only to have a knife held at his throat before he reached it. The wiry warrior looked about him for a stone or other weapon; his eye rested upon a sharp stalagmite growing up from the cave floor. Suddenly, a snarling sound was heard followed by a blurring leap of an animal at the knife bearer. Thus freed, Long Branch instantly leapt, broke off the sharp end of the stalagmite, and slashed at the throat of Falling Leaf's assailant. Blood spurted out of the man's carotid artery. The blur was the wolf returning to save those who had saved him. Two of the would be plunderers lay in the repose of the death their attack had earned them; the third had fled.

The next day the trio prepared to leave their lair to ascend the heights and to find their destiny. They cremated the bodies of the intruders. They gave their new companion the name. Paw. He only entered their shelter when the elements outside created a need, but he was always ahead of or behind them, in case they needed his protection. On one stormy night, he found out about human habits. Long Branch and Falling Leaf were in the middle of lovemaking when Paw burst in on them to get out of the rain. He heard Falling Leaf letting out a God awful moan and Long Branch looking like he was attacking her while they attached to each other in some bizarre manner. Not understanding this because of never having seen it, Paw began to snarl and poised for attack. Long Branch quickly broke away and poured water on his pet, which he probably needed to do to himself. Falling Leaf did not try too hard to stifle the laugh welling up inside of her, no one provided a lecture on the indelicacy of Coitus Interruptus, but Paw eventually got the message that sometimes mommy and daddy wanted to be alone. Long Branch wouldn't talk to Paw for two days; Falling Leaf either stifled giggles or laughed uproariously for the same time period. The three of them had transformed from three individuals seeking the convenience of companionship to a household looking for a house.

During the day climbing was sloppy, but at night everything froze again so that climbing at night was dangerously icy. As the time in the peaks increased, the couple started to become acquainted with mountain folk. Some had difficulty tolerating the collection of bizarre rules and limits to self expression that accumulated as aggregates of people assemble in an area. Some had encountered betrayals and become bitter at any influx of others into the perimeters of their decreed space. Others wanted to find roots as they did. Thus, their search for their singular destiny soon became a caravan looking for their collective answers. One person saw a way to profit out of the fact that some are weak and some are strong. He approached Long Branch about paying him a fee so that his goods and woman would not be harmed. Long

Branch put his arm around him in comradely fashion and stepped to the edge of the precipice they had just climbed. "I have considered your ingeniously devised offer and decided if anything happens to my woman or my goods, I will throw you off of this cliff or any other one we stand upon. Does that make sense to you?" He then shook the exhorter's head in agreement and said, "I'm glad we agree on terms." There was no more talk of protection money. The real significance of this so-called offer was that a need was pointed out for establishment of a minimum code of group ethics. Hence a loose federation was formed that was amenable to a firmer change once a final place of settlement. Was reached. The members of this pilgrimage were free to drift off if a preferred area was decided upon by anyone. Though not permanent, each was beginning to develop a sense of community.

For two years, they slogged their way through hot, muggy weather, through the difficult breathing of elevated altitudes. Some of them left, some died, some new people joined them. Some of these had measurable and sensible goals; some were exploiters and rooters. Finally, the descent began. Red Earth began to be prevalent, which hinted at some kind of mineral being in the soil. Flat precipices were there with green foliage on their plateaus.

These people had had enough of hiding under ledges to hold back the elements. They wanted permanent homes and wanted to stop chasing animals that had as much chance to kill them for food as the humans did them. Plenty of vegetation was available. Someone learned to make containers for the berries and herbs they picked; others learned to carve firepots out of the earth to cook meat. One inventive soul learned to divert the mountain streams down to where the new migrants were. Building permanent homes required the development new implements. As did growing corn and other staples. The areas where game was available were further away and required longer-range bows and arrows. In fact, a new type of spear was developed with a throwing shaft. It was known as an atalatl. The houses started out being long rows of flat houses made of adobe with posts. In time, they became more complex and subterranean. They eventually became 2-3 stories high and were connected by tunnels. The culture established became what is known as a basket culture because baskets were made from the vegetation to hold berries and other vegetables and herbs. Later this gave way to pottery making after the settlers found they would have to store water. These people became aware of other peoples through wars and marauding, but also through needing what others had and having what others needed. Thus did trade develop between the peoples of the area. The development of trade generated the development of a marketable line of products: a jewelry industry grew up in the area; cotton was bartered along with salt, seashells, and turquoise. However, knowing of other cultures via war was also motivation for erecting defenses to keep out invaders. Perhaps for this reason, the kiva was devised. This structure was a 2-3-story dwelling that had towers above to see who was coming and tunnels connecting to other kivas to allow escape. The need to depend on each other and the need to stand on your own against a common enemy dramatically came to pass when a decision to settle down was made.

All these changes did not originate with Long Branch and Falling Leaf. They came in time, as following generations had to adapt to what their needs became, or perish. These original settlers had overcome and survived the danger and frustration of battling the elements to create a solid home for themselves in a way that was different from a bear or a wolf. The belief emerged that God or the Gods through a spiritual love connected Man and land. Maintaining this connection allowed a condition in which Man and Land nurtured each other. If the connections were kept in balance, both Man and land would prosper. This belief system was handed down from Long Branch and Falling Leaf from one generation to the next by a class of men known as the priesthood. They were the medicine men and shamans. They led isolated lives and survived by the support of the rest of the tribe. They were the link between God and Man.

These changes and organization of their society took place over generations and centuries. The foundations were laid by this group of initial arrivals because they had the experience of breaking away from where they came and starting with nothing but which the immediate surround provided. They knew that something with more knowledge and strength guided the adaptation of what had been put in nature for their use. The God or Gods had provided the land for them to adapt to their needs by discovering the connection between God, Man, and Land. Once the connect was discovered, and a harmony established, the class of shamans protected this balance. The tribe supported them because they held the key to avoiding the restoration of their former state of chaos. The position of guardian of the link between chaos and organization was a seat of power that the priest class came to enjoy, as they did in other tribes and gatherings of men.

In time, a culture was established; the Pueblo culture, named after the intricate style of home carved from the cliffs. No written language was in evidence, nor was the wheel or metal in use. Yet, a people grew out of chaos, a people that survived its enemies and did business with its friends. Into the aura of these changes walked Long Branch and Falling Leaf. They were fruitful and multiplied. Communication with Elk Horn and Fawn Eyes was not maintained due to the time and differences that grew between them. As progeny followed from his union with Falling Leaf, Long Branch thought less and less and less of his sister and her family, but a connection was to briefly restore remembrance.

One winter day a lone figure clad in animal skins came out of the mountains. He did not run, walk, or hobble out as others had. To the contrary, he rowed in a hollowed out log with oars that had attached to springs that propelled him forward each stroke. He was very original and brought, at least a smile, if not an outright guffaw, from anyone he met. He brought homemade playthings for children; trinkets made from seashells and bits of turquoise for the ladies, and arrows and tomahawks for the menfolk. He was a trader that used gifts to create an interest in his wares. He was tired and asked to sit by their fire and eat with them. He had brought a few mountain hares, various birds, and fish to contribute to a communal meal if they would have him. One brave noticed a peculiar case that resembled a quiver. He hinted that he might like to barter for it. The trader indicated that this was of special value to him, and he would not trade it. Hearing this, Long Branch began to have the feeling that he should know this man. Seated at the fire, where his features were visible Long Branch noticed huskiness about the shoulders and flashing, dark eyes. There was something about how this man made people smile and chuckle at him or at themselves. All of it hit the Tall, wiry warrior; without realizing, he was doing it. Long Branch stood up and shouted, "He-who-makes-smiles.' The stranger looked up astonished and asked how this man knew his name. Long Branch told him who he was. Uncle and nephew embraced and they wept for the happy occasion of their reunion.

He-Who-Makes-Smiles related a turbulent set of events. A nomadic tribe had invaded from out of the mountains. Elk Horn and his two brothers were in the forest hunting when the attack had hit. They were taken prisoner by the rear wing of the invaders. Their fate was to hang on the rack of torture. They were tied to vertical poles separated by connecting bars joining them at the ends, left to die in the sun. That night He-Who-Makes-Smiles cut them free and told them to hide in the woods until the time to retake their village. This battle took place, but without He-Who-Makes-Smiles, because he saw one of the enemy seize his mother. He skewed the would be rapist on an atalatl, lifted him in the air and threw the victim and its connecting spear into the fire. His mother had taught him the Phoenician script so that he could become the scribe if anything happened to her. He knew that unless the war was immediately begun, he could expect an immediate, brutal execution. Hence, he kissed his mother goodbye, took the quiver, and became the merry trader for two years. Unjustifiably, the agricultural and fishing oriented Puget Sound dwellers did not maintain a defense to withstand aggressive, desperate nomads. They were decimated. He-Who-Makes-Smiles was the only one of Long Branch's family that was left. The wept together.

Because he knew Phoenician and kept the scrolls, He-Who-Makes-Smiles became the tribe historian and shaman. He changed his name to Spirit Maker. It was by his design that the kivas had towers added and that tunnels connected them. He also maintained an arms cache inside these tunnels. He had experienced the horror and devastation of not being prepared for invasion. The businessperson part of him diverted the tribal barter he had established for himself to that of his tribe. Trade was built up with Arapaho, Kiowa, Apache Ute, and Paiute. This was He-Who-Makes-Smiles' last worldly act. Hence forward, he was the ascetic, Spirit Maker. Many men and women came to him in their spiritual trouble. He spoke at the elders' meetings as the voice of the

God, and he prayed over plantings and harvests. In time, he took a woman and she bore him sons and daughters that were related to Long Branch's sons and daughters. But they were connected to the sect of shaman. Policy for the tribes was determined by the shaman's communications with the Deities. They did not have to hunt or do battle as others did. The foundation was built for a theocracy to flourish that established a base in the belief of symbiosis between Soil, Man, and God.

In addition to their religious and policy, making powers the shamans of this tribe carried the function of historians because of possession of the quiver of scrolls and because of knowledge of Phoenician. Spirit Maker also kept one other memento of his past: The phylacteries his father brought from the east coast. He would never understand their religious significance, but he wound them around his head and left forearm, as he had seen his father do every morning and night in the way Elk Horn had seen the Phoenician do. Spirit Maker did not know the connections that later day people would make about the origin of this population upon finding these religious objects in his burial mound.

The years went by, wars and famines occurred, as well as years of abundance. The community survived the centuries and all at once became abandoned. However, some stalwart people stayed and mingled with other nomadic tribes that settled in the area. A time occurred when mingling occurred with a race of Caucasians. The Christians, whom Long Branch saw persecuted in Rome, came to dominate Europe. In obtaining power and wealth, these people seemed to forget their origins. Wars occurred over land and wealth, which provided security and ease of life where fear of terror had existed. The doctrine of religious and cultural superiority became an excuse to pillage and take from others by deceit. As men mingled with others, the greed and deception was introduced them. Now the contagion was to assume an interracial character. For the vastness of the American continent was to be opened up to the White man.

The original Pueblo inhabitants migrated to the New Mexico area, and the stalwarts that remained formed a new generation. The doctrine of "Love the Land, and it will love you back" continued to prevail. As the years turned to centuries, generations of strong men and weak men continued to populate the kiva and the outlanders beyond. Some of the nomadic tribes began to envy the security of a village closed off from these, who had no one but themselves for which to fend. As a result, raids took place. Since most folks don not like anyone grabbing that for which they have struggled, defenses and fortifications arose to meet villagers and ravagers.

These barricades against invasion were built by the planning of the shaman warrior alliance that had been passed on from the days of Long Brach and Spirit Maker. Attention was paid to the increasing numbers of Frenchmen and Spaniards who were taking an interest in the area. They were allying themselves with some of the nomadic, envious tribes in their cause of taking the place of this culture so that they could have permanent homes cut into the rock. What their White allies wanted was to expropriate resources and to seek souls of converts to achieve their own salvation.

A great grandson of Spirit Maker came to his majority during this time. He became aware that another White nation was interested in this "New World," as it was called; England was this nation. A sailor had deserted from one of the ships, seeking a Northwest Passage; Macon Gibblet was his name. He had stolen several barrels of whale oil and traded them for a home made sleigh and beasts to haul himself and his cargo to the west from the St. Lawrence valley. When winter was over, he converted his sled to a wagon by attaching tree trunks that had fallen to its bottom. After almost eight months of traveling, Macon arrived to the mountains north of the Pueblo village. He had two barrels of whale oil left. There he met Great Puma, the great grandson. He traded these last two barrels for help in building himself a house. He also had to promise to help undermine any Spanish or French attempts at a permanent settlement or forced religious conversion. This barter served as a way of starting the latter. The Pueblos got word that a renegade part off the Apaches were to meet with a Spanish delegation to plan a raid. Anticipating this move, Great Puma, the night of the meeting, led a band of men who pushed Giblet's flaming wagon into their meeting. All were destroyed.

The Spaniards skulked around and tried to gain whatever information they could. This uneasy suspicious truce lasted for several decades. Great Puma had joined his ancestors, but a son followed him, Lion Claw. He was a shaman and, very much believed in the symbiosis of the land and man. When he saw Apache renegades, in collusion with White men trying to poison the Mountain River that had been diverted to the village, he knew that the time had arrived to teach another lesson. Outside of the Apache encampment were the lair of a pride of lions and the den of a pack of wolves. He and several Pueblos killed several deer and placed them at the perimeter of the encampment and in the center. They then used fire to scare the animals to the Apache settlement. The animals attacked the village, and smelling man, attacked the tents while the stunned Apaches struggled to rouse themselves from sleep and roust their offenders. At the same time, the poison, taken from the mountain stream, was mixed into the soil of the Spanish mission's vegetable garden. This action was enough to calm the aggressive acts for a while, but Lion Claw was not a favorite with the Apaches or the Spaniards. The uneasy peace was maintained. Macon Giblet had maintained no interest in the area and left, while the Apaches and Spaniards stewed into heir greedy juices and plotted.

Up until this time, the numbers of Whites in the area was small, but a legend of golden cities became distorted by servants of the Spaniards, the Apaches had endured a winter of scarcity of game, and a son was born to Lion Claw. His name was Watering Ground. Watering Ground was a peaceful man, providing his family was not hurt. He also grew to be a compassionate man, but a man that would put down the ploughshare and pick up the sword readily.

The legend spoke of seven cities of gold built by bishops on an island called Antilla. The Spaniards, in their greed, sought these cities, according to a story related by survivors of a shipwreck off the coast of Florida after the natives of the area repulsed a landing attempt. The survivors of the repulsion and shipwreck were servants, who feared for their lives due to punishment for failure of their mission; as a result, they made up a story about a settlement to the North of Mexico where there were golden towers. An expedition was sent to the Zuni to take these cherished cities for Spain. A man named Francisco Coronado headed the expedition. Despite many wanton acts of cruelty and blatant racism, no wealth was found, and Coronado returned to Mexico as a failure. Now a son of one of servants, who told the lie in the first place, was organizing a second expedition further north, to the land of the red earth, to the Green plateau. The Apaches were massing for another raid because of their winter of paucity of game and because they remembered, how Lion claw had turned the beasts of the forest on them.

Lion Claw had done his warfare. He was now an elder on the tribe council. A sixth sense seemed to tell him that the Apaches were up to something. He sent his son out with a small band of warriors to investigate. In the meantime, the Apache had learned from the days of Great Puma. They traded with their allies, the Spanish to get a wagon and whale oil. A burning wagon with hay in it was propelled into the Pueblo village in the middle of the night. Much damage was done by the mass attack following this fire. Among those killed was Lion Claw. When Watering ground returned from his expedition and found his father dead, he vowed revenge and to leave this area, for it was cursed by the Spaniards poisoning the water; he believed this act had destroyed the symbiosis between Man and Land.

Watering Ground called council meetings of the elders and of the elders of neighboring tribes. He spoke of the bands of renegade Apaches as a menace to them all and felt something had to be done to curtail the periodic raids. Discussions about the alarming number of White people coming to the area. The rebirth of the idiotic Spanish legend was named as the cause. Perhaps alliance with their rivals could provide an answer. Englishmen, such as Sir Francis Drake and John Hawkins were engaged in their own war with Spain and attacked Mexican ports. The French were in the area. They might be persuaded to trade for weapons. A cannon was obtained by this trading. Two days after the gun was received firebrands torched the Apache camp. A raining of cannon shot on the site for another two days followed the firing. This village was devastated.

On the way, back to the Pueblo village Watering Ground and his band discovered another victim of Apache aggression. For they had raided other tribes than the Pueblos.

A young lady was wandering around in a distraught manner. She swayed as she walked, as if she were in a daze. She passed out. A stretcher was made, and she was wrapped in blankets and placed on it. She had an ugly gash on her head. A cloth was wrapped around it. Watering Ground's mother tended the woman. Her name was Mountain Dove.

She was a kiowa, whose village had been attacked by the Apache on their return from the raid, in which Lion Claw had been killed. All of her people were wiped out. Her man had also been killed. Slender and appearing frail, she was encouraged to become part of their tribe. A new hybrid vegetable was grown from the bean and squash under Mountain dove's tutelage. People in the area enjoyed this vegetable, and it soon became sought after in inter tribal bartering. Even in embittered Watering Ground, a faith in the symbiosis was restored. In fact, an increasing attraction was developing between Mountain Dove and her rescuer. Within a year, a tribal wedding was held.

Watering Ground was a very caring and gentle husband. However, he was extremely shy and inexperienced in matters pertaining to womankind. One night by their fire, Mountain Dove changed this. She took Watering Ground's hand and placed it upon her breast asking him if he liked women the way other men did. He said that he did, but he was afraid of hurting her after her injury. He also told her that the sexual encounter might be painful to her. Smiling at his innocence, she reminded him that she had a man before the Apache raid. Her eyes grew sad at the mention of this. Touched by this, Watering Ground told her she would never be sad again and gently undressed her, as she did to him. They made love, at first with tenderness and then with a raging passion that grew within them. As time progressed, lovemaking became fun and sometimes very beautiful and poetic to them. Mountain Dove became pregnant and listening for and feeling for signs of the baby's growth became a part of their love. While Watering Ground was away at a hunt, mountain Dove went into labor. Very sadly, Watering Ground's prediction about his wife's frailty was accurate. Mountain Dove died in his arms upon his return giving birth to a beautiful baby girl.

Though the child was beautiful, Watering Ground could not bear to look at her and see his wife's beautiful brown eyes and the dark hair he had loved so much. A widow who had loved Watering Ground from afar came to him in his need. But she also said to him, "Go to your daughter; give her a name. You are all she has. I will help you raise her in the ways of a woman, and I will be here for you. She still needs to know her father." He named her Dark Waters because her eyes looked like the pools of a mountain spring. As she grew older, she became precious to him. He would let nothing hurt her. He interceded to teach her the discipline she needed and let her suffer the pain she needed to learn how to cope with life, but when malice was directed to her, it had to go through him. She became a strong, yet a sensitive girl. She mingled with other outside traders, even the Spanish, and French ones. Under her quiet exterior, she seemed to know that her way of life was about to be inalterably changed. She, as did all the others, fearfully awaited this change. It became more apparent as more white men began to appear in the village. To restore a sense of security, she began to look for signs of strength she could rely on to be able to muster her own when she needed it.

As a child, Dark Waters was thoughtful and gentle. She was also very observant. She knew her father loved her very much, but that there was an ache in him, sometimes for her mother, sometimes for a woman in general. During both times, he would visit the widow. She could not discuss the need to establish a new order to replace the one that was crumbling in front of her eyes. She too believed in the symbiosis of the Land and Man. However, working the land that was supposed to yield in abundance for whoever worked it, it didn't make sense to fight back when someone else was confiscating the yield. She saw her father go to a quiver, make some marks on large sheets of bark, then put it away. He explained that he was the tribe historian and how this position was created. He added that right now the tribe was going through tribulations and that talking about this matter was dangerous in front of white strangers. They would use any knowledge they obtained to justify their unjust seizure of this land. He did agree to tell her what he had learned of tribal history and how to read and write the mysterious language. Nightly discussions of the ancient wanderings began because Watering Ground feared that their culture would die at the hands of the Spaniards.

Living with this fear had a destructive effect to her ego. She loved the relationship between God, Man, and the world in which she had lived. She could see no natural sense of being that these greedy, insensitive, brutish invaders brought with them. A philosophy that had allowed so many diverse populations to survive for centuries had to have enough merit to survive this onslaught of barbarism, which was in the offing. The philosophy would start with, "Reaffirm the beliefs that you stood for and that stood for you. Provide belief in the ways of God, and these beliefs will drive you to purge your lives of what goes against these ways. The faith and the driving energy has to come from man to God via the nature of the world God has wrought." Some say this is done by way of Jesus; some say it is by a way of the Messiah. Some say we reach God through the teachings of Mohammed Confucius, or Buddha. The name is different, but the path is the same. Follow the route of being in tune with the world, as it shows you it is made. It will lead you to its maker, The God in all of us. The ones that force their ways on us are not following natural paths. If the answer to the world is do it my way because I have reached God and you have not, then our obligation is to say: Get thee from my soul and find your way for yourself. Where was the one, who would arise and remove the impediment? Whoever he/she was would have to find a clean way to God. In the end, it would be a man and a woman combining the warrior instincts of the ancient kushite fighter with the love of generations of those who strove only for a home as a base to build their way back to the God that brought them to the world of nature.

This deliverer came in the form of a tall, wiry, ebon colored man that carried the emptiness of a home that was destroyed, perhaps of the one sidedness that clung to it, and a homeland that could not acknowledge his people as individuals. Intuitively Dark Waters recognized this when she saw Gideon Retta. He seemed to recognize it also, but he also seemed to fear it. Time would correct this myopic vision. At this point in his life, he was so blinded by having to fight the world alone with only hate for oppressors to drive him, he could not see that cherishing yourself and building a path to God with another through negotiating the world God provided to find the route to Him was the direction that had to be taken. The fight was definitely part of reaching the goal, but the other part of the journey was to have something for which to fight. As the depression at being overwhelmed by a racist usurper took the fight out of Dark Waters, the draining need to keep fighting a sea of enemies dept Gideon Retta from building a life that would give him something for which to fight only to protect.

All culture seeks its place in the sun and invests hopes in a deliverer. The great paradox becomes that the deliverer is the people themselves by altering the culture to give it both the fight and the reason to fight. This takes culture from the realm of a fixed structure that dictates to a flexible tool that it's creator, Man, adapts to His needs. This concept of change is a difficult process; it involves clarity of purpose and a willingness to challenge the vested interests that resist the change. It can mean establishing a new cultural imperative and being willing to fight for it.

Dark Waters did not know from whence she came, but the beginning was established when her father started to tell her about the Assyrians and the trek through Siberia to Tatary and Mongolia, followed by wandering up the coast of Russia and the crossing of the Bering Strait to Alaska. He told her about fighting the mountains to settle in Puget Sound. She learned about Kurilia's and Adolphus' thirst to learn of her origin, and why it developed. She learned why Kamnchatka had changed his name to Panther Slayer, and what led Long Branch to the land of the red earth. She learned why Brynna wanted no name until Tamakar gave her an identity. She felt that these horrible intruders robbed her of this. She blocked out her history and could not summon it forth when Gideon asked her about it. Many years later when she felt a sense of being somebody, did the knowledge her father gave her return to her conscious mind. The search for a sense of having an anchor, a home base from which to emerge had been passed on through the centuries, was it connected to all people needing a deliverer? Is this search for a deliverer a phase that all people go through to find that each is his own Messiah?

The courage to build one's own culture is an outgrowth of fighting for the culture into which one is born and finding it does not provide what one needs. As Dark Waters and Gideon found that fighting for the sense of peoplehood of their ancestors did not contribute to their sense of peoplehood, they developed a sense of accepting what they wanted to take out of the world they knew to reach the view of God they had.

In other words, when Gideon realized that his battle to liberate the Jews from Gentile oppression would end with fearing retaliation from the oppressor more than valuing the freedom achieved, or when Gideon's helping the Pueblos remove the Spanish intruder was not sufficient to buy acceptance into their brotherhood perhaps a new culture had to appear to include their needs. This new culture had to be created by them. A new culture diversified by Gideon's fighting prowess and Dark Water's love for him to be the reason, for which to fight. To find this combination, one had to see through the blind spots. Seeking a home for centuries had been passed down to Dark Waters; fighting for recognition in a home that had been there for centuries was Gideon's heritage. Finding there complimentarity was the first step in creating their own path to God. Valuing the home, she never quite had made Dark Waters reach out to turn a violent man away from violence and subsequent self-destruction. For this reason, the two of them and their son were able to negotiate the creation of a trading post, where all people who did right to themselves and others were welcome. It was a melting pot, as was pre Isabellan Spain.

# Chapter 5

Dark Waters evolved out of several generations of women that wanted to be rescued as other women had. However, men also sought deliverance. Freedom from the need to have an external deliverer can only motivate the self-reliance needed to change how the doctrines that inhibit us. Brynna had no brother to protect her. She chose to have no name until she found a new life for herself. Kurilia had to take her own stance to stop the whale that terrorized her village; she also had to create a matrix of love that held her and Kamchatka so that she could have a reason to kill the whale after her people showed her they chose the security of a phony orthodoxy over the common sense solution that God spoke to her people through her . Green Fawn and Fawn Eyes lived within the safety and security of the Puget Sound culture only to have it torn from them. Long Branch and Falling Leaf had no one to whom they could turn but each other. Hence, they looked for their home to build where the path they trod led to the reunion with Spirit Maker who completed a path to God.

Dark Waters could see the disciplined soldier in Gideon Retta, and she saw the depth of his hatred for the Spaniards. She also saw that he was attracted to her; what she didn't understand was why he withheld from her. She could see him smolder with rage every time a Spanish conquistador fawned over her or became aggressive with her. She knew he did not want to deter himself from his task of creating a fighting force, but there was something else that she could not fathom. She did not understand why he did not, at least, act friendly to her despite curtailing his attraction to her. It was not until they started walking back to the village that she learned of the cold militarism that had been his life, or that his hurt had been so deep that he had estranged himself from the world of nature, which was the basis of all that she knew about life. It took time before the rage in him subsided, and his love became gentle. She saw the change more once Fiery Water was born. The gentleness grew as he taught his son the ways of natural law and learned them himself.

During this time, Dark Waters began to learn the Phoenician and the history of the wanderings of her people. However, several events started to take place that inhibited these efforts. One was the depression and death of Watering Ground. His longing for his wife had been lifelong. The widow that had been his link to the past died of her old age and loneliness; the rejection of his comrades was the final straw that drove him over the edge. She also sensed the uncomfortable uncertainty in her husband as he saw more and more inidcations of a return of the conquistadores. This also produced a state of unease within her. She remembered the cajoling and aggressive importuning of the soldiers. As Gideon reassured himself that a return to soldierly discipline would not mean a restoration to the cold, hating thing that he was, Dark Waters reassured herself that she would not have to relive the terror that she had once known. They both took a measure of contentment with the fact that they had each other. They could lie abed and hold or touch each other or mumble about their mutual concerns together. Just knowing the other was there was of comfort and mutual love. They thought that this could never be taken from them.

A certain sadness seemed to overtake Dark Waters. Her son was a man and growing away from her. She knew that he had a set of his own stubborn views that clashed with her" and his father". But she also knew that women played a role in his life. She also was concerned that beyond her and Gideon, no one would be able to tell the story of her people. Dark Waters resolved to have a talk with her son.

Fiery Water had kept a secret from his mother. One day, he happened to notice his grandfather taking his mother to a hidden place and showing her something in what looked like a quiver. After they left, he went back there and found several sheets of bark with strange marks on them. The next day he asked his grandfather about the quiver and its contents. Once Watering Ground had explained the purpose, his grandson wanted to learn how to use the mysterious language and to learn from whence he came. Watering Ground began to teach him because he could see that Dark Waters was otherwise preoccupied. He did not want the knowledge to die with him. Together with what his father had taught him about Falasha customs and Amharic history, Fiery Water was able to piece together a clear picture of his ancestry. Another secret he kept was Ismalia.

Ismalia was born to a Pueblo woman and a conquistador. In a state of drunkenness, he had raped her. When the Pope visited, he was afraid of the consequences of exposure. He enticed an aged midwife and her into a cave and bade them to stay there and have the baby. He said he would stop in every day and bring food or meet whatever needs they had. He did no such thing, and he left them to starve.

The midwife taught the young mother to be how to hunt for her own food and how to make weapons, as well how to survive on the vegetation around her.

A few months after Ismalia was born, a leopard became interested in the cave. The two ladies hid the baby under a rock and prepared to face the leopard. The leopard sprang at the young mother because she was closest and mortally mauled her. While this was happening, the midwife with surprisingly movement sprang on the cat's back and jammed a broken stalactite between its shoulder blades killing the beast instantly. Now she and Ismalia had to face the world alone.

Several months had gone by when the errant father had returned to hide from the retaliatory war, born of Spanish arrogance. He sought respite from his warrior like desertion. He was surprised to find the cave empty, as the midwife and baby were hidden behind him on a flat ledge. While he slept, the elderly woman crept down the ledge and watched to be sure he was asleep. Then remembering the rape, in the aftermath of which she had to nurture his victim through pregnancy and childbirth and remembering the murder of her man and her subsequent detachment at conquistadorian hands, she picked up his sword and plunged it into his diaphragm in mid inhale. She had the eternal satisfaction of leaving a man breathless. Single handedly she dragged the body out of the cave, and gave the wolves a treat.

By the time she was ten, Ismalia could hunt, kill, cook, and make clothing and weapons and utensils out of any animal that crossed her path. This included a man. When she was sixteen, the midwife's heart burst while they were climbing to an aerie to obtain eagle's eggs. Is-malia wept for three days. After this, she built a pyre and chanted over the burning remains, committing her to the home of the Great Spirits.

Shortly after this, while on a hunt for otters, she encountered three people, one was a tall, wiry Black man with a beard and numerous scars on his body; one was a beautiful, coppery skinned Pueblo wom-an; the third was a black-haired youth about her age, slender of build with dark eyes and hair. He was tallish, but not as tall or tough looking as the Black man. He seemed to her as beautiful as the God of wind. They seemed to be very happy with each other as they bathed in the river. An otter came up to them, and the young man played in a frolic-some way with it. Her preference for dinner changed to berries. About a month later, she saw him again in the mountains at another river res-cuing a White man from a capsized raft. She began to go to the river more often so that she might encounter him alone.

Ismalia did have a lone encounter with this dark-haired young man, but it was not of her choosing; nor was it brought about by plea-sant circumstances. She was swimming at the site where she had wit-nessed the rescue, when a large snake swam toward her. In a panic, she swam away and banged her head on a rock protruding out of the water. She started to get dizzy but managed to force her way to shore. As soon as she reached land, she swooned and fainted.

Fiery Water went down to the river after an exploring excursion in the mountains. He ran toward it when he saw what appeared to be a body on the shore. He saw a pretty, young woman lying unconscious. Upon getting closer, he saw a big gash on her forehead. He used his shirt as a blanket to prevent shock and put a dressing of herbs and leaves on the wound. Then he went back to the trading post to get help. In a few days she was restored in health and went back to her cave. Unbeknownst to his family he went back with her, at first, by sneaking behind her. She heard a twig snapping behind her, hid behind a log, and invited him to join her after she had caught him. He started to visit her at home, but he neglected to let his family know.

Over a period of two years, they saw each other more frequently, and their tryst became intensely passionate. For all his stealth in battle, Gideon was extremely naïve about the manifestations of a young boy growing to manhood. This was probably because he didn't have his own boyhood for too long. However, his mother did not share this naïveté. She caught him red-handed, if that's what the extremity could be called. Dark Waters had followed them to the cave numerous times and had gone inside when they weren't there. Hence, she knew where to hide. They were in the middle of lovemaking when they heard a voice shout, "You better bring me a man child." The mother/son talk was about to begin.

Dark Waters expressed her concern about gaps developing between Fiery Water and his parents and about a nation being unknown in history because no one could pass it on. Her son reminded her that the life he had to build was to be his. He indicated that he loved his parents for sharing their perception of the world with him. He also indicated that his world was not quite the same as theirs.

To survive in a changing world, he had to adapt what he had learned from them to what he had to experience and process alone. He further added that he did not want to see Ismalia through their eyes, but through his own. The final expression of this need to grown as an individual was his need to sort out whether or not he and Ismalia were compatible on what they were able to sort out about themselves, just as Dark Waters and Gideon did. On the issue of no one being able to pass on the Pueblo history, Fiery Water told her about his following her and his grandfather and about Watering Ground teaching him the Phoenician. He told her about the entries he had made. Ismalia joined in and made her feelings known about the need to build a new existence because the Spaniards introduction into their society meant a new structure had to develop to learn to deal with the interlopers or a means of realistic communication had to evolve. At this juncture, mother, son, and potential daughter-in-law joined hands and thanked God for each other and Gideon. Suddenly, a noise was heard, and Gideon strode in and said, "I can thank for myself." He had followed his wife and had heard the entire production. They all laughed, as if it might be the last enjoyment they had of each other for a while.

This multi centuried Diaspora may well be one of the ways that Israel was rebuilt. For are not the lessons of the Bible that since Man could not be satisfied with having the Garden of Eden bestowed upon him, as a gift, then he must work to rebuild his own Eden. The fruit from the Tree of knowledge was sought because Man wanted to be the center of the universe, but the centricity comes from wanting for your own kind because this brings the control of the universe closer to you. This is an error in thought. Bringing resources close to you makes you more aware that you don't have them.

On the other hand, loving the land that provides for you speaks of finding a path to God through building to mutuality. What took the beauty of the Garden from Adam and Eve was their becoming divided from each other through the plotting of the snake. If Man wants Eden restored, He will have to develop a unity out of duality so that the efforts we make are directed to driving the treachery of ego motivation at another's expense out of our soul. In other words, we have to drive the snake in us back to Hell from whence it came. This is what Israel had to do, and the world is Israel. The lost tribes are making their Diaspora back home. Some went directly back to their "Promised Land." Some took the centuries to wander from the Assyrian in their lives through the Siberia's of life and the hordes of Tatary to the Alaskan snows to the cold and terror of the Rockies to Mesa Verde. Others of us have yet to discover how to fight our way back to the paradise Lucifer lost.

The progenitors of Dark Waters found that communion with God came through communion with nature. To establish a communion she needed a Gideon in her life, a protector of the cherished light she bore, and he needed to know that if you save one life, you blend should and can reach for God by pulling both your souls to Him.

This is the lesson that Dark Waters and Gideon carried to each other. The land is good because it meets our needs and allows us to build a home and hearth from which we can feel safe and secure in our own identity and reach out to another to reach out to Him who provided the base of security out of His love for us. The lesson is so simple, yet so complex. As basic as this lesson is, straying from it is easy. All we have to do is forget that we are not perfect beings and direct our energies as if the world centers around us and not God.

For this reason imperial, Spain did not look to its defeat as a message from the One on High that empire and converted souls in huge numbers or magnificent edifices were not the way to God. Instead, they distorted their own erring to allow them to believe they were struggling to enrich mankind by forcing their right thinking on pagans. By doing this, the basic relationship of humans to the land, their home was altered so that man learned to reach for a false concept of God through a graven image. This may be another way of saying that as mankind sought the security to reach for God, it also erected its own barrier to reaching Him. A jealousy for control of the resources of the world that had its roots in the Garden impelled humans to divide from each other due to greed for resources, contrive rules for acceptance into a structure called culture, and to allow these rules to assume a value beyond that of their designer.

Stepping from Gideon and Dark Waters from the past to Mark and Kiona in the present, the struggle is part of Kiona's battle to free her people from a misnomer and a false abomination and part of Mark's battle to find himself and to free himself from the world of obligation to his parents. By reaching for each other, despite parental warnings and being cast out to survive on their own, they challenged a cultural directive and lived to allow their forebears to choose to incorporate them rather than lose them. To accomplish this deed, they not only needed each other, as Gideon and Dark Water did, but they needed this referent to the past to let them know they had chosen the path to life, in the midst of the pressure to conform to norms that were deemed beyond mankind because mankind let them become so. The poison of false dogma didn't start with Jack and Bert or with Spain's demand for empire. It started in The Garden of Eden and has been the source of a wrestling match within our own soul ever since.

To fully grasp the meaning of the union of Dark Waters and Gideon, Mark and Kiona had to become familiar with the final destination that Dark Waters' ancestors reached via the underlying spirit that drove them to get there. This knowledge was forthcoming from an unexpected source.

# Chapter 6

A letter with good and bad tidings came for Mark and Kiona; it was from Helga Seredensky. After their experience in Yucatan, she and Henry were planning to marry. He had taken a boat to Port Au Prince to bring his parents to Miami for the wedding, and Helga took a plane to Kiev to bring her family back. A cocaine distributor was on the run from federal officials, who had exposed the drug ring, of which he was the center. He was on board the same ship as Henry. One of his victims had lost a daughter due to an overdose. An inner voice told him to plant a bomb on the ship. He did this and set it off to fire when the boat was two miles out to sea. The passengers, including Henry, were blown to bits. The police apprehended the crazed father, but Helga had spent the last two years grieving and trying to mend her broken heart. Mark and Kiona both wept for the kind Ukrainian girl, who in many ways was responsible for their finding each other. Helga had immersed herself in several archeological projects.

By a strange coincidence, she had contact with a Mr. Grady Almederson, who was in search of projects in which he could engage groups of retired or near retiring businessmen. She recognized the name and inquired if he were related to Kiona. Her father updated Helga about Mark and Kiona and about their work in the Pueblo village in Colorado. She, in turn, told him about a project, in which she had worked in Saskatchewan. Helga and a team of archeologists had found a scroll or several scrolls of bark inside what appeared to be a quiver for arrows. It was written in Phoenician, an ancient Mediterranean language. The scrolls told of the migrations of people that traced their origin to ancient Israel and settled in the Mesa Verde area, in Colorado. The last portion described a relationship between a Pueblo woman and a Falasha Jew, of Ethiopia. She accepted Mr. Almederson's offer of a consultancy and agreed to write Kiona to see whether the documents were useful. Once this was established, she sent Mark and Kiona an English translation of the scripts. For the first time in two years, she was able to smile again as she added this note: "Mark, are you still looking where you're not supposed to look and finding snakes' heads to snap off." When they read these lines, Mark and Kiona laughed for the happy days of their courtship and hugged each other for the love they shared. Mark touched Kiona's growing belly tenderly and said with mock sadness, "Now the red nightie will be just a memory to me." He left the room singing "Echoes of My Mind," by Glenn Campbell.

Rachel was very excited about meeting Helga because, she was encountering bouts of depression due to her taking a sabbatical from medical school and now was having doubts about returning as she unearthed more and more of Gideon's and Dark Waters' story. She suggested that Helga and some of their other friends have a get together. Mark and Kiona were all excited about this and began to plan it. Arne, Michelle and Reed, Amy and Ron were all sent invitations with the mysterious note that Mark and Kiona had a surprise for everyone.

However, Mark and Kiona were not the only ones with surprises. Reed and Michelle were pregnant, as were Amy and Ron. Ron had passed his Med Boards and he was about to begin a residency in space medicine at Cape Hatteras, N.C. The biggest surprise, was Arne. He had a large gash down the side of his face and a small child with him. The child was a small Black little boy, of about five years old. Arne related that he was working with U.N.R.R.A. in the relief camps in Zaire, when he heard a cry. He turned toward the sound and saw a starving woman about to throw the child into the river. She said she was about to die and did not want the Tutus to get her baby and kill him. Arne was so moved by this that he reassured the woman that he would raise the baby until she could. She smiled and passed out of existence from this earthly realm. Arne adopted the youngster and took him wherever was stationed making sure he was safe from harm. His name was Yusseff. Touching his face, Rachel asked him where he got the scar. With a bizarre grin, he peeled it off and said, "At a novelty store in the Bronx." The loudest laughter came from Yusseff. Rachel, at first angered and felt she had been played for a fool, then she picked up a lampshade, put it over his head, and sang, "You Are the Light of My Life." Someone had finally beaten Arne at his own game. Yusseff was allowed to partake of ice cream and cake to celebrate the new babies' birthdays and played twister with the grownups. He beat Ron at checkers and portrayed a charade of "The Littlest Mermaid" before he had to go to bed. With him upstairs, the girls had a wet "T Shirt" contest to see who had the biggest belly. After this, Rachel served Arne his scar mixed in with salami in a sandwich. They both laughed about the turnabout to the joke. They stepped out on the steps for some fresh air. Somehow Arne sensed that Rachel wanted to talk.

Rachel sat beside Arne on the steps and told him how she knew that her country had a great need for physicians, and she had thought she wanted to help fulfill that need. However, she saw how big the story of Gideon Retta and Dark Waters was. She saw it as striking back at racism; the racism that had crippled her people in their own land or that had caused a small boy like Yusseff to be an orphan at five. She was not sure that medicine was the right way for her to serve.

For a brief moment, Arne felt some anger. "Let's be clear about one thing. Yussef is not an orphan. He's my son. No label of problem child or not belonging because he's not really my kid if he does bad is going to mess him up, as it has so many others." Rachel looked as if she was about to cry, and Arne saw this. He took her shoulder and apologized, adding that he gets defensive and carried away by any reference to Yusseff being other than a normal kid with normal chances to be loved. He acknowledged that she didn't mean to be offensive, but she didn't realize that Arne was paranoid about this issue. He hugged her as he said, "I understand your need to directly confront racism and how evil it is, but you have to keep in mind that if people are not kept alive no one will be around to fight racism or anything else. Maybe if there would have been another Doctor around, Yusseff might be playing in the veldt with his mother and father watching over him to grow, marry, and bring other kids into this world."

Rachel said that she did not realize how level headed and serious minded Arne was. She guessed his humor was a cover for a lot of deep feeling. She further indicated that she deeply respected what she had just heard. Her belief in medicine was restored. She said she didn't have that much left to translate and would return to Case Western Reserve University in the fall. She had already told them this. She thanked Arne for his help and reached out to shake his hand. His hand lingered in hers, and he said, "I want to see more of you, may I call you?" She agreed to this and turned to go back to the party, when he turned her to him and very gently kissed her. She was surprised to feel herself responding shyly at first, then more seemingly. Without further adieu, she took his hand, and they rejoined the party.

The next day they all devoured the contents of the quiver, the history of the pilgrimage across Asia through Siberia, Tatary, Mongolia, Alaska to Mesa Verde had created an impression of evolving strength of character that raised questions about who was really civilized, and who was barbaric. Was there a message for people of all ages and eras here? Just where do we create a haven for a heaven, a hell, or ourselves for ourselves? What is Man reaching for when he reaches for God? These were questions that Man asks universally, but must find answers for self. Dark Waters and Gideon found their own set of answers. If their strivings are an example, then our strings must originate with creating our base line to our maker by individual acts that will guide us where we want to go or will divert us from our own destruction.

The time had come for the reunion to end and for all the friends to return to the lives that they lived day by day. The blossoming relationship between Rachel and Arne had made itself evident by their lingering alone, apart from the others, or by their whispered conversations. Helga was at loose ends, having finished her project in Saskatchewan. She offered to work with Rachel until her sabbatical was over or until Rachel and Arne had made a decision about the direction of their relationship. Besides, a new wrinkle was thrown into Mark and Kiona's project. What happened that the quiverful of knowledge about how people had migrated across Asia to Colorado showed up in Saskatchewan? To allow for her own mobility, Helga had accepted a consultancy with Grady and Jack's firm. She was encouraged by Mark and Kiona to make an appointment to talk to Aaron Donleavy about coming aboard their project.

Out on the steps, Rachel and Arne were saying their good-byes.

Before Arne could voice his concerns about whether or not Yusseff could adapt to Rachel, the youngster stepped between them, hugged Rachel, and said, "My dad and I need a woman around." Left alone for a few minutes, they took hands, looked deep into each other's eyes, and kissed softly.

These friends were charting directions: Directions that would have to adapt to the tragedies and successes that would happen to them. This was most obvious in the cases of Helga and Rachel, but the uncertainty of adaptation stood before them all, as it stands before each of us; as it stood before Gideon Retta and his family.

# Chapter 7

Ismalia and Dark Waters became very close friends. They shared female confidences, helped each other with doing chores, planned excursions to the desert or mountains; they even hunted game or fished together. On one such expedition, the sight they beheld astounded them. At the fork of a mountain stream, they saw a ship, which bore an insignia on it they could not read. They heard the sound of footsteps approaching and hid. The footsteps they heard were Gideon's. A swarthy White man got out of the vessel and greeted Dark Waters' husband warmly. "My friend, it has been many years. How are you/" The language was like Spanish, but not quite the same. Neither of the women understood it. Gideon asked how he got the ship over the mountains. The stranger, who responded to a name that sounded like Ericio, told him he dismantled it and carried the parts by mule train. When he got to the designated point, he and his crew reconstructed the boat. Its name was "Enigma of the East." Its cannons and harpoon guns were intact, as they were when the two of them had fought the pirates in the Mediterranean Sea. Of course, the ladies did not understand a word of the conversation, and Gideon had to explain everything to Dark Waters that night. He also explained that the ship was there to shoot at the fort that the Spaniards would build. His spies had overheard Spanish missionaries discussing the sites of forts, which were to be erected. The next day Dark Waters told Ismalia what she had learned. The ship was camouflaged with shrubs and mountain brush. Another one was being built and camouflaged in a similar manner. Gideon hoped that they would have enough time before the invasion to prepare. The war was in the making.

In turn, Ismalia told Fiery Water, who told her he already knew and that he and Joaquim had been training fighters secretly for months and that Ericio DePelunis had landed six months ago, made the trip over the mountains in another four months, and had been working on the reconstruction of his vessel for two months. The work was done at night and the intent was to create a disciplined cadre of fighters to counter the blind fanaticism of the colonists that drove them to so un-feelingly tramp on anything different from them and to bombard their fortifications before they launched attacks with superior weapons, fi-nanced by the ill gotten gains of the inquisition.

Another strategy that was devised was to make use of economic ri-valries to harass Spain from outside Mesa Verde. British privateer's shot at coastal ports of New Spain to reduce the wealth used to prose-cute the war by directing its use to repairing the damage they did. Tri-bes that had allied themselves with French hunters, trappers, and ex-plorers were cultivated through trade and defensive agreements. The anti colonial forces also wooed the mountain men, who resented the tribute exacted by the Spaniards.

Spain, on the other hand, was developing its on counter measures. Ignatius Loyola had founded the Society of Jesus. He was an ex-soldier and added militancy and zeal to the missionaries and the con-quistadors who went forth for Spain and Christianity Larger cannons with longer trajectories were developed. More spies were recruited from tribes hostile to the Pueblos. Crooked Hand and other Pueblos, who had left Gideon and Dark Waters to starve were encouraged to engage in trade with people that did business with Gideon's Dark Wa-tering Ground, to monitor the movements of the Rettas. Uniforms were designed that were less cumbersome and that blended in with the desert or mountain terrain. Men, such as the former Inquisitor of Por-tugal, John De Melo, were sent to firmly implant propaganda to build large numbers of Converts and a loyal following for Spain and Portug-al. John De Melo was chosen specifically because of the emotional role he had played in Gideon's past.

An uneasy truce pervaded the Mesa Verde area, as in the ancient days of the Apaches raids. War seemed to be at the back of everyone's mind, but no one wanted to talk about it. Some hoped the thought would go away. Gideon had heard that John De Melo was in the area. He considered searching him out and repaying the debt, he owed him then he remembered Dark Waters and Fiery Waters and the love he had learned from them both. He talked to them about the feelings he had inside of him for this creature of the jails. Consequently, he could cool part of this longstanding anger. After all, he put the angry, hating part of him away for good once he had met Dark Waters. He really wanted to be finished with hate, but there were some things that were beyond forgiveness. When he spoke to his wife about it, she stroked his arm and tried to soothe the fire resurging in his eyes. He touched her cheek gently and said, "I have to recall the demon in me to fight a war, but once my war is over I will turn it back to peace and loving God in His natural world the way you taught me." She took his arm and kissed him. "I know you will," she said.

The southern Pueblo sent Gideon an emissary asking him to join them in their fight against their common enemy of old. The message he sent back was "I don't need fair weather friends," When Fiery Waters heard this, he reminded his father that to save a life is to save humanity. To this Gideon replied, "The blood of Abel arises in me." He had even sent spies out to locate where De Melo was staying. He was in an Apache camp in the Plains to the northeast of Mesa Verde, in what would become Montana or Idaho. Despite his struggle to contain his rage, he felt he had to remove this menace to humanity. He did not want to be identified and carefully developed a disguise. He learned to walk on his knees in order to reduce his height. He then had special shoes fitted to them. He died his beard and hair red with berries, as well as his face covered it with war paint. He also cut a gash in his face. He also changed the way he parted his hair and learned a walk that at least looked natural. He did not tell his wife or son about it, but kept this entirely to himself so that his family was not vulnerable. He had prepared a change of clothes and a horse in a cave outside the encampment. When he was ready, he explained to his family that he would be gone a couple days. He explained the gash on his face as being from a low hanging branch, as he rode by. He excused this murder in his own mind, as necessary for war.

He secured entrance to the camp in the guise of a trader. His legs were tied to his thighs so that the reduced height seemed real. Walking on his knees was painful. He kept his mind on his goal to forget the pain. De Melo was blessing a group of people. He waited at the northern periphery on his horse, in order to speed to the cave with dispatch. As the religious Icon approached him, a brief recognition of Gideon's dark eyes flashed before his mind's eye an instant before the dagger struck his throat. Before the supplicants realized what had happened, the horseman was well on his way. Upon reaching the cave, Gideon untied his calves tore off, burned his clothes, and washed the dye off him in an underground river. He then put on his change of clothes and rode his fresh mount back to Mesa Verde after using a branch to wipe away footprints. There might be tortures and burning at the stake, but John De Melo would not be doing them. Gideon muttered to himself, "May God rest his soul."

The Spaniards mourned the loss of their pious son and cast suspicions on Gideon Retta, but they could prove nothing. He never told his family a word about it. He had thoughts of Guintera and Nahum of Gondar. He wondered what had become of them, or how they would feel about what he had done. For the first time since he had fought at the side of Redai, he felt as if he had violated a holy sanction. He did not know whether God would bless or damn him; he had learned that killing was an abomination, but De Melo had killed in the name of God. Why was it a heinous act in the one instance and an act of salvation in the other?

An uneasy state existed throughout the areas. The tribes on both sides were on edge looking for someone to trigger off a provocation. The Spaniards had troops massed at the Rio Grande. When they or their allies came into the trading post, they seemed to have a chip on their shoulder, but the model of the day was business as usual. One other source of tension was the Pueblos watching for any abuse of women or children

He had thoughts of Guintera and Nahum of Gondar. He wondered what had become of them, or how they would feel about what he had done. For the first time since he had fought by the side of Redai, he felt as if he had violated a holy sanction. He did not know whether God would bless or damn him; he had learned that killing was an abomination, but De Melo had killed in the name of God. Why was it a heinous act in the one instance and an act of salvation in the other?

An uneasy state existed throughout the areas. The tribes on both sides were on edge looking for someone to trigger off a provocation. The Spaniards had troops massed at the Rio Grande. When they or their allies came into the trading post, they seemed to have a chip on their shoulder, but the model of the day was business as usual. One other source of tension was the Pueblos watching for any abuse of women or children. A conquistador was eyeing Dark Waters and Ismalia and had made a snide remark to Gideon about De Melo being murdered to prevent these ignorant "Noble Savages" from learning the True Word. Gideon got on one side and Fiery Water got on the other, picked him up, and threw him on the porch. In the next few minutes the commandant came in with soldiers bearing arms. Gideon's reply was that the trading post was a place of business, and rude behavior was not tolerated. His nonverbal communication indicated that if the commandant wanted a fight, Gideon was game for it. Fortunately, the incident passed. In a mountain stream, two camouflaged ship cannons were poised to fight. Warriors were ready to hit the trees to ambush any battalion sent against them. The air could be cut with a knife.

Dark Waters asked Gideon, when they were alone, if he knew anything about the murder. Without a blink, he said, "Woman, I don't hold anything back from you, but do not ask me about that." She said, "you did it; why surely, it will mean war!" "War is coming anyway. He not only tortured me beyond any forgiveness, but he is a dangerous firebrand and propagandist. He would be responsible for a lot of atrocities. I still shake whenever I remember those lashings, skin burning, screw turnings, while I was hanging on that wall. Believe me, the world is a lot better off with that bastard dead." Then he went outside to cool off. The night was crisp and the sky was filled with stars. Despite this, one look at the campfires filled him with pending terror.

Suddenly, he was not alone. He felt a hand on his thigh and looked to his wife as she took his hand and asked him to love her tonight. She was naked and pulled both of them down to the earth. She thrust herself against him and drew him to her. She moaned as he entered, as did he, and they rocked. Afterward she stroked his face and said, "Fight hard, my love, it is our home for which we fight. I will be in every battle with you."

243

The death of John De Melo became a rallying cry to the Spaniards. It was a rallying cry because they had been beaten back by those they had labeled as inferior, because rivals were challenging Spain's rule of the sea, because the Church was aware of the inhumanity with which native inhabitants were treated and couldn't call itself moral in the face of wanton exploitation. Besides, Spain was under economic strain. The Protestants in the Netherlands were revolting; Britain was raiding Spanish shipping and Spanish ports. The Jews were not standing back to be exterminated, but they were allying themselves with the Protestants. Of course, retaliation for the murder of a Christian's saint, such as De Melo, served as a cover for the conditions that led to the act. The rallying point was beginning to peak to a crescendo.

The fear of war that was permeating the area had also spread to the Pueblo dwellers to the south. They had already begun to make entreaties to Gideon and had been spurned due to their previous rejection. Of course, Dark Waters and Fiery Water were constantly after Gideon with "If you save one life, you save humanity." Gideon chuckled at this and thought what a humanity there would be if someone had saved De Melo's life. Personally, he was glad the scum bucket was dead. That thought frightened him; he did not want to return to being that type of person. Yet, he knew what war can do to those with high ideals. He was worried about his wife and son, in this regard. He remembered the bitterness he felt after Redai's defeat. A tear ran down his cheek, and he said, "Dear God, I know now that you are a God of love, and all the bitterness and hatred I felt was for naught. Dark Waters taught me that. Please spare her and my son the bitterness and the cold heart that became the sustenance of my life for so many years." Dark Waters saved the tear trickling down his cheek and moved to his side. She surprised him when she said in Amharic, "Why weepest thou, my man." Before he could respond, she told him she had met a friend of his. From behind a tree stepped Ericio De Pelunis. In mock anger, Gideon stated "Why have you taught my wife the language of the desert, "Ericio grimly replied, "Unless we are extremely organized, we will be running for the desert. We will be facing a power with a lot more might than the Pirates of the Barbary Coast."

Dark Waters interrupted this dialogue and asked why he had a tear in his eye. The old fighter sighed and said he had forgotten. She took his arm and told him he was a liar. Devastated, he sat on a rock, and the tears were back. "I was remembering how all I had in my life was fighting. With your help I could deprogram myself. I am afraid for you and Fiery Water. Who will help deprogram you from the hate and killing if I am killed? Ericio was right, our cause is right, but we are going up against a decadent power, but a power, none the less. When they were here throwing atrocities in our face, our rage and some organization was enough to throw them out, but they have not been here doing that. They have also modernized their defenses."

His wife encircled him with her arms and said, "whatever happens, Fiery and I are with you. God helped you program and deprogram yourself and will do the same for us. We have lived in unity with the Land and nature, for which God gave us the world. These people are not real and do not follow The Way of the Land. Even if they beat us in battle, they will destroy themselves. We will be together in defeat or victory because we have woven our spirits to nature and to each other. There will never be another man in my life that can equal what you are. I have never met anyone that lived through the Hell that you have and still can have the capacity to love. You are like my ancestors of old; the mountain blizzards, the pretentious love to gain and had never stopped you. You just plowed your way through it until you got to me. Well, now you have me, and I'll never let you go. If I perish, you must go on; if you perish before me, then I must go on. The result of wars we have already fought must go on. Otherwise, no one will know about how Man finds his way to God through Nature and about being natural to each other. Mankind will only know the world of the user, the exploiter, and we all will be expendable things to each other. This will be our destruction; that we found the true God and chose to worship the false ones."

The answer found by Dark Waters is the same one that drove Mark Engler to go to the earth to find out how he ticked. What made him tick was brought out by the complimentarity that Kiona brought to him. She had a need to right the great wrong, or at least, part of the wrong done to her people. In the righting of this wrong, she found the wrong that Man has contrived to turn a tool designed to make adaptation to the world easier, into a monster that defined and limited intellectual and emotional growth. By attaching ourselves to rigid definitions of our selves, we have built our own mental prisons. This connection to God through Nature has screamed to our deaf ears from Genesis to Nebuchadnezzar to the Spanish Inquisition to Hitler's Germany to the Cold War to now.

With this message in their hearts, spanning the generations, Dark Waters and Gideon Retta stood as a precedent for the Mark Englers and Kiona Almedersons so that they could see alternatives to locking themselves into the mental stagnation that was being imposed upon them. Cultural imperatives are tools to help Man survive the changing demands of the larger society, but once they outwear their use or need to adapt so that Man might grow, their precepts need to be questioned. Cultural norms are tools designed by human beings, not fixed principles above them. That is God's role. Thus, the magic charm that Dark Waters brought to Gideon Retta needs to be distilled through the cooker of time to emerge as the purifier of our spirit. It was done by her making her mark, as she understood it from The One on High. Through all the wanderings they did to finally find their homes, her ancestors always believed that if they took care of the land the land would show them the way to God.

In contrast to this pantheism of nature, the Mayan and Aztecs civilizations built massive shrines to their Gods and gave up human sacrifices. Elements of their cultures survive, but all that is left of them are relics, an empty shell of what once was. The Pueblo tribes never achieved an empirical greatness because they didn't look for it, but they are still part of the heritage of the West.

# Chapter 8

The referent to the past had a function to bind its generation to a survival and to provide a matrix from which future generations could build their own survival. The combined elements of this developmental springboard came from Gideon's inward drive to fight for what was his and from Dark Waters centuries old will to fight for the love she had wrested from the land. To discover and maintain the essence of this sustaining principal, Helga and Rachel did a lot of sharing. Helga taught Rachel Phoenician, and Rachel taught Helga Amharic. Once the information was distilled through each other it was discussed with Mark and Kiona and the rest of the archeology group.

From the group discussions came a heightened sense of the blend of spirituality involved in Darwinian principles. The sense was that the fittest for survival were those that anticipated the changing courses of nature and adapted to them to reach the view of God that lay along the path of their adaptation. They did not impose a sense about moral rightness or egotistical superiority to their belief; they just practiced it for themselves. At the fore front of this philosophy was Mattanni Bmgai, the archeologist from the Union of South Africa. She had long lived with the double standard of the Dutch Reformed Church that preached about Godliness and God's love for man and practiced the Apartheid that condoned dividing the population into an empowered and powerless, disenfranchised mass. She had been seeking a sincere road to God for most of her life that included all peoples without dictating what the belief of others should be. Her summation thought was that how we view God is the individual process by which we feel we reach Him, not what an organized religious body tells us is the truth about how to strive to match their reaching for God and holiness.

The whole doctrine, espoused by Dark Waters and Gideon, was attractive to the group because it played down emphasizing how correct my group is, but emphasized that the only bond that needed emphasis was in putting this project into the perspective of history. In a sense Mattanni was fighting a battle in her heart that we all fight: How do I contribute to making myself and my people free, yet respect the freedom of others. This is a lesson that America never learned. The British replaced Spain as queen of the seas. When its Puritan sons fled to their freedom; they gave neither Roger William's religious freedom nor Squanto or Pocahontas recognition as equals. Thus, in a land of freedom, lynching and disenfranchisement were tolerated in the South, Japanese Nisei were incarcerated for what they were racially, and a state could develop in which Jack Engler and Grady Almederson would keep from knowing one another until Mark and Kiona brought them together. We have preserved the right to be what you want in the sense of being left alone due to paying our own way, but we ostracize people for not fitting the norms we prescribe for them. We do not consider whether or not the failure to conform does harm or represents a healthy growth.

Into this distorted sense of freedom walked Mark and Kiona. After them would walk the baby they would bring into the world. They had their imaginings whether they'd have a boy or girl, but they wanted two gifts for their child. Good health and a sense of freedom and respect for the right to be different. Every night Mark stroked Kiona's belly and listened and felt for movement. Then he'd say, "That's what you get for having sex! You can't have sex." Kiona laughed at him and added, "See, Smarty, you did it to yourself." Then Mark would say, yeah, you're right. I thought I did it to you, but I did it to myself." She next threw a pillow at him. When they were ready for sleep. They hugged each other and woke up that way into the morning. Because they learned about Gideon's risk and Dark Waters' reading it by incorporating it into walking a path of faith, these two were building their security from the matrix of a precedent established through history. How did it endure stresses in its own time, and what made it adapt and endure through the years so that other Marks and Kiona's can learn to believe in each other beyond what the cultural norms dictate for ethnic, racial, religious, or any sectarian safety?

With the help of Helga and Rachel translating the material and Mark and Kiona digesting it then presenting for further distillation by Mattanni and the rest of the group, principles were being explored and developed that could unravel the riddle of life. To penetrate the core of the solution of the riddle might mean stopping the time honored practice of being a replica of our fathers and be our own men/women in search of the right way for us, as individuals, to find the way to "dwell in the house of the Lord forever." To dwell in this house, we need to be free to find our way there. As a well known song says "You got to walk that lonesome valley; you got to walk it by yourself." As Rachel began to communicate more with Arne and was brought more in touch with her goal of becoming a physician, she began to detach from the project and to rely on Helga's growing knowledge of Gideon Retta and Amharic. She was surprised at how she had not defended against identifying with this figure out of her past. At this point in time, she had to permit herself to pull back from the conception that elicited her return to the past so that she could learn to walk her own path in the present. The time had come in her life when she had to free herself from the protective bonds of Amy and Ron, Reed and Kiona, then walk her own path without forgetting them. She smiled about the student that had harassed her about a million years ago and had ended up blindfolded, wearing a garbage can in front of the police station. She believed that the connection of Dark Waters with Gideon was one of the straws that broke the camel's back and caused her to want to resume her old life back with her right partner to compliment her set of goals, and needs.

Helga, on the other hand, had stood and reached toward her path and had her signposts torn out from under her. With Henri's death, she felt like an aimless adolescent thrown on the ocean of life. She found Dark Waters a model of how to make an enduring love survive in a world of hate, but she had to learn to hate what threatened love before she could find it again for herself or anyone else. She needed to go back and walk in Gideon Retta's shoes before she could try on Dark Waters' moccasins and find a fit. She did not have to tread the trails of violence, but she had to be in touch with the part of her grief that was violent in order to find peace. She was not a violent person, as was Gideon Retta. Subsequently, she unconsciously began to look for victims of violent crimes, in order to help her deal with her own victimization. She began to campaign against use of drugs/alcohol use by teenagers and argue publicly for strict enforcement of gun control laws. Her activities put her in the public eye. The resultant effect was to attract attention of fanatic elements of the opposing view to attempt to silence her.

On a hot, summer evening she had left an anti gun rally to meet Mattanni and Jonos for a cooling can of beer. On the way there, she was waylaid by a gang with knives drawn and Billy clubs poised for action. Her purse was immediately snatched to prevent her from reaching for the mace she kept there. She felt the cigarette lighter in her shoe and saw a filled trash can nearby, and an idea from her translations of the quiver documents clicked in her head. She remembered how one of Dark Waters' ancestors stifled an Apache raid by attracting wild animals to the encampment and burning the perimeter to prevent escape. This led her to remember an earlier incident in which a burning wagon was pushed into the camp to prevent another raid. She kicked off her shoe, picked up her lighter threw the trashcan in the middle of the ring around her, and lit it. The fleeing gang dropped her purse, as the burning can rolled toward them. One fleeing figure ran by her, and she snatched him by the collar and slammed him against the nearest building. She got to her feet just as the policeman came through the alley. After Helga explained what had happened, the officer cuffed and collared the ruffian, who did not appear so formidable alone. His last words before entering the paddy wagon were, "Didn't know we had tackled such a bull dyke." The last feeling he had on the way into the wagon came with Helga's foot hitting his posterior. The police officer did not seem much older than her assailant did. His name was Julio Barsta. He was twenty-three years old and lived alone in an apartment. He had actually lived there with his parents. They had immigrated from Mexico three years ago. His parents were murdered two years ago. As part of his quest to find their murderer, he joined the police academy and scored extremely high scores in marksmanship and knowledge of karate. All he had been able to discover about the murder was that they had been attacked on the way to a friend's for a Saturday night of playing Parcheesi. He knew that a lot of anti Hispanic feeling was condensing in this particular neighborhood because at one factory, illegal immigrants were used to break a strike of assembly line workers. Helga noticed the roguish way he grinned and the attractive dark brown eyes that seemed to shoot flames when he spoke of his parents. Helga knew they'd see each other again.

Helga and Julio became close to each other, in that, they would be instrumental in breaking up this gang and that he would contribute to the project. The gang member they had apprehended turned out to be a family member of one of the employees, who had lost a job due to the scabbing of the illegal immigrants. Several irate adolescents had met and vowed to avenge the job displacement by terrorist acts against the influx of illegal aliens. The immigrants, in turn, began to arm themselves and give the gang measure for measure. Julio's parents were caught in the melee of the street warfare. The young man was interested in saving his own hide and gave up names, areas where weapons were cached, officers' addresses, etc. In breaking up the gang, Julio needed an excuse to bring the gang together. He and Helga were seeing more and more of each other, and he began to unburden his dilemma to her. She and he together framed a plan; Helga would continue to attend controversial meetings in the neighborhood, while Julio approached his superiors about recruiting a special crew of officers to be part of an easily aroused mob that would assemble outside the meeting place, then close in on the gang at the right time and make the arrests.

Helga just now realized that the plan she had helped devise came from the "Quiver Documents." The specific source was Kurilia's suggestion that the federation of fishing villages lure the whale to an island and assemble en masse to kill it. She marveled at how interconnected humanity is in the past and present. In the course of events another linkage was to unfold.

Mattanni and Jonos found themselves concerned for their friend and volunteered to be part of the crew. Julio's supervisor did not like this, but he gave way because he had never seen such zeal and inventiveness in one so recently out of the academy. The next occasion was being set up; a boycott of the N.R.A. meeting taking place in the same alley where Helga had been attacked. The crew was agitating, and gang members, lurking in the neighborhood, heard it. As Helga, Jonos, and Mattanni raised their placards of protest, they were met by an angry mass of teens, wielding baseball bats and brass knuckles. These were met by a group of older citizens wielding fire hoses and blowtorches. The entire gang was captured without firing a shot. Mattanni began to call Jonos Sergeant York, and he began to call her Irving. Julio was promoted to lieutenant and given his own gang unit in The Juvenile Squad.

The linkage that unfolded involved Julio and Helga, a resolution of the murder of Julio's parents, and an emergent connection between Helga, Mark, and Kiona. In questioning, it was found that this gang was involved in the murder, and it was in reprisal for an attack launched by the immigrants on a grocery that charged exorbitant prices to the Mexicans. In the attack, the store was burned, and the owner died of a heart attack. Surprisingly the killer stepped forward, saying he could live with his guilt no longer. He was the grocer's nephew, and the sight of these aliens right after the death of his uncle enraged him to the point of not knowing what he was doing. Other gang members told him what he had done. Julio picked him up by his neck and prepared to end both their ordeals, when a voice came from his throat; "When you save a life, you save humanity." Helga's mouth dropped open, and she said, "Where did you hear that?" Julio did not know from where the quotation came and swore he had never before heard it anywhere. The young man was remanded to the homicide unit. Now Julio was left with two gangs tearing up a neighborhood where he resided. A dim memory out of his past came back to him that offered a solution. He wanted to discuss this, among other things with Helga.

After the arrests were over, Helga lingered by Julio's side. She invited him to join Jonos, Mattanni, and her for a beer, since he was off duty and not in uniform, He agreed, and they went off to a nearby sandwich place. He was so excited that he blurted out a plan he had been hatching in his head. He wanted to meet regularly with both gangs and talk about common problems in the neighborhood. After the meetings, different members of the meeting or committees would look into developing solutions. It was their neighborhood; they should decide what was needed for it and present the needs to the city fathers, instead of waiting for them to develop an opportunistic conscience and hand down their ideas of reform to the masses. Mattanni and Jonos asked where he had gotten such a splendid idea; Julio told them that he had come from a part of Mexico, called Yucatan. A couple of years ago some Yankee students came to his town, near Chichen Itza to dig at some of the temples. They were a diverse and extremely fair-minded group. They were trying to find the truth about one of the nature legends. They involved them in looking for this truth, he thought because violence was about to erupt, due to the fact that outsiders were coming in and imposing their views of the villagers' history. Helga seemed impressed by this tale and asked Julio to take her home.

When they got to her apartment, Helga turned to Julio and said, "I was part of that group. In fact two of my friends from there are part of the project, in which I am now engaged. I think you know them; my memory was jogged by what you said. I recalled an ugly incident. My friends, who are an interracial couple, were in it. A villager became jealous and angry and charged the Black lady with a knife. The White man charged the villager with a log and knocked the knife from his hand. A thin teenager picked up that knife and gave it to one of the guides. That teenager had intensely brown, beautiful eyes. He was you." Julio just stood there with his lower jaw agape. She took his hand and said, "Can I offer you a cup of me before we retire."

During the next couple of weeks three things happened; Julio became re-acquainted with Kiona and Mark. The Spanish gang was rounded up, and both gangs were given the choice of standing for trial or being put on unofficial probation for a year and participating in the neighborhood meetings; last but not least, a new couple was welcomed into the group's dialogue.

The riddle of the source of the quotation made by Julio was never answered, as Kurilia's utterance of centuries ago was not as Kiona's finding the gemstone that symbolized that Mark and she would stay together was not.

Julio worked with Helga and Rachel. He did not have sufficient linguistic skill to engage in any translation, but he could work with some of the others in trying to locate or excavate artifacts that Helga or Rachel found not worthy in their work. For example, he went to the site of the sound settlement and to Saskatchewan, to look for the phylacteries that Fawn Eyes' husband brought with him from the East Coast. He did find them. He also looked for what may have been an Apache camp to locate any remains of the burning log wagon that was sent hurtling through the site. He found what might have been a steering rudder that guided the direction of the log wheels. He also located the cave where Fiery Water and Ismalia had their trysts and, later, lived. He was now engaged in trying to find out what the plate with the moniker Enigma on it meant. Returning to the site where the piece of wood was found. Another piece of wood of the same texture with the word, Este, was found on it. Julio was thinking what would connect the words enigma and east. Looking further, he found more pieces of wood with some metal attached, several feet further, a bad rusted piece of metal that looked like part of an anchor was in what appeared to have been a river bed. Suddenly, a thought struck him. All these bits and pieces pointed out that somehow a boat, a sea faring boat, was in this mountain river, what on earth would a sea faring ship be doing in a mountain river?

Dutifully, Julio informed Rachel and Helga about his findings of the day. Excitedly, Rachel told him that he had made a remarkable find. She told him the story about a Portuguese sailor that rescued Gideon and several other Falasha from reprisal from an Amharic, victorious army, filled with bloodlust after a fierce battle. His name was Ericio De Pelunis, and his ship was known as, Enigma of the East. He had somehow come by way of the Pacific, beached his ships, and took them over the mountains, and helped Gideon's war effort. The final artifact that Julio retrieved was several pages of bark drawings of what appeared to be diagrams of a tool that resembled huge buttocks. When he brought this back to the girls, he said with a chuckle, "Someone must have been reading "Playboy" back then. Look at these drawings! I sure would have liked to see the model that posed for this. You could probably park a truck on that bottom."

Laughing uproariously, the girls explained about Gideon's plan to discredit Father Benedetto. They also told him about the final outcome of the escapade. The workday was over, and Helga and Julio went to their group meeting. The topic was to be how to discourage the neighborhood drug peddler from making his wares attractive to the teenagers in the neighborhood and from inspiring fear in their parents with the threat of bringing outside gangsters into the community. Helga was focusing on how Lion Claw had avoided an Apache raid by putting animal meat in the center of the camp and sent wild animals in to destroy the camp. She worked on how to apply this scheme to the present. One youth came up with a plan. A phony buy would be set up; the buy would be rejected by a show of force of the two gangs. Then the same buyer would make a more attractive offer and tell him to bring in his muscle. At the point of consummation of the deal, a pack of trained dogs was to be let loose, and the air near the sellers sprayed with female dog hormone. A line of gang members, Lieutenant Barsta's men, and parents of the neighborhood teens were to be at the periphery of the area fire hoses attached to fire hydrants blasting at full pressure. These were to be flanked by three army tanks, on loan from a nearby army base, firing at them. A helicopter, also on loan from the army base, was to drop buckets of burning oil on their cars. Beyond the cars were to be a squad of D.E.A. agents awaiting the surrenders of the drugsters. The plan worked like clockwork, and the drug lords stayed out of Durango and Mesa Verde for quite a while.

# Chapter 9

Kiona was having difficulty straddling the fence between her obligations to the project and the demands pregnancy made upon her body. After the nausea of morning sickness, she found herself becoming tired easily; apologetically, she would have to leave digs early. To take up her fair share of the burden she began to do more of the research and reading between the lines of the translations. She began assisting Rachel and Helga more and was working more with Julio. Since her experience with Reed and Michelle, she made sure that there are no gaps left open for suspicions or jealousies. In conversations with Helga, she always made reference to him as your man, your lieutenant, etc. Both of them were included in the socializing with Mattanni and Jonos.

Halloween weekend carried memories for Rachel and Kiona: The Ma Trash Episode. They were laughing about it when Julio and a surprise visitor and a little surprise visitor walked into the room. Arne and Yusseff walked into the room and helped Rachel to her feet by each kissing either cheek and gently taking her hand. Arne handed her a gift-wrapped small box. He said, "This is to end the scars of misunderstanding that clouded our life together." He waited while she opened the box. Inside was the scar that he had at their last get-together. With mock severity, he then said, "Here is the healing balm to forever take away that ugly scar." Then he handed her another box. It held a sapphire ring of gold. Arne then said, "Will you be my old lady? I can't cook worth a damn." Without a word, Rachel kissed them both and said, "Yes, but who do you think you are to interrupt my reminiscing. We were talking about the Ma Trash Episode." She sat Yusseff on her lap, as if to resume conversation. Arne nudged her and asked where he would sit. Rachel smiled and said, "Later!"

Mark no sooner strode into the room from outside, when they all heard a gasp from Kiona. They all turned to her. "My water!" she yelled. They all scurried around her to get her things together and to support her. She told Mark to get the car ready. A caravan brought her to the hospital, and the astounded medical staff almost let them wheel the gurney into the maternity ward. The nurses almost went crazy trying to calm down seven people, who kept pacing back and forth all night long. In fact, an elderly lady on a walk from her ward was so attracted by the hubbub that she joined them in their pace, making excellent time with her walker.

After seven hours of labor, a beautiful baby girl was born to Mark and Kiona. The input for the naming was tremendous. Both sets of in-laws, the archeology group, the Mayan study group, and friends from college all contributed. The name they decided upon was Articulata Ruby Engler-Almederson. She was a beautiful child with jet black eyes and hair against a tawny skin coloration. In time she would be a combination of her mother's quiet strength and her father's flippant humor. She would be the most spoiled and the most loved little girl "West of the Pecos."

Whatever Articulata's future would be will depend on the base of love she learns to have for herself within the realm of all mankind; she can learn to feel she is better than others and to exploit others, or she can live her life in a natural way and build for herself without hurting those around her. This sort of self-love comes from being loved and having the strength and the faith in a loving God to be willing to take a risk based on self and mutual respect. The love that raises a child to this level must be possessive and non-possessive. A child must know that he/she will still be loved, regardless of the path chosen, but must also know that stepping over others is akin to stepping on one's self. For this to be learned, this child has to be able to weigh the cost of the violation. In other words, he/she needs to feel enough pain from their choices to curtail intrusions on others rights.

Mark's and Kiona's battle to vindicate Black people from a false and evil doctrine and the level of understanding they were striving for to understand humanity by understanding how thought processes evolved from history was presenting the pattern they would organize for their daughter. They were fortunate to be able to draw from that which Dark Waters and Gideon laid before them.

That this model survived the war, in which Gideon and his wife were about to engage is illustrative that a path to God is not through the numbers of converts or through edifices left behind in His honor, but by a simple love for the world, in which we live and for each other. The fight went beyond Imperial Spain vs. the Pueblo Nation. It dealt with how we relate to each other. The battle for the manner in which we tie in to each other goes on in many arenas of our daily living.

# Chapter 10

We may develop the most beautiful philosophies for our lives, but we also have to live with the ugly realities. We drift apart from those that share our ideals, and their values change. Others do not hear the calls to a natural existence we do, or hear calls we don't. Others are discontented because they cannot stand to see that our challenge to adopt the ways God wants us to adopt for us, instead of following their lead. Gideon and Dark Waters and their band were about to take the ultimate risk: To put yourself on the line for the precious lot you have reaped from the seeds you have planted. The offending blow had been struck; John De Melo was dead. When Kurilia stood against the whale, she had to accept the risk that she might be no more. Gideon and Dark Waters were steeling themselves for just that danger.

The quiet was the lull before the storm. The mighty tiger could not lie still while the ant slapped it. An ant can sting, and it can also sting more than once. In fact it can sting enough to bring its prey down. History and Howard Fast have showed us that this is true. Rome defeated Spartacus in a bloody slave rebellion, but his son ran to the hills and carried on the war, and his son did the same after him. Eventually mighty Rome toppled and left its magnificent monuments crumbling. This also was the demise of Imperial Spain and its holocaust of an inquisition. It was a long time coming, and it did not come with this war. The natural spirit of Man eventually won out.

Gideon had dispatched mountain men to establish trade with French forts in the area. They were to trade furs for guns and other weapons, gunpowder, foodstuffs, oil. These were to be hidden under blankets, clothing, and material for tents. The object was to keep the preparations for war as secret as possible. Training was held within the kivas or in caves in the mountains, but never in the open.

The Spaniards also began to make crafty preparations. The commander of the army was a man that had fought under Escobar as a soldier. He remained in the guise of an ordinary trooper, while Escobar was placed in a masquerade commander role. The Spanish taught the tribes with whom they had allied Spanish so that there would be a unification pattern in communication. Skills were developed for night raids. A scorched earth policy was to be pursued. One area, in which Gideon had surmised correctly, was in the use of John De Melo as a propagandist.

Though the old warrior had other motivations in eliminating the cleric, this was a smart, but risky move. For the propagandist and the terror tactics were gone, but the motivation to avenge a martyr was not. The missionaries fanned their hatred for this act amongst their allies and soldados alike. Not even these men of God knew who the real commander was. His name was Emilio Trocadero. His father, before him, had been a Jesuit soldier in his youth. He had been mortally wounded in one of the Papal wars. Emilio cherished his memory and prosecuted any war effort with a fanatic zeal. With this emphasis on the martyrdom of the Inquisitor, he was filled with a single purposed rage. He initiated what he thought would start a war by stampeding a herd of horses into the Pueblo village at night to claim horse stealing as an excuse for a raid.

Gideon was kept informed of this plan via a spy and avoided the war's outbreak by his own slyness. As soon as the horses were left at Mesa Verde, he stampeded them back to the Spaniards. Trocadero surmised that Retta must have had inside information and proceeded to try to ferret out the spy. The spy was Ismalia, who was fully aware of the circumstances of her birth. She thoroughly hated the White intruder and vowed to use any deception or other means to drive him from the land she had come to regard as the path to reaching God. She worked in a mill that ground wheat into bread for the Spaniards and carried it to the bakery and the finished bread to Escobar's hacienda. By talking to other mill hands or bakery workers, she was able to learn that Escobar was only a figurehead commander, but she was not able to learn, who the real leader was. She did learn about the plot to goad the Pueblos into war. Through a shipment of bread for trade with the trading post, she was able to send a message to Gideon. Hence, the horses were able to be re-stampeded back to their source. One night she enticed a guard away from the arms magazine so that guns, ammunition and oil could be stolen. The guard was frustrated and remained suspicious of her movements. One night he followed her back to her cave and observed her meeting with Fiery Water. His movement was heard, and he was captured and brought before Gideon and Fiery Water. They could not let him go back to his camp and could not raise suspicion or the uproar of another martyrdom. The plan that was devised was to take him to a bear's hunting spot near the mission and let the animal catch him at his food while feeding. The enraged animal attacked and made short work of the guard, who bore no weapon. Afterward the bear was shot with the soldado's gun in two spots, one in the leg and once in the head. The fired gun was placed in the guard's hand at a sufficient distance to make the encounter look real.

A Shoshonean on his way back to what would be Wyoming stopped at the trading post. He had no goods to trade and tried to use currency to pay for his goods. The currency was in doubloons, Spanish coins. He was followed and seen in conversation with Escobar. What had transpired in this conversation was not overheard.

He was allowed free movement through the village and closely followed. No untoward behavior was observed. Yet there was something eerie about the man. He seemed very stealthy and sneaky in manner. They knew he had some connection with the Spaniards, but they could not put their finger on it. Eventually he left their village. Twilight settled on the village at the time of his leaving. However the peace of the evening was shattered by a lone Apache rider speeding into Mesa Verde at breakneck speed. He bore wounds, and an arrow was lodged in his leg. He was carried inside and had his wounds tended. He said who he was did not matter, but what he had to say did. He identified the man who came to them. He was not a Shoshonean, but Storm Cloud, a renegade Apache that was cast off from his tribe for molesting a young maiden. He was left in the desert to die and saved by the Spanish missionaries. He had been training raiders in the mountains. He was launching a raid tonight. The man before them was the girl's father. He had been spying on Storm Cloud and was caught and had to flee. The man died without their even knowing his name. Gideon started to marshal his forces when he heard the screams and saw the fire. Storm Cloud was upon them. Luckily, Gideon thought, he had sent Fiery Water and Dark Waters to negotiate with an Apache encampment nearby to help in the pending war, which was no longer pending.

Trocadero knew of this pending alliance and decided to raid the Apache camp while Storm Cloud kept Mesa Verde preoccupied. Fiery Water seized a wagon of arms that the Spaniards had used to seduce the Apache into their camp and yanked his mother into the wagon. Three horses were tethered to the wagon, and Fiery Water got them moving, but not before a conquistador hurled a torch onto the wagon that caused a rocking explosion that hurled them through space. The last memory that Fiery Water had was screaming, "Mother!" and viewing her broken body lying still. Then followed oblivion.

Two days later after this while the smoke was clearing from Storm Cloud's attack, Gideon found them. Fiery Water was still alive, but Dark Waters was dead. After his son was taken to have his wounds tended, Gideon screamed at the top of his lungs and cursed God with every vile and violent word he knew. He vowed a vengeance against Spain and her allies for all time. He could not bear to be with people or without them. He felt like the stripling he was when he sought out Redai. He wanted his mother or Guintera. He felt as he did when he left the Falasha community to seek out Guintera because he felt empty, useless, and devoid of function. His grief was bottomless. He cursed the God that gave him Dark Waters and took her away. Gideon was experienced enough to know that Escobar was not the leader because he could not draw up a plan to tie his shoe, let alone devise a strategy, such as the one that had crushed them. He made a vow to find the real commander and to destroy him for taking his wife.

Three interventions occurred in Gideon's life that aided his grieving: The first was a plea for leadership, the second was a cementing of a painful difference, and the third was a message from beyond the realm of the living world. Fiery Water came forward and spoke to his father, as he had never spoke before; "My father, you have led us in dubious battle to a victory we may never have enjoyed without the training or spark of life you put into us. I know that the ingratitude of men you called brothers, who could not even acknowledge your humanity, made you bitter of spirit. My mother and I realized that you did not hate these men. You went back to them, not because of Mother and me, but because you believed in a doctrine in which you pretended not to believe. For your soul knows that one human being has value for all of us. I believe that you know that whether we win or not is of less importance than standing up for our own dignity is. Please lead us now so that we may either pass out of history like men or take our place in it as those who stood against our oppressors."

The next event proved to be something that the old Gideon Retta would not have done. A young man he had crippled for life came forward to him. Crooked Hand approached him and said, "I speak this with difficulty, for I attacked you from behind and bear the mark of my folly. I admit my error in thought; only you could mobilize us in the past to deliver ourselves; only you can do so now." The young and the old warrior embraced and wept away the bitterness that had set them against each other.

The third intervention came to him in a dream. His wife appeared before him and said, "I am now with our God of Nature, and I am safe. You need to live your life for you now. Part of this is to pass on the message to those beyond us that no oppression or refusal to acknowledge the right of individuals to exist side by side will be tolerated. In this age of enlightenment and rebirth of knowledge, no excuse exists to allow the creation of a supreme and a subservient class, based upon false assumptions and very real greed. Yes, my Love, with new knowledge comes the responsibility of chaining that knowledge so it remains a tool and does not become a master. We need to become our father's equal and friend, and not remain his son, a puppet of his will. Only in this way, by standing up to a tyrant can we get this message across. My life was not in vain, for I helped you let out the man in you to be able to forgive and not tie up your energies in useless hates that would've let our history be one of barbarism and savagery. Goodbye, my Love, we will be together soon."

That a New Spain was fighting this war was evidenced by hiding who the real commander was. This was a sore spot for Gideon because he had to give his enemy credit for having brains. He had sent numerous spies into Spanish strongholds to try to extract this vital information to no avail. Several traps were set with this obsession to know, as a basis. On one occasion a conquistador feigning drunkenness announced in an inn abounding with planted spies that he was the leader. Several of these espionage agents followed him right into an ambush. Seductive young ladies were used to try to extract information from lonely soldados. Since biological attraction is a two way process, the seduction could be reversed. This did happen on one occasion. An impetuous young lady, who was not schooled in the intricacies of espionage, found herself enamored with the target she had chosen, and, instead of extracting information, became guilt ridden and revealed herself. The officer turned her over to the authorities. She was to be tortured for information then hanged. Because he knew the appropriate demeanor from such a person via his incarceration, Gideon decided to undertake the rescue himself. He had access to a hooded cassock, left by Father Benedetto. The first task was to intercept the mission with a band of men. The torturer was held prisoner on board Ericio's ship in the mountains. He was only blind folded and not tortured. Gideon rode to the Spaniard's camp on a mule with his face hidden from view by the hood and a large cross hanging from his neck on a heavy chain. A wagon full of hay was waiting behind the mission a few feet from the torture cell. It was placed there by her brother, another spy. Gideon entered the cell with would be torture instruments in a case and a barbed whip in his hand. He spoke softly and compassionately the way he remembered De Melo used to speak to him until provoked. He opened his case of instruments while the guard was there and acted as if he were choosing one of them. After the guard left, he instructed the girl to scream loudly and agonizingly as he cracked the whip on the wall a couple times. He lowered his hood so that she might recognize him, then quickly raised it again. He told the young lady to run as fast as she could when the door swung open and called the guard. When the guard opened the door, Gideon hit him across the face with the butt end of the whip and drew a knife out of his robe and plunged it into the guard in one fluid motion. He took the maiden by the hand, ran at lightning speed, and picked her up and dumped her into the hay wagon. While they were moving, she burrowed down into the hay.

That night when they were back at Mesa Verde, she came to his bed. He asked her not to do this, but she was persistent. He cried out inside for his wife and companion of years who would not return, and he saw her image telling him to live his life for himself. He gave in to her ministrations. After three days of this, he sent her away, but the guilt still was within him.

Gideon made his way to "Enigma of the East" to interrogate the prisoner. He was brought before Gideon blindfolded. "You can not see me, but I assume you know who I am, do you not?" The man indicated his recognition and the old soldier continued, "You have tortured many to extract information or to force confessions or rejection of Judaism or Islam?" Again the captive nodded his head. "I have been your victim and know about torture. I also know that you profess to call yourself a man of God. Does your God speak of torture or love! I have also seen and been a recipient of your kind of love. At this point in time, whether you lose that worthless scrap you have called life and spend eternity in Hell for what you have done to my brothers and sisters and my wife (Gideon choked back a sob) or get a chance to redeem yourself is up to me. The torture you will bear will be to do right by those you have wronged. I know that you do not know your leader's identity, but I want you to find it out and give it to me. I know the mission where you serve, and I have men and women serving our cause that can reach you and hasten your journey to Hell if you think you can deceive me. You will be taken to a mule with enough provisions to get you to your mission. Then your blindfold will be removed. Now, what is your name?" The cleric was actually sweating in fear then relief that he would live, then in fear for his soul, "Father Nico De Avila", He stammered. Fiery Water led him off of the ship and to the mule. He was bursting with pride for his father, who had resisted the easy way out to torture and kill, as he had witnessed, and through which he had lived.

The memory of a glimpse of a new weapon Gideon had seen began to stimulate his thought processes. He saw a wagon with cannons at either end on moveable turrets with portholes on the sides for additional weapons hidden beneath a bale of hay. The hay wagon, stolen from the mission was still at Mesa Verde. He called a meeting of Fiery Water and Ismalia, Ericio, and Joaquim La Rouxe. He related what he had seen and what was available to create a weapon to surpass this. Ericio's suggestion was to deploy a two-team effort: One to destroy the Spaniards' weapon and the other to build a weapon of their own. A second wagon would have to be built so that the cannons from the Spanish weapon could be stolen and used in the weapon. Joaquim asked if it would not be more sensible to steal the Spanish weapon intact and improve upon it. Fiery Water remembered something he had read in the quiver scrolls about and Englishman that modified a boat into a sleigh on rollers and sent into an Apache camp. Ericio was the only one of the Lieutenants not known to the Spaniards.

He could drive one of these long roller wagons into the area under the guise of making it his home and either steal parts and destroy the weapon or steal the weapon intact and attach it to his "home," Ericio did not want to expose himself to the Spaniards because he was still unknown and wanted this protection in case he was needed for more strategic espionage. However, he was outvoted, and work began on the long roller wagon.

In a month's time the roller wagon was done, and the hay wagon was lengthened for what its new purpose would be. Turrets were placed in the center to mount a system of multi-firing guns, such as was used at the base of the tunnels in the last war. Two cannons could be placed at either end on moveable turrets at either end. These operated like a ship's capstan that was revolved by a system of pulleys once a string was released. Portholes on the sides would allow the use of other weapons, such as harpoon guns or rifles.

Crooked Hand had elected to go with Ericio because the job seemed too big for one man alone. They made their camp on a hill about five miles from the site Gideon had described to them. Their appearance raised suspicions; a quiet, sneaky Shoshone appearing officer was dispatched to keep an eye on their activities. Crooked Hand observed him following them at a distance. About a mile from the weapon site the two decided to split directions. Storm Cloud followed Ericio because he was assumed to be less trail wise. When the sailor paused for a moment Storm Cloud followed behind him, only for his throat to meet the blade of Crooked Hand. They disposed of the body in a back handed way; they burned it to the point of unrecognizability. Later that evening, they brought the long roller wagon, to the site of the weapon. The killing took the luxury of time away from them. The only choice left to them was to dismantle the weapon, destroy what was left, and run. They loaded the two cannons and their mounting turrets in the roller, covered them with hay, and began to move. Crooked Hand knew of Storm Cloud and that he would be missed even if the body was unidentifiable. They set fire to the wagon and were well out of the area by dawn. However, soldiers were still out looking for them. They spotted a cave in a plateau and hid there for two days until the search had died down. Afterwards they made their way back to a warm welcome by their comrades in arms. Crooked Hand did tell Gideon that Storm Cloud was no more. The next day the cannons were mounted at either end of the lengthened wagon. Ericio slept on his ship for two days.

Gideon had not spoken to his son about how his mother's death affected him. He took some time now. He told him about feeling alone with his anchor gone: he articulated feeling like an aimless adolescent searching for an identity or how he could not endure the empty space where there was companionship, the comfort of a warm body to snuggle and with which they made love when they chose. There were no more needs for comfort or giving comfort; no one with whom to take a walk. He felt that he would have rather died in battle than have her exposed to its horrors. He wept, and his son wept with him. Fiery spoke of her gentle eyes and her kindly, sometimes impish smile, her patience with him, and her protectiveness when something or someone threatened him. He smiled in spite of himself, when he thought of her getting flustered and turning him away, when they saw two deer having sex one day on a walk in the mountains. Arm in arm, they came to the realization that they and Gideon were all they had and vowed never to abuse each other. They also vowed to protect each other in battle.

If a barracks can be said to afford any privacy, Soldado Trocadero devised his private plans about pulling Retta out into open warfare. He thought about engaging Storm Cloud in another two pronged attack.

To his dismay, he had heard that the renegade was missing, probably looking for some squaw with which to dispel his energies. Suddenly, a tumult was heard throughout the camp. The alarm was sounded, and the troops were roused from slumber and stumbling into their clothes and groping for their rifles. The horses were stampeding, and fire was all about. A note was pinned to the corral in Portuguese. It said, "Now I have stolen your horses. Come get them if you are man enough." Infuriated, the Spanish troopers charged into a ring of flame with a circle of soldiers behind it firing muskets behind the flames. For those that went beyond to Mesa Verde. Another note was found on the corral in the same language that said, "Commander Escobar has brought another glorious victory to Mother Isabella and Father Ferdinand." During the night the bodies were picked clean of weapons, ammunition, and uniforms. This was the first act of open war.

# Section VII

# Spain Returns

*Empires built on others' backs are like
the sands of time; they run out; they collapse*

# Chapter 1

Emilio Trocadero disliked showing the qualities of a disciplined officer and having to hide behind the ineptitude of a newly recruited private, or it's equivalent in the Spanish army. For this reason Gideon's second note had a particularly irritating effect on him. It was if he were mocking him by saying, "I know that an imbecile like Escobar cannot be your commander, and it is only a matter of time before I find out who he really is. He also knew that De Melo tortured him and ended up dead and that he lost his wife at the hands of the commander. A wave of sweat passed from his eyebrows down his forehead. He also disliked formulating strategic maneuvers, translating them to that, rhino's hindquarters, Escobar, and watching them become botched. His exalted Jesuit father had probably developed a new abdominal scar from turning over in his grave so many times due to the nonmilitary sub functional status of whatever structure served as the nominal commander's cerebral counterpart.

The night was windy across the desert between Mesa Verde and the Spaniard Fort. Gideon was entertaining a notion for a follow-up attack if the wind kept up. He went across the desert, propelled by wind. Ericio was against this proposal. He felt that the ship should be used later in the war because of the high powered cannons. However, he did offer an alternative plan. He told Gideon about a cave in a plateau not far from the fort where he and Crooked Hand hid with the long wagon. A raiding party could fit sails to canoes, carry catapults, harpoons, barrels of oil, and a supply of rags and logs. The war materials could be hidden in that cave so that an attack could be launched at the spur of the moment. The only drawback to this could be that to return they would have to wait for a shift of wind. Diversions would also have to be created to hold back retaliatory advances of the enemy. The masts of the canoes would have to be of light wood, and roller logs would be used to navigate the sand. Defensive weapons and weapons to be used against a pursuing army would be hidden in an adjoining cave, to be dug by Gideon's fighters.

The preparations took a couple months. Trocadero was going insane wondering what Gideon could be doing all this time. He organized a scouting party to go and have a look. They found a group of farmers growing a cross between green beans and asparagus. It turned to be so tasty; they put in the Spaniards' drinking water.

At length, Gideon was ready. A force of canoes on rollers with sails set into the wind late on an April night. They surrounded the fort and shot harpoons with burning rags on them onto the fort. They ascended the ramparts to find a deserted structure. The soldiers within had hidden outside behind plateaus and dunes and attacked the canoes from behind. This attack would be one of hand to hand combat in the desert. The savior that prevented a total rout was Fiery Water who had led an army following the canoes from the rear, spotted the Spaniards, and attacked from behind. Thus, the Spaniards had to fight on two fronts. The wind shifted directions. The canoes were able to tach and escape without too much loss. The fort would have to be repaired, but both sides had a chance to learn the danger of under estimating the other. This could be a long and bloody war.

Gideon was a product of an old system that had inspired a lot of hatred inside him: That of torturing prisoners to get information. When prisoners were taken, they were given the choice of joining him and providing whatever information they could or sent far into the mountains or desert with a few days supply of water and food and told to make it the best way they could. Some made it back to their own commands, some found a way to build their own lives, some died, some fought behind Gideon loyally; others treacherously. Occasionally Gideon had to make an example. One prisoner had tried to kill Gideon. His body was found in the desert with his hands and feet bound together to kill or fight no more.

A young Soldado had very much intrigued the old fighter. His name was Porifirio De Guma. Upon capture, he was brought before this fear-inspiring commander. He was small and wiry. When he stood to his full height, Gideon was astounded, and almost more than that. The prisoner tried to knee him in the groin and proceeded to attempt to kick him in the knee. Gideon took a second look at the prisoner and saw, out of the long ago, a skinny stripling attacking the huge fighter Redai. "How old are you?" queried the commander. Porifirio said, "I am old enough to fight." Not knowing what to say, Gideon sternly said, "You are my prisoner, I can force information I want out of you!" "Go ahead, Bastardo," menaced the diminutive captive. Unbelieving of the brass of this midget, Gideon asked what was being said of him that this prisoner should respond to him like this. The response was, "You are a cowardly Jew that murders Christian children for their blood for wine at his festivals; that you pray in a foreign language to the Devil, that you practice black arts, such as usury and smithery." Gideon was mortified and steeled with remembrance that this lad seemed still a child. He seemed dark in appearance. When the anger between them subsided, Porifirio told his story. He appeared fifteen years old but he was twenty-five. He had lived in a Moorish village in North Africa when the Spanish ship arrived. They traded, but they also examined military strengths and weaknesses. Suddenly, they attacked. He was taken aboard a ship and put in the hold with other slaves. Chaining him was overlooked, and when the ship docked and the hold was opened, he ran to the deck and threw himself into the water; he would rather be dead than a slave.

He made his way to a piece of a log and drifted into the harbor of Cadiz. This was a port of southern Spain with a large Moorish population. A priest took him in and fed him. He became an altar boy in the church. When he was old enough to understand that at puberty, he would be castrated to preserve that fine alto voice, he fled to live in the alleys. He had to steal to survive and came to know all he could expect was the gallows. He learned that he could fight for Spain and God in the new colonies, but he would have to make himself older appearing and act older to fool the authorities. He grew a mustache and acquired some facial scarring from several skirmishes along the waterfront.

When Porifirio felt he had a sufficiently matured appearance, he stowed away on a ship bound for the New World. On board this were three prisoners. A short Black man, a very tall Black man, and a White woman. Only the tall Black man was in chains. The other two were let off on Majorca. Gideon's jaw dropped when he heard this. He was dying to know what had happened to Nahum of Gondar and Guintera, but he didn't ask the young captive about it. As the years went by, Porifirio had learned the tricks that would keep him out of combat. Though his youth was behind him, he retained a youthful appearance and demeanor. His diminutive size also contributed to this guise. Gideon admired the fight of the soldier, but he did not feel he could trust him. Yet he genuinely liked this small fighter. The hostility had faded within the small Soldado, but he was aware that Gideon was a powerful man, as an enemy, he also saw that this commandant liked something about him and did not want to let him languish in a dungeon or kill him. Therefore, he saw an opportunity to save his own life and to be useful to his captor. "I am youthful in appearance. I can serve your cause by relaying military information, by freeing prisoners, and many other activities. I can return to looking like a boy, and I can return to camp as your man. There is no reason to torture me; I have no information to give. Killing me would be stupid since I can be useful to you." Smiling at the crafty Leprechaun tactics before him, Gideon said, "I thought I was a cowardly Jew that drank your blood at my festivals. All of a sudden I am supposed to be your benefactor. Just why is this alteration in our relationship supposed to take place." Porifirio's answer was thought out with lightning speed: "At this point in time, a war is going on, a war with you on the losing odds higher on your side. I have lived on that side of the coin most of my life, but I am still alive. I really bear no one any loyalty or fealty, but I am true to myself. I know you have been in battle before and would not trust me so much that you would not watch me. My life would be forfeit if I deceived you. I also know you were the tall man on the ship and I saw how you can hate. I also spent much time in dungeons and was able to escape because of my size. I am familiar with John De Melo and his tactics. You did the world a favor. In short, you don't trust me, but you like me and are trying to spare me because of the intelligence you've just heard." Gideon laughed heartily and sent him out with Ericio to learn to transform the use of a sea faring vessel to a weapon on land. Ericio put his arm around the pseudo stripling and took him to his boat. While "acquiring his sea legs", Porifirio was starting to hatch a scheme: He would shave off his body hair so that he could go back to looking like a teenager again. He could enter the fort under the guise of being a child laborer. After the entrance, he could let in the ship with its multiplicity of guns, which would arrive the same way the canoes had. The canoes could arrive with the ship and wait on the outside to pick off the fleeing troops from the fort. About a month later, a fleet of five canoes and the ship had rolled across the desert, propelled by the wind. The plan worked like clockwork. Trocadero never knew what hit him. The fort was in shambles. The slender young man found himself among friends. Rumors spread of troop movement along the Rio Grande. Gideon was there to meet them in the narrow trails of the Mexican Mountains. The hoots of success were short lived. The Spaniards had found the cave and demolished the canoes. This avenue was closed as a means of surprise assault. Trocadero now occupied the cavern.

The escape tunnels, used in the first war, were also dug in this cavern. Gideon tried to make use of the tactic of sending troops through the top into the cave. The enemy was waiting for them and picked them off. Joaquim was wounded in this foray, and Crooked Hand and Fiery Water rescued him. They were part of a frontal attack. Joaquim was hit in the shoulder, as he emerged from the tunnel, just as the force led by Crooked Hand and the one led by Fiery Water converged outside the cave. They had defeated the forces trying to advance on Mesa Verde. Joaquim's piercing cry could be heard when the arrow hit. The Spaniard, who was about to finish him off, found a dagger in his neck. After a two-day skirmish, most of which occurred within the labyrinths of the cavern; The Colonizer was driven out.

This cave was a strategic point for both sides, and, throughout the course of the war, it changed hands several times. On one such endeavor, Escobar was bringing up fresh troops from the southern stronghold in what is now New Mexico. Porifirio lay in wait for him with the wagon reinforced with the four turrets. He decimated the army of new recruits, but the remnant, led by Escobar fled to the cave. They were able to hold out for about ten days, due to finding a supply of oil, as the Jews, of ancient times, were able to hold out against the armies of

Antiochus. In his pursuit, Porifirio made an important discovery. He found out who the leader of the Spanish army was.

Laying in wait with the army, which was about to go into siege formation, the versatile young officer, (For that is what he had become), shaved his body hair off and disguised himself as a woman. He then sneaked into the desert and had a small squad of men chase him to the cave. He was come upon by one of the soldiers within and questioned. He then was admitted into the confidence and taken further into the depths of the cavern and admitted to the army as a confidante. He saw Escobar conferring with an ordinary appearing Soldado. He drew closer and heard the non-official looking man start giving orders. This plain, little man was the commanding officer of the army. Porifirio only had to learn his name. He knew he had a certain attraction as a male or as a female, and he made his way to the officer and feigned an interest in meeting the man while he was on sentry duty. His time of guarding was 3:00 -6:00 at the cave's entrance. Stroking his face with a lascivious grin, Porifirio said he'd see him at the post.

At the appointed hour, the supposed tryst took place, but a lot more occurred with it. While Porifirio kept Trocadero preoccupied, Gideon and a group of raiders made their way to the cave and entered through the roof and the tunnel. In silence they gathered up the weapons and ammunition and passed them through the same tunnel through which they entered. Porifirio led Trocadero away from the entrance into a bush of brambles and briars and coaxed him to shed his clothing. He gathered them up as the garments were shed; he had learned the name and had no further need of the commandant. Therefore, he left him in the prickly bushes Au Naturel, put his clothes in a pile, and set fire to it. The raiders similarly gathered up the soldiers' attire, made their way to the outside, piled up the clothes, set fire to them, and waited for the nude, weaponless fighters to burst through the entrance. A wagon was waiting to take them back across the Rio Grande. As the raiders went by the bramble bush, they each respectfully saluted the unclad commander.

A small contingency accompanied the wagon to the Rio Grande. Reinforcements waited on the other side. As soon as the wagon was on the Mexican side, they stormed the contingency unit and slaughtered them. Broken was the restraint and mercy. The Spanish military machine felt only they had the right to slap at an enemy's dignity. Crooked Hand was among those slain. His maimed hand was sent to Gideon via courtier. The sense of rage that the fighter felt was unsurpassed. He vowed as brutal a retaliation. His son, even, couldn't stem the tide of it. "Father, are we in a war presently because we can not tolerate abuses, such as we have just seen. What is the point of this war if it is not so?" "The point, my son, is that a no good Bastard walked into our land as if it were his and treated us as if we were vassals on it. What I have sown, I will reap, not some dandified, European, who does not know where the beauty of our life on the land will lead us. Instead, he buries himself in his own greed. I feel the time has come to show him that he can't force this on us by sending him a reflection of what his behavior looks like."

Trocadero had moved men to the mountain on the night previous to a proposed attack. Ericio had spotted them and shelled them into submission from his ship while Porifirio and Fiery Water shot at them from the turrets of the long wagon. Among the prisoners was Escobar. Gideon wanted to send Trocadero his head to restore the head to the army's rightful head, in anger Fiery Water stepped forward. "I fought for this victory, and it should be through me that it is conveyed to the commandant!" As Gideon saw the stern resolve in his son's eyes along with the others, he gave way. "What is your proposal, Fiery Water," he interjected. His son stated, "Send the fool back on foot with a note in his hat that we do not have to kill or maim innocent prisoners to win a war. Along with this, we should address him by name to let him know we know who he is." Grudgingly, Gideon gave in. Escobar was sweating and fearful, but he did show his gratitude. His usefulness to the war was ended, and he was relieved to return to Mexico, or, as it was then called, New Spain.

Now that Trocadero was exposed, he knew that his prowess was on the line. For every victory or failure carried with it the judgment of who was moral or immoral or which doctrine had the eyes of God or of Satan. He was sick inside that he had let his lust for a woman overpower him into revealing himself to the Pueblo, as well as to the painful aspects of the bramble bushes. In a fervor, he began to import mercenaries, to learn about theoretical formulations for weaponry via thinkers, such as Leonardo Da Vinci and others. He also began to use the heinous devices of the Inquisition used to propagandize against Jewry in Spain and elsewhere against the Pueblo. Stories were invented depicting barbaric tortures and paganistic rituals, practiced by his foe in battle. The purpose of this stratagem was twofold: It created a cover for his own indiscretionatory behavior, and it motivated a hatred for the enemy that would excuse its own brand of torture against a sub human monster who occupied land undeservedly. A converse effect was beginning to make itself felt within the ranks of the Pueblo. The reasoning behind it was, "If we are thought of as beasts, we can fight back as abused beasts and create a real fear in the Spaniard. Then and only then will he leave us alone." Gideon found himself attracted to this thought more and more frequently.

The injection of feelings of vengeance and righting perceived dishonors is not new to mankind; nor is it always wrong to adopt it as a tactic. What is wrong is to attribute such behavior to noble purposes and to use it as an excuse to subject others to it and to repeat the same behavior against, which one is fighting. From the Ranks of the Pueblo nation, emerged the leader of an opposing faction and a strong ally with him. Ericio De Pelunis and Fiery Water began this movement away from vengeance; a battle hardened fighter, spat at Gideon's show of leniency upon his capture as cowardice. He did not want to live like a Pagan in a pagan's land. After all, God and Christ wanted the White man to rule as the vanguard of what is cultured and civilized. In a rage, Gideon rose to his full height and roared, "Maybe you'd like to die on a cross the way your savior did!" Then Ericio stepped forward. "Was it not you that stayed the hand of others and stated we are only fighting for decency? Did you not allow our prisoners to choose to live a life of their own in peace with us? Did I not join you and try to put the world of rot and profiteering at others' cost behind me? What has happened to the man I knew in the Mediterranean, who fought like a madman when he fought, but hung up his sword to find a place where his people could live in peace?

What happened to the man that learned life could be beautiful if one strives to make it so? If worthwhile causes are so easily discarded, then I go to keep my life comfortable for me and mine."

In a rage equal to Gideon's, he started to leave, but Fiery Water bade him stay. He turned to his father for the first time with tears in his eyes and said, "My father, if Ericio, who believed in you before I was and before my mother helped you to see what love was about, leaves, I go with him. I knew not cruelty until that trapper went after my mother. You taught me that kindness in the face of bestiality, was a human act that day. Though he spoke in ignorance, let this prisoner have his final day as a man, instead of a life of self disrespect." Gideon's next response was long remembered. He picked up two atalatls, threw one to the Spaniard, and screamed, "Fight or run for your life!" The Soldado threw and missed. Then he ran, and Gideon threw with a thrust that sent the shaft through him. Both Fiery Water and Ericio De Pelunis embraced him.

# Chapter 2

The annals of history have long periods that are vacuous, and the empty spaces are filled by men who are filled with a desire to equivocate for a point of view be the reason moral, professional, or rationalization. Fiery Water understood the rudiments of these motivations and kept documentation of what had happened in the quiver documents. He feared for his survival and began to entrust the writing to Ismalia. Ismalia began to crave sexual encounters more frequently once he began to teach her how to write Phoenician and to encourage her to record more.

Sometimes their lovemaking assumed an almost desperate proportion. Finally Fiery Water had to ask her about it. Ismalia began to cry and said she feared two phenomena: The demise of their people and that no one would be there to tell the tale to posterity when this war was lost, and the Pueblos were no more. Fiery Water held her close and said, "There will always be a Pueblo people. Always will those who are living decently and love the land stand up against unrighteousness. In our quiver enough has been said to speak out for what and how we stood so those that follow us will know of us, know for what we fought. Win or lose, corruption and greed will continue until human beings learn that all we have is each other. With the corruption will also continue oppression that cannot be tolerated, and a Pueblo people will arise against it, through Pueblo be not their name. Now let's make the baby you want, but let's make it because we love while we are here and will love him/her the same way. Because my father and mother loved each other and me, we can learn from each other. If the love is repeated, we will not die out." They left their cave and went into the mountain woodlands where they undressed each other and marveled at how beautiful their bodies were in the sight of God before they lay together in His grass and flowers and enjoyed what the Lord hath wrought.

Something in Gideon began to reconnect with humanity when he left the Soldado die a fighter's death. He was starting to feel that Dark Waters had the right idea, the only reason to fight was to protect your home and hearth. There is no inherent label assigned as good or evil; just the judgment is my house or family vulnerable. Because a soldier tries to fight for the cause for which he entered a war does not necessarily create an evil design in his head to pass on the evil. Every enemy soldier does not have to be a war criminal.

Some can be there because of duress; others may be there out of a sense of fanaticism. These are the ones that need to be watched, curtailed. For instance, saving Father Nico proved to be a very beneficial idea.

Gideon was in the forest in the mountains, when he saw the Father with three small children building a cabin. "Father," yelled Gideon; "What are you doing here?" Father Nico looked up from his work and addressed the fighter, "You can see that I have left the priesthood. I could not bear the burden you laid on me. I was unable to face the false and cruel things I did in the name of God and called noble. I have adopted these boys because their parents were killed in this war. My flock will be the motherless and fatherless youth that this war creates. I was not able to discover the commander's identity, as you bade me. If you do not release me from my bond to you and wish to kill me, I have naught to say about it, I can only do my penance the way my God has shown me to do it. Now, if you will excuse me, I'll be on with my work."

Gideon did not know what to say. He said that he was not a Holy man, vested with the power of absolution, but, by whatever powers God gave to him, he was absolved. Father Nico thanked him. They were never to meet again.

Now that he had begun to purge his soul, Gideon could redirect himself back to the war. Father Nico had shown remorse. Maybe there were some human Spaniards after all. The Spanish soldiers were being trained at a Franciscan mission in Northern Mexico. Gideon wanted to engage in a twofold operation: He wanted to see just what the colonizers were being trained to do. Then he wanted to stop others on their tracks. He sent his long wagon with the turrets with the newly de- signed guns on it and Ericio with Enigma of the East and its cannon multiplicity and its rollers on it. With stolen binoculars, he observed the men being trained in hand to hand combat, learning to fake being wounded, in order to fall quickly, get to one's feet quickly with more than one weapon drawn and ready for use. Unfortunately, Trocadero had heard that Gideon was sending a force and sent one of his own.

The out of the closet commandant had spies follow Gideon's troop movements and keep him informed. He then had two long cannons brought along behind an army that began following the Pueblo force to the mission outside San Antonio. He also sent word to the troops being trained that an ambush was awaiting them. Thus, Gideon had made a serious blunder; he was trapped between two armies. The cannons were pummeling him from the rear, and the troops were attacking frontally. The weaponry from the ship and the rotary gunnery wagon could hold the armies at bay, but their numbers were great on both sides; one led by Joaquim and one led by Ismalia rescued him. The ensuing battle spilled much blood on the desert floor, and green shrubs turned red. Gideon was able to get his weapons back to base, and Tro- cadero was able to retreat with his cannons intact; However, a clear message was sent to both sides: This war was going to be Hell. Whats more, the secret weapons were used. Their presence was known. Find- ing their location was only a matter of time.

Ismalia and Joaquim pursued Trocadero into a narrow canyon be- tween two plateaus. Then they split in two. One army attacked them from above and threw an avalanche of rocks, while Ismalia attacked them frontally and blocked exit. The army from the south was able to advance unimpededly and attacked Ismalia forcing her to split her force and run. Joaquim had done his damage and joined Ismalia in re- treat. The days of easy pickings were over for both sides.

The Spaniards launched an attack on the mountain terrain looking for the camouflaged Enigma of the East and the rotary-gunned wagon. They employed their wagon with cannons at either end. Rather than expose the hidden weapons, the Pueblos climbed high in the trees and fired burning harpoons down at the conquistadors. There was no room for massive troop movements in the narrow mountain trails, and Joaquim's Mountain Men could get the Spanish soldiers in traps then pick them off. This cost Trocadero the loss of considerable manpower and the destruction of a strategic weapon. He had to make the next battle cost the Pueblos heavily.

Trocadero began a siege of Mesa Verde. Catapults were used to hurl incendiary objects at the kivas. Apache and other tribes with which alliances had been made engaged the mountain men and tribes with which the Pueblos were allied, to keep the siege from being broken. At night Gideon would sneak out and hunt food or raid the siege forces.

The British privateers began to lose interest in shelling the Spanish, as they became more interested in seeking a Northwest Passage and in populating Canada. The Frenchmen began to see the Spaniards as allies because of their common Catholic heritage.

The old alliances and common grounds for fighting Spanish oppression were beginning to grow old. New alliances had to be effected or old ones had to be strengthened. The burden was carried to the peripheral posts. These were comprised of Joaquim and the Mountain Men, Ericio, and Porifirio, and Fiery Water and Ismalia. Russian fur traders and British adventurers began to penetrate the area. Their interests were no less exploitative than the Spaniards, but they were eager to obtain goods via trade agreements, rather than become engaged in an all out war. Besides the Englishmen were bitter rivals of Spain. What was to become the Oregon Territory attracted these hunters and trappers, who had no love for Spain, and saw her as an economic rival. Some of the tribes that had allied themselves with Spain began to feel more and more oppressed by the racist, greedy side of her. There was potential for inciting a rebellion from within. As the prisoners of war were released to the mountains to build their own lives, some began to realize the justice of the Pueblo cause. Joaquim served as a trainer and recruiter for these new settlers. Father Nico would not engage in the warfare directly because of his commitment to the children (Whose numbers had increased logarithmically due to the more aggressive pursuit of the war). Yet he was sympathetic enough to shelter wounded soldiers, recruit and train physicians, and show Gideon's men routes by which to attack the besieging Spaniards from the rear. Considerable efforts were made to shore up the defenses because of belief in their cause and the threat of inquisitor "justice" awaited them if they were defeated. Therefore, morale was high.

There were always thoughts of Dark Waters. Her image always floated before Gideon. Dreams occurred, in which she spurred him on to continue his battle. Sometimes he became disillusioned with a war that started out for justice and fairness and seemed to acquire an impetus of its own: The drive to kill for the sake of killing was one way this showed itself. Another way was one of which he had been guilty in his early years. The enemy is an object to kill before he kills you. There are no Father Nicos; all Spaniards want to exploit and defile. They need to be wiped out. When these thoughts occurred, he would see an image of his wife. She would repeat what the fight was concerning and that letting the war assume its own prerogatives was turning it into a living entity that controlled its creator, instead of vice versa, as was intended. Then she would vanish. He was returned to his solitary, lonely military command.

Fiery Water had just finished a negotiating session with some Kiowa and Arapaho elders. Anger against the way in which the arrogance of the Spaniards and their allies, the French, showed itself was discussed. A method was devised to deal with the return to their previous behavior. Rebellion was to be created from within by hoarding foodstuffs and weapons and ammunition. Wherever or whenever dissension occurred, themes of expulsion of the intruder were brought up as hints of alternative measures. When the time was ripe, contact was to be made with Gideon, Fiery Water or Ismalia, or Porifirio, Ericio, or Joaquim. A force would be sent to reinforce any expulsion efforts from within.

The conquistadors had anticipated such moves and encouraged the missionaries to provide food and medical help to the people in question. They approached Father Nico. He told him that he was a part of a nation at war and owed that nation his loyalty. In anger, he said, "My loyalty is to God! This war of imperialism is unholy. It consists of usurping land settled by others long ago. I'll not be part of it." Joaquim La Rouxe overheard this and reported this to Gideon. A band of mountain men was to occupy the territory around the cabin, and the new weapons were to be ready to be mobilized at a moment's notice. This was never discussed with Father Nico. For Gideon knew that Father Nico did not want the children in his home to know any more about the ravages of war than they ha already learned. Due to this merciful stance, Gideon vowed to make his intervention as non-violent as he could.

The intervention came as expected. A Company of soldados was sent to Father Nico's door with a cannon and siege equipment. Father Nico prepared to defend himself when he saw wild appearing men approach from the rear, several hundred braves approaching from the front, a ship on rollers with cannon poised on the east flank, and a long wagon with rotary guns at the sides and cannon at either end on the west flank. A youthful appearing Moor and a wizened appearing sailor/soldier got out of the vessels and walked to the surrounded company of men. Father Nico joined them, his face beet-red with fury. Ericio spoke: "You are to leave your weaponry and armor on the ground and go back to your camp, as you came into the world, naked. If you don't do as I say, there will be a mass of blood and gore where you stood. I will give you twenty minutes to prepare and make your exit from this place. After this, we will begin firing." He turned around and boarded his ship. Father Nico mounted the cannon and raged, "My religion is these children. If they are ever to know the horrors of war again, I will re awaken my priestly powers and pray for all of your eternal damnations. The eternal army of "Civilization's Way" divested themselves of their armor and raiment and proceeded upon its well-disciplined march home. The mountain men and braves confiscated the cannon, siege equipment, rifles, ammo, and armor. Father Nico laughed, in spite of himself, and Trocadero almost burst a carotid artery and a jugular vein in his tantrum.

As the numbers of White men in the New World multiplied, the numbers of Indi Americans that were displaced from their homes increased. The Spaniards did not have a monopoly on greed and exploitation. Whole tribes moved west, only to find more treachery, exploitation, and being driven off of their own land by other Whites. When they came to Mesa Verde and outlying areas, they were ripe for discussions about joining the Pueblo, but the failure to unite against a common enemy was diluted by cultural differences and the sense of disorganization and defeatism that comes from being driven from one's home of centuries and having no equivalent permanent arrangements that could be the seed of rejuvenation of what they had. This was also occurring with Black people ripped from their lives and taken by force in the holds of slave's ships. It was for leaders to emerge at later dates to mobilize fighting forces to assert their own freedom.

Yet Ismalia and Fiery Water continued to try to create fifth columns and to try and effect alliances with rivals of Spain. More and more the trading post became a meeting site for these meetings between tribes that could not seem to find common ground among the potential for European alliances, the Russians, and British hardy enough to brave the cold of the western areas of Canada were enticed: however, to the migrating tribes, trusting the White Man's word was difficult after their experiences.

# Chapter 3

Despite the fervor to build alliances, the war seemed to be stagnating. Trocadero was seething after the insult at Father Nico's. He was looking for a way to return it to Gideon. When he heard about the gatherings at the trading post, he knew that his point of retaliation had to be centered there. He conferred with his advisors almost daily to author a workable strategy. One plan that was presented was that a gift of a stuffed animal full of explosives be left at the foot of the mesa. At night the army was to use it to blast open an entrance through which tunnels could be dug. When Trocadero heard this, at first he giggled, then he turned his invective on the presenter. "It's generous of our government to employ retarded planners. Maybe your carcass should hold the explosives. Would you like your beard neatly combed out for the presentation? We are dealing with men driven by high ideals led by able, experienced leaders. If they would be fooled by such a proposal as what I just heard this war would not have lasted a week. Let's all pretend we were endowed with an intelligence greater than a desert newt."

A plan was proposed; a plan that would take some time, but one that had the possibility of turning the direction of the war in favor of the Spaniards. The fighting in the southern stronghold was at a standstill. Troops could be moved from the West Coast with impunity. If they could get within a mile of the mountain stronghold, by marching at night and hiding in caves in the mountains during the day undetected, they could tunnel through the mountains and come out behind the areas where the Enigma of the East and the Long Wagon were suspected to lie. These formidable weapons could be located by search and destroyed, not to mention the by-product of decimating the mountain men that had denuded his attack force at Father Nico's.

As Trocadero heard this plan, his eyes started to glitter, and his lips curled in a snarl. Once the mountain stronghold was knocked out, the trading post would be easy pickings. He thought to take his troops from California because the British privateers were raiding further south, and he did not want to attract their attention unduly. Besides, the further north he was the less hiding in caves his army would have to do. What he did not know was that a Russian army was poised to strike in what would be the Oregon territory. Gideon had anticipated some form of attack from the West. The Russians were very self-seeking and their reliability was questionable. To ensure the trustworthy response of these soldiers of the tundra, use was made of a distant connection in history, the connection between Spirit Maker and Long Branch. This connected the Pueblos to the People of the Sound. The Sound People had access to where the seals aggregated, and the Russians were interested in seal furs. Trocadero knew nothing about these arrangements and began his troop movements from California to the mountains. He even allowed them to travel in civilian clothes to create the image of civilian travel, as opposed to movement of military personnel. The ruse was effective.

The Russians were not very schooled in the kind of warfare in mountainous and desert terrains in combination. Therefore, Gideon thought that perhaps some mutual training sessions would be beneficial. This also entailed renewing acquaintanceship with the Sound People. The Sound People were awed by Gideon's appearance. They were awed by the fierce appearance then further awed by the gentleness that emanated from him. Fiery Water was a distant relative by the genealogy from Long Branch and Spirit Maker to Watering Ground to Dark Waters. For this reason they related to him easier than to his father. They did feel the racial difference, but Gideon had expected this and was prepared for it. The Russians had something to teach that was implemented in battle along with what they had to learn. They brought a dance from their native land, the kazatski; in this dance, the dancer squatted down and kicked his legs out. With a knife in each shoe, and by virtue of the squatting position, unreachable by a sword or rifle due to closeness of quarters, quick killing could ensue if the motion was rapid enough. The equalizing factor was this kazatski. Both Russians and braves alike practiced this movement until it became rote; the Russians learned how to fight from trees, while they also learned to fight with more than one weapon at a time. They also had to learn how to cover up their tracks on mountain trails, the propitious time to start an avalanche, how to use herds of animal to do the fighting. In addition they had to learn to discipline themselves to do without water, to learn to time when a dust storm would hit and make use of it in launching an attack. The Russians brought with them knowledge about how to deploy oneself to withstand long periods of cold, how to reduce a large army into small bands. In order to build an army all factions found their common ground and built on it.

These wild men from across the sea impressed Gideon and, in turn, they were impressed by his awesome appearance, as well as his fighting skills. Looking at this tall, Black man with the scarred body and ebony eyes that sometimes-flashed mirth and kindness and sometimes a rage that could sere the land for miles around. He was agile and strong for one of his years. Two husky soldiers: One, a brave, and the other a Russian, disputed his authority because they assumed he hadn't seen battle in years. He picked one up by his beard with one hand and the other by his waistband with the other then threw them down and said menacingly, "Next time either of you dispute my authority, I'll throw both of your corpses to Hell." Ericio saw this and saw the Russian reach for his saber. He stopped him and told him the story of Crooked Hand.

As the Russian troops and the mountain men and braves drilled and learned skills from each other, they began to warm up to each other. They engaged in mock selling of tickets to the "performances of the dance". The appearances of these barbaric White Men and this wiry giant killer of a Black Man stunned the peaceful Sound People until they got to know each other. The bad effect was that vodka was beginning to flow too freely. Gideon put a dramatic stop to this; upon seeing a bottle being passed, he shot it out of the two hands in mid exchange. "A drunken army is a weak army, and I do not have time to indulge weakness," he roared. In one swift motion, he cast off his shirt and showed them all his whiplash scars. "I got these in a Portuguese dungeon. Do you think I want it for you? There will be time for play when we have won!" No one questioned his courage, his savvy, or his leadership after that.

Emilio Trocadero was becoming increasingly annoyed with his army. He wanted this march to be one of stealth and silent advance to maintain the surprise that would finally topple Gideon Retta from the pinnacles of power. Instead, even without the bulk of armor, they sounded like the movement of a herd of pregnant llamas. He was even expecting them to bleat, or whatever sound llamas made. Battle drills were held in the caves where they hid during the day. At least, discipline was not lax. The army had to climb up fairly high to avoid detection, and adaptations had to be made to the thinner mountain air. Until the appropriate breathing rate was established drill had to be kept at a minimum. Their Indian guides tried to instruct them in proper breathing techniques and activity levels to allow them to breathe at all. Moreover, the nights were cold, and this did not seem to be the best time to march. As of yet, they were still undetected.

Ismalia still retained her libidinal fervor, and Fiery Water certainly was not a slouch, but they did so because they loved their cause and they loved each other. After a tough negotiation with the Cheyenne, whose territory was at the junction of two rivers, where Spanish troops coming from the South could be shelled by the Enigma of the East, Fiery Water voiced his frustration with the proceedings, "Can't this fool see that by not stopping the Spaniard's advance, he is not avoiding the White Man's war. He is allowing himself to be callously absorbed into New Spain when the greed pushes Trocadero, or the viceroy of that colony wants to push us out. Why can't he see that the only way to keep them from wiping us out is to provide a united front? He resents us so much because our kivas are a protestation against the nomadic pillaging that this tribe wants to do instead of staying in one place and growing the food we eat. How will the Cheyenne hunt when the Spaniard discovers that his lady likes buffalo hats and coats, and he slaughters this would be hunter's means of food, clothing, shelter, and a hundred other life necessities for the furs. What can our God of Nature show me to pierce this wily coyote's stubborn resistance." Ismalia put her arms around his exhausted, discouraged frame and murmured to him: "Come to our home and fight to master me, then we'll figure out how to master the Cheyenne." Deftly she led him by the hand into their cave and began to nuzzle his face with hers until she could feel his arousal, then she let him attack her. They lay together, arms about each other in the morning and did not think, or wonder, or even hunger. That afternoon both of them approached the stubborn chief and equally obstinate council of elders. Fiery Water said very tersely, "I can not ask you to put aside your centuries old mistrust of us because we closed ourselves off from you years ago, but the only sensible course of action when we have a common enemy, is to throw him out. He is a common enemy because he only wants to use us to get the land and resources and not love them, as we have, but to bleed them dry for his own greed. If I can not help you see this, then my wisdom is not great enough. May our God of Nature pity you! I go." He returned to his cave that night a saddened man, and his wife loved him tenderly. In the morning, the Cheyenne sent word that they accepted the alliance. Ericio moved one ship to the river junction and camouflaged it, but he kept Enigma of the East in its moorings in the mountains.

Gideon had noticed an attractive young lady eyeing him while he went through training maneuvers. Trying to be as unostensible as possible, he drew close enough to her to see who she was.

She turned out to be the young woman whom he had saved from hanging and who had come to his bed shortly after his wife had died. Her name was Flower Petal. After Gideon had rejected her advances, in desolation, she had left Mesa Verde and headed into the mountains. For weeks she wandered until she came out of the mountains to a fishing village, at whose outskirts she had passed out and was found by the villagers. It was the village of the Sound People. She became a part of them and fished, prepared meals, and joined in all phases of their lives. She came again to his bed that night. He did not send her away. While they made love, he was taken with bizarre fantasy. He saw Dark Waters before the consummation and she vanished. Then he saw Guintera, only he was Guintera, and Flower Petal was he. Then he became aggressive, and he was himself, and Flower Petal was Guintera and then herself. He thought he was going mad and sorted out his violent and love feelings from their entanglement. Before he fell off to sleep, he saw Dark Waters image. She said to him, "Do not worry, my love, you are confusing your new violence with that of the old. It is part of your letting go to free you and me until we meet again as whole souls in God's house." Then she vanished, and he slept. He still felt a sense of unease with Flower Petal, but he could not put his finger on why.

Trocadero was growing impatient. His troops had hid in numerous caves and were becoming used to the mountain air. They were becoming restless and had to be worked hard on military operations to keep them from mutinying due to anxiousness to engage an enemy. They could not locate the sector that would lead to the back door of the weapons cache. Besides, a hay wagon was hauling around the disassembled cannons and ammunition; this was getting increasingly difficult to do on the narrow mountain trails. That night one of his agent's provacateurs reported that Gideon was in the village of the Sound People training some wild men from another White nation across the sea and the Sound People in some new strategy of warfare. The last time, Gideon had fouled up their plan to operate as a double agent by rescuing her from her supposed hanging. Thus far, she was unable to learn about any channel of communication from the Western Rockies to the hideout of the ship and the Long Wagon. She agreed to meet Trocadero in a month with any information she was able to discover. She had to get back to the village before she was missed. She did not know this, but because some premonition told Gideon not to trust her, he had her followed. The spy who tailed her was her own brother, who had been part of Gideon's saving her from her contrived journey with the hangman.

He relayed the news of Trocadero's presence in the mountains and of her being a double agent to Gideon. He dispatched a messenger to Ericio and Porifirio and decided to use her to convey misinformation to Trocadero. The gloom that settled over Gideon at the aspect of treachery in his midst for a second overwhelmed him. However, he surmised that for some people nobility of purpose was not enough to motivate loyalty. His ego was also wounded because he felt used sexually and violated.

Some of Gideon's cynicism began to return. He also began to enjoy their encounters less and less. Flower Petal began to question him about her no longer pleasing him. Because he needed her as an instrument, he evaded her questions. This was another aspect of their relationship he disliked. He did not believe in using people. He felt that most of his past life was expressed as being an instrument for others. When he stood up to those bullies so long ago, he did not stand up as an individual who was wronged by a label, but as a Jew who was not given full participation in nation. Flower Petal did not come to him as a woman comes to a man, but as a female object going to a male object to gain information for yet another object. Was this war losing its idealistic meaning and assuming a life all its own, independent of the men who engaged in it?

Trocadero began to feel ill at ease. He was afraid that Gideon knew he was in the area and would surprise him. As a result he began to house his men in two caves, so that if one set was caught, the other could come to its rescue. He always kept the cannons in the hay wagon to the rear. He was trying to develop a new weapon from this wagon after a drawing made by Leonardo Da Vinci: It was closed off except for a gun turret in the center and could run in rugged terrain because the wheels were replaced with a covered system of pulleys that moved unstoppably because of the momentum of the forces pushing it from behind. Therefore, it could be used as a moving battering ram that could shoot down what got in its path on the way to the target to be rammed. In much later years this would be called a tank. The idea that developed was to use roller logs and bind them together with leather thongs. He did not know if this would be workable on the narrow mountain passes. Several shields were placed on the surface to provide armor plating. How successful this weapon would remain to be seen.

Flower Petal could not understand how her cleverly worked ruse had fallen apart; she knew that she was an attractive woman. When she asked Gideon if she no longer pleased him, he was noncommittal. Hence, she felt she had the answer she needed. The next night she tried to act pouty at Gideon. He said in a very penitent voice, "I have a present for you" and called for a soldier to give it to her. Astoundedly, she greeted her brother. The two military men told her about her antics and gave her a choice of serving as a double agent or drinking the cup of snake venom placed before her. She was also warned that she would be followed on her treks into the mountains and held accountable for

any treachery. A squad of five Russians and five Sound braves followed her one night. From a cliff they observed a huge army on the
march. They were dressed as civilians. While the two armies entered
their respective caves, some (about fifteen men) had separated from
the others. The squad had instructions to engage a small party to test
out their new techniques. A brave approached one of the conquistadors. When he failed to give the password, the guard attempted to
bayonet him. The brave ducked and squatted then kicked him in the
jaw. Without rising to his feet, he threw a knife in his neck and watched him drop. He no sooner recovered his weapon and got the guard's
rifle, when another guard approached him. The brave squatted down
again and kicked out again. This time the knife blade was in his shoe
and struck its mark. A third guard approached, and without changing
from his squat he bayoneted him. The fighter picked up all three sets
of weapons and made his way back to the cliff. Each one picked off
the Spaniards one at a time in the same manner and built a stockpile of
weapons. In the morning, Trocadero discovered the bodies. In his rage
he shot Flower Petal.

Gideon felt a sense of outrage at this, but she had made her bed
and had to sleep in it the way she had chosen to make it. He had, not
long after he left his father's house, learned that if you live by using
people, this will be the way you die. He pitied her, but she would have
to answer to God for how she had lived. At least, the new fighting
technique worked.

Trocadero was dismayed to know that Gideon knew his whereabouts, and he resolved to find the outlet to the mountain stronghold as
quickly as possible. His lure was to capture a mountain family and
spread a rumor that they were to be tortured for information and
hanged. As expected Gideon was incensed and prepared to attack. But
as unexpected he did not unleash the ships and long wagon or send for
mountain men to let Trocadero know where the pass was. Instead he
started a fire in the area and attacked under its cover to rescue the family under its cover. Trocadero did not flee in a panic, but he and his
men climbed out of the tunnels and surrounded Gideon's small band of
fighters forcing a retreat. Gideon retreated into a canyon and found
himself and his band boxed in by Trocadero's army. there was virtually

no way out. Gideon prepared to make what he thought would be his last stand, when another army appeared. It was led by a raging young man followed by Joaquim La Rouxe and his mountain men. The raging leader was Flower Petal's brother. Despite her treachery he had deeply loved his sister. They drove off Trocadero's army, but it had been a close call, and many a brave warrior had been lost. Gideon began to feel the sober realization that he could not stand any more losses such as this one.

Gideon realized that he had to get Trocadero out of the mountains, or he would come upon the hiding place of the weapons and destroy them. He had tried having Ericio and Porifirio move them around and to shell Trocadero from atop a plateau. They also kept a watch on the movements of Trocadero's army. Gideon also used frontal attacks to harass the advance of the Spanish forces. The new close quarters fighting techniques and the Russians helped, but the fighting was fierce and costly to both sides. Oftentimes he felt he was back at the hill of Jews with Redai. He could see him being led away in defeat. He began to sweat at these times and tried to divert himself by devising new strategies. His men were getting tired of night fighting, and he attacked once in the day while Trocadero's army was drilling in the cave. Right in front of the cavern stood the long wagon, and it mowed down the fleeing troops. From a precipice behind the battle site the long cannons were assembled and fired on the long wagon, severely damaging it. Porifirio barely was able to get it out of there to be repaired. The Pueblo army was stunned to find that their new weapon was not invincible.

The technique that finally drove a retreat from the mountains was another costly episode. While the daytime drill took place, Gideon's army threw brush all over the trail. Then when the army tried to move out at night, they fired burning arrows and harpoons with flaming rags on them and charged them through the burning brush. After a few hours, the mountain rains put out the fires. Trocadero was able to advance his position but not without having his rear flank harassed.

The new alliance with the Cheyenne was about to be tested. A joint force was to advance over the plateau at Mesa Verde into the Rockies and join a combined unit of mountain men and Russians and Sound People attacking frontally from the west. The Long Wagon was still being repaired and could not be utilized. Ericio moved one of the ships into a narrow pass between two cliffs and covered it with brush and tree limbs. The ship was placed so that it could withstand either an offensive from the rear or front and also be able to shell the cave or troops on the march. Torches were placed at several points along the narrow mountain passes, but they were not lit to prevent awareness of the new plan. Now they were lit, as the army of conquistadors was getting ready to move. The Cheyenne and Fiery Waters' troops descended upon the troops, and Ericio began shelling them. The Spaniards began firing back in the dark, and the battle raged until dawn. Then about ten wagons covered with shields with rotary gun turrets in the center showed up advancing up the mountain terrain on log rollers tied with thongs, firing in the direction of the camouflaged ship. They tried to pin point its position from the trajectories of the shells. Joaquim began advancing behind the roller wagons because they could only advance in a forward direction. However, they were moving in a curved arc and began to fire on the mountain man, as their positions became reversed. Thus, a circle was formed with half of the new weapons, firing at the ship and half firing at the mountain men advancing up the slope. From the southeast corner emerged an army led by Gideon, which came together with one led by Ismalia from the southwest. Trocadero was surrounded until two Comanche armies approached behind Ismalia and Gideon's armies. Each of them was wielding a long cannon and began shelling them from the rear. The battle raged for three days, and the dead were piling up on both sides. Yet the fighting went on and on. Neither side wanted to yield to the other. They seemed determined to not yield an inch of ground to the other. The Spaniards' new weapons held off Joaquim and Fiery Water and the Cheyenne up to the time that Ericio found their range in his guns then blew them apart. However, the delay caused by their intervention allowed Trocadero's men to advance and split up Fiery Waters' men from the Cheyenne. They were not schooled in the new techniques and had difficulty standing off the endless sea of Spanish infantry in undating them.

The tide of the battle was beginning to turn in favor of the Spaniards. Trocadero began to employ some of the tactics used by the Pueblos. He had seen a pride of mountain lions stalking a herd of deer and used torches to direct the herd between Ismalia and Gideon's armies with the lions following them. The stampeding army engaged the two diminished bands and caused them to have to retreat instead of meeting the armies of Fiery Water, the Cheyenne, and Joaquim's mountain men. Besides, the two long guns were also impeding Ismalia and Gideon. Suddenly Porifirio appeared with the second ship and took out one of the long cannons, manned by the Comanches. Having driven off the clumsy tank forerunners, Ericio was able to direct his attention again to the troops harassing Fiery Water and Joaquim. Trocadero was able to find a pass out of the mountains, and the battle was a draw. Had the Spaniard been able to push five hundred yards further, he would have found the pass to the weapons cache.

# Chapter 4

Both adversaries needed to take time to tend their dead and wounded and to let time heal them from the rigors of battle. Joaquim, Porifirio, and Ericio went into the mountains for some fishing. At a small river encampment, they happened upon a band of children both White and Indian that survived by stealing from hunters, trappers, and runaway soldiers. They spoke an amalgam of Spanish, various tribal dialects, and Amharic. When word was relayed to Gideon, he was excited to meet this band. He found that in Spain and Portugal, the Falasha communities, as well as Amer-Indians brought home as curiosities were being eliminated, and their children were left to survive in the alleys and streets then incarcerated and shipped to New Spain to be used as slaves. When they could run off, these youngsters did so and formed companies of mountain brigands. He asked if any of them would be willing to volunteer to serve a continuation of their function by sneaking back to their villages and stealing from the Soldados. He found an interested group; one of them gave him back his dagger, watch, and two doubloons he carried in his trousers. The other fighters continued on their fishing trip.

Having recruited the children, Gideon went to visit Father Nico to see if he would cooperate in providing housing for some of them. "I do not provide a barracks for thieves here. I do not want your war touching my children! I cherish your friendship, but keep this battleground away from my doors." Then he beat the fighter at three games of chess. Gideon clapped him on the back and went on his way.

Fiery Water jumped up with a startled yell. He felt his wife sneak up behind him and pinch him on the bottom. "Whatever might you want?", He asked with a smile. "Why don't you come into my cave and find out, Big Boy," she teasingly laughed. They kept this pattern up for about a week, and Ismalia announced she was pregnant. Fiery Water playfully admonished her, "See where all that sex gets you."

Sadly, she hung her head and said, "Yes, let's go have some more." That's just what they did. After that they began to update the quiver, which they kept hidden in their cave. They told of the recent battle for the mountains. They also acknowledged that this was not showing itself to be an easy war. The Spaniards had, in the ranks of their army, a small band of rebels. These were youngsters, who were born in New Spain. They did not like fighting for the Mother Country, only to be slaves.

They observed the converted Mountain brigands' activities and sought out Gideon Retta to join up with his junior fifth column, thus, there was a unit of spies and saboteurs operating within the stronghold of the enemy. However, the Pueblo leadership was soon to discover that cautions were required in recruiting these youngsters. They provided evidence that a book cannot be judged by its cover.

This evidence was provided by a young man that was seen to be beaten by a Soldado for not shining his boots to satisfaction. He was a good natured, pudgy kid, named El Gato Gordo, by the street urchins, for his movements were swift and skillful, despite his rotund appearance. He was the illegitimate son of Father Benedetto and a Sister of the Church. He did not know his parentage, but he did know that he was a Bastardo and had to constantly have his origin and need to unceasingly strive for salvation in the loving soul of God thrown at him. He was to travel the mountain roads from the south and render them impassable to the Spaniards. However, the need to earn salvation was imprinted on his psyche. He would observe troop movements and various fortifications to the officers of Trocadero or agents of tribes allied to him. He was also shown the kazatski attack movement and presented a demonstration of its operation to Trocadero himself. However, because the youth's body was undergoing puberty, and the swift movements drained energy that was used for growth, the technique looked ineffective to the commander; unknowingly the son of a Jesuit fighter dismissed this knowledge as magic gyrations to some pagan Russian God. He had the Fat Cat beaten for taking up his precious time with nonsense. From then on, El Gato Gordo was loyal to Gideon, and he gave Trocadero only false or misleading information. Gideon never learned about his earlier treacheries and had no need to doubt his loyalty. Perhaps these rebellious youngsters were the forerunners of America's Latino and Chicano cultures that fight so hard to be recognized in their own proud rights as Americans. Perhaps El Gato Gordo represented a movement away from unquestioned cultural loyalties to adapting functioning to survival of ones own soul; maybe this generation was not their fathers' sons. Indeed a book cannot be judged by its cover. The interlude in the fighting provided a chance for relaxation and diversion into the non military aspects of their lives by the combatants of both sets of adversaries, but it also gave them an opportunity to examine their own motivations to enter and pursue a war, such as this one. Ericio De Pelunis was a skillful navigator and knew much about military strategy and history. He grew up on the docks of Lisbon, having been raised by a drunken father after abandonment by his mother at the age of two. His father was often in barroom brawls and showed other elements of little or no respect for the law. By the age of ten, he knew well the feel of his father's foot. He was not altogether mortified with sadness when some officials hauled him off to the gallows. He stowed away on a ship that had established trade with India. In a bar fight in Goa, he was stabbed by a rajah whose daughter he had ravished and almost died on the way to the missionary hospital. Once he was admitted and sewn upon, he had time on his hands, in his mind's eye, or maybe it was his mind's nose he told himself, "Your values stink." On his way to recovery, he got into a card game with another sailor, as degenerate as he was. He won a boat from him, called "Enigma of the East." After he healed, he left India post haste, as he had convinced the pretty sister, charged with his care to share his bed; she found herself pregnant. He took his new acquisition to explore how he could use the world to his advantage. On the way to India he had passed through Ethiopia and had seen the fanatical religious wars that involved Moslems, Jews, and Christians. He had noticed a proud, tall commander, named Redai and an equally tall young soldier that seemed to be sitting on an insurmountable amount of rage. He made his way back to Ethiopia and saw the broken spirits of the Falasha after the battle of The Hill of the Jews. He made himself indifferent to the sufferings of the vanquished. After all, the world was not so kind to him; he resolved to become a businessman and reap what the world allowed to reap. While negotiating a trade deal worth Sarsa Dengal, the victorious Amhara commander, he happened upon Redai's lieutenant, Gideon Retta. From an alley, he saw a band of six Amhara approach him: "Cowardly Jew! Where is your champion woman empress, Judith now? Where is her deformed eye, her Buda, with which she killed our priests? Go study her victory tactics in the books we have burned." With this, they laughed. The Falasha seized one of their swords out of its haft and cut its owner in two. The other five charged him. He killed them all. "As my people's blood is on your hands, so will yours be on mine. You'll never wipe us out. God has chosen us to survive. From that day on, Ericio knew he could not sell out humanity for a shekel. He became ready to put aside the material world because he saw one man that was willing to fight, not for an advantage over another, but for his own right to respect himself for living his own life the way he saw fit and to reach for God the way he felt, not the way he was told and forced to reach for Him. Any man has a right to rise by his own mettle. It would be done in the guise of business: You pay your own way, and we are not beholden to each other. If we are bound, it is love of the humanity we all share.

When he dropped the Falasha off on Portugal's shore, he did not know that his motherland had become a Spanish vassal and carried on its own form of the Inquisition. If Christianity meant the arms of a loving God, then why was there a loved and a hated faction. Could it be that when brought to grips with his own need man becomes the Adam that blamed Eve for his own greed so that he could have more? If that is what makes up a man, what redemption had Christ brought to mankind? Ericio operated on this assumption: That man is powerless to alter the basic greedy structure of the universe and had to either act as an aggressor and take a better piece of the world and let the weaklings, who didn't do so, suffer. Or he had to convince the suckers to give him more, as a businessman does. Then he met Gideon Retta, who hated the world of the conniver and cheat. He was strong enough to take for himself, but he reached into his heart and never took without giving back.

The toughened, wizened sailor saw the fighter's spirit against the Barbary pirates, and from a distance, he saw it diminished, when his own people, instead of loving him for, as standing up to the devious mannerisms of the oppressor, held him culpable for starting a pogrom that had already been planned. He also saw this spirit replenished by the first war and by Dark Waters' love in the aftermath. In the wake of her death, Ericio saw a disappearance of his compassion and took it upon himself to awaken it by anger. At the point of engagement in the first war, Ericio knew that, despite a fiery anger at the abuses he had received, the tall, Kushitic battler believed in his fellow man behind the obvious greed that motivated most men. Because he wanted his soul to flourish instead of rot, the stormer of the seas made a decision to join this battle when the risk of victory was low in actual physical terms due to Spain being powerful, but high in spiritual terms because the message that came across was that the way of God was not the way of deception and ignoring the pain caused by the racism, covering covetousness. Win or lose, he was with Gideon to the end.

Ericio was not the only one touched by the sheer justice of the Pueblos' cause. The diminutive, Porifirio, fiery product of the Moorish community of Northern Africa, the docks of Cadiz, and the pious hypocrisy that wanted his manhood to maintain an alto voice had as much hatred in him as the Ethiopian, but he saw a love of man underneath this. At first he took it for weakness until he had heard what he had done to the Russian and brave that challenged him and because he knew about the combination of strength and genius it took to kill John De Melo right in his own lair.

He also knew that if Gideon Retta ever felt betrayed, his retaliation would be swift and merciless. He saw the old soldier send Flower Petal to her own death without even conscious awareness, but thorough knowledge that Trocadero would shoot her in his rage. The tale he heard about giving the Spanish prisoner a chance to fight for his life also moved him. Porifirio had never known the love of his fellow man because of his small stature and his explosive fighting spirit. He knew the love of a woman, but it was only the kind of woman who found the non-bonding love of a soldier satisfactory to her needs. He found himself not only feeling strongly for this brave, but compassionate fighter, but also placing himself by his side to protect him. He even developed a sixth sense that could tell when Gideon was in danger. He was bitter to the extent that he only acknowledged God, as a bitter, vengeance creation of Man until he met Gideon on that fateful day his life was spared.

Father Nico knew that he owed Gideon his life. Whatsmore, he tremendously admired the gallantry of his fight, but he was sacred to his vow to protect the children because he knew in his heart that he had earned damnation; he also knew that one didn't get a second chance every day. But short of becoming a combatant, he would do anything to help him or his cause. He silently thanked Gideon for respecting his vow. He also knew that he owed the soldier his life. Every child that would walk the forest trails or the mountain paths of Colorado, or fish, or mine for gold or silver in free dignity owed it to this reincarnation of the Kushitic warrior that made Rome tremble.

Joaquim La Rouxe owed his life to Fiery Water for the rescue from the river so long ago, but also to Gideon, himself, for that daring foray into a Spanish settlement to save him from the gallows. He would never be far behind Porifirio or Ericio when it came to protecting Gideon or Fiery Water. The war showed the fierce loyalties that can evolve from mutual unity against a common enemy. What was not predictable was how long the cement of bonding would endure after the cataclysm was over. The loyalty of a family member is either maintained with a ferocity or broken off with an intensity that usually carries a depth of feeling, either good or bad, that adds color to the relationship. So was it with Fiery Water and his wife.

They were deeply loyal to Gideon because they knew of the loss that dominated his thoughts, the hatred for the hypocrisy and greed the inquisition created, and the double standard of humanity that rejected him because he dared to stand alone by his own standards, yet sought him out readily enough when their needs became unmanageable. They also believed in the same ideals he did and stood up to him when he went against these self devised norms. There was a dimension of the loyalty that Ismalia and Fiery Water carried a bit further. Perhaps, it developed because Gideon confided more with his family. He had hinted that, win or lose, as he and Dark Waters had agreed before the war, their life style had to go on even if it meant the war had to never end. Fiery even added this principle to the quiver documents.

# Chapter 5

Most of the time Articulata was a good baby. However, though she did not have a curl in the middle of her forehead, when she was horrid, she was horrid. Mark had to bear the brunt of changing her in the middle of the night because Kiona was a sound sleeper. Most of the time during the day Articulata enjoyed the company of her numerous uncles and aunts at archeology meetings or even digs that kept uncovering more and more artifacts from further and further away. In fact, artifact would, in all probability, be the third word she learned. Rachel, who was beginning to get antsy about getting back to medical school and Arne and Yusseff, spent a lot of time with Articulata; she even started singing her lullabies in Amharic and even Geez. Helga was busy with Julio, but not too busy to take a hand in the endless mothering and spoiling of his daughter, along with Mattani's ministrations in that area. Her two sets of grandparents made things worse. Mark knew they were visiting when he would come home to gurgling and cooing that meant the baby language was in full chorus. One time he came home to such an ungodly babble that he bought a bandleader's baton and spent a half-hour conducting the cackle before anyone noticed he was in the room. On another occasion he entered his house wearing a diaper so he could get some attention: Kiona put a bottle in his mouth. They both laughed at this. However, the next day after Mark saw Kiona bending over to make their bed, he tackled her onto it. Laughingly, she asked if she had done anything to warrant such aggression. Mark despairingly said, "It's what we haven't done that's the problem. I am so horny, I could sexually attack a basket of fruit." With a smile on her face, Kiona offered him a box of raisins. Mark groaned and said, "I may never be able to walk a straight line again. This behavior may get me arrested for intoxication, and I don't even drink." Kiona hugged him to her and told him she loved him, but they'd have to wait a few more weeks until she was all healed from the episiotomy. "But I'm getting allergic to abstinence and to cold showers. I'm developing a rash on my optic nerve, and it's giving me an unhealthy outlook on life," pleaded Mark.

That weekend, Reed and Michelle and Amy and Ron visited and brought their new babies. Reed had a son, Aaron, and Amy also had a son, Gideon. They hired a baby sitter for the three kids and went out for a night on the town with Arne and Rachel and Julio and Helga. They went to a Karioke bar, and the men had to put on a wet tee-shirt act while singing "Gypsy." Mark started to take his cap off, then his shoes and socks. Reed kept pulling his suspenders up and down; Arne wiggled his ears and dropped his tee shirt to his shoulder, while Julio uncrossed and crossed his eyes and bobbed his Adam's Apple up and down in time to the music. The girls booed them and threw peanuts and broccoli at them. Mark ate a piece of the broccoli, as it landed on the stage. Reed put a peanut between two pieces of bread he had secretly brought and ate it. Arne threw olives at the audience. The grand finale was Arne doing a solo of "Snoopy and the Red Baron" while Mark, Julio, and Reed did a chorus of chicken clucks.

When the boisterous crowd came home they saw Aaron, Gideon, Yusseff, all asleep in the arms of their sixteen-year-old baby-sitter. Kiona took a picture of it for posterity. Next to them was Articulata with her free arm around Yusseff. Mark nudged Arne and said, "Don't come here and start a UN meeting. We only want our own kind." Then he and Arne hugged, and tears were in both their eyes, tears that tore away at the pain of racism. It was this type of tear shedding that Mark and Kiona had spent in their battle, that Professor Owens had poured forth in defense of his family, and that Gideon Retta and Dark Waters had issued when they were left alone to starve. It was akin to Grady Almederson's time at sea, when the searing pain racism had carved onto his soul was scrubbed clean. Maybe this new generation could clean the ugly stain that mankind had placed upon itself to cover the failure to see beyond one's self. Perhaps parents and children can work together to eradicate this foul weed from our thinking so that, as God's children we can build our own Garden of Eden and return to it. At any rate, this moment of love between children was beautiful to behold.

However, there were other elements in the neighborhood and in the community that frowned at co-mingling of children of different racial background; they talked about the horrors of inter marriage and mixing, of a race losing its identity, and of the terrible mongrelization that such contacts produced. Community meetings were being held blaming the archeologists for starting the disruption by delving into the past that God had seen fit to bury.

One of the community meetings that took place was the group of youngsters that met with Helga and Julio. There was a lot of divisiveness among the former gang members over these issues because each had grown up with his/her identity establishment patterns. The debates dominated the last few meetings. Several adults from some of the community factions that were developing, including the archeologists began to participate in the meetings and express their views. The meetings that had brought kids together and driven out drug lords were turning into brawls until Julio and Arne combined their intelligence to combat the ugliness that was pervading the community. They approached Aaron Donleavy about finding tapes of the work of Heinrich Schliemann, who uncovered the city of Troy and shed light on the Trojan War that was the beginning of East meeting West. Professor Horton was brought in to lecture on his group's work on finding the truth of the Quetzalcoatl history/legend and how his study group had broken the barriers to communication down to pursue a common truth. Arne brought films of the Rwandan War and the hatred between the Tutsies and Hotis and how it almost destroyed these segments of humanity in the refugee camps in Zaire; last but not least, Julio brought a tape of "Rocky IV", a Sylvester Stallone movie, in which Rocky Balboa, an American boxer defeats a Russian champion. He hated and feared the Russians, and they hated and feared him until he said, "I hated you, and you hated me. But I changed, and you changed. If I can change, and you can change, we can all change." It was slow in developing, but the next couple of months saw a change in the face of the Durango community, Rachel and Arne were married and returned to the wilds of Cleveland and medical education, Helga took Rachel's place with competencies since she had learned Amharic; Julio began to enjoy unprecedented sex, and Mark began to win some of the chases around the bed with Kiona. He didn't even cheat; she did.

# Chapter 6

Grady Almederson stood from his position, bent over his lawn mower to repair it with a startled yell. Ruthena had sneaked up behind him and pinched him while he was preoccupied with mechanical thoughts. "Damn it, woman, my world does not revolve romance when I can't mow my lawn because something is wrong with this raggedy ass tool of the devil." She said, "Mousie, I know you're covering up your appetites with that pseudo-anger, but we can discuss that later." Then they both laughed. She laughed at his response to a later discussion and told him Jack Engler, and Professors Owen and Horton were there to discuss business proposition. The tour of archeological Sites Corporation had done the six friends well, but the market was getting played out since Helga was involved with the Gideon Retta project and Julio Barsta. Jack had the idea and contacted Maxim Horton and Alexander Owens to have a brainstorming session on how to find some income to sustain the corporation. Jack and Grady and Bert and Ruthie hugged each other and the two professors, then they started talking business right away. Ideas ranged from putting tapes from some of the exotic digs on TV commercials, preparing narratives for shows, such as "Twenty Minutes", and approaching retirement communities with plans for group trips for purposes of getting tax breaks. The most attractive idea that came out of the think tank was Ruthie's and Bert's idea of finding a writer and a movie producer to make movies out of the Quetzalcoatl and Gideon Retta stories and giving the author of the scripts and producer advice and technical assistance. The income might have to be split with the Mexican government and with Aaron Donleavy's group, but the estimated potential was a gold mine. It could even mean money for Mark, Kiona, and Articulata.

The next step was for the partners to split into groups and to divide up the tasks. They agreed to meet again in six months to evaluate their progress and to see where they went from there. Professor's Horton and Owens were to find movie writers and producers, while Bert and Ruthie were to negotiate with Mark and Kiona, as a way to approach Aaron Donleavy with their proposition. Jack and Grady were to negotiate with the Mexican government for rights to publication, copyrights, etc. Needless to say, this proposition was fraught with complications.

When they approached the Mexican government, Jack began to feel uncomfortable. A young man kept staring at him. After he could stand it no more, he went up to the man and said, "Do you know me? Why are you obsessed with staring at me?" He said, "Excuse me, Senor, you look like a much younger man with whom I had dealings a few years ago back in my village in Yucatan. He was a very nice man and an honest one. He helped the people of the village in which I was born, to get a realistic view of their history so that they could hold their heads up in self respect." "My name is Jack Engler, and this is my friend and business partner Mr. Grady Almederson." "I am Provincial legislator from Yucatan, my name is Jiminez Bartomas. Senor Grady, if I may call you that, I also knew your daughter. She was as honest as your son, Senor Jack, and just as fiery, but she could not fight with the love and ferocity he did." He went on to explain how Mark had disarmed the jealous young man with the flame-thrower.

Jiminez and Grady and Jack sat down at a sidewalk cantino and exchanged Mark and Kiona stories until far into the night, laughing and clapping each other on the back. Jiminez very much wanted to help these Americanos, whose son and daughter had shown what a real American is supposed to stand for. He could see some of the fiber and guts had passed from one generation to the next, but also gentleness and compassion had echoed back from the son and daughter to the parents. From the anecdotes he had heard, the passage was fraught with strife and anger, but their tales also reflected a lot of love and pride in their children. Jiminez agreed to back the two of them in their venture and to seek the cooperation of the Mexican government in selling rights to any movie they would make. Thus, this part of the plan appeared to be in the bag.

Finding a producer and a scriptwriter also seemed to encounter both breaks and difficulties. An amateur writer, by the name of Freddy Gauland claimed a distant descent from a tribe that had settled in the Puget Sound area and had been allied with and distantly related to the Pueblos. He was interested in tracing his roots. He alleged to be descended from a refugee from an eastern tribe that had had contact with a Phoenician trader, of Jewish extraction, who had left phylacteries with the family with whom he had established a relationship. The wanderer's name was Elk Horn. Freddy was interested in the phylacteries because he was Jewish and had done much research to connect himself with the Sound People. He had heard about Julio's discovery of the phylacteries in a museum of artifacts in Saskatchewan. He was also related by marriage to a small producer, who had acquired a small failing film company through an inheritance. The name of the company was Tripod Productions.

In order to survive, Tripod had to be attached to a larger company to be able to meet expenses. A good reason had to present itself for a larger company to be willing to back Tripod. A sound idea for a movie that would generate profits was a good reason. Professor's Horton and Owens congratulated themselves on a task well done.

At the last minute, all six of the partners decided they wanted to see Mark, Kiona and the baby. Ruthena and Bert had already begun to talk to their children, who had begun to whet Aaron Donleavy's appetite for money. The Professors brought Fred and his uncle with them to further acceptance of this greedy, yet creative plan. Negotiations were tough, and arguments were fierce. Jiminez was brought forth from Mexico to be part of the bargaining, haggling and down right cussing that caused the windows to have to be closed. Jiminez nudged Mark and Kiona and laughed, "Just like the old days, isn't it." Mark and Kiona laughingly acknowledged this. At one point, the heat from within was as stifling as from without, and the windows had to be opened, verbiage or not. To cool down the tempers, Kiona brought Articulata into the room; she said, "My baby needs to see her friends and family. Could she see them acting like something else besides drunken sailors?" All of a sudden, the room became still. Everyone smiled, as Kiona danced her around the room. She then let each one hold her. The discussion resumed at a politer level.

After three fun-filled days of hammering out an agreement (This statement may be literal), the group agreed to pursue the venture. Now they only had to work out international protocols, implications of mergers develop a formula for respecting publishing rights and filming rights. hire a crew to start working, find-funding sources, and do a lot of praying.

# Chapter 7

The time of year was Christmas. Trocadero was saddened because his mother had died in Spain, and he was here in New Spain fighting the heathen instead of saying good-bye to her and wishing her God speed to the arms of the Lord. A tear fell down his cheek. His face turned beet red, and he screamed, "Damn that heathen scum, Retta. Why can't he admit he is of the inferior stock of the Black man and the cunning stock of the Devil Jew and admit he cannot war against his betters and win!" He returned to the mold of self-pity and thought about his wife and child across the accursed mountains, deserts and seas. God, how he wanted this war to end.

In Gideon's camp, the spirits were high, but they too wanted to see the fighting and dying at an end, however, they did not want the end to be a condition of servitude to the aggressive colonizer. They realized that the Spaniard was no different than any other exploiter. They would not admit the evil of their ways unless the cost of maintaining the status quo outweighed the cost of change. Therefore, a fiery blood-lust had to be maintained for a war which was doomed because the exploiters had prepared for lengthy duration by continuing to accumulate and apply the wealth of its ill gotten gains, and the plundered were becoming more and more drained of their own resources. The leadership met to explore new sources. The monarchy in Spain had passed to Phillip, and he was making a series of enemies: The British were building their navy and defeated Spain at the battle of the Armada; The Netherlanders threw the Gauntlet down against Spain because they had felt the Spanish Inquisition because they had adopted Protestantism and began to fight for their own self government. Negotiations were sought to encourage privateering ventures with both the British and the Dutch. However, they were White men with White men's greed and their own set of hidden agendas for their relationship to the Amerindian.

The Russians fled the tyranny of the Autocratic Tsars. Their makeup consisted of wild Cossacks from the Ukraine, Mongols who rode with Genghis Khan, and their counterparts the Tatars, left to rule conquered Russia. However, to their consternation, they heard of Russia prospering under these tyrants since the growth of the Byzantine Church in their land. They began to miss their homeland and to desert.

They had respect for Gideon because he certainly was a strong man and a military genius to be able to wield an army that could threaten the Queen of the Seas and its renowned army with makeshift weaponry and loyalty to a cause. However, it was not their cause. They had learned many military skills for the time when they would seek furs and seals for themselves. Their craftiness was not unlike these White men that the Pueblo Nation was fighting. This link would have an impact on the outcome of the war.

Trocadero was very rapid and very secretive about getting the cannon repaired. He had also added three more to his repertoire. A garrison was stationed at a church to the south of Mesa Verde. This locale was a receiving site for strangers of all types of military and church personnel. New weapons were tested here, espionage missions and raids were launched from this site, Gideon reasoned that he could damage the Spanish war effort by destroying this impediment so close to his home. He could not send Ismalia, who began to show the effects of her pregnancy and was ordered to stay in her cave with a midwife both by her man and his towering protector father. She could not lead this raid. El Gato with his troop of youngsters was causing damage to armaments from within. He was spotted from within by a Soldado, who reported the information to Trocadero. A sadistic smile showed on his face, as he planned his strategy. It was a strategy based on the Pueblo thinking that had thrown Spain out of the Pueblo country in the last war.

An army that had marched through the mountains was to approach from the south. It was led by Fiery Water. It was joined by one of Ericio's ships, carrying troops to invade from the northern sector. The ship was to locate itself on the periphery and shell the fort. A back up army, led by Porifirio was to shadow Fiery Water and provide cover if needed. The attack was to take place in two nights.

At the last minute, Gideon decided to join Fiery Water's army to protect his son and father to his grandson or granddaughter. He felt a need to do this because, for the first time in his military life, he felt something in the air. It was something ominous. And ominous it was.

The land Armada launched itself at about 3:00 a.m. The troops found they had attacked an empty fortress, picked clean of ammunition, artillery, and foodstuffs. All that there was to see was a dangling body swinging from a rope on the guard tower, which was the steeple when the structure had a holier purpose. The body was El Gato Gordo. The Comanche that had filed out of the tunnels they had dug were now filing back in and wreaking havoc. On the outside, Porifirio and Fiery Water were engaging an army that had shadowed them, flanked by three cannons, one of which was concentrating on Ericio's ship. The troops had no cover to get out of the ship to join their comrades in the fort. The one saving device for those within the Church was the multiple firing of the several rifles connected together. This allowed the warriors to hold those emerging from the tunnels at bay. Gideon noticed the convergence point of the tunnels in the ceiling. He took a torch from its holder and a bucket of tar that had been left behind, ran out of the building, ascended one of the ladders to the roof. He kept his hands free for climbing by holding the torch with his teeth. When he reached the roof, he found the tunnel opening and poured the tar into it. He then threw the torch in after it. He then went back into the Church, rallied his men until they had established control of the inner fortress and pushed their way out to join the two armies engaged with Trocadero's army at their rear. In the heat of battle, Porifirio slipped away to Ericio's ship, climbed the mast to the crow's nest and began firing harpoons with flaming rags at the long cannon which had them trapped with its shelling. He hit his mark, and the wagon holding the cannon burst into flames but it sent out its ball of death and blew apart the crow's nest bearing the small warrior. Pausing a moment to weep, Ericio joined his troops in leaving the ship to engage their adversaries. The combined number drove off Trocadero's army, but this was no victory, and it was not a draw.

The loss of these two mighty fighters cut Gideon to the quick. One was just a boy who would never grow to be a man. The other would never laugh, scheme, or fight the tyrant or the hypocrite again. Was the cost of recognition as an individual and dignity worth this price? He got his answer in two ways: Ismalia gave birth to an eight and a half-pound, twenty-one inch baby boy; they named him Running Lion. Gideon was bursting with pride, that his line would continue with the way of life that gave its respect to nature and extracted respect from it. The next answer came from the world beyond. A vision of his wife came before him: "Our victory will not be measured on the scale of body counts, possession of territory, or immediate control of population. It will be measured by how one man acts towards another two hundred years from now. Our war was fought for our sons and their sons. Gato Gordo and Porifirio stayed in the battle because they knew what our fight was about. The sons of our grandsons and great-grandsons will realize the fruits of our war. Trocadero won't realize them until he has to make his choice when he meets his God." With that said, she was gone.

Gato Gordo was indeed just a boy, but was that all he was? Gideon was once a boy, a boy that would not learn the wisdom and patience of a man, or, at least, the kind of a man about which he was taught. Perhaps Gideon was wiser than Gato Gordo, for he had known the love of a father before the discipline of life. Perhaps, not having paternal or maternal love, El Gato Gordo was able to create his own kind of love for himself, based on how he saw justice and the real pursuit of Godliness. Porifirio also had learned to survive with this self-actualized kind of love. Maybe this is what Dark Waters' spirit was telling him. As Jesus gave is life to make men holy, Man had to love to make himself free to learn about which way to be holy. Unfortunately, one of the choices Man must make is whether or not that struggle is worth giving up the comforts that go with being His Fathers' son. In the inevitable conflict that emerges, some must die. The towering fighter sadly acknowledged that two of his best warriors were gone because of their spirits as fighters, and that his and many more such spirits would join theirs. Gideon wept for his fallen comrades.

There would be more dead comrades, and there would be the neverending grief for his wife. He knew he'd have to stay active as the commander and could not grieve in public because it would dampen the spirits of the men under him. He also knew he could not surrender because it would mean the enemy had to save its face and wipe them out; the defeats had been humiliating ones for the Spaniards. He remembered the viciousness of the victorious Amhara: The burning of all Falasha literature, the humiliation heaped upon his people by the bands of Sarsa Dengle's rapine motivated soldiers, and the murder of his family. Would being similarly annihilated and dismembered as a people be the fate of these fine warriors? No! No! Not ever! Gideon went to the cave of his son and told him to get out the quiver. For a week he dictated the story of him and Dark Waters, starting with his entrance into the Pueblo village in chains. He dictated the atrocities he had witnessed, the victory over the Spaniards, the humiliation of the rejection by those he had helped become victors, the struggles to establish an independent community and to unite the warriors of the area against a common enemy, and the progression of the war itself. Now no matter what propagandists and face-savers said, someone somewhere would know the truth. Now, he could enjoy a moment of play with Running Lion, his new grandson.

Greedy for bloodlust, Trocadero launched an attack that would draw out all the leadership of the rebellious nations and leave themselves vulnerable to a larger army approaching behind it.

Remembering how his army was forced to leave this battle site naked and embarrassed, the proud Jesuit's son launched an attack on Father Nico's home for the war displaced children. The senseless seeming massacre enraged the entire alliance against Trocadero. The Sound People and Russians attacked his rear approaching army, The Cheyenne ventured South and destroyed the Church/fort and any other camp that the Spanish or their allies could use as a place to retreat. All fifth column or espionage units were evacuated ahead of time. Trocadero was left with a desert in front of him and mountains behind him with two armies struggling for mastery of their peaks. The Long Wagon and Enigma of the East lay in the woods behind what was once Father Nico's farm. A skillful and loyal Russian gunner, named Komarovski manned the Long Wagon. He had a lot of respect for Porifirio and had cultivated a friendship with him. The diminutive spy and fighter came to trust him and taught him to use the weapons of the Long Wagon at the time it had to be repaired. Komarovski learned the intricacies of the weapon while he took part in repairing it. The Cheyenne had completed their scorched earth policy and were met by Gideon's army and Joaquim's, who would converge on Nico's plain, as it was now called and drive the Spaniards South, either into their own men or into the victorious army of the Sound People and Russians. Gideon composed the following note and sent it to Trocadero:

Commander of the Dog Droppings Army:
    Have you extended your holy war against us heathen to children who could not have any intent to do you harm? I promise you that for this act, if our Nation is victorious, your entrails will hang from a cactus.
    You're loving mother,
    The Hyena of Cairo

At first Trocadero felt outrage; then it turned to a cold, unrelenting fear. This man would not make such a statement unless he planned to follow through with it.

Gideon did not want Trocadero to have the satisfaction of claiming he could out fight him by claiming this last victory, and he wanted him to pay for attacking The Padre, as this protector of children was called. Trocadero tried to get out of Nico's Plain by stealth at night; suddenly a fire lightened up the mountain clearing, and Enigma of the East began mercilessly shelling the retreating army. At the other extremity, Komarovski was gunning down the troops that had made it through the flames. Ericio had brought a company of Utes in the hold of his ship that had brought packs of dogs, trained for combat with them. They stationed themselves in the southeastern periphery of the fire and dug a trench. They used the multiple firing rifle packets of the last war and the long cannon that Porifirio had sacrificed his life to take out of the last battle. This canyon was to prevent any escape. The bands of dogs almost sent the Spaniards into their arms. As the rage at the loss of Father Nico was being dissipated, the battle in the South raged.

The snowy world of the White Christmas, welcomed by worldwide Christendom, was not such a welcome sight to these adversaries. The mountains were cold, and bulky attire had to be worn that made movement clumsy. The snowfall had been heavy and damp, impeding the battle to a few feet or miles at a time. Fighting was close and many times hand to hand. During this time, the Kazatski maneuver was well used. Losses on both sides were heavy, as one army slogged against the other. Out of the Southern flank emerged three of the long cannon that shelled the Russians and Sound People from precipices above. Three of the new tanks began to roll toward the warriors into a clearing preceding the mountain passes in which the two armies inched forward. They had been waiting behind the precipices for the cannons to begin firing. At this point both armies were diminished, cold, and battle weary. The Spaniards began to become rejuvenated in their fighting by the new weaponry and to push their enemy into the clearing ahead of them and the waiting tanks. Swooping down from the Northeast and Northwest flanks were two armies: One led by Fiery Water, and the other led by Ismalia, who had chosen to leave Running Lion with a midwife so that she could join her man in battle. Her army began to ascend the precipice to get at least one cannon, while Fiery Water moved on the tanks from behind. Now history intervened on Spain's behalf. England had been under Rome's domination and emerged as a Catholic nation until the time of the Protestant Revolution. Henry VIII had ideas about the right to divorce, and, as a result, she became Protestant State. However, the island of Ireland was settled by a tribe, the Galicians, which had migrated from the western shores of Spain. In addition to not liking a foreign invader forcing their ways on them, strong Catholic roots were established, and Catholic alliances were organized and forged with strong bonds. Spain could count on the bond of this alliance. Thus, a bond was established with Ireland, and a Celtic leader's army joined ranks with Trocadero. His name was Entamor Donovan. What, at this point in time, was indicative of a Pueblo victory, turned into a rout by the appearance of this Irish army. As a result the Pueblo leaders that could muster their armies together were forced to retreat. The army had been smuggled to the area by the same route that Gideon was brought to the Pueblos years ago. An alliance was sought with France, who was becoming interested in the fur trade in the Oregon valley.

Ismalia had ascended the first plateau and taken over the first position of the three cannons when the Celtic army struck behind her husband's army. She directed the cannon fire behind Fiery Waters' troops, but she could not be sure that they were not caught in some of the fire. She also had to either knock out the other two cannons or allow them to continue firing at her husband while he struggled with another army behind him plus the one in front of him which he had attacked to disable the tanks. Part of Joaquim's army had to cut itself off from Gideon and come to the assistance of Fiery Water. The Russians and Sound People had pushed Trocadero's men back sufficiently so that they could engage Entamor's army and free Fiery Waters from the trap for long enough to allow his retreat to a cave from where he could take a stance against the two remaining cannons and return her favor to him. In the end this massive retaliatory effort turned out to be a standoff with many dead on both sides. Only the Pueblos could not tolerate too many more losses.

Trocadero smiled to himself for the first time in months. This battle had cost him, and cost him severely, but the tide had turned. He knew the war was his and it was just a matter of time. The intent of the alliance with Entamor was to forage a unity against British sea power. Religion was only the means of establishing the link. Entamor's only strong principle was to transplant Eire away from the hungry jaws of exploitatory England. Komarovski proved invaluable in negotiating with the Irishman. He had fled Russia because the increasing nationalism was giving the Tsars more and more arbitrary power over the peasantry, from whence he sprang. They negotiated in secret and devised an assassination plot with a small band of Russian and Irish troops. They sneaked into the Spaniard's encampment at night only to slash the throat of an aide. Trocadero had sensed a growing mutinous movement among his soldiers and changed his head quarters. Entamor, not an intriguer by nature, was caught and hanged, but Komarovski escaped to fight again. The remainder of the Irish troops settled in what became British Columbia. Trocadero still wore his smile, but it was a little thinner. Win or lose the war, Gideon was no easy foe. He also remembered the warrior's written warning to him.

The Spaniards were superstitious, as were many people invested in their religion. Gideon commissioned an artist to carve a huge face in the desert sand with huge, gaping eyes and a large open mouth that evoked a combination of terror and a bottomless pity. When Spanish troops were on maneuvers, groups of braves on maneuvers would hide behind cactuses and moan hideously, as if undergoing the tortures of the damned. The conquistadors trembled in fear every time they passed by the face. The conditioning for fear was so complete that when the Pueblos finally did attack, the Spaniards practically ran all the way to the sea. At night Komarovski led one expeditionary force, and Ismalia another one that took the two ridges where the two cannons were raining shells on the Pueblo army. Now all three poured shells on the colonizers. Trocadero had stopped smiling.

The mountain streams began thawing as spring approached; the earth assumed a messy, sloshy consistency. No one wanted to even walk through the bog, yet engage in hand to hand combat in it, but the time for the surprise element to operate was never more opportune. What is known as the Santa Fe Trail stretches from Independence, Mo. into New Mexico. However, it forks and one tine goes into Southern Colorado for a short stretch. This trail was not known in those days. By means of forced marches Trocadero hoped to surprise Mesa Verde. However, Komarovski and Ericio were waiting for them at one end and the three cannons at the other. The advancing army was easy pickings.

The victory felt good, but the victory dance was short lived. For, in the Sound People's camp, a silent night raid resulted in the murder of an entire barracks of Russian and Sound Peoples' troops. Komarovski, who was on guard duty, discovered the Perpetrators in the middle of their acts. He could not get help soon enough to stop the assault, but he did manage to wound Trocadero in his shoulder and thigh. The Russians were now beginning to talk about abandoning the war effort. News of a bitter pogrom at home kept them from abandoning Gideon's cause altogether. A mission in the northern provinces of New Spain, at the mouth of the San Jacinto was hoarding arms for the Spanish soldiers. Ericio, in the uniform of a captured officer posed as Generalissimo Francobar Dengali, and brought back fourteen cannons, thirty two muskets, four hundred rounds of ammunition, and six barrels of whale oil. He left enough explosives and gunpowder to destroy the mission after he had evacuated it and took the men of the garrison prisoner. Trocadero was following Ericio, who stopped off at Mesa Verde to deposit off his goods and prisoners instead of his mountain lair. While he was in this process, Trocadero put his siege apparatus in place. A ring of a large number surrounded the cliff dwelling with its multiple tunnels and compartments. Most of his soldados were in the brush immediately outside the fortification, camouflaged in uniforms that resembled the brush around them. As they discovered openings from the tunnels, they were to stuff burning rags into them. Once the organization of the siege pattern was discerned, the responsibilities for defense were assigned to Joaquim and Fiery Water. They had to hide in trees to avoid detection and to attack via coordinated swinging down from vines while the Spaniards looked for the exit. Learning such maneuvering was complicated and expensive to this army. It also involved several hundreds of men training themselves almost instantaneously to be the first air force in America. It was, in reality, an ingenious way to hold the siegers at bay, but it was short lived. Komarovski was hurrying to bring the multi-weapon Long Wagon into the fray to join Ericio's cannoneers from the inside, shelling the camouflaged Spaniards in the brush. Joaquim and Fiery Water had to time their vine swoops between shellings and hope they could hold back the siege until Komarovski arrived with the wagon. Ismalia launched an attack behind a Ring of Fire set to contain the camouflaged brush men. The defense was valiant, but the defenders were spread out too thin; the fighting was close, deadly, and intense.

The soldiers from the sky had foreseen a long vicious battle and made use of a nighttime ally, the bat. The rampant fear that ran through the Army of the Conquistadors drove them from the safety of the mountain brush. Komarovski arrived with the Long Wagon, and he and Ismalia picked them off as they came into the open. By luck, the day was saved. Yet luck has a way of running out. The besiegers had become entrenched, despite all the efforts made. Breaking the siege had to be a combination of sneaking through smoke clogged tunnels to get food and leading raids against the siege works. The only ship left was Enigma of the East. The Long Wagon frequently raided, but Komarovski had to frequently keep it on the move. Trocadero was always looking for their hideaways. The flying men came down from the trees because smoking the tunnels had lowered the numbers sneaking out.

Despair became a prevalent mood with the siegers so firmly entrenched. Despite the gallantry and ingenuity used in trying to break the strangle hold the Spaniards had on their periphery and, subsequently, the food and water supplies, the Pueblos began to physically show the effects of the deprivation. Morale was at an all-time low. The combined efforts of Ismalia, Fiery Water, and Joaquim could not get through the siege works. The Russians and Sound People were preoccupied by two Spanish armies. Ericio and Komarovski could only make spot raids because Trocadero's soldiers were continuously hounding them looking for their hideaways. The captured cannons were of little use because while attacking the siege works, they also shot at their own men trying to get at them. The gloom was beginning to create a self-fulfilling prophecy.

Gideon was beginning to realize that he had to find a way to cure his own sense of defeatism before he could help his army to manage theirs. He turned to the spirit of his wife for an answer. "I know that you have guided me to come to understand that our victory will be in the hearts of men that value the struggle against oppression for greed covered by the shoddy view of themselves being better than us. I cannot reconcile the surrendering up of the souls of the vital young men with whom I planned, worked, laughed, and ultimately buried." A night owl got his attention and flew to a cave in the nearby mountains. The tall, wiry fighter followed him into the huge cavern. The bird found a roost and stared at the veteran of many battles and spoke with the voices of Dark Waters, Porifirio, Gato Gordo, Watering Ground, Gideon's murdered father, Father Nico. This superimposition of voices called out "Yea, though I walk the valley of the shadow of Death, I shall fear no evil." He dropped to his knees and joined the reverberating voices and finished the prayer. Here was his answer: God provided all; just muster your faith and the courage to face the unknown would follow. It was so simple, yet so complex.

The siege breakers renewed their efforts. They continued to use bats at night and to burn the brush beneath the siege works. Joaquim managed to lead a band of men right up to the base of the scaling ladders and set fire to them while the climbers were ascending. A battering ram was captured and used to damage one of the catapults, to put it out of commission. Suddenly reinforcements appeared in the form of several Apache bands with torches to light their way. They picked off the siege breakers. All that saved them from annihilation was the appearance of the Long Wagon and the Enigma of the East. Joaquim was severely injured in this siege-breaking attempt. He was in a delirium from a fever for several days. A poultice was applied to his head until the fever broke.

# Chapter 8

The siege was severely battered, but it went on. The resistance also went on, but it was also more costly. The mountain men went on fighting, but they had to be incorporated into Fiery Waters' army while Joaquim recovered. The Sound People and the Russians were growing tired of the war and its slaughter. They began to defect and to sneak away from their encampments back to their lands of peace. A unit of Trocadero's soldiers masqueraded as a group interested in helping the escapees find escape routes through the mountains. When they were far away enough from their comrades, the soldiers brought them all together and shot the entire band. Several of Fiery Waters' soldiers posed as deserters and led the Spaniards into a trap. Their corpses were sent to Trocadero's camp in a wagon that was also packed with a wagonload of captured wolves. A note was attached that read, "Greetings, O slayer of children. May your overstuffed ranks provide an excellent dessert for these inhabitants of our mountain forests. At least they have earned their position in our population, not stolen a place." For a while the desertion stopped due to this note that served as a reminder as to why the war was undertaken.

Despite the resumption of the will to fight, Morale was low. The wounding and subsequent debilitation of Joaquim and the growing number of casualties gave a real credence to what the outcome of war usually is. No one likes to think of friendships ending by a body count or numbers diminished by starvation and disease. For this reason, depression and despair began to make marked penetrations into Trocadero's ranks, as well. Soldados began to run back to Mexico; sometimes their numbers equaled the replacements coming from there. A stop had to be put to this practice. One band of deserters crossed the river into Mexico to be met by a band of new recruits going the other way; only they were not new recruits. They were executioners; they shot the deserters, as they crossed the river. Morale did not improve any, but, for the moment, desertions stopped. Instead, many allies, as well as soldados, went over to the other side. The reminders of the goals of the war kept this from occurring on the Pueblo side because they knew they had nowhere else to go, but to struggle for their freedom and integrity to the end. Thus, both armies plodded on in a state of despair and gloom, fighting by the rote memorization of habit.

Gideon had experienced this phenomenon years ago at the defeat at the Hill of the Jews. To keep the despair down, he pushed his men hard. Yet he walked the ranks during lulls in battle, asking about loved ones, reminding them of their proud and free heritages, and time and persistence would drive the tyrant out. He pointed out that mighty Hispania would be plagued with rebellions from within and without until it crumbled into the sea, as the reptilian behemoths had, as Spain herself had done against the tiny island of Britain in 1588. He spoke encouragingly, almost entertainingly to get them to hang on by their eyeteeth because the freedom would come, if not in their generation, perhaps in the next, but it would come.

Needless to say, Gideon had the pulse of his army. Because they had seen his justice to foe and friend alike, because he had stopped them from turning into savage beasts in their victories, they knew that, in the end, mercy and decency would triumph. To go on, they had to blind themselves to the fact that the road to victory is littered with a lot of bloody defeats on the way to it. That one can advance mankind by one's sacrifice of him/herself is noble, but it is also hard to accept. The early Christian martyrs accepted this; yet their position became that of imperial Spain. David accepted this possibility when he went up against Goliath. But time and power corrupted him to focus on his lust for Bathsheba rather on his former moral rectitude. By redirecting this army from bestiality and defeatism, Gideon created a motivation to take up arms again until the dragon of tyranny was slain. Who was there to let other men in his time and into the future know what he had done? Ismalia, Fiery Water, and, much later, Running Lion told the tale. Ismalia had to make a larger quiver to hold all the documentation: But it was passed on.

The sky men continued to swoop down on the Spaniards with fire-brands, harpoons with burning rags, and nests full of bats. The besiegers resisted with cannons and the primitive tanks from Da Vinci's drawings aimed at the trees, on whose vines they swung down. Ground troops led by Ismalia and Fiery Water tried to force their way up behind the siege makers, while Ericio and Kamorovski bombarded them from the east and west flanks. The siege was slowed by these efforts, but it was not stopped. Sharp-eyed Comancheros started watching from which trees the most sky men swung down and they began to cut the vines and branches that yielded the highest numbers. They also unleashed bats-fire on them. Some of the battering rams were turned on trees with a lot of vines or where nests of sky men seemed to be spawned.

Both sides wanted to end the war, but neither wanted to concede to the other. At one point, Trocadero offered Gideon a truce to work out a peace proposal. Gideon's answer was, "Remember, slayer of children, I told you about your entrails. That is the only peace there will ever be between you and me. Besides, you don't view me as your equal, and I would not believe a word you say." That he spoke the truth did not matter to Trocadero, but the blow to his pride to have a non-white address him so, was more than his ego would bear. He hotheadedly acknowledged, "If this sub-human wants more war, war it will be." When he was asked why he couldn't bring himself to talk truce with the son of the Jesuit, he repeated his answer and stated a peace without mutual respect was not a peace, but an abdication of enmity to stop killing. It was an acknowledgment of superiority of the opponent, a one sided acknowledgment that could and, usually, would be taken back once strength was re-established. A sad event occurred that made Gideon wonder if he had decided incorrectly. Joaquim La Rouxe died after a long siege with fever and pneumonia. Gideon wondered if this would be all their fates. In his dreams at night, a confusing blend of Guintera and Dark Waters spoke to him and said, "The road to God is fraught with the cadavers who meant well but let error lead them astray. Couldn't his short sightedness in battle have led him to the wound that killed him?" Then the images separated and his wife said, "Nay, he was a casualty in a war that had to be fought. Weep for your friend and brave soul, but remember why you both fought the war." Joaquim's body was sent up river in a burning canoe for his soul to find new mountain horizons where he could be independent forever. Gone, was a true soldier and a loyal friend. Gideon and Gabriel Fiery Water Retta wept deeply with an inside crying that went on for many months.

In the last battle in the brush before the siege makers, a man that was half Aztec and half Spaniard ran from the heat of battle to board the Enigma of the East. He declared that he wanted no more of the war and offered an assassination plan that he and a company of soldiers had created that would eliminate Trocadero and bring the war to a quick close. He brought plans of the internal layout of the barracks where Trocadero slept, as well as where the munitions and weapons were kept. A captured Cheyenne was to be shot at midnight by a special detachment of guards that wore a uniform of a particular demarcation that showed their special status. He had stolen a box of these uniforms before he left, and Ericio had them aboard his ship. The executioner's helmet had a visor that hid his face from view so that other soldiers could not recognize him. If four men could be smuggled to the gate of the barracks where a tunnel could be dug twenty feet right beneath the barracks door, the entrance would be theirs. Finding Trocadero's bed was just a matter of following the map. He then could be slain and the ammunition dump set afire; the war's end could be brought about. Gideon liked the idea, but he was leery of trusting the captive.

The man's name was Tomas Aguinaldo. Ericio, Fiery Water, a Sound People's chief, Komarovski all met with him, both to interrogate him and to discuss the feasibility of this plan. His father had been a conquistador and his mother had been a laborer in the gold mines. He had a beautiful sister that was sent to Portugal to pay part of his father's debts. He never saw her; her name was Guintera. Gideon blanched at the mention of Guintera's name. Her younger brother stated that the last he had heard about her was about thirty years ago; she was sent to Majorca. The Spaniards had used her name as a threat to make someone join their war. He had never seen his beautiful sister, and both of his parents were dead. He wanted to find her and acquaint himself with her. The others accepted his story. Ericio remained skeptical. Gideon's hand shook as Tomas related his story. He felt he owed this lady from his bitter past so much. Was faith in the truth of her alleged younger brother's story too far-fetched a gamble? The enticement of ending the slaughters that were taking his close companions from him one by one also ran through his mind. He, Ericio, despite his skepticism, Fiery Water, and Komarovski agreed to go. The mission was scheduled for two weeks from that day. Tomas would also join them. He'd be the first shot, if he were lying.

The five men set out for the Spanish fort the night of the assassination attempt. The first task was to confiscate all the useable weapons they could find and put them in their wagon, next they dug their tunnel to the barracks door. Once out of the tunnel they took a length of fusing from the door of the munitions dump to where the gunpowder lay. They left Komarovski there to light the fuse on their way out. Trocadero lay in a room separated from the others. Tomas guarded the other soldiers, making sure other soldiers couldn't interfere. To do this, he had laid lengths of fusing down each aisle. In the event anyone woke up he was to light the length of fusing nearest him. Fiery Water patrolled one side of the building, while Ericio patrolled the opposite side. Gideon was to sneak into the office and slit Trocadero's throat. He was forewarned that he was a very light sleeper and very tricky. Stealthily, Gideon crept up to the bed, dagger in hand. He slashed at a pillow, while Trocadero sprang out of nowhere upon him. By instinct Gideon dodged him and missed the slash at his own throat. He jabbed Trocadero in the shoulder and drew the blade across his chest inflicting a long, deep gash. The Spaniard screamed for help and slashed Gideon across his face and down his neck. Gideon quickly exited through a window and ran to the wagon with Ericio and Fiery Water. Tomas lit the fuse and ran out to join them. As they drove past the munitions dump, Komarovski lit the fuses, ran, and jumped onto the wagon. Trocadero lived, but he received a serious wound that would bear him a scar and a memory of Gideon Retta. They were a distance from the fort when they heard the powder go off. Whether he had set this up with Trocadero was never established, but all else had gone as planned. Tomas never gave any evidence of being a Spanish agent in any subsequent behavior. He became a trusted officer in Gideon's army.

Trocadero had been warned by a sixth sense not to get in his bed right away, but he was not expecting a move as bold as this one from Gideon. With a twinge of conscience, he thought to himself that he might have gone too far in raiding Father Nico's farm and killing the children. A dribble of sweat trickled down his forehead as he thought about Gideon's remark about his entrails. He had referred to this twice. Therefore, he must mean it. He had to win this war to leave New Spain intact with all his parts.

Gideon felt some relief from his depression, but he knew he had to reconcile himself to a moral victory because more and more countries that found that they could profit from trade and exploitation did so with an increasing demand for cheap goods to export because the cost of production was kept down by the use of cheap labor and slaves. Those that were classified into these menial categories were looked down upon to cover the dirt of using another person as an object. As countries grew wealthier by this system, they had more of a stake in maintaining it. As they competed with each other, they became the monolithic structure that differed from others only by its name or special format, such as autocracy, plutocracy, and even republican democracy. This form of monolith was becoming a gigantic creature that required a tireless effort and an endless coffer of wealth dumped into it. Because their wealth had been exploited, it was not available to be used as a war chest. As a result the exploiting colonials had the resources for war, whereas the native populations wealth was depleted.

For this reason and this reason alone, lengthy war would deplete indigenous peoples from enjoying a physical victory, but the justice and decency would be remembered and sung of by the souls of those that lived after the vanquished. A victory that no one can physically see may sound noble, but it is not readily seen by those seeking relief from oppression.

While he was walking through and observing the flora and fauna around him, he saw a pretty dark-haired woman feeding deer. She would stroke and pet them after they ate from her hand. As she turned her face toward him, his mind saw a pretty, young girl of years ago, a pretty lady with whom he feared involvement would destroy his mission to avenge himself against his jailers. He watched her intently and noticed three Apache fighters surround her. He circled around behind one of them and broke his neck. He sneaked behind the second and stabbed him in the chest piercing the heart. The third heard him and lunged at him. Gideon seized the arm and broke it at the elbow. He screamed, and the young lady turned startled from her preoccupation with the deer. She saw the veteran soldier reach for the brave's toma-hawk and plant it in his neck. Gideon stated, "Young lady, we all appreciate nature around us, but it would be good sense to remember we are presently engaged in a war."

The young woman thanked him and introduced herself, as Purple Flower. He did not want to tell her that she looked like his wife when she was a young maiden. Purple Flower startled him when she said, "I know you! you are Gideon Retta, our leader." "Yes, I am he. What makes you take leave of your senses and feed the deer unprotected when enemy soldiers are lurking about these woods. What if I did not happen along and see your plight because I am trained to look for such things." She answered that she would be more careful next time. He walked her back to her parents' home. He asked why she still lived with her parents. Purple Flower tried to hide the tear as she spoke about her man, Tusk of the Boar. He was in Ismalia's army that was scaling the cliff to get the cannons from the Spaniards. He had reached the plateau, only to stop a harpoon that had been aimed at his chest. Undauntedly he pulled the harpoon out and threw a dagger at his assailant and killed him. The blood loss was too great to accommodate this heroic act, and he fell dead on the spot. He left a two-week-old son behind. Gideon sadly caressed her cheek to wipe away the tear. She brushed his hand away and said, "What he did was both gallant and foolish.

Foolish because my son is without a father and gallant because someday we will be free from the White invader's yoke. Rav Retta, we all believe in you, and your war is our war, win or lose."

Gideon did not know how to take these words, and he let a tear trickle down his cheek. She brushed it away with her lips and was gone. He touched the spot and walked back to the now lonely trading post he had loved so dearly and could not approach for months because of the memories. During the next months he would long for, yet fear that kiss. With all the courage he could muster, Gideon could make himself go back to the trading post. He entered the bed that he and Dark Waters had shared and began to envision the loneliness that replaced the warm love that had been there for which he would ache for the rest of his days. He at first thought he was dreaming, as he saw a beautiful apparition enter his room. She shed her raiment and came to his bed. "Dark Waters!" There was no answer but real lips touched his; a real body embraced him and said "I am Purple Flower, the life you saved today is yours." With a wave of fear and guilt, Gideon tried to draw away. "I cannot love you with the memory of my treasure hanging over my soul. Don't you see that?" "Of course I see that! I am not blind or insensitive, but I am a woman and know that no woman that ever loved her man would condemn him to solitude. I know that you can not lead an army with the loneliness eating away at you, as it is. I do not expect us to have a long or eternal love. For I know that odds are against us winning this war. I know that you may not return from battle, but I want us to have this night because you risked your life to save mine." As she caressed him and gave herself to him, there was no more conversation between them. The needs were mutual despite Gideon's grief, guilt, and protestation. In the morning she left and carried her unspoken love with her.

Though Gideon bore a strong attraction for Purple Flower, he knew he could not give in to his vanity because his life belonged to the war. He went so far to tell his son the Falasha burial ritual if he was killed in battle. He told him he wanted to die as the Jew he never was because his faith sprang from this, whether he observed it or not. He wanted to die in battle and be interred in the home for which he had fought. He'd never give it up he also made up his mind that if he was killed he would not let himself die until he took Trocadero with him: For his wife, for the innocent children of Father Nico, for Porifirio, and for Joaquim.

The assault and battering of the siege had stopped one night when the Spaniards were battle weary. Gideon took a company of braves and Russians outside Mesa Verde stole a siege ladder, a catapult, and a cannon. The company made its way to the Spanish fortress and hurled incendiaries onto the barricaded walls. He followed this up with cannon shot. The fortress buckled to the surprise attack, but a combination of new army recruits arrived from the south. Apache bands heard the noise and trapped Gideon's band inside the ravaged fort. Their number was great enough so that they could split into two armies, one attacking from the rear and the other from the front. They captured the siege equipment and turned it on the attackers and shot burning rags into the rear of the fort with harpoon guns. The survivors of the company stole a horse and wagon and fled back to their own camp. Luckily Gideon was among them.

Being unwilling to accept defeat in their retreat, they hid behind a butte and attacked the returning army that attempted to restore the siege armament. They were joined by their flying men and finally broke the siege. Once again the cost of this gallant venture was high. Gideon's depression returned with a vengeance. Only the ministrations of Purple Flower were able to give him some relief. He began to have dreams of marching conquistadors, led by John De Mello laughing at him for fighting a war he was destined to lose; a war in which Porifirio arose to manhood and had it shot from under him, in which innocent babies were slain and an obese, older and braver one was hanged, in which Joaquim, of the free mountain spirit died in a sick bed. All their spirits were led to a shining light by the most beautiful spirit of all, Dark Waters. God pointed an icy stalactite down and said in a voice as icy as the falling stone knife, "Thou art damned. You fell with Redai and brought death upon the Pueblo nation."

The torment and the dreams did not stop. De Mello's laugh turned into the slap he got in the prison. In turn it turned into the slap his father gave him. It turned into the Nazir pointing his finger saying you brought us a pogrom. His finger turned into the icy stalactite that God pointed at him. An image of Elijah Tanndela talking with the church and government officials appeared before him with the knife Gideon had thrown in his neck. He smiled and drew it out. It became the stalactite God pointed at him. Guintera's image appeared before him. She was weeping before him and said, "The love that might have been." Then a final image appeared: Dark Waters holding Guintera's hand with Purple Flower's hand joining them. All three said, "Yea, though I walk through the valley of the shadow of death, I shall fear no evil. For thou art with me; they rod and thy staff they comfort me." Fiery Water joined them with Gideon's father and all five said, "If you save one life, you save humanity." The vision disappeared and Gideon awoke to Purple Flower's arms around him in sleep holding back his pain with her body. Gently he woke her and said, "I cannot love you the way I once loved, but I will do right by you for whatever time on Earth I have left."

Gideon left the safety of the trading post and met with Komarovski, Ericio, Fiery Water, and Ismalia. He also included a chief of the Sound People and the commander of the Russians: "We all know how this war must end. White people will band together because they are of the mind that we are to be used to satisfy their greed and power drives. I do not know why Ericio and your Russians have stood with us, but I and the God of Nature thank you for it. During our last months together, or perhaps, our last months on Earth, we must make Spain's venture in ambition and greed memorable and fearful to the Spaniards. Otherwise, the Spaniards of the world will eat our land up. Because their greed makes acquisition and exploitation attractive, I am guessing the lesson we are sacrificing ourselves to teach, will have to be taught many times. I hope beyond hope that there will be enough of us left to carry on his fight after I am gone. This fateful council all formed a circle and took hands and prayed. Some wept, some said nothing, but their eyes smoldered their rage; some made a quiet, but determined vow. The God of Nature who had told them centuries ago if they loved the Land, the Land would love them heard their prayers that day, as he heard them at Masada, Thermopylae, and much later, at the Warsaw Ghetto.

For the next three days the Long Wagon, the Enigma of the East, and the captured cannons hammered Trocadero's fort. At the siege, soldados burned the trees and the brush to drive out the flying men and the bats while they attempted to rebuild the siege structures. Da Vinci's primitive tanks were once again used in this connection. From the cactus plant, a drug was extracted that made men dreamy and hallucinogenic; it was known as peyote. It was put in the streams outside Spanish fortresses. The young fifth columnists, who well remembered the murder of Father Nico's children and the hanging of Gato Gordo smuggled a gum that could be modified into a paste out of southern colonies of New Spain. It was known as coca gum; it was ground into the maize that the Spaniards ate.

In turn, the enemy had accumulated many rattlesnake and Gila monster corpses. They drained the venom and put it into the irrigation wells outside the village.

In retaliation for the barrage on their own fort, the Spaniards were massing for a frontal assault on Mesa Verde. Ismalia and Fiery Water got advance notice, and, at the periphery of a butte the Spanish army had to negotiate, the Pueblo fighters dug a trench. They filled it full of whale oil and spaced several lengths of fusing at ten-foot intervals for lengths of five hundred yards away from the trench. When the troops descended the butte into the trench, the lengths of fusing were lit. The descended soldiers made an excellent omelet. Gideon led an army up behind the soldados and picked off those lucky enough to be able to retreat. He caught a glimpse of Trocadero on horseback and whirled around to pursue him, only to find him gone. He was reminded of his vow by the incident.

That night Gideon was tired, bone weary, in fact, but headiness seemed to pervade his spirit because this victory was not costly. When Purple Flower came to him, he found himself relishing her charms. She drew him to her and told him his lovemaking was beautiful. Suddenly an assassin sprung through the tunnel and fired an arrow into Gideon's shoulder. The wounded warrior grabbed a dagger with his good hand and hit his would be assailant between the eyes. Losing blood, he collapsed after his successful thrust. Another had been captured at Fiery Water's cave and two more were captured at Ericio's ship and at Komarovski's wagon site. In answer to the obvious question, one of the assassins handed Gideon a packet. In it was the head of one of the flying men, who had been captured while the Spaniards were burning the brush. The men had confessed to being mercenary mountain men, who had infiltrated Joaquim's army. The would-be murderers were not slain.

They were immersed in a wagon of manure for the healing period it took Gideon to heal, had to eat their meals and drink the water they

were allotted in the wagon, and were made to walk back to Trocadero's camp across the desert in their fragrant condition. Gideon attached
a note to the first one:

My Dearest Trocadero,
  To put it mildly your archers stink.
    Your Worst Nightmare

Trocadero was fit to be tied that Gideon still lived. He knew that
the boat and the Long Wagon would, in all probability, be moved.
Gideon, on the other hand, felt relieved. He had come to believe that in
military terms, the victory meant nothing in terms of spirit, the right to
believe in a natural connection between Man and God and to reach for
Him through this connection and not through another's imposition
would pass onto other hands in following generations until it was won;
for perceiving God in one's own way is part of the human condition: A
condition that Imperial Spain did not have a right to dictate to others.
His quarrel with Trocadero came from his killing innocent children.
For this act he would have to pay the way Gideon had told him he
would have to pay.

Gideon sent Purple Flower into Trocadero's camp as a servant to
learn his weak spots as a man. She happened upon a private, or its
equivalent in the Spanish army, who had grown up with Trocadero. He
was envious of his rise to power. His father had been a Jesuit, as had
been Trocadero's. This order of the Catholic Reformation was founded
by an ex-soldier, who fought for his Lord, by the trade he knew. This
started to be the way Christianity was spread, but a system of education and preaching evolved out of it. Before this evolution took place
there were several papal wars in which papal unity was brought into
conflict. The soldier, from whom Purple Flower extracted information,
accused Trocadero's father of being a follower of Savanarola, one of
the Papal heretics, who was hanged. The accusation deeply embarrassed the family and caused the young Emilio to leave Jesuit training
and become a soldier. The man was bitter because this castoff Jesuit,
whom he had surpassed in school, was chosen as his commander after
he, himself, rejected the priesthood as too passive a vocation in this

assertive world. He told her of a liaison with a barmaid in Lisbon, initiated by Trocadero telling three sailors to approach her because he was angered by her spurning him. The lady's rescuer was a tall, Black man, who became involved in a murder.

Purple Flower went to Gideon with this tale without knowing how significant or insignificant it was. When she saw Gideon's reaction, she knew the data was invaluable. He winced when he first heard the tale. His mind went back to that night at the Turtle Shell. He remembered the faces of the three sailors admiring Guintera's slim body and long, muscular legs. A dim memory re-awakened, a remembrance of a puny runt sitting in a corner with a smirk and a bitter look in his eyes. Was this to be the initiation of a fatal relationship, or would there be a peace with God to end it in amiability? A tear entered Gideon's eye, as he thought of Guintera, so recently brought back in his dream. By automatic reflex, Gideon snarled his hatred for this sanctimonious, little cur. He would use the inflated ego of this invader to draw him out.

Two days later, an arrow was shot into Trocadero's camp: The message it contained was written on a piece of bark with a stone attached for weight. It said:

> I have discovered we have a connection out of our pasts. I once engaged three brutes in combat that got one maimed over a lady's honor. These three men were enticed by you to approach her. You enticed them because you were not man enough to successfully carry on your own seduction. Add this to your prideful murder of children. Be assured that you will pay for both of these acts. Your presence on the land, I and those for whom I fight have come to love, is an abomination! An abomination I will end personally.
>
> A son of Moses and The God of Nature

Trocadero did not take this communication lightly. He guessed the identity of the informant and had him executed. He then wrote a reply and sent via a courier that climbed Mesa Verde at night, threw the reply, attached to a rock through the tunnel, and was shot through the neck with an arrow. He was one of the returned assassins.

The message said:

My dearest Pagan's Buttocks,
 Enclosed are the ears of your informant. May your success match his.
 Your Superior in intelligence and battle

After this, the war was not conducted with any restraint at either end. The exception was that Gideon did not kill prisoners unless it was an unavoidable necessity. Though he spoke boldly, Trocadero lived in constant fear. This was in part because he feared retaliation for his racism and greed, as well as exploitation, and, in part, due to the anger that had been generated in this fierce fighting warrior. He reminded him of the Kushitic fighter of old or of the Carthaginian, Hannibal, whom, even mighty Rome feared. He was also troubled with nightmares. At night he saw an image of Gideon shouting, "Where is Abel." He saw himself sending Bathsheba's husband to a battle from which he would not return, out of his own lust. Trocadero sweated profusely through these dreams and awoke with a tic in his eye and tremor in his hand. The last frightening thought he remembered dreaming was, "At what price did we unify our nation? Are we still men, who do these deeds?"

Whatever foul thoughts he had about what he had become, Trocadero knew two things: He could expect no mercy from Gideon Retta, and he could not go back to Spain if he lost this war. Christopher Columbus, the discoverer of the new colonies, had introduced the concept of cruel practices, and once word had spread to the Church publicly, he was brought back to Spain in chains. A Spanish commander, who brought back failure to defeat a pagan culture, could expect no better. Therefore, he began to devise schemes that only desperation could entertain. Likewise Gideon, who knew he was fighting for his life put into practice one harebrained scheme after another. The siegers began to hurl wasps' nests into the village with their catapults. The flymen were, for the most part grounded due to the destruction of the trees; but they crawled on the ground camouflaged to blend with the earth. When they arose close to the siegers, it was with incendiary harpoon guns or arrows with lit dynamite attached. Arrows and atalatls were dipped in poison from Gila monster; and rattlesnakes' venom. Captured cannons and the Long Wagon and Enigma of the East were used to drive the siegers away and to destroy siege equipment. The war was assuming a character of murderous proportions. There was no breakdown of hostile spirit between participants because this war was started with the fundamental that our opponents are not men like us, and we have to wipe them off of the Earth for our own survival. No format for compromise was devised because the underlying motives were not addressed, but hidden in a myth meant to cover a lie. As a result, this war would be a fight to the finish.

In this atmosphere Gideon survived because Purple Flower was there for him. Guilt, remembrance, and consciousness that the base of this feeling was not a communication of love, but of mutual need, always seemed to riddle Gideon.

One day, she seemed to read his thoughts:

"I know you do not love me the way you loved Dark Waters, maybe because of the years between us, or maybe because you rescuing me obligated me to you. But I have come to admire the strong, yet gentle man that you are. I love this in you for as long as we have it. For I know you will not survive to see our people grovel before we rise up again. I want you to understand I will love you from beyond your home with our ancestors, as you continue to love your wife's memory while you try to love me enough not to hurt me. Because the time is right and because of how I feel, I want your son. Come to me now so that you may live on after we are separated by your journey to the land of our ancestors."

She shed her maiden's attire and left his bed a fulfilled woman. She would bear him a beautiful daughter to find her way to love, as Dark Waters and Purple Flower had before her.

# Chapter 9

The war was becoming a series of murderous exploits, as Gideon and Trocadero mounted excursions to eliminate each other. It was a matter of time until one or the other or both killed their leadership. This would be the inevitable end of the war. The direction of their activities seemed to indicate that this is the way they wanted to end it. A Spanish detachment went into the mountains looking for Enigma of the East and the Long Wagon. They toppled over when they found them behind the trees at their rear shooting down these troops. A soldier from this band looked remarkably like Trocadero. He was captured and revealed that the wily commander was employing doubles. He did not know how many or in what units they were located. In exchange for his life, he had to find the others and eliminate them. A spy in the fort would be watching and would eliminate him if he failed to do so. He did not know the identity of this spy or when or where he/she would strike. Under these conditions, he was released. This double actually was a highly placed officer, who was the only double used. He followed a band of Russians to the home of the Sound People and led an attack that devastated their village. Luckily Komarovski was not with them. The damage took them out of the war for, at least a month. Russians were beginning to desert again. Though the enterprise was successful, the double was killed in the battle.

Fiery Water was looking forward to the war ending and returning to the trading post in peaceful coexistence with whoever was left, when he found a disturbing turn of events. He had been away on a hunting trip due to the siege causing a food shortage. Upon his return, he saw horses tethered in front of the cave and sentries in the rear. He discovered his wife and son had been taken prisoner. The Spaniards did not know his identity. Tunneling inside while the soldados slept, he extricated them both and took them to the trading post with his father. He and Gideon returned with a band of men. While he was reconnoitering, he had counted fifty-two men. The horses were confiscated and hidden with the other Pueblo horses. The sleeping soldados were jabbed with poisoned atalatls, and the cave burned to purify it. From then on Fiery Water and his family resided with his father, but they maintained separate quarters for privacy purposes. The old cave was sealed shut. Only the growing quiver was taken out. This time seemed to be a restoration of the olden time when they were a family learning and enjoying the ways of nature. Gideon even began to take Running Lion for walks in the woods, as he had done with Fiery Water years ago; the woods had the same freshness he remembered. Suddenly a tomahawk flew through the air and just missed Running Lion. Instinctively Gideon threw his knife, and a body pitched forward. He wore the markings of an Apache. The man was not yet dead, and Gideon ordered him to be treated. He visited him while he was still recovering. His name was Roaring Bear. Gideon, Komarovski, Fiery Water, and Ericio all were there to interrogate, as was Ismalia. Roaring Bear was expelled from his tribe along with his family for refusal to surrender his oldest daughter to a Spanish officer, who employed their tribe to grow crops and tend their horses. His family lived off of the game of the forest. They wanted to fight against the Spaniards. Gideon asked to meet the rest of the family. Roaring Bear took the party to a cliff where a tent was pitched before a cave. In the tent, Ismalia noticed European boots. She nudged Komarovski, who nudged Fiery Water, who nudged Ericio, who nudged Gideon. Roaring Bear noticed the nudging and was shot as he fled. Then they all opened fire on the tent and shot incendiary arrows into the cave. They fled back to the woods.

When they got back to the trading post, Gideon found Purple Flower waiting. She whispered that the time was right and pulled him into their boudoir. Afterwards she lay snuggled against Gideon and told him that leading an army was good for his manliness and that he would be a father soon. He smiled and drew her to him. "I have my son to live after me and a grandson. Our child will live after us. I knew before you entered my life that we were fighting a lost cause in terms of the here and now. There have been strong women and men on my wife's side but you have a new kind of strength, the strength to with-stand a defeat that is coming and to live with the hope that the future will bring a new dawn in which we can all walk on ground that we love according to God's natural laws. I once felt that I had a mission to fight the Cains to avenge the Abels of the world, but I found that Cains and Abels are within us all. The Pueblos for whom I fought and for whom I am fighting are all within me. I learned this by acquiring the wisdom from my first wife and to carry it on from my second, you. I don't love her the same way I love you, but I love you both." With that they kissed each other tenderly and fell asleep in each other's arms.

Trocadero was disgusted that his last scheme was foiled. This was not a war that would bring him honor. In fact, it had brought him a lot of gray hairs. He did not like admitting that his foe could get out of the traps he devised. With the failure of Roaring Bear's attempt to deliver Gideon into their hands, came a bitterness. However, it was short lived. That Gideon respected people who fought their own way up and that he admired people who valued their own freedom were known facts about him. Such a character was invented by Trocadero and his protégées. The character they created was Alcalde De Bartolome, sai-lor on a Spanish Merchant ship that transported slaves from the North West Coast of Africa. Alcalde became disgusted with the slave trade and sneaked off the ship after freeing the hold of the slaves. He ran to the mountains and built a log cabin for himself in a clearing and began to attract mountain goats to him by feeding the herds as they ambled past his cabin. An already made cabin was transported in pieces by mule to a place in the mountains near to the camp of the Russians and Sound People, who were recovering from the last attack. When the weakened allies had informed Gideon, Alcalde represented his story and the herd brought from a Spanish mission. He said he wanted noth-ing more than to start a goat ranch because he could build a monopoly in an area in which no one had ventured and would hurt no one. Gide-on could not feel comfortable, though his story seemed logical. He had built up a trade with the fur seeking French hunters in the territory of what is now Oregon, as well as some of the intrepid Britisher's that raided the Spanish colonies of the coast of the Pacific. The bold Dutch traders and sailors were interested in the goat meat and cheese that could be obtained. The growing British colonies along the Atlantic seaboard were also potential markets. Had this invented tale been true, a millionaire would have been in the making by his sheer genius and nerve. But he was a creation of Trocadero's to inveigle his way into Gideon's heart and become the instrument of his demise.

Gideon genuinely liked the little farmer, and he also began to like Gideon, who respected his brains and chutzpah. In contrast Ericio did not trust him. He had in his travels about the countryside observed and had noted that the herds of goats were mostly European strains that were common in regions of the Southern Alps and Pyrenees, areas with which he had conducted trade when was a businessman, himself. While observing his travels through the mountains, Tomas Aguinaldo saw him meeting with four or five thuggish appearing men in the cave where the long wagon and Enigma of the East were first hidden.

Drawing as near as he could, he overheard them asking for details about how many people were in the trading post with Gideon and how many and what kinds of weaponry were there. He carried this information to Ericio. A council of the leaders was called to share this information and to develop a counter plot. Tomas was to be an unemployed herder seeking work as a herder in return for room and board. Since he was from a silver mining town in the Andes, allegedly, he invented the name, Juan De La Argentum, as an alias and a code name, through which information was sent to Ericio to Gideon. Gideon's affection for this bright, little plotter was genuine, and he was hurt when the deception was revealed to him. He resolved to let the Entrepreneurial genius live because of his apparent brainpower shown both by the brilliancy of his plot and the skill by which it was acted out. As more and more information was relayed to him, he found himself amused by the antics of deception and discovery. This served to make the war's grinding to its ultimate conclusion less aggravating to his soul. Purple Flower laughed to herself also because the entertainment not only eased her man's depression, but it also enhanced his performance in the war and to bring a new baby into the world. Because of the anxiety, the pregnancy was difficult to achieve. Now it seemed to be ready to come about because of the easing of tension.

None the less, the time arrived to confront the diminutive farmer.

One day Ericio accompanied Tomas with Fiery Water, Ismalia, Komarovski and Gideon to Alcalde's cabin. He seemed surprised at the assemblage of leadership brought before him, and he made preparation for a hasty exit. he also cursed himself for not realizing that a name like Juan De La Argentum had to be contrived. Perhaps, the ego of the imperialist had blinded his perception to the fact that he was dealing with men, who had every bit of the brainpower that he did. Gideon spoke first: "My friend, we have a proposition to offer you." "What may this be," said the man whose name meant mayor in Spanish. With an amused smile on his face, the tall, ebony fighter answered, "Change the focus of your loyalty from Trocadero to us, and you will live to be a prosperous goat farmer with your own goat herd; we have someone watching you and reporting the progress of Trocadero's plot that you tell him, to us. I want you to know that we spare your life because your plan is brilliant to use goat products as a commodity. After the destruction of this war is over, your skills can be used to help my people learn to feed themselves. It will be another way of showing that if you love the land, it will love you."

Gideon knew that he would accept the proposition because anyone that is given a choice between life and death would choose life if he/she were in their right mind. Briefly he remembered a time when he would have preferred death. He remembered his disillusion with mankind for creating cultures based on lies and subjugation and with his own people for whom he had fought and for whom he had killed a perpetrator of an intrigue, only to be blamed for that intrigue. The old Gideon would never have had any conversation with Alcalde, but this purpose was t value life, not to destroy it. Time had come around to show him that he was not Abel's avenger, and that to save one life was to save humanity.

With Alcalde working both sides of the fence with Gideon as a benefactor, Trocadero was led into several traps and started to suspect some sort of treachery. Therefore, he sent his own spy with orders to kill the bogus goat rancher. Tomas spotted the spy and tied him to a team of mules captured from the Spaniards that dragged him back to his leader, while Ismalia led a small band to Valparaiso, on the Pacific coast of Mexico, where they set fire to a troopship about to drop off new troops from Spain. At the same time Ericio attacked a mission near him that had been a site for recruit shipments to Mesa Verde and a base for poisoning arrows and spears. Instead it became a site for attacking the fort commanded by Trocadero. The purpose of these attacks was to goad the Jesuit into open battle to increase the risk of his being slain. The Spaniards decided to use more northern routes to dock their troops. They were met by Sound People and kazatski dancing Russians, who slaughtered them as they disembarked from the ships. The feeling a new Soldado would get by getting kicked backward and shot full of bullets must have felt unusual, to say the least.

Alcalde was a product of his environment until he met Gideon Retta. His sparing the life of the potential assassin in his midst would have marked him as a naive weakling to be used. However, Gideon had trod the roads of battle for a large enough number of years to know how to wield power effectively. Others that did not know him stood in judgment of his decisions, the way gossips are wont to do. Long years in battle had taught him on whom he could rely and to be able to decide this quickly. He felt that his trust should be rewarded with loyalty. In the wake of these mutual resolutions a beautiful friendship grew.

Beautiful as their friendship was, it was to be short lived. In his thirst for vengeance, Trocadero kept raiding the mountains. His men found Alcalde's cabin; subsequently they burned it to the ground with him in it, screaming to his fiery death. Gideon was crushed by this move, especially since Tomas was also a victim of the pyre.

Gideon was aware that Trocadero frequented a particular saloon in the vicinity of what is eastern edge of New Mexico. He had a penchant for a dancing girl, named Sussalita. Gideon dyed his hair red and made a plaster mask from the skull of a Soldado whose corpse was found in the woods. The appropriate mix of herbs was used to affect a Caucasian pigment, and he wore gloves on his hands. He became Francisco Pentajeno, a wealthy ranchero from the Los Angeles area, looking for an evening's companionship. he journeyed to the saloon and flirted with Sussalita until she enticed him to her boudoir. She was shocked when she saw that the color of his body did not match that of his face. He said that he had to do this for security reasons, but he was about to share a military secret with her. He indicated that he had fought for

342

Gideon Retta and was fed up with the self- sacrifice that he demanded of his men. He had made arrangements to flee to the Southern part of the empire. He would not be seen again, but he wanted to avenge himself against Gideon for never recognizing what a sacrifice he had made by giving up the profits of his ranchero to serve as a financier to this rag tag army. He told her the location of the Enigma of the East and that the Long Wagon was right there with it. After a quick night of satisfying the lust, that her part in the intrigue excited in her, as well as his own, Gideon left her with a note to inform commandant Trocadero of this information. He also added that he hoped to encounter her beautiful form again in the future. He hurried back to meet with his council of leaders; for they had much to prepare in a short time.

The plan that had been evolved was that the long wagon and Enigma of the East would be waiting in a grassy plain that lay to the east of Mesa Verde with armies led by Ericio, Komarovski, Fiery Water, and Ismalia hidden in the grass with four long range cannon. Approaching from the rear of the Spanish army would be an army composed of Sound People, Russians, Cheyenne and Ute warriors. Gideon wanted Trocadero to know that he would pay for Alcalde and Tomas. The die had been cast.

Ericio did not realize how territorial he had become. He was violent in his assault on Trocadero's troops at the thought of having his ship attacked; to him it was more than a ship. It was his home: The home, where he settled in to shut out the world. He led a charge around his home. There were mounds of Spanish bodies about Enigma's peripheries. Likewise, Komarovski charged the hordes with his wagon. He had stolen several battering rams from the siegers and a catapult. When the Spaniards were still a long ways off, he set the ram afire and threw it at them with the catapult. Though Gideon led several insane appearing charges to find and engage Trocadero in battle, the crafty Jesuit never openly showed himself. The Sound People, Russians, and Cheyenne/Ute army were preventing escape from the rear, while Fiery Waters and Ismalia's armies pounded the East and West flanks and rained cannon shells on the invaders from across the sea. It seemed that the war would end this day. Suddenly a herd of buffalo, deer, several prides of lions appeared from the North with flames behind them. The fire and the stampede caused the defenders that were on the offense to have to flee and allowed the invaders the option of retreating themselves or pursuing their attackers. They chose to pursue, and at this time, Gideon and Trocadero met in hand to hand combat. Gideon's horse's hoof hit a root and threw him. Trocadero, seeing this, charged him, sword in hand. Gideon picked up a fallen atalatl and threw it into his foe's shoulder. Trocadero fell from his steed and charged Gideon with his sword, striking a glancing blow to his chest. Gideon fell to the earth and rolled down a hill. Trocadero advanced on him but was stopped by a dagger thrown into his thigh. By this time men on either side pulled them away from the battle so that they would both live to fight another day. Their parting words to one another were "Next time. Next time!"

While they both healed, their hatreds flowered with each pain, but a grudging respect was beginning to emerge: Respect for courage, skill in battle, respect for the ability to make a commitment. Yet the thought persisted that one had to destroy the other. This was not the time or place for mutual admiration. Did their encounter act to soften the impact of war? Only time and eternity would measure this. Their earthly tasks were defined. There could be no quarter between them.

Where do we draw the line at what is others to dictate and ours to live? The causes of this war were rooted in decency and justice and respect for individual integrity versus the right to impose our ways on others. However, wars, as well as any other instrumentation, designed by Man, meets needs then assumes a meaning independent of the means for which it was designed. At this point, the man becomes the tool, and right then, the tool rules by a power that seems to be its own. This self assumed power is power that deluded Man may be creating to promote the covering up of ugly motives. I have gone at length to explain how the Imperial Spains of the world have created false images to motivate themselves to do wrong to another for gain. The other side is how does a righteous sufferer become twisted in this same bizarre pattern of thought. Releases of pent up anger at an oppressor feel good. Hence, there is a penchant to repeat these releases. The penchant grows into almost an addiction, once the natural inhibition is removed by sanction. Gideon sensed this himself when he feared returning to war would reawaken his addiction to kill and that his wife and son would pick up this addiction with no one to help deprogram them, as he had had to learn to struggle with it to become his own de-programmer.

Because he was in the throes of his kill addiction, Gideon would not let go of his thirst for Trocadero's blood. The original cause and the causative injustices were there as initial causes, but the impetus was maintained by the addictive like force. In such a way, instrumentalities that are built by Man to ease His way become more powerful than their designer and run a course independent of Him. It happens because we let it happen or because we subtly create it to happen unaware of our unconscious plans. At any rate Gideon sensed that the aims of the war had become obscured behind the release of the inhibition on killing. He also sensed that neither he nor Trocadero would be around to either witness or be victim of the spoils of war. They were too fanatical in prosecuting the individual war between themselves. The emotional conflict between them became a motivating force in maintaining the status quo that brought a sense of balance and comfort within each one. This is the most baneful effect of warring, and the very one that must be targeted in de-programming. Mankind has been warring from before the inquisition and still has not resolved this issue.

The age old problem of addiction to war and de-programming from it will probably always be with us, but the cultural imperatives that give norms power beyond mutual protection and allowing compromise between differing peoples to be able to live together create a self destructive state of affairs. The ability to adapt and allow for each other's separate existence within a larger mutual framework is as evolutionary a function as development of a flexible thumb. But it encompasses an awareness of the defenses we use and the lies we tell ourselves to maintain the status quo to keep getting the benefits we get from it, despite the inevitability of destruction by pursuing the same path. When the Christ told his Disciples to "love one another as I have loved you" he did not mean to keep it confined to one cultural group. However, to step beyond this is risky because it involves a blind faith in a supreme being who cannot share complete knowledge with us because we are

345

less perfect than He and cannot absorb it all, but can do so in increasing doses if we open ourselves to this absorption process.

Gideon and Trocadero could not back off of their positions in the power spectrum because both their individual egos and the societal egos would not let them. Thus, they were committed to pursuing their courses of action to the bitter end, with one side receiving an earthly victory and the other undermining it to achieve its own justice and recognition. As a result, Trocadero continued to scheme about how to depose this infidel from blocking righteous United Christian Spain from achieving its God supported destiny, while, Gideon Retta, focused his energies on pushing the importunate invader back where he belonged, if, not in his time, in his son's or grandson's. The violence and bloodshed was not finished between the two adversaries. Their evolutionary developments had stopped at being their fathers' sons.

Neither Gideon nor Trocadero wanted to go beyond questioning the cultural imperatives that drove them to the war. Perhaps the change would be too damaging to the balance that their nervous systems had achieved with nature. The result was that both slunk back to their cubbyholes to heal their wounds and to plot. A waiting period ensued during which each healed from wounds that were close to being fatal. As this healing took place, the two fighters had time on their hands, and the minds of each smoldered with remembrances of injustices and evils of the other. Given the immutability of both combatants, each began to look for excuses to return to the field of battle. That the tide of the fray could be easily turned and that victory could be easily turned aside was forgotten in the thirst of their blood lust. Battle was the only sedative that could assuage their angers. Gideon did not stop to remember that it was Nature that had stepped in to snatch a victory from him, the nature that was synonymous with loving the land to reach God. Trocadero also forgot tat the God that saved him from a slaughter by sending a fire and a stampede did not provide the foresight on how to turn this into a victory. He did not think that if he would have followed the animals, he could have routed Gideon's composite army. Nor did either consider that they both survived the murderous fighting because this was what God wanted. Was there a lesson here?

The wounding of egos beyond the viewable physical maiming of war was put on hold by the development of a renewed capacity to love as Purple Flower's pregnancy grew. The couple enjoyed walks in the forest or just sitting on a rock looking at the beautiful world around them. It was a beautiful time to be alive; even in the enemy camp; Trocadero couldn't help but notice the opening up of flowers and the greening of the forests. He longed to be at home with his wife and children in his beloved Hispania and began to leave the security of the fortress to enjoy the feminine pulchritude in the village. For both adversaries this interlude of passive appreciation of the world they were tearing apart for their respective goals was occurring. It certainly raised the question of whether or not these goals were worth the violence and the upheavals.

As Caesar's Gallic wars continued, this one renewed itself; for it had been allowed to assume a life of its own. The reawakening came simultaneously to both camps: A lone Soldado on a patrol encountered a Pueblo maiden picking flowers in the woods and decided to avail himself of her. A nearby warrior heard her screams and slew the assailant. An attractive young lady that took Trocadero's fancy arranged to be invited to his quarters. After exhausting him by demanding lovemaking, she tried to plunge a knife in him, but just missed, as he quickly moved. Between clenched teeth, he snarled, "Now for you, my love!" He then smothered her with a pillow. The interlude was over; there would be periods of plotting and counter plotting, then the slaughter would resume. The price would go up: More bodies would cover the mountains or the desert; more strategic leaders would be slain; more tears would be shed.

A series of terrorist attacks were launched to bring Trocadero into an open fight. First the fort was raided at night, and the horses were stampeded by a fire causing damage tot he barracks where the soldiers slept. Next herbs that caused diarrhea were put into the drinking water by spies planted among the peon laborers. While suffering the effects of the weakness caused by the chemicals, the warriors struck. The soldados were slaughtered and the munitions dump burned. Infuriated by this humiliation, Trocadero led a retaliatory army. However, it was not the picnic Gideon had planned because this army was followed by Da

Vinci tanks and cannons that stayed far enough behind to not be seen and to be able to attack any army waiting for them. Komarovski and Ericio were also waiting in the wings, but the artillery launched against them was too massive and attacked too suddenly.

The battle raged for three days: Three days of pure hell for both sides, but more severe for Gideon because he had let himself get caught undermanned. An army of Sound People and Russians provided backup, so that a retreat could take place.

Gideon returned from battle tired to the bone, saddened beyond tears, and trying to maintain a brave front in the face of imminent defeat. He recognized a difference between what he endured years ago after the defeat of Redai and what Redai had endured. Redai had to carry the defeat on his shoulders so that suffering could be minimized to the others. Gideon carried only his sense of loss and emptiness. Now Gideon had to serve Redai's function; He was the commander: It fell to him to comfort widows and orphans. There was no Father Nico anymore. He had to implant memories of gallant war deeds in younger brothers and sisters left behind. He also had to pass on belief in a war so that others would take it up after he was gone. Only now he was beginning to question the merits. Other Whites were beginning to take the banner that Spain took later. They would mouth the same self lies and justify stepping on someone else with the same trashy explanation of inferiority of pagan, primitive belief systems. Wearily, the old fighter reconciled himself to the fact that this battle would have to be fought many times before mankind grew up enough to accept each other. To give meaning to his people's struggle to throw out an oppressor, Gideon had to continue to believe in what he knew what he would never see. He had fought for three days straight and slept for two days straight to recover. Would the outcome be worth all of this pain?

Gideon tried a reversal of Trocadero's Mo.'s. At night he and his men stole the siege equipment and set it up outside his fortress. His soldados tried to sleep through catapulting fire and explosives, some of which hit the replenished or attempting to be replenished ammo dump followed by catapulting containers of gila monsters and rattle snakes over the walls to smash on the ground and release their venomous denizens. They also catapulted crates of bananas infested with tarantula spiders and some Black Widows. The Spaniards were not locked inside the fort but came running out to be met by the long wagon and archers firing arrows laced with poison. Trocadero knew that Gideon would be looking for him. Therefore, he hid in a hay wagon and slowly inched his way out of the fort and turned to the south where he could meet the oncoming recruits and lead them to a smashing victory over the siegers.

His effort was greatly helped by an approaching sandstorm. Once again the routers were routed. Gideon was too buried in a sand dune to be found.

The sand of the dune was packed around him by the air pressure from the wind; what drove him to dig himself out was the claustrophobic feeling of being trapped. Once out of the dune, an image appeared before him. It was Dark Waters. An aura and a glow was about her. "I am wholly with God, but I came to you to tell you that you will be blessed for two reasons: You have sustained the spiritual lives of us all by finding another and bringing a new life into your world. I can now let you go. We will be together soon in God's house for this. The second task for which you are blessed is that you maintained the holiness of our cause in your soul, despite the ugliness and brutality of war. Man was created by God to learn to master the Earth to work his way back to Paradise. he was not designed as a monolithic tool for someone to use to circumvent the path we must all find on our own. You have done well, my Love." Then she vanished.

# Chapter 10

Gideon carried a remnant of shame back to the war with him. He knew what had to be done; he just didn't like the pleasure, the thought of killing another human being gave him. Then he thought of his wife that was gone and of Father Nico, and the shameful pleasure and rage returned enough to set his course until it was over, one way or another. Gideon felt the gentle presence of his son in contrast to this being that let warfare become an addiction. More and more, he began to turn to Fiery Water as a guide or a mentor to remind himself of the gentle side of his nature that Dark Waters had elicited from him. He feared going before his maker as a luster of death, a warmonger. Then he stopped the depressive chain of thought; in spite of his violent penchant, he did not kill senselessly or viciously. He had spared life where he could. He was, after all, prosecuting a war and could only be so gentle. His son would live behind him and could testify to God that he was more good than bad. He was a fighter and had to dispense with elements of conscience if he was to lead men into battle.

More and more this war was becoming a game of cat and mouse. Each antagonist would try to lure the other into open battle under adverse conditions to increase the losses of his foe. Where adversities did not exist, they were created. Trocadero used his catapults to hurl wasps' nests into Mesa Verde and placed them into the outlets of the tunnels on the outer perimeter. when the warriors ran out, his soldados picked them off like flies. Trocadero tried to use the remains of Alcalde's farm and Tomas's cabin as outposts to locate the new sites for the Long Wagon and Enigma of the East. Ericio and Komarovski used dynamite to rain an avalanche down on them. Each side was afraid of exposing itself to the ravages of the other.

While on one of his raids to the Spaniard's camps, Gideon found a book called "Macbeth". Since it was written in English, he brought it to Ericio, who was more worldly than most of his troops, due to his travels as a sailor. Upon piecing together a translation, a passage of military interest was found: "A forest had come to Dunsinane." In this passage MacDuff's troops attacked Mac Beth's fortress disguised as trees near Trocadero's camp in the mountains lay a valley between two cliffs. If one end could be closed off by troops, covered by branches to look like trees, they could trap an army within this self-made cul-de-sac.

Spies that had infiltrated the village around Trocadero's camp spread a rumor that a cave in one of these cliffs could be a point from which attacks could be launched against the braves' fortifications in the mountains. "A guide" led them to the two cliffs. Atop each cliff were two armies, one led by Fiery Water, and one led by Ericio. From the forest around the cliffs, moved in Komarovski and the Long Wagon followed by cannoneers. Trocadero's army was wiped out.

Gideon was not the only one capable of devising intricate schemes of battle. A spy had gotten into the village, connected several hoses together to where the ammunition was, buried them beneath the dirt and run them through an upper kivas to the outside. He attached the end to a container of whale oil and ignited a pile of rags in front of the ammunition dump where the oil had flowed through the hose. After he lit the hose, this infiltrator ran and disappeared into history. While the conflagration raged, a siege was launched, and several soldados penetrated before Komarovski and Ericio broke it up with Enigma and the Long Wagon. The soldados that had entered the village began to express their feelings of ego by sexually harassing the womenfolk of the village. The warriors were so enraged that they captured them all, tied them to a wagon yoke, and sent them back to their fort, pulling the wagon across the desert without water. Despite the breaking of the siege and the capture of the penetrators, considerable damage was done to the village.

The soldiers tied to the wagon made their way with extreme difficulty, as far as the first sand dune, where one of them managed to extradite himself from the bonds and freed the others. They opened up a cactus and took the water from it. They set up a station from which fresh rested troops could be relayed to front lines. This provided the Spaniards with the advantage of not using exhausted troops in battle. It may have been the advantage that brought them victory, victory they little deserved by any moral standards. The basis of starting this relay station was not that it was a logical battle strategy, but a way to avenge themselves for being held accountable for atrocious behavior by someone who was not their equal. Ultimately the victory would belong to whoever could muster the most firepower.

Though Komarovski and Ericio pounded at the relay stop, they could do little damage to a cave cut into a mountain and protected by the Da Vinci tanks, which had been streamlined so that the shields were laid on the frame like plates rather than standing upright and obscuring the vision of the gunner. Gideon hoped to negate the modernization of the tanks via an adaptation of an ancient weapon: David, of biblical times, slew Goliath with a sling shot; why could not young saplings grown in pots and carried in wagons be used to fire boulders and other projectiles at the tanks. Flaming atalatls or harpoons, cannon balls, or poison arrows were some of the possibilities that could be employed. The disadvantage to this weapon was that it was easily found by a long-range cannon unless it could be skillfully camouflaged.

A partial answer to this dilemma was to use this catapult only in forested areas. Another solution was to create a wagon train, by which other wagons bearing long-range cannon surrounded the catapult wagon and fired on the counterpart guns of the enemy. This was attempted with a surprising amount of success in reducing the threat of the tanks. The new rains of projectiles from the air forced the enemy troops to huddle closer together and left them vulnerable to the Long Wagon with its multiple muskets bound together. The men of the relay station protected themselves further from such attacks by digging a trench around the cliff filled with oil that could be ignited by torches kept nearby. The relay station proved to be a formidable bit of strategy: The distance to Mesa Verde was short and troops could be replaced before battle fatigue or great reduction in numbers could turn the tide of battle.

The task fell to Gideon's forces to either disarm this battle instrument or to destroy it. The cave was the target of many raids and seemed to withstand all of them. Draining the cactus plants in the periphery of the cliff led to the discovery of an underground river that surfaced in juxtaposition to the cave through a grotto hidden by rocks and layers of packed sand. The river was not too far beneath the surface. It seemed to disappear in a canyon that was once a riverbed. A little digging traced it to the grotto from what was the far bank. Several canoes of dynamite with long fuses were floated into the antrim to the cave. When the fuses were lit, the cave was buried by the ensuing avalanche, and the relay station was no more. A positive by product was that a new source of water was discovered to make the desert bloom. The grotto at the other end was sealed. In destroying the relay cave, a nearly fatal accident occurred. Gideon was thrown from his horse just before the cave was blasted shut. A boulder had to be pried off of his leg and had crushed his ankle. The condition was worsened by an inflammation. The ankle became swollen, and Gideon was the worst patient in the universe. He howled, demanded round the clock attention, and barked commands at the one who loved him the most. Purple Flower became so outraged at his behavior that she poured scalding hot water on his genitalia in return for his demand for an immediate serving of a warm drink. "If your demands to me get hot, mine can get hotter!" she replied in anger. Later, he took her hand in his and voiced his realization that he was being unbearable. She kissed him like a petulant child and hugged him to her. They shyly smiled at one another and ended their fight. He had to endure two weeks of this healing, but the yelling and demands stopped.

Gideon was unbearable because the conditions of his life were precarious. He did not know when an assassination attempt would be made, whether a stray bullet would find him, or whether Trocadero would beat him in battle. He had tried to prevent the blast by attacking him, by goading him to attack, by seeking him out on the battlefield. Still the war and the strategy of constantly being cagier than his adversary seemed to endlessly drag on. The wily Spaniard was also growing weary of this chess·game and wanted to end the hostilities and go home. However, neither side wanted to acknowledge the humanity of his opponent, be it good or bad. The deadlock would remain as long as each was able to fight.

The tender ministrations of Purple Flower and the time to enjoy his son and grandson took some of the sting away. He enjoyed their talks about their plans after the war or about their explanations of the constellation in the sky. He even enjoyed Running Lion's endless stream of questions about the world of nature. On this particular day, Running Lion had found a beautiful blue stone. It was a clear stone, and it made objects bigger than they were. Running Lion did not resist being picked up and sat down on his grandfather's lap because he knew an interesting story would follow: "Out of the early days of our people comes the story of Big Eye, the giant killer. He was a small boy from a poor mother in hilly, rough land that was hard to farm; here were many rocks because the Earth God stumbled there and got his foot caught in a rabbit hole and had to work very hard to pry it loose. Big Eye picked up a pretty blue stone, just like the one you found. When he held to his eye and looked at a snake or an ant, the image was much bigger than the snake or the ant. He kept this stone because it was special. A tribe of one-eyed Giants occupied the land next to Big Eye's tribe. They did not have enough water and liked the taste of the "Little Ones" as they called Big Eye's people. They were always afraid the giants would raid them to empty their wells and to pick up a snack. On one of these snack days, a giant picked Big Eyes and drooled over him. He told his tiny victim that he'd make a nice sandwich with rice and cactus sauce. At this point, Big Eyes turned to him and said, "I bet my father can beat up your father!" The giant said he could do no such thing. Big Eyes said he could because he had a magic stone that made him grow. In fact, he saw one of the stones right now and could get it and show him. when the giant released him, Big Eyes picked up a huge thorn, which the giant could not see while he got the magic stone.

The giant picked up Big Eyes, the thorn, and the stone. When the giant looked through the stone Big Eyes, grew to about ten times his normal size. The huge behemoth became frightened and dropped Big Eyes, but not before the little fella jabbed him in the eye with the thorn. The giant experienced a fuzzy vision and split his head open on a rock as he stumbled."

One day Running Lion asked his grand father why they were fighting the White Man. he said because they did not come and respect the Land by putting some of themselves into it then say where they gave of themselves was theirs. Instead they came and took Land that the tribes had blessed by giving of themselves to it then claiming it. Furthermore, they acted as if the Land they stole was theirs through their God's giving it to them. The youth asked if all white men were described as he thought fully, Gideon stated that he hoped that there were some who were different but he hadn't seen them yet. The sadness and futility of battle began to fill him again. He had already broken normative taboos. He did not understand what this war could teach human beings. Perhaps the value lay in the fact that Dark Waters, Watering Ground, and so many others were lost due to this skirmish, and he did not want his dear ones to have died in vain. The boy could see that the grand father he admired so much had trouble convincing himself that what he once had felt he did not feel now, at least not with the same intensity, as then.

On one occasion, Gideon was on a footpath he had not seen before. It led to a wider road that led to a riverbed. At the shoreline, he saw flat tailed beavers building a dam to trap water for their community. A school of otters also had their eyes on the dam site. They began to swim playfully with the beavers to coax them over to where they were. All of a sudden, one beaver carried his branches over to where the otters were. The otters nearest him helped him move the branches to their site. The other beavers and otters noticed that they could control more of the river if they controlled it together. he also noted that when gathering branches and twigs on the shore the otter/beaver teams lined up in a vee shaped line and pushed everything into one pile. Gideon knew there was something to be learned from this, but he could not see what it was. One of the otters wanted to build his own estate at a point nearer to the leeward shore. The beavers and otters formed a vee around the otter and literally forced him back on the path they wanted him to take. Gideon recalled reading of the Roman phalanx, a marching vee that stopped for nothing in its path. he also recalled that he had found people in the villages that felt the same way about the Spaniards that the Pueblos did. Perhaps they could be recruited to join in their battle the way the beavers and otters united. Several villages were in the perimeter of the troopship landing sites. As the troops were marching to their campsites, recruits were being trained in marching with shields and spears overlapping in the vee formation. Soon they had perfected the technique and were impeding the troop movements of the Spaniards to the extent that there was beginning to be a feeling that the war could be turned around.

When the new maneuver was taught to the Sound People and Russians, the kazatski motion was added. Trocadero's soldiers did not have any conception of how to cope with these styles. They were being slaughtered right off of the troop ships. Trocadero realized he'd have to come up with a pretty powerful weapon to keep the tide of the war on his side. Trocadero went back to the writings of Leonardo Da Vinci, Galileo, and an earlier Moslem mathematician, named Alhazen. They had done work in the sciences of optics and astronomy. Of interest to him was the phenomenon of light and heat refraction and reflection. A concave lens would bend light waves outward, increasing the light and, subsequently, the heat sent to a given area by the sun. If this intensified light could be brought to a focus at a spot on the ground, Trocadero reasoned, it would heat up the spot where it was focused. A convex lens would be used to bring the divergent light rays from the concave lens together. They could connect by a cylinder, open at either end and placed within a circle, whose position could be positioned to vary the angle. Cylindrical tubes were available from Galileo's experiments. If explosives could be buried at marked points, this instrument could be used to ignite them. (There was an error in thought in this thinking here. Diverging light rays does not, to my knowledge, increase their magnitude.

However, directing light to a focus also brings heat to same site). At any rate, Trocadero had found a way to neutralize the effect of the Roman phalanx. The only defense that Gideon had against this device was to deploy either the Long Wagon or Enigma of the East against it, but he had to be able to surmise the site at which it would be used ahead of time. He also had to learn to decipher Trocadero's marking code to detect the minefields, as they came to be called in later wars. The renaissance age had caught up with the Pueblo Army, and they did not have the wealth to bring its advances to them. The native ability was there; as evidenced by their ingenious use of what was available to keep Spain at bay as long as they had. As has occurred through many wars in the history, the side with the resources prevailed, but a war that is won, but which leaves an unjustly treated minority is not quite a finished war.

The appeal to the masses that were trampled upon in the Spanish strongholds restimulated the sabotage activities in the forts and villages, but it also evoked out and out rebellions. A raiding party, composed of people forced to labor in mines, spend long hours tilling soil for crops they did not eat, women and children sexually abused by the invaders joined the phalanx of warriors. They sneaked along the cliffs above the marching Vee and located the refractor, angled toward the sun. Several of the ladies, having been ravaged by the soldados, sauntered by the guards, while another band attacked them from behind. The weapon was seized and hidden in the village for use by Gideon's men.

# Chapter 11

Mark and Kiona were beginning a depression. All their latest work pointed to Gideon's defeat at the hands of the takers of the world. The moral victory that brought their parents together, sharing a business venture and the cooperative system they had initiated in Mexico all seemed obscure to them. Perhaps they needed to revisit some of what they had accomplished and could accomplish to establish what is and what isn't a victory, as their Ethiopian forebear had to establish.

For this reason, they were eager to accept Grady's invitation to join him and Ruthie on a vacation/business trip to Yucatan and Mexico. Aaron and the rest of the group had been riding them about taking a vacation and replenishing their commitment to each other and the project. A mental note they had made with each other was to decide how they would implement Kiona's project and when they would do it.

Articulata was approaching one year old. She was a little chatterbox and was learning the verbal skills that were to drive her parents crazy for the rest of their lives. They knew they would have to take her with them because neither could stand to be anywhere without her. Mark had a memory flashback to a restaurant in Chichen Itza and called his daughter, Snoopy, playfully. He remembered dancing a little old lady around the room to the tune of Snoopy and the Red Baron. That seemed like about a million years ago. He smiled at the memory. Kiona looked at him; wondering what he was smiling about. He told her about his recollection, and she smiled fondly. For this, their first evening alone together. In a gesture of sentimentality, she took his hand and led him upstairs to her jewelry box and showed him the stone she had found in front of her tent in the silver surround with the inscription on it. He said, "Listen, I know your ways. That's just an excuse to get me in bed." Kiona smiled and told him she didn't need any excuse and pulled him down to her.

Grady and Ruthena were all excited about seeing the baby, as well as Mark and Kiona. They also wanted to share their adventures with them and wanted to get to know Jiminez Bartomas. He was very touched by two events, as per Jiminez. The first was the courage with which Mark protected his daughter from a jealous racist. As courageous as he had been in his youth, Grady doubted if he would've charged a knife wielding mad man with a blowtorch, as Mark had done. He also admired the way Kiona and he had dealt with the prejudice and anger the village residents had shown for challenging their legends in pursuit of truth. Grady also, thought that they had shown a stroke of genius in making the villagers a part of the truth seeking team. Both of these memorable events would have repercussions during this visit.

Jiminez greeted his old and new friends warmly. He related to them in an excited, yet apprehensive manner. He advised them that the Mexican government was going through an isolationist phase because several American tourists had been vacationing in the Cancun area and caused problems. They had had affairs with local womenfolk, and the families were irate and put marijuana in the tire rims of their cars. They then informed the border guards that they were smuggling drugs out of the country. The Americans were detained with a great deal of furor before they were allowed to go home. One of the primary agitators was the man with whom Mark had encountered the incident with the blowtorch years ago. His name was Fulviemo La Marca. He had been released from prison, due to serving his sentence; he was re-incarcerated as a political agitator and was operating a clandestine movement from within the prison. Jiminez told Mark that La Marca was very vocal and very respected in the community. He added that neutralizing his influence was an integral part of reversing the current isolationist policy and allowing their agency to conduct tours. The four Americans had their work cut out for them.

Upon returning to their campsite, they found deserted huts and memories that this was once a bustling camp where an ancient language was pieced together, where adversity of cultures mixed and found each other. Now all their memories were overgrown with weeds.

In four short years, the creativity of learning had returned to the indifferent remains of the site where a culture had flourished. Was this what Man struggled to leave behind him? Was this the purpose of Gideon Retta's battle to be recognized, as a human being, equal to others who earned their own way? Do people fight for their own history, just to throw it away? Both Kiona and Mark had tears in their eyes. Grady sensed the pain in the youngsters' eyes (At least to him, they were youngsters,) and told them that we do not always understand what God's plan for Man is. It would take time and effort to be able to piece it together and to rebuild what had been destroyed. He suggested that the four of them enjoy what there was to see in Chichen Itza. They went to the restaurant where Mark and Kiona had fallen in love.

Surprisingly, they were met by Jiminez. He had acknowledged that the world they had come to know and love had been abandoned. In its place was the idea the Nord Americanos only viewed Latins as peasants, whose women were subject to their wants, who derived their livings by providing drugs, sex, or other accommodations to their base natures. Jiminez knew that this was not true of all Americans by what he had experienced, but those that had not witnessed what he and Mark and Kiona had shared with each other judged by their own experiences and by what was said about them. Fulvielmo had an organization in the community that preyed on public weaknesses by providing a drug market to bring drugs into the community and to bring money-making jobs with this market. The income from honoring their heritage was dismissed as small potatoes and North American apologetic for creating a culture of illegal aliens by their greed for cheap labor, then making them victims of their immigration laws. From jail, Fulvielmo waged his propaganda via national television and via the leaflets he printed and had distributed by his organization. Now they all knew what they were up against. All that remained for them to do was to develop a counter machine to Fulvielmo's machine.

The five of them met with those few people who had remained at the old campsite. They met to plan their counter offensive. Those that had remained would provide drug education materials to the families that they obtained from the government and distribute them to the adolescents the way Fulvielmo's organization did. American drug agencies would also be contracted in Washington DC and Texas to provide information. Jiminez would contact his governmental connections to bring drug programs and motivational speakers into the community to meet with parents and students in the schools and churches. The church would be involved in the meetings with them and direct sermons toward remembering their heritage and rebuilding the tourist industry. Kiona and Mark would be available speakers and to help with site restoration. Grady and Ruth would help the public understand the benefits of creating the program for the businessmen and work with Jiminez to get government backing for the project. They had a month to turn a degeneration that took place over four years into a success.

In addition, Mark and Kiona elected to handle a counter propaganda move to discredit Fulvielmo. This meant that his drug sources would have to be found and the structure of his organization would have to be defined. Unknown to them this carried an unknown danger.

To carry out this last function, this couple needed assistance from friends. Julio and Helga came down a couple weekends to talk to the kids about drugs and to inform them about how to get a clear message of no across to the pushers. (This involved using the same terror tactics against the pushers that they used). Reed and Michelle, as well as Ron and Amy and Rachel offered to provide some of the counseling via medical rotations through the medical school at Guadalajara or by donating time from existing medical practices. Yusseff and Arne also provided company for Articulata, which made her visible to the community, including Fulvielmo's drug pushers. The pushers were toughs from the community where Fulvielmo had grown up. On a visit to the prison where he was incarcerated, one of these youths relayed this information to his superior. Fulvielmo reconnected himself with his hatred and anger towards Mark and chose to take his revenge through Articulata. Together they devised a kidnapping scheme.

Articulata was induced to talk about herself by a young lady, who saw her strolling with her mother in the park with some other young mothers. After three days of such friendly palaver, Kiona had gotten used to the appearance of the young lady and greeted her new friend. She was in the park by herself with Articulata, but she was surprised because this friend pointed a gun at her and bade her to get into a van parked nearby with the baby. A note was left at Mark's door warning him to stay out of business that was not within his realm. Once Fulvielmo was assured that Mark and his party was out of the country, his woman and child would be returned upon payment of $500,000 ransom to the lady in the park, who would also view their airline tickets.

With a trembling hand, Mark showed the note to Grady. He immediately phoned Jiminez, who was there in fifteen minutes. Julio and Helga were about to return to Colorado, when they received a phone call from Mark. They hurried right over, and he filled them in.

Julio was really angry when he found out what was afoot. He said he knew Fulvielmo's family well. He asked Mark to come with him and to bring the blowtorch. He asked Jiminez to get him and Mark security clearance to see Fulvielmo in prison. When Julio and Mark got to the La Marca residence, they were up in arms about a visitor at this late hour. Julio showed them the note from their son. He also asked the whereabouts of Raoul, Fulvielmo's younger brother. They went and roused their sixteen-year old son from sleep. Julio showed him the note. "What do you expect me to do about it," He snarled in a surly tone. At this point, Mark went right where Julio's initiative had led him. He grabbed the hooligan by his nightshirt with one hand and raised the blowtorch with the other. "Did you ever hear the story about what happened between me and your brother?" I better find out where my wife and daughter are, or history will repeat itself." Raoul turned to Julio for support. All he found was a blank stare. His swarthy features paled with the torch at the level of his eyes. He blurted out; "They are at the Temple of Kukulcan, where you found the library." Mark took away the torch and made a phone call. "Hello, dad, we found them, call the polizia and tell them the story of what happened. Ask them to take you to the Temple of Kukulcan. Julio and I will meet you there." Julio told him he also had more information, but it would have to wait until they confronted Fulvielmo in prison. He also asked Jiminez to accompany him to the prison visitation. When they had their audience with this self-styled crime kingpin, he had a smug look on his face and a sneer for Mark: "Well, do you come to appeal to my decency as a person that was with you in our formative years."

"Not at all," chimed in Julio. "We came to let you know that Kiona and the baby are free, and that your brother and his girlfriend are in jail. I also have documentation that include photographs of you together linking you to the Somoza Cartel in Ecuador that has been involved in the heroin and cocaine trade for years. Several other inmates of this facility are in for lengthy stays. If any misfortune should befall my friends while here or after their return to their country, my friend, Senor Bartomas will see to it that his copy or copies he has made will reach the Somozas and their friends in here. Do I make myself clear to you, Vulture Dropping?" Fulvielmo indicated his full understanding; Julio hugged Jiminez and Mark, and said, "Helga and I have a plane to catch. By the way, you referred to Kiona as your wife." Mark only grinned.

The rest of the month was not uneventful, nor was it traumatic. The sites that depicted Mayan history were cleaned up and once again became a source of community pride. As Julio had taught the drug pushers to stay away from Durango, they learned to stay away from Chichen Itza. The populace began to judge some Americans as not being worth the genome that created them and others as worthwhile human beings, dependent upon their actions. Kiona and her parents took Mark and Grady over their old stomping grounds. They traveled to Belize where they had camped out with Helga and Henri. Kiona told her mother about all the flora and fauna they had seen and what had happened to Henri after they had gone their separate ways. She also mentioned how crushed Helga was by the experience. Mark and Kiona had to stop at their waterfall. Kiona showed Articulata the falls and said to her, "Sweet Heart, this is where Daddy and I realized that we loved each other." Ruthena nudged Mark and asked, how did this come about, Big Boy." Mark tried to hide the blush that came over him, and said, "Mind your own business", with a grin. Ruthena noticed a similar grin and blush on Kiona's face. She and Grady exchanged smiles, then she added, "I bet I know." They all laughed. Alone, she asked Kiona what the experience was like. The only reply that Kiona could make was the truth: "Mother, it was like returning to the Garden of Eden." Then mother and daughter hugged. Articulata wanted a hug too, so they both hugged her.

The only real task was to negotiate with the Mexican Government.

Drs. Horton and Owens, as well as Jack and Bert and several federal officials from the State Department and Bureau of Foreign affairs were also present. They met with Jiminez and the Committees of Foreign Activities and Historical Artifacts. A big question that the Mexican and American Governments posed was why should Mexico allow its history to become an item of export to American businessmen who had no connection with its development. A corollary that sprang off of this what gains would each government receive from these transactions. Now the defense would begin.

Professor Horton addressed the issue first. He described how he had brought an international group of students to discover historical truths about a past culture. Where there had been a mingling of superstition and knowledge, a blend was created because the people, themselves were involved in the uncovering of this history. He further stated that the good feeling that the search together and the pool of data had beneficial effects on both, or all the cultures. He stated that what appeared to be an erosion of this good feeling would not have been able to have been repaired, as it was, if some permanent good feeling had not been laid down the first time. He then called on Kiona to relate what her experience had taught her. She described how she still maintained friendships that spanned the two borders because two plus several other nations had met as equals, debated issues, compromised philosophies for the common good, and learned the basic truth that we, together, are all that we have. Mark took the floor next. He related how people of evil intent arose and were held in check, while he was a student in the project. They were held in check, because mutually digging out the facts gave people a sense of pride in what they are because they have dug out what they were from the pages of their history.

Grady spoke next about how he had scrubbed hatred and isolation out of his system alone to find that he had to mingle with others and help them discover this facility in themselves for the cleansing to last. When the self-searching stops, we tend to fall back in to old habits, as was done with Adolph Hitler and Fulvielmo La Marca seeing this happen and drawing the old habits out of the vacuum. He further stated that the plan, his company had developed would spread the art of getting to know yourself and being able to learn to get to know others.

Income would be diverted to communities for what they were to produce in others by producing and reinforcing their feelings of well being in themselves. Ruthena spoke about how the message also was in the media. She elaborated upon how Tripod, a movie producing company, was negotiating with the company on another dig to recreate truths that another culture of the past had made available and that they were willing to share royalties. The possibility of including the Mayan project under this banner was very good. Jack added that he had learned to negotiate with his son, as a man with a brain of his own through the experience of returning to the past via his son's work and coordinating it with the present. This is an ability needed in all cultures. He also spoke of increasing the flow of money between countries via a transportation industry built up in both countries. Bert related how the merciful boxing in of Fulvielmo was related to what going into the past had taught her about people. She went on to elaborate upon the theme that the Mayans had eliminated a leader of a defeated army only to contribute to their own destruction. Her son was an instrument of discovering this information and sharing it. This sharing helped evolve a philosophy that stressed spending less time and energy on eliminating the negatives than on building the positives because the positives are what causes a culture to survive, not just be remembered. All her life she heard a song from her youth about "accentuating the positives and eliminating the negatives and not messing with Mr. In Between." Yet she did not grasp that this meant hold negatives at a standstill and go on building. Fulvielmo grew out of a Mr. In Between attitude taking over. The program she and her colleagues proposed is continuation of building with each other because we need each other. She did not tell anyone that the start of her thinking in this direction was Mark's giving a perfectly good raincoat to that hoodlum. She finally understood her son. Last to speak was Professor Owens. He related publicizing what Fulvielmo represented to what he had endured at Colorado University. He stated that the evils of racism plague all cultures.

The only way to accentuate the positives and eliminate the negatives is to scrutinize the negatives that have destroyed others and to find the positives that are or can be passed on to others.

The committees and bureaucrats of both nations met with each other and separately. They concluded that the premises of this endeavor were based upon morally sound and financially sound precepts. They also felt that this endeavor had many creative possibilities for both nations.

After it was all over, Jack and Grady and Bert and Ruthie sat down and talked. Jack said, " Our kids certainly turned out O.K. Did you see how they fought for our cause as if it were theirs!" Grady said, "In a way, it was. We put them in the position to have to fight for the right to have their own minds then to fight for each other. Regardless, I am proud of both of them."

Jiminez warmly invited them all to his home in Chichen Itza for a reunion and a victory party. Reed ad Michelle, Arne and Rachel, Amy and Ron, and Julio and Helga were also invited. They had also contributed to the success of the mission. The restaurant in Chichen Itza had catered the affair, and the wares of the establishment were displayed on a table in the middle of the lawn. They all took pictures for their family albums. The wandering musicians were also there and led them in songs of their choosing. The first song was La Paloma. Julio, Jiminez, several committee members, and Articulata had tears in their eyes. When she was asked why she cried, she said because Yusseff was on her foot. According to protocol, "The Star Spangled Banner" was played. Arne cried because his wife bit him for laughing too loud at Articulata's answer. Without even asking 'Snoopy and the Red Baron" was played for Mark. Mark and Julio surprised everyone by playing a duet of "You Are My Sunshine" on the guitars and singing the refrains. Kiona was trying to hide her beaming expression, as she asked why they chose that song. Julio said Mark chose it; Mark said he chose it to honor the last solar eclipse. He dropped down on one knee, picked up his guitar as if to play and said, "Kiona, will you marry me?" Her jaw dropped, and she ran forward, saying, "Yes, yes, yes." He swung her through the air as she reached him. They were smiling ear to ear. Everyone in the yard cheered. Mark called out: "One year from today, right here." Jiminez nodded his assent. The parents were elated hugged and kissed them both. Everyone joined hands in a circle and sang a verse of "This is your Land; This is My Land." The quality would've made Woody Guthrie turn over in his grave, but the feeling was there.

A precedent had served as a building block for the perceptions that brought about the self and the others configurations into a successful pattern of thought. This precedent was the knowledge of Gideon Retta's struggle with himself, and the valuable lesson he learned that turned an immediate defeat into a victory over the course of time. Because they were to learn from Gideon's making violence his God and from his finding a way to God, they were able to comprehend that violence begets violence. This ultimately means that once the realization that violence carries destruction with it occurs, alternatives to the use of violent solutions must be found. However, as long as negotiations remain myopic one sided compromises for the defeated, the seeds for violence will remain firmly implanted in the souls of both adversaries; neither will find their ways to a return to Eden on the path to God. By going back to see what Gideon left us as an individual, not as the carrier of a dictated imperative, we can learn what we can do to find our own individual path to God and how far we can break from the stagnation of cultural limitation. Now, let us probe into how a defeat became the search for the beginning of an individual path to the ultimate essence of our being.

# Chapter 12

Now that Gideon had begun a revolt by some of the subjects of the Spanish colonization and captured the refractor, he began an aggressive pursuit of Trocadero's new recruits. Use of the phalanx, mining the ground in the forefront of the troops, and igniting the explosives with the refractor were creating a serious shortage of replacements. The quelling of local rebellions also created a drain on his manpower. Trocadero was beginning to squirm. His only way to decisively and quickly win this war was to take and destroy Mesa Verde. He also had to break up the alliances that were there to harass his advance. To free himself of the phalanx and the mining, Trocadero began to use the northern routes through the mountains again, as well as employing more northern landing points. This eliminated the phalanx and the mines ignited by the refractor, but he had to face the Russian and their close combat techniques, the Long Wagon and the Enigma, the marksmanship of Komarovski, and the Sound People. History was about to intervene on Spain's behalf and turn the victory to her lap.

As has been indirectly mentioned, with the passage into the seventeenth century Spain was reduced to a second rate power fighting for its identity on seas against a growing British and Dutch naval power and an increasingly skillful and disciplined French army. As the English established a foothold on the Atlantic seaboard, they began to practice their disguised intolerance for differing factions of their own kind, as well as, for the indigenous populations. One member of a dissenting religious faction was descended from the man who had deserted Frobisher's ship in the St. Lawrence to make his way to the Pueblo Village. Unable to tolerate the insane persecution at Salem, he fled to Rhode Island and the same craziness under Roger William's. At the port of Providence, he stole a ship and decided the only freedom he could have was at sea. He made his way around Cape Horn and preyed on Spanish, shipping, since he still considered himself Loyal British subject, and he didn't want to starve. He made his way up to about San Francisco along the Pacific Coast, when he was spotted and identified as one of the British pests harassing Spanish ports. Ironically, it was one of Trocadero's troop ships that captured him. Now Trocadero could implement his plan to take the Sound People and Russians out of the war. To prevent identification he left the Union jack on the mast and pulled into what would become Puget Sound. He arrived in the dark of night. At dawn he began shelling the village.

The implementation of some technology kept the Sound Settlement from being completely wiped out. Komarovski had been present when the refractor was captured. He made two replicas: One for the Long Wagon, one for the Enigma. While the boat was shelling the village, Komarovski lined up the refractor with the sunlight and burned the boat to a cinder, but not before considerable damage had been done, which would take the Sound People out of the war for a long time. However, this had been done previously, and they had still returned.

A second part of Trocadero's strategy was to move his troops in from further north now that the Sound People's base was immobilized, and the terrain was more mountainous precluding use of the phalanx. The disadvantage to this maneuver was that his men were vulnerable to the kazatski fighting at close quarters. After he came out of the mountains he had to turn south to face the even more steep mountains to get to Mesa Verde. They were also harassed by the mountain fighters of Fiery Water and Ismalia and by cannon fire from captured guns. An advantage that Trocadero had was that he did not put all his eggs in one basket. While he was marching one army through the mountains, he had another marching up from Texas (there was no geographic area known as Texas at that time). Gideon could not spare the Russians to help rebuild the Sound Settlement. Therefore, Komarovski became their commander and brought his Long Wagon with him to the mountain. The fighting assumed vicious proportions.

The viciousness produced its own set of repercussions. A battalion was trapped on a ridge by a burning trench to its front. Ericio was able to sneak behind them with the Enigma and carried a shipload of troopers that was led by Ismalia. The troopers joined Ericio's attack. The soldados were in a hopeless position and knew it. Yet they could not bring themselves to lay down their arms and surrender to people that did not acknowledge the superiority of the White Man's way of life. Instead, they chose to either be burned from the front or blasted off of the earth from behind. That is exactly what did happen to them. They were wiped out. After a seven-hour battle, not a Soldado remained on the ridge. The wiped out battalion became martyrs to the Spaniards and, subsequently, a motivating force. The force was so great that Men were agitating to raid Mesa Verde at 3:00 a.m.

The Pueblos were taken by surprise. No siege equipment was needed. Ladders were mounted and soldados carrying oil, fusing, and other incendiary devices had silently gained access to the village and set everything ablaze. They then exited through the kivas. They did this again a second night. On the third day they were met by an armed force led by Gideon. He let them get away with the army following at a discreet distance until the gates of the fort were opened to admit the raiders. Then Gideon pounced with his own firebrands. They gave as much burning as they got. Even before the burning had stopped, long cannons shelled the fortress and doubled the damage done.

A long interim occurred while each adversary licked his wounds. During this time Purple Flower was sitting with Gideon enjoying the water life in a mountain stream, when she stood up with a startled gasp. "My water, she screamed." Gideon stood straight up like an arrow shot from a bow before it hits its trajectory. He made Purple Flower lie down on the shore with a blanket and ran for the midwife. The time had been a nerve wracking one for Purple Flower during the raids. She encountered difficulty relaxing and had a long, difficult labor. Finally after two days, she finally gave birth to a tall, coppery toned little lady. They named her Red Earth. She had deep brown eyes set in high cheekbones and jet-black hair. Gideon sadly acknowledged that for most of her life he would not be there; he vowed to let her know how much he loved her before that time went by.

Running Lion became Red Earth's protector, as soon as she was able to be separated from her mother. She clung to him when her mother was not available. In turn, Gideon spent as much time as he could with the babies. He sometimes wondered what their world would be like.

He wanted them to have the security his son had known. At least, Fiery Water had known how loved he was. He grew up during a time when the enemy had to have respect for the warrior that threw him out of his land. That time would come again, but not without the humiliation of a defeat a time like that of the Hill of the Jews. Would Gideon be there to guide his people through the darkness and hopelessness of the defeat? Would another leader emerge? Gideon decided that he would meet with his officers and strategize with his officers about how to prosecute their own defense.

At the meeting were Fiery Water, Ismalia, Ericio, and Komarovski. Gideon started out sadly: "We already know that this is a war that we will have to lose because we do not have the resources that our enemy has to put to it. We also that our foe is not alone in its greed and cannot tolerate to look weak in the eyes of rivals looking for what Spain once had and is losing more daily. For this reason those of us that remain will have to wait and watch for the right time, place, and method to strike. Make no mistakes! This is not a war that is won in one breath. It is a war that all of mankind will fight as long as one-man uses another. To stop this senseless killing, we have to stop the senseless living that led us to it. We need to question the models of behavior that we allow to be set down as our patterns before they evolve from a pattern, designed by us to a way of life that is dictated to us. The freedom to choose realistic patterns comes from living apart from the mainstream, observing that mainstream, challenging its inequities, and striking at the weaknesses caused by these inequities. Once we have struck our blow, we must guard against the same power lust that our oppressor had becoming our guiding principle. In many respects, my son has kept me from becoming so blinded. Let your sons and daughters help prevent your blindness, but be careful not to be led astray by their short sightedness. In the long run the world we build has to be our own taken from what has been there and our estimate of what will be there. We, who are now here, cannot back up from fighting our own doctrines of racism and exploitation."

Komarovski spoke next: "My Land is a nation trying to mold to-

371

gether far apart tribes conquered by a strong man that puts us together by force and forgets we are people. I have seen this Trocadero try to do the same to you but I have also seen a brave and a strong man rise up against him and say just because you are used to thinking of those that are different than you as things does not mean we will be things, and my way is to start the way of life that says you must remember that I am a person with my own set of ideas to be able to deal with me. My men and I rode across the tundra brandishing our swords against Tatar, Prince of Muscovy, and would be Tsar alike so that we could stand on our own land and call it ours. I left there to find this here because the people there want this strong man to take care of them from the snow and cold wind. I knew I would face the strong man again to call what I take for mine, as mine. By Gideon Retta's side, I have a chance to build for myself because he showed me how. I know he is a brave and good man, and he can die, as well as I can; if he is gone, his shadow will follow me the rest of my days. If we do not win now, we will win later because he has shown us who and why to fight." With that said, he held out a goblet of vodka he had hidden and bellowed, "Nas Drovzia."

Ericio spoke next about how he had entered a hopeless war, a war with the odds against it because he saw a tall, gaunt fighter stand up against several times his number to let them know that "you may defeat me in battle, but you are no better than me nor can you walk on me. I realized that I was abandoning a life in which I would be gaining the wealth, for which Trocadero now fights so entrenchably, without firing a shot. Maybe I owe the children I left behind in Goa, Portugal, or Ethiopia the sense of honor to go down for a cause that espouses the reason we are all here: To love one another to the extent of not tolerating the indignities and abuses that prevent us from rebuilding the Eden we once threw away. To find the paradise we lost, we must diminish the minions of Satan. Exploitation and racism are the cornerstones of these minions. Diminishing them will take more than one war and more than one generation. This fight started before Gideon Retta, and it will be taken up by a lot of self-sacrificing men and women after him, but he sure gave us a helluva start. I've never seen anyone like him, but I know at least three that have the makings." Ericio further

372

elaborated that once when Gideon had shown the human element of reacting in a well-provoked anger at a prisoner, he and Fiery Water helped him curtail it by reminding him of their cause.

Ismalia now addressed the council. She spoke upon her awareness of what the view of the Spaniards of their role to the Pueblos was. She had fire in her eye, as she reiterated the circumstances of her birth; altering her view of herself, as worthy of a good man, Fiery Water, and of being other than a product of a usurper's vent to meet his needs were brought about by the stance Gideon took against this parasite from a distant land. She went on to exposit that her Man's father had shown her oppressed people how to stand, and that she would continue to stand for her son's and her dignity, as long as oppression in her own land kept her home and hearth from being just that; she maintained that as long as she was able to draw a breath, no tyrant could walk safely by her with his arrogant head erect. In fact, he probably couldn't walk by her at all without a shot being taken at him. She was also an excellent shot with about three weapons. In short, her war would go on because its continuation was right.

Fiery Water let the council know that he was raised to be gentle and to try to love and understand the world around him, but he was also taught that there were those who responded to gentleness as weakness. His father showed him this, as a boy and as a fighter that he did not take or destroy a life unnecessarily. However, defining other people in terms of one's own needs, and, what's worse, defining their worth in terms of these needs is a hideous crime upon humanity and such premises should be warred upon for as long a time as Man walks the face of the earth. This Fiery Water was prepared to do. His only regret was to give such a low enemy the material semblance of a victory. Yet he saw that the Pueblos had no other choice.

Nothing would be handed to Trocadero. Whatever he won would be wrested from the soil and paid for with Spaniards' blood. This was a vow that they all took and that they all meant. This would be a New World Masada or an earlier version of the Warsaw Ghetto. There might be bloodied heads, but they would never be bowed: At least, not to Man.

Word was passed that a troop ship would be docking at Vera Cruz.

Normally Gideon did not go so far into New Spain; nor would Trocadero expect him to make this march. He received help from some of the victims of Spanish tyranny that wanted to cast off their yoke. A herd of Llamas was smuggled to the cave that the Spaniards had used for their relay stations. They were stolen and sneaked across the border at night. Then they were marched at night to the cave. they were marched to the mountains at night, where Ismalia's army mounted them and rode them to Veracruz. In the meantime Ericio took his ship and Russian troops to raid three Apache strongholds to the southeast, while Gideon and Fiery Water raided the fort that housed Trocadero with Komarovski's army waiting with a back up army and the Long Wagon. A vicious series of battles was expected, but the direction of the viciousness was miscalculated.

Ericio succeeded in sufficiently crippling the Apache strongholds without any problem. He packed up his troops and went to join Gideon at Trocadero's fort. Gideon had found this bastion deserted and proceeded to demolish it then join Komarovski to strategize a useful deployment of their forces. When Ericio had joined them, they began to wonder if Trocadero hadn't tricked them. Ericio went on home to protect Mesa Verde from attack since it was newly rebuilt. Gideon went on to the mountains with Komarovski, in case Ismalia was in trouble. They found her trying to fight her way out of a circle of entrapment. The Russian bore into the battle with his Long Wagon firing into the Spanish troops, flanked by his fighters moving for close fighting. Though they were not Russians, they had been trained in kazatski fighting. Gideon and Fiery Water moved in on the opposite flank with Fiery Water's troops covering the rear. Ismalia was now able to make use of her cannons to help break up the ring around her. In the fighting she was wounded in the shoulder, but the ring was broken. The Spaniards were outnumbered and had to flee. Ismalia had lost heavily in the battle. Since their fort was destroyed, the Spaniards hid in caves in the mountains and raided the Pueblos and their allies from their new strongholds. Both sides were tired of war and killing and destruction; neither side would capitulate.

Imperial Spain was laying out more monies to fight the Dutch and British on the seas and on the Land. The Jews were not submitting to pogroms and buying their way out of trouble any more; they were leaving Spain to ally themselves with Protestant nations and showing their persecutors what happens when a person is pushed too far and stops turning the other cheek. Hence, Philip II communicated to Trocadero that he wanted this war ended, or there would be consequences to pay. He knew that unless he brought about an end he had to fear for himself and his family. He remembered that at one time a Trojan Horse strategy had been suggested to him. He thought about using a variant of this plan. The Cheyenne village was not far from his present mountain stronghold. In a night foray he captured their settlement by surrounding it and offering to burn it to the ground unless everyone surrendered. He executed the chief and his family along with the shaman and gave the rest an ultimatum of following his directives or joining the body count. The majority of the tribe was marched to Mesa Verde and instructed to plead for entrance because Trocadero had burned them out. As soon as the Cheyenne were let in, cannons were fired at the portal, and Spaniards came pouring through the enlarged breach. Others went down the tunnels with exits to the outside firing harpoon guns with burning rags attached to ward off the multi firing muskets. Mesa Verde was stormed. Soldados were rounding up people in house to house raids. Ismalia, Purple Flower, and the two children were moved to the cave behind the trading post and told to go through the exit tunnel to Ismalia's old cave temporarily. Ismalia insisted on staying because was she was an officer. Sharply, Gideon told her that her wound was not healed and that she could only bring help if she was outside. She heeded her command.

Ismalia arrived at her former abode to find it covered with the boulders that one by one they removed enough to gain entrance. Then Ismalia fainted because her wound opened up. Purple Flower brought her to a dry spot inside and put a new poultice on her arm. She found two Cheyenne women in a wagon, who had escaped the pillage; she brought one back to tend to Ismalia and the children, and she sent the other one in the wagon to find more women, children, and wounded or escaped people. She went to the mountains to bring back Ericio, Komarovski, or both. A band of deserting soldados was looking for strays while she was making for the mountains. Purple Flower remembered that she met Gideon through his rescuing her. She crawled into a hollow log at the sound of their voices. Inside at the other end was a sleeping bear cub, whose mother had set him free that day. He started to growl at her, but she gave him some pieces of bark to munch on. The soldiers heard the noise. One of them saw her feet sticking out of the log. He grabbed the feet and pulled her out. He reached for Purple Flower and whirled her around and twisted her arm. With her free arm, she grabbed a low hanging branch and raked it across his face. She ran, and he followed raging after her. He ran right into the arms of the young bear, which Purple Flower had fed the chips of bark. She heard the soldier's ribs crack as the bear squeezed him. The other soldados had run off. Now she was free to make her way to the mountains. First she took the soldados armor and weapons. She put on the armor, placed the weapons on the Spaniard's horse, and mounted the steed. The young bear followed behind his new friend.

She thought of Ismalia and the two kids left to the care of a stranger then had a flashback of the fires and pillaging at Mesa Verde. Her thoughts were interrupted by the sound of more male voices. A squad of dragoons was out looking for runaways. She stayed hidden in the shrubbery to avoid detection and had a very hard time having her mount remain still, especially since the smell of the bear was in his nostrils. The stallion complied with her pressure to remain silent until the squad was out of sight and out of earshot. Once out of the forest, she sneaked by Mesa to see a wagonload of women, children, and old folks move stealthily toward the cave where she had left Ismalia. She quickly and silently went by her home because she knew she had to reach her destination to even help to save it. She rode as fast as her horse could move through the narrow mountain trails. Finally she spotted a boat and a wagon with guns at both ends and rifles in the portholes at the sides. She knew that she would have Ericio and Komarovski at her side when she returned to Mesa Verde She tied the horse to the ship and mounted the rope ladder. She found Ericio passed out from rum and roused him. Komarovski was aboard and looking at the stars amidships. She got them both together and explained the situation. A piercing whistle screeched into the air, and two battalions of warriors appeared out of nowhere. Komarovski bellowed, "Gentlemen, we are needed at Mesa Verde. Keep silent on our approach, then blast a welcome for Trocadero when we greet his big, fat ass." The armies split into those for the boat and those with Russian. They followed Purple Flower on the horse. The bear followed her peripherally at a higher level of tree line.

Mesa Verde was in shambles, but there were more Spanish dead than Pueblo. Komarovski turned his immediate attention to the tanks. He began blasting them with his cannons. The sun was not yet up, and the refractor could not yet be used. When he had knocked the tanks out, he had his gunners fire the multiple muskets through the masses of soldados. Ericio kept his guns on the tanks so that they were penned in. The combined army, under Fiery Water was able to move behind the tanks and hurl jars of burning oil and rags into their openings. Purple Flower crawled through the tunnel to fight by her man's side. The bear did not want to be around these crazy humans so he looked for a hollow log in which to curl up. Purple Flower picked up one of the bundles of rifles that were triggered to multiple fire. She saw Gideon fighting about twenty men and began firing at the crowd, which began to thin between the two of them. Gideon was armed with atalatls, harpoon, guns, rifle bundles, swords, and axes. As the two of them advanced they had no compunction about walking over the corpses in their path. This battle had been raging for a week.

In the cave, away from Mesa Verde, Ismalia was recovering under the auspices of the nurse sent back by Purple Flower. She lay in a swoon for two days and was fed by mouth berries and warm broth made from various herbs in the area. The dressing, on her wound was changed twice daily. She had dreams about fighting at Fiery Water's side Mixed with a dream about fighting the conquistador that had raped her mother. Along with delirium, Ismalia spiked a high fever that was constantly in need of cold compresses. A rattlesnake had made its way to her bedside and was rearing back its head to strike when three-year-old Running Lion charged the head with a burning torch. "You can't hurt my mommie," bellowed the toddler as the snake burned. The noise startled Ismalia out of her reverie; the other women explained Purple Flower's heroic role in saving them and going for help. They assumed that she had joined the battle if she had made it for help.

From this point on, Ismalia began to recover. The wagon that brought the women and children was hidden by brush. Under Ismalia's direction, it was brought into the cave and stocked with water and food, boulders, and branches sharpened by the kids with broken pieces of stalagmites. Ismalia and three other women and an older, harmless, appearing man set out on a supply-securing mission.

A squad of dragoons was out looking for deserters. Ismalia heard them while they were too far to see them. The old man lay down in the road and groaned while the others lurked in the bushes with their makeshift weapons poised to strike. The leader and several others stopped to see what was wrong; the others leapt on them from behind and wiped them out. They took their weapons, armor, and horses to pull the wagon now and to ride in battle later.

Fiery Water could not help but worry over his wife and son. Did they make it to the cave? Was her wound tended to sufficiently? Was Running Lion all right? After all he carried the burden of trying to be a man and protect his mother. This thought made him smile a little; who could be so presumptuous as to be Ismalia's protector. She probably had to be tied down to allow ministrations to her wound. The tanks were finished. Dawn was arriving with a vengeance. Out of the corner of his eye, Fiery saw Komarovski adjusting the refractor towards a bluff where a cannon was firing down on some warrior troops trying to advance. Fiery Water formed a phalanx with his army and began to move toward the bluff. It seemed to mop up what was in its path. When he got close enough, he took a squad of kazatski fighters up the bluff and engaged the cannoneers in hand to hand combat, while the phalanx advanced up behind the squadron. The army, though unwieldy because it was two combined armies, was holding its own.

Komarovski and Ericio had crippled the tanks from the front and set a trench to their front afire to withhold troop advance at a standstill. They headed toward Mesa Verde with the ship and Long Wagon. Their troops followed them. The refractors were angled to manage the siege ladders and catapults. The advance was slow, but progress was being made.

From the edge of the forest, Ismalia could see a double army advancing up a bluff with a few men ahead of it. The bulk of this army was in a series of phalanges. They were all moving towards a long cannon firing from atop the bluff. In the other direction, she saw the Long Wagon and Enigma moving on the outside edges of a large number of men moving toward Mesa Verde.

There were a lot of flames where the siege works were. She knew the children were safe in the cave and turned her wagon full of weapons and a scouting party of four toward the opposite side of the bluff where her husband was. The others were preparing torches and dipping rags in oil and putting them at the tips of the arrows. They began throwing them and shooting as they ascended the cliff. Both factions reached the cannon at the same time. The cannon was captured.

Inside Mesa Verde Purple Flower and Gideon had accumulated a small, but determined minority that was beginning to push the enemy to the outside. Less were coming in due to the activity of four armies against the conquistadors. It appeared that the Pueblos had turned the tide of battle and maybe the war itself. The Spaniards were repulsed on all fronts; none of the leaders had been slain or seriously wounded; Gideon and Fiery Water were able to embrace their wives, to ask how the kids were bearing up under the pressure. Perhaps there would be the opportunity for some sleep and some moments for tenderness and lovemaking. Other skirmishes were dangerous, draining, and exhausting, but this one had been murderous. Gideon felt the tension ease between his shoulder blades. He took Purple Flower's hand and started back to Fiery Water and Ismalia's cave to go back to the children. The sun was out, and the day was warm. The plants were budding above the green carpet that was their spawning ground. It seemed that Man and God were at peace with one another. Gideon hugged his two babies to him and stroked their faces ever so gently. His world was no longer kindly; though there were times of gentleness and beauty. He had to cherish them because he did not know how many he would have left. He sat Red Earth on one shoulder and Running Lion on the other and pranced around the greenery around the cave. Suddenly they heard a sound like the sound of distant thunder.

Gideon put the children down and motioned Fiery Water to go with him. They gathered weapons and went back to the battlefield. They looked toward the crest where they had wrested the cannon from the enemy. Fiery counted 5000 troops wearing Spanish helmets. The war was back on their doorstop. Gideon sent couriers out to mobilize the other armies. There was more fighting to do. An inward part of him quaked. "We just finished the most draining battle of this stupid war. Can we stand another onslaught like the last one?" he thought with a wave of exhaustion. Ismalia circled around behind the ridge, flanked by Komarovski into he Long Wagon and Ericio in the Enigma with each leading an army. Gideon and Fiery assaulted them from the front, while Sound People and Russians split to hit the thundering host from either flank. Hell was getting ready to spit its fire.

Behind his troops Trocadero had heavy artillery: Tanks and cannon. They were facing the rear and mounted on inflexible turrets. Komarovski and Ericio positioned themselves between the soldiers and the guns, able to face either direction with their refractors burning the brush between the infantry and the gunnery units. Then these two leaders could split their armies into one attacking the artillery unit and one attacking the infantry from the rear. Ismalia and Gideon would lead a frontal assault, while Fiery and the Cheyenne would frontally attack the two flanks despite an excellent strategy planning scheme with such short notice, this would promise to be a blood bath. If Trocadero lost this one, he knew what Philip had in mind upon his return to Spain.

The opposing forces were entrenched frontally and stretched to their maximally utilized manpower in the rear. A stalemate appeared imminent, when Trocadero appeared at the head of a horde of Apache over the mountain crests. The horde split into left and right flanks at the rear and frontal armies. The fire between the frontal and rear armies had burnt itself out allowing the tanks to advance. The Apache swarmed over Gideon's army. Ismalia, Fiery Water, and the Cheyenne tried to support them with part of their armies, but they were also trying to fight their way out of their own traps. The Spanish cannons had almost disabled themselves by facing the rear with fixed turrets. However, a shot from a tank gun split the Long Wagon in half. Komarovski was able to procure some bottles of oil from the wreckage and hid under the axle until a tank separated itself from the others. He leapt onto it, opened the port, and threw a flaming bottle of oil inside. He took the wheel, as the driver burned to death and rammed the next tank. This started a chain reaction that caused them to ram each other in turn and recreate the fire effect. Komarovski sustained a severe chest wound. He let one of his Lieutenants wrap him with a bandage dipped in herbs and kept right in the fight. He retreated to his Long Wagon's remains and pushed one half of it into two tanks. Then he lit the last bottle of oil and threw it into the wagon hold so that it burned and took the two tanks with it. From the second half he focused the refractor on the advancing army of soldados so that they unbearably burned their feet as they marched and could be picked off by Ericio's guns. Ericio had to contend with attempts to board his vessel from both sides.

A flaming harpoon burned one of his masts, and as it fell, it took fifty men with it. His shoulder took another harpoon, but he fought on as his brachial artery spewed blood. Gideon, Ismalia, and Fiery Water were able to push back enough Spaniards to come to his aid. They broke up the attempts to board on his port side. In defending his star-board side, Ericio fell overboard, pushing the harpoon in further, and also, breaking his leg. Ismalia quickly grabbed two atalatls, broke off the points, and splinted his leg. She secured the splints with strips she tore from her clothing. She then prepared an herb poultice and made him grab a boulder, gritting his teeth. She cut around the harpoon in his shoulder and yanked out the offending javelin. She then applied and fixed the poultice to the wound. Fiery Water and the Cheyenne converged in the center and began to box the Spaniards between them and Gideon and Ismalia. Both sides were sore and aching from a battle fought too soon after the last one. They stretched their manpower to the maximum because they felt there was something prophetic about this battle.

Apart from feeling prophetic, events occurred to cause the men to view prophecy. As Gideon pushed to be part of the boxing in process, he encountered his sworn enemy leading a band of Apache warriors. He led his men after them scramming, "Trocadero, you vermin, I'm coming for your entrails." The son of Jesuit militancy heard the blood-curdling scream and ran with his band. Gideon followed in hot pursuit. At the foot of a cliff, Trocadero whirled around and began charging his opponent. They engaged each other fiercely with spear, Lance, sword, hatchet, and knife. Each bled, as neither had bled before. Each was filled with a fanaticism that would not allow death until the other dropped.

The deranged hatred brought about the prophecy. Ismalia and Fiery Water and The Cheyenne could not box in the Spaniards without the fourth leg of the quadrangle. Komarovski and Ericio were effectively removed from battle. Ismalia tried to form a phalanx, but it was not big enough to contain the soldados driven toward her. She had to retreat to a cave and hold off her attackers until Fiery and the Cheyenne could catch up with her. Komarovski's kazatski fighters joined Fiery Water's brigade and were able to reduce the Spanish number enough to bring Ismalia and her fighters out of the cave. The heat Komarovski had generated was enough to cause spontaneous combustion. Both sides fled the flames. But he heat generated in another part of the battlefield continued to flare. Gideon and Trocadero both realized that this would be a fight to the finish. For the Spaniard, it would be a proclamation that Christianity was a war for Jesus, no matter that the soul sent to God were not sent in love. For Gideon, it was a vindication of his rights as a man that were granted by a God that rewarded loyalty with protection and preservation, regardless whether the defender survived to enjoy the benefits of this protection or had no more preservation than the concept that people are allowed to love their God and each other in their own way, as long as oppression and exploitation are not factors. They would stand to the end for their hypotheses, and stand to the end, they did. Gideon had sustained stabbing, gouging, burning, spear piercing, some of whose instruments still protruded from him; Trocadero had similar badges of courage (or foolhardiness) marking him corporeally. The band of Apaches multiplied, as they appeared from behind the rocks. Yet the two fought on. Trocadero had pierced Gideon's sub-clavian area with a dagger, causing him to buckle over, but not before he put an atalatl in the Spaniard's throat. Then the Ethiopian, the kushite fighter turned with his few remaining men and went back to Mesa Verde. He went on foot, for his steed had been shot or stabbed out from under him. He was a walking picture of one who id dead, but he would not let himself die until he was with his people, his family. He was not a Falasha, nor was he a Pueblo. He was just a man, that wanted to live, love, and find God his own way. This he would leave behind him because had worked and fought for it.

When Gideon arrived at Mesa Verde and was inside its confines he was greeted by his son and woman and his child and grandchild and his companions in love and war. He asked that he be taken to his cave and that Purple Flower and Fiery Water, as well as Komarovski and Ericio stay with him there. Ismalia and Purple Flower cleaned him and dressed his wounds. He told himself that, at least, Trocadero would never see home again. Nor would he see Mesa Verde be a vassal state to Spain.

Gideon knew that his days on earth were numbered. He called Fiery Water to him and bade him to act as Nazir. The instructions were in the scroll, which was to be left at his gravesite. The quiver documents were to be kept with Fiery Water and passed on to his next of kin (Ismalia). Purple Flower was to be taught the ancient Phoenician Language, keep the history of their people, and pass on the skills to Running Lion and Red Earth when they grew old enough. His body was to be preserved, as per instructions in the scroll. Fiery Water demonstrated to him that he had retained the Amharic and Geez his father had taught him when he was young. He indicated that he also understood about the seven days of mourning and about the offering being made on the third day. He also was aware of the customs of cutting themselves and putting dust on their heads that the mourners had to observe and that the grave had to be lined with stones. Gideon also specified that his coffin be placed in a crypt with a hinged door. In addition, Purple Flower was to recite Pueblo prayers for the dead in her and Dark Waters' name. Gideon had Running Lion and Red Earth brought to him, and he explained the history of his family and his people to them. He told them he loved them very much as he had loved his son, daughter-in-law, and Purple Flower. He told them that when he was with the natural God he would look down on them and be there for their joys and sorrows. Now there was peace in his soul; he had made peace with his God. Gideon called Ismalia and Purple Flower to his bedside and told them that they had been his back bones because they were there as fighters, and they were there as nurturers of the ones that could fight with their accepting the courage to fight after this war was lost. He told Purple Flower that his love for her was not different in quality or quantity from the one he held for Dark Waters, but different because it had come at a different point in time. He went on to tell her that whatever earthly soul he had inside him in the next world would love her forever, as he had loved Dark Waters. She smiled at the simple beauty and honesty of this statement through her tears and pressed his hand to her lips. His final farewell was to his comrades in arms; he told Komarovski that he was made of the stuff of courage and honor. If he made his way back to Russia, the Tsar would never rule his soul. To Ericio he said, "Despite the cynicism with you speak of man, you are a true believer in the natural love human beings have for one another. If anyone carries the message for which we fought to other peoples, you will do so. God blessed me when he sent me such fighters as you two and my son and daughter by marriage. I am sorry that Father Nico, Porifirio, El Gato Gordo, and Joaquim did not see us through to the end, but their souls will join our fight, as mine will join yours and my son's and daughters by birth and marriage. Our fight will go on, as long as one man uses another. I am not sorry for the wars I fought. they are part of what we have to do as children of our God; we have to grow to meet Him not stay frozen as Our Father's Son's." Three days later Gideon Retta was dead. There was much weeping for a good man, but there was also much pride, and there was a thin veneer of politeness to Spanish patrone, who came to find out what had happened to the glorious commander, Gideon Retta.

The landowner still had the smirk on his face when he was brought before Fiery Water, Ismalia, Purple Flower, Komarovski, and Ericio. Their eyes were still wet with tears. The former fighter, who brought the swaggering victor to them, told them what he wanted. Fiery Water's reply was uncontrolled and full of the fire that such grief brings. "Go and ask Trocadero where he is." The Patrone slapped Fiery Water for his insolence. Fiery Water snarled and seized his arm and twisted it while holding a knife to his throat. Through clenched teeth, he said, "We did not have to end the war and have the means to continue if you have not learned manners from it. If you think cowardice or inability to fight made us quit; maybe you should talk to your soldados. If you expect to stay here any length of time, you better lose your attitude.

We threw you out once, and we can do it again!" With that he withdrew the knife blade from his neck and released his arm. The patrone walked out with an air of hauteur. All in the room realized that someday arms would be taken up again.

The week of mourning had passed, and the real pain and anger associated with loss had set in. Every act that had taken place in the village for the last twenty years had somehow involved Gideon. Now Gideon was no more. On the third day, the day of offering, Komarovski stated, "We, who loved and depended upon him, will have to learn to stand on our own and keep him as a beautiful memory. My offering to him will be to never look at a man as if he is beneath me unless his action towards me puts him beneath me. I shall miss him deeply, and I shall never forget him. I have to leave this area because the memories hurt too badly. I.... I don't know where I'll be or what I'll be doing. I just know I love you all deeply, but I can't stay here." Likewise Ericio sadly looked them in the eyes then stared into space then he spoke in a voice not recognizable as his own, "The only roots I have ever had were those of the sea with a deck beneath my feet. The first man I met that showed me he was worth his salt was Gideon. He was so filled with hate when I first met him that he practically wiped out an entire crew of Barbary Pirates single handedly. Dark Waters worked a miracle and instilled so much love in that soul that the original was nowhere to be found. Even though he sometimes looked like a ruthless leader, I saw the quality of mercy exercised where I never would've dreamt to do so. I can't stay here and remember the brilliant war moves coupled with the faith in people and the uncanny knack of being right about them most of the time. With all this he listened to my opinions and feelings about how he conducted himself.

God knows I'll carry his and your memories to whatever port I travel, but I can't stay here and see where it began with so much hope and ended in such tragedy." The departure was tearful. Neither one knew where they would end up or what they would do with their lives. Komarovski headed east, and Ericio somehow got his ship seaworthy, hauled it over the mountains, and was only heard from indirectly by rumor, where a Spanish galleon carrying gold or silver was sunk. He became dreaded in the Spanish colonies in the South Pacific. His son was said to have had an encounter with Captain Cook, and a great grandson was said to have been involved in an assassination attempt on Napoleon Bona Parte. Descendants of Komarovski were said to have fought with Ethan Allan and his Green Mountain Boys. Some had a peculiar habit of carrying a knife in their shoe and a style of fighting, by kicking out. Thus, did this war fade into obscurity; or did it?

Those that remained at Mesa Verde had a difficult time accepting Spanish authority since all they seemed to show was the same arrogant disrespect for their captors. Several rancheros and government officials were murdered. Christian churches were desecrated and even robbed. Once Fiery Water had words with the Alcalde over paying a tax to Imperial Spain for the privilege of maintaining a trading post on Spanish Land. For the first time in a long time his responses matched his name. He reached for a weapon, whatever weapon he could find. Fortunately there was none available. The Spanish overlords offered sad looks and narratives about the spoils of war as explanations for their shoddy, racist behavior. Fiery Water did three things to keep himself calm on the outside. He kept his family close to him, kept his weapons sharpened and in good condition, and be began to hoard food and water in an old wagon. Ismalia and Running Lion tried to be sensitive to his moods, but they could see his strain. Besides Ismalia was a fighter and encountered difficulty stifling her outrage. Purple Flower and Red Earth were helpful in the planning to leave and wanted to accompany them. Bit by bit they brought their plans closer to implementation, and the rage continued to build up.

As the racism and false ego served more and more to antagonize the tribes in the area, bands of raiders formed and directed attacks against the rancheros. At first Fiery Water tried to avoid these raids, but the haughty Patrone and the Alcalde, whose greed for tax money had been thwarted kept casting suspicions upon him. One day, he had reached the threshold of his tolerance level. He went to Ismalia and Purple Flower, expressing his frustration in a single statement: "Tonight we leave, but we will make two stops."

The first stop was at the Alcalde's ranchero. He torched his house and stampeded his horses and left a receipt on the corral: "Paid in full." The next stop was to the patrone. He stampeded his cattle, broke down the corral that held his horses, setting them free. Free as he was now, free to start a new life, put the stench of Spanish greed behind him. He and his family moved to the East and North. They came to a land that would be called Saskatchewan. The soil was fertile, but the climates varied between extremes of hot and cold. British, Russians, and Frenchmen settled there, but there were not permanent White settlements until 1774. Because of the climate extremes, people did not want to form communities. Settlements were far apart. At a much later date, social experiments took place here. Contacts with the lands to the south brought back the competitive, racist aura of the White Man. Fiery Water and his family set the precedent that such contacts were to be superficial unless importunism presented itself. Then it was to be resisted. In his older years when his son and baby sister were grown with their own families, he and Ismalia journeyed back to what was being called Colorado, due to the redness of the earth. The couple found that the Spaniards had not found the wealth they wanted, but they tried to hang onto the land simply because France was starting to express an interest in the area. Mesa Verde was just an empty shell where people had once lived. From out of the mountains a huge bear-like figure dressed in animal skins stared at them. They stared back, and a sprinkle that neither could quite place seemed to drip between them and draw them closer. It became a creek then a rivulet as they drew closer together. They screamed each other's names as they drew nearer and hugged each other. It was Komarovski. They laughed and talked about what the years had brought them. Both found that they preferred an isolation that shut out comparison and manufactured inequalities. The brotherhood of man that each sought was a long time in coming and could only be brought about by those that had the energy to fight for it. The trio laughed over the battles, the daring raids, the escapes and espionage's, they wept over the friends they had lost. They finally sensed that there was unspoken bond between them. They made a pilgrimage to a cave that stood behind what was left of a once prosperous trading post. Through a tunnel they entered the cave and gave their reverence to the man that bound them together. For a brief moment in time, they felt strong and young and righteous. The years seemed to drift away.

Then they came back to who they had become. The jogging of memory let them know that what they are or were will emerge when it is needed.

On the way back Ismalia and he encountered a small man caught in a trap holding a torch to fend off a pack of wolves that had formed a ring around him. At his side lay an empty musket that he had used to hold off his invaders. Fiery Water and Ismalia looked at one another with an understanding of what had to be done. Each took a flank and began shooting at the wolves until they lay dead at their feet. The trapper was in pain, and they freed him and dressed his wound. He was a hunter and a trapper. His name was Fuego Del Capeto. He told them the tale of his origin. Years ago a vicious war had been fought between the Pueblo nation and Spaniards. His parents were trying to get away from the fighting with him when they encountered a squad of dragoons who commandeered their wagon after they killed them and left him to perish on the rocks. He was found by a priest, Father Nico. This lasted until the home was destroyed by the Spaniards. He ran off into the woods and lived off of berries until he learned to make weapons and hunt. Fuego had had his fill of living the life of using others or being used. He preferred to maintain his own self-sufficiency. For a while, he lived in an area to the north where there was a large body of water opening into the sea. They lived side by side with White men called Russians. He genuinely liked these people, but the war came to them. One night he saddled his horse and left. In fact he was headed back that way when he had walked into a trap, and they found him. Fiery Waters and Ismalia decided they would visit the Sound People and took Fuego with them. On the way there, a squad of Spanish troopers looking for French spies spotted them and began interrogating them. Fiery Water was starting to get irritated. The officer did not like Fiery Water's apparent dislike of being questioned as if he were a criminal. He grew hostile and Fiery Water pulled him off of his horse and put his knee on his chest. The others prepared to defend their leader, but Ismalia had the multiple muskets aimed at their chests. They sat where they were. "I am a man as you are. I am not a criminal or a subhuman that I have to be talked down to because you can't live side by side with someone different than what you are. Now I am doing no wrong to anyone. If you continue to bother me and my party, you may not be so fortunate the next time." With that he returned to his horse and left. No one whom he had known was at the Sound People's village. The Russians had long since developed other interests and moved on. Nothing seemed the same except he same colonial patronizing and prejudice. Fuego seemed to like the ladies, and they seemed to crowd around him. The fishing and hunting were abundant; no Spanish or other White men were there to make him feel like a vassal living off of he noblesse oblige of the Lord of the manor, who was more of a usurper than a Lord. Fuego thought he might stay there a while.

Fiery Water and Ismalia had other ideas. This country was too strange and with too many bad memories. Saskatchewan had bitter cold, but so did The Land of the Red Earth. Saskatchewan was not yet heavily populated, and people kept a respectful distance from each other. On the way back the couple encountered the same espionage chasers. He had his hand on his dagger, and Ismalia held her hand beneath her blanket on he multi-firing rifle. The officer looked at him a moment then stepped forward: "Buenos Dias, Senor Fiery Water and Senora Ismalia! We fought against each other many years ago. Maybe we can learn to be friends now. I apologize to you for my rude behavior." Both of their jaws dropped. Maybe that bloody war did accomplish something. They stopped and thought a minute. Perhaps the country had changed, and they might remain and recapture some of the innocent beauty of youth; they changed their minds and kept moving. It wasn't part of them anymore.

Fiery Water did not cognitively understand how he had grown, but he had intuitively grasped how to respond to a bully. Something else made him draw back from his violent response. The missing item was that he did not feel tied to one culture or the other. Spaniards had abused his people. Pueblos had left his father and mother to starve and dismissed his father's warnings to them about the Spaniards return. Consequently, he had learned to rely on his own wit plus the positive inputs he had received from his parents and culture. He had had help in making a decision to live by an independent course; he was loved for what he was and encouraged to reason for himself with the stipulation that he was responsible for learning from his error.

Part of this learning was discussion with those who had experienced the same set of circumstances so that he could distill their own experience in his learning process. He had learned to be more than his father's son. He was not the total mindless automation of what was around him and what was imposed upon him, but a thinking being that put together what he saw with what he wanted and needed to build his own sense of person-hood. This type of being evolved from the stresses that a life in harmony with nature brings.

When the opportunity or need arose to stand up to tyranny, Fiery Water and his family did so. Ousting the invader was left to later generations; the initiator and model for support was Gideon. These hills and cliffs once rang with the shouts and the clangs of swords or the shots of guns, slapping back at the sneers of the tyrant. The anger behind these clangs, shouts, and shots was stilled unless expropriation, using people as objects, and blatant racism reared their ugly heads. No one wanted green fields and rivers turning to bodies piled upon bodies, caked with the red of blood; but if this was needed to bring respect, it was done once and could be done again. In fact, it was done again, not necessarily to Spaniards, but also to Frenchmen, Britishers, and later to Americanos. Perhaps this is the way that Americans learned that they do not have the right to hold themselves above minorities that their legacy of greed has created. Perhaps the echoes of Gideon Retta, Dark Waters, Fiery Waters, Joaquim La Rouxe, Martin Luther King, Malcolm X, and many more have evolved a generation that is finding the ears to listen because the price of not listening is war and destruction.

The hypothesizing and philosophizing won't change a tyrant, but enhances the development of a culture that is willing to say "I belong to me and not to what someone else tells me is best and safe for me because that's the way it's always been done." The way it's always been done implies a maintenance function that puts rules above people and ignores the fact that conditions change. Gideon's battle and the postwar Spaniard's reply to Fiery Water is exemplary of the ability to recognize the error of dysfunctional fixed thoughts about people that are different. This ability comes from seeing that persistence of the same way of thinking will mean self-destruction, whether by war, economic reprisal, or some subtle way of making people feel tramped upon. Does the symbol of a snake that is broken by such trampling as a suggestion for an American flag with the words "Don't tread on me", inscribed on it suggest that a society can emerge that won't tolerate being used. The War of Gideon Retta and hundreds of other wars before and after him convey this message. The survivors of these cataclysms are those that have survived the ordeals of a cultural pattern and understand that something is needed. A culture is nothing more than an organic structuring of us all. When we allow this structure to be controlled by an oligarchy that manipulates it to their will, we are allowing the few to make the decisions for the many.

Gideon Retta is one who broke this pyramid of command because he realized that if he can so easily be made a victim, so can we all. We have to guard against this type of tyranny if we are to have any future at all.

Purple Flower did not stay in Saskatchewan. She and Red Earth had wandered east and south until they reached a river. They stayed in the teepees of a tribe that had befriended them and worked on a project: Hollowing out a tree to make a canoe and be on their way. In three months the tree was hollowed out, and they moved further east. They went from one river to another that emptied into five lakes and followed one of them until they found an island. The British and French continued a rivalry that had its start in Europe in the New World and tried to involve the indigenous tribes in their war via treacherous and deceptive alliances. Purple Flower had secreted away a harpoon gun and a set of multi-fire muskets. She had good use for them, for she found herself in the middle of a crossfire between Englishmen and Frenchmen across the creek in which she rowed. She was getting ready to let loose with a volley when she saw two figures on one side and one on the other side burning brush ahead of them and charging the soldiers with rifle shots until they were driven off. Purple Flower thanked the God of Nature that she and Red Earth would live another day.

The two men from the leeward side were Amerindian. The third was a tall, lanky White man. He introduced himself, as Thomas Engler, a runaway from Plymouth Colony. The other two introduced themselves as Unias and Squamtor, of the Erie Tribe. Purple Flower could only understand by inflections when names were mentioned. Via a primitive sign language, they decided to go back to the hunters' cabin and take the time to learn to communicate. After about a couple months they were conversant enough to tell their stories. Purple Flower told of the usurpation of her land by the Spaniards and of Gideon's heroism through two wars. She related how there was nothing left and of the Diaspora of the leaders. Squamtor told of the usurpation of their lands by the French and Britons and their fighting like babies over it; then they had the temerity to further insult the tribes with lies, false treaties, and teaching their two languages to them, as if these two nasal and guttural intonations imparted some sort of cultural superiority. They came to the island to get away from both sets of jackasses. Let them kill each other and be gone. Now the imbeciles had followed them here. Tom, as they had come to call him, told a story of calling people names; assigning bizarre symbols to have an excuse to burn or hang people then seize their property. The name was witch. His minister called his wife this name and she and their children were hanged while he was away on a trip negotiating for rights to a waterway that he and a neighbor were contesting. The minister and the neighbor were to split Tom's land after the family was "removed from contention." Tom invited them to his home to negotiate their portions of the land, which he indicated he was willing to give up. He had them stand back to back so he could give the taller the greater share, and then he shot them both between the eyes and left Plymouth for the island. Before he left town, he tied both corpses together back to back with a note attached stating: "Which is a witch?"

The island was supposed to be his refuge from the stupidity of mankind. He could not understand how two nations were fighting for the sovereign rights of territory that was not theirs in the first place. It seemed quaintly reminiscent of the logic of the witch trials: All that counts is what I want, and people opposed to this want deserved to be defined as inferior or in league with the devil for committing the foul sin of not yielding to greed. They became fast friends until Tom saw Purple Flower taking a bath beneath a waterfall. Unias and Squantor sensed that the couple had found one another and moved on because couple-hood meant responsibility and towns populated by pipe smoking, bifocal wearing White men that hollered vehemently about the prices of rum and tobacco while they slaughtered each other over ownership of a well or a cow. Red Earth came to love her new father and mother as a team, and they loved her and taught her the ways of the world; yet, there was always time for the waterfall. As Red Earth grew to womanhood, restlessness pervaded her. She learned English at home and began to go into the town across the lake and to mingle with some of the town-folk. Several young Frenchmen began to notice her coppery skin tones surrounding doe brown eyes and, in turn, surrounded by a beautiful shock of long black hair with a short, feminine torso and firmly muscled, athletic legs. They began to follow her home, which frightened her to the point that she told her father. Tom met the young men firing burning arrows at them. They ran and told the commander of the French garrison. Another townsman told the British commander. Both armies were poised for battle at the shore, when Tom greeted them with a cannon he had stolen from Salem. He said, "I'll blow both of your bastardy armies back to the slot in Hell from whence you came if you do not get your fermented arse away from my home. Can't I even protect my daughter without it being part of your infantile politics? Be gone with you, or you can have your innards mailed back to Britain or Brittany".

Unbeknownst to Tom, other voices were saying the same thing to themselves in the forest part of the island behind him. Now they silently but determinedly stepped forward armed to the teeth. They were visible to the Britons and French. Standing with them was Purple Flower, Unias, and Squamtor. There would be no retreat, no lying negotiation. For once those who wanted to be left alone would be, or there would be war to the last man. The two companies, who would meet in battle, tonight, went back to their respective barracks.

Tom did not know this, but his prideful stance for his own freedom would be a demarcation point of a new phase in history: The evolution of a minority that said, "I am not yours to manipulate for your needs." Colonies do not exist for the good of the so-called, mother country. In fact, many colonies in the Americas would cast off the breed of rotters

393

and stranglers that called themselves mother countries. It seemed that God was in the process of decreeing unto man that the road to the return to Eden was to cast off oppressors. However, enough of selfishness and greed were interfaced with this new emergent doctrine to cause Non White, Non Christians to remain outside of its embrace. Needless to say this sore would fester. For it became a doctrine of change that fundamentally offered no change. Tom represented a change in history on a smaller scale. He and Purple Flower had children, and Red Earth had a child. Through the centuries, a Jack Engler then a Mark Engler then an Articulata Engler Almederson came into the world.

The doctrine of mercantilism involved the trading of rum for slaves. Hence, a thriving industry developed: It involved Europeans bringing slaves to the New World in exchange of sugar, cocoa, rum, and gold and silver. One ship owner had wandered the South American and West African coasts. He saw people herded into the holds of ships or crushed by avalanches or sweated to death in silver mines. Lucrative or not, he would not sell his soul to the devil to engage in such an industry. He had been part of a struggle for freedom that had been lost in all but spirit, and this spirit pervaded his core of being. Ericio docked Enigma of the East II at the port of Tripoli to find recruits for a crew. Not far from the pier, was a crowd of men. The sailor moved closer to learn what was happening. He saw men and women in chairs being bought and sold to make a land journey chained together to board a ship on the West Coast.

In the midst of such human horror, the ship captain saw a beautiful woman in chains. She had light skin, auburn hair, and gorgeous green eyes. She was a Mandingo from the Sudan. Ericio watched the proceedings with horror and knew what course his life would take. He followed the caravan until it was out of town and strew brush ahead of them. Then he turned the refractor on the brush and freed the slaves while the slavers were preoccupied with the fire. On the way back to Enigma, he noticed two figures following him at a distance from each other. He turned into an alley once he had returned to Tripoli. He surprised the slave trader, who had his dagger drawn. He was not expecting the harpoon in his neck. Behind him slunk another that had the intelligence to duck when the second harpoon was fired. Ericio rushed the figure and tackled his would be assailant. To his surprise he felt female breasts. He let the figure rise to her feet and discovered the Mandingo woman.

Without stopping to think that she might not understand him, he blurted out, "Why did you follow me after I set you free?" To his further shock, she said, "Maybe it's because you set me free." She gave him her name as Rafana. She stated that she was the daughter of a Mali chieftain, who had traded with Spaniards, Portuguese, British, and French. As a result, she learned many languages. She then said to him that he had saved her life; now according to custom, she belonged to him. With a look of sadness, he replied, "I fought a war and lost, probably, the best friend I ever had over the issue of how much control one person has a right to have over another. You are very intelligent and very beautiful, and I would be delighted to have such power. To take it under such terms is to deny that you are a human being." She stroked his chest through the thin cloth of his shirt and took his hand, saying, "Come with me then because I think you are a dark-haired, curly headed man with beautiful dark eyes, and I want you to be my father." With that said, he picked her up and carried her to his ship. She bore him two sons and never left his side, as they built a career of terrorizing slavers of all nations and relieving Spanish treasure ships of their ill gotten gains from Mexico to the coast of Chile.

One day Enigma raided a Spanish slave ship and another galleon came out from behind an atoll, armed to the teeth spitting fire at its opponent. The slaver turned its guns on Ericio's ship. He felt caught in the middle because he was. Suddenly a Yankee ship began firing at the galleon closest to it and sank it.

As the American drifted by, Ericio saw the nameplate, Islander, on the prow, and he saw a tall, lanky White man, next to a darker woman, who looked like Purple Flower, His jaw dropped with the recognition, but the moment passed too quickly. As they passed, the White man and Rafana seemed to stare at each other prophetically. Ericio and Rafana continued their attack on the slaver, putting the crew in the hold to figure their way out to re-navigate their ship and to steer the freed slaves to an island where they could rebuild their own lives. Perhaps these fighters who came to know, learn and understand their destinies, as well as to free themselves, from the miasma of exploitation, had intertwined themselves on this day.

# Section VIII

# A Soul's Durability

*We are remembered by our works, and their measurement is passed from one man to another*

# Chapter 1

The wedding had Ruthie, Bert, Rachel, Helga, and Amy in tears. Each row on either side of the aisle held a candle that was lit by the last person in the row to leave. The wedding was preceded by Julio and Helga singing "The Unchained Melody". Yusseff received the wedding rings on a silken pillow. Arne, who stood opposite his son released a trained dove to pick up the ring and place it on the bride's and groom' fingers. This was followed by an organ rendition of "La Paloma". The priest pronounced them man and wife, and they kissed. Then they read their vows to each other. After that they kissed each other again. As Mark took his vows, he knelt before Kiona and took her hand in his. Then said, "Our names have been tied together for as long as we tread the earth. You will never take a step without knowing that nothing can hurt you, as you walk the path of my tall, lanky shadow. It will be a shadow as long as you want it to be because I'll love you the way you want to be loved." He then picked a Lily of the Valley up off of the altar and put it in her hair. Kiona took both his hands in hers, smiled gently, and said, "Me and my Shadow Walling down the Avenue is the name of our song. It speaks of our oneness that stands under the protection of God, while we uncover His wisdom together. Today I vow to make our life with each other into our own treasure. Mark, I love you with all the womanly heart I have." The best memory of this wedding was the proud beaming smiles of Jack and Bert, Grady and Ruthena and an innocent baby about a little more than a year old.

Jiminez was very proud and very sensitive of the friendship that had opened up his mind to the difference between legend and history about his own culture and rescued his people from being overtaken by a foreign drug Lord. He was delighted to make the business deal that would bring more into his country in the name of intercultural exchange and good feeling between nations. The Bartomas name would be a name that stood for Pan Americanism for a long time. It would also be a name that would be battled by Fulvielmo LA Marca, who had just been pardoned from prison. As the friends strolled about Chichen Itza, a bullet whizzed between Reed Hymer and his son, Aaron. Simultaneously, Mark and Reed raced to the site of the bullet and tackled the assailant. He turned out to be Raoul, Fulvielmo's brother. When he was interrogated by the police, Mark, Reed, and Julio. They didn't ask him who put him up to the shooting incident. They told him to call his brother to come get him. When Fulviemo got there, he was handcuffed to his brother, and they were put on a boat to Quito, Ecuador under armed guard. Fulvielmo's dossier was faxed to the Somozas and to the Ecuadorian polizia. Reed and Mark went up to him and pinched his cheek. They then said, "Good-bye old friend, have a safe trip." The rest of the La Barcas never really caused the community any problem. No one ever heard anything about Fulvielmo or Raoul La Barca again.

The friends of so many years had enjoyed this wedding which, in all reality, was long overdue because they all knew that Mark and Kiona were meant for each other. Still they enjoyed getting together again and, ruefully prepared to return to their busy lives. The group felt that they had put together all the material they could about Gideon Retta and the Pueblo wars to present a clear picture of what had happened at Mesa Verde and what mankind could learn from what had happened there. The time to move on had come. Grady and Jack were already beginning discussions with Aaron Donleavy about tours, making a movie, writing a book, etc.

Mark and Kiona sneaked down to Belize and found a waterfall that made them feel as if they had returned to the Garden of Eden. This time when they returned to shore there was no attempt, not even the slightest interest in putting their clothes back on. They loved each other the way Adam and Eve and Gideon and Dark Waters did so many years ago. They knew they could make a life together because another couple had made one in the face of not only ostracism but also in the face of starvation and war.

The time had come for Mark and Kiona to gather the data that would dismiss the story of Ham as a construct to create racial prejudice rather than as a statement from God. They began to research areas that were suitable to demonstrate that viable civilizations emerged from what was known as Black Africa. To the South of the Egyptian Empire lay Nubia, which came to be known as the Sudan. This culture spread to the south and west. From it sprang several empires and trade centers: (1) Elephantine-Said to be the site of a departure of a sect of Hebrews from the Biblical Exodus from Egypt. These Hebrews are said to have mingled with the Agau, a Kushitic tribe of the area, to be the Progenitors of the Falasha Jews, along with Danite migrants from Aden. (2) The Mali civilization of Western Africa that built an enduring Trade Center at Timbuktu. the culture, under the Mandingo's, was noted for its sense of justice and order. (3) The civilization at Ghana, which began as a White area of control that was absorbed by Blacks, who established the first trade center of the Western Sudan. (4) The Songhai, who developed a Trade Center at Gao, on the Niger. (5) The Zimbabwean civilization which brought prominence to the southern portion of Africa. There was also much work that had to be done to show the effects of the Moslem invasion of Sub Saharan Africa and the devastating impact of the slave trade on the development of these aforesaid cultures. At the basis of this heinous industry was fear of the Black warrior, which stemmed from the fear Rome held for Carthage and, perhaps, the fear the North African Whites held for the Kushitic warrior. The curse allegedly made by Noah on his son, allegedly, for sodomization of the elder when in a drunken state had to be proven to be part of an ancient scheme to hold this fear of the Black warrior of old in check by creating a slave trade to control him. Although, Mark had done much research on modern day Blacks to provide evidence that the giants of his studies were sufficiently numerous in American society to warrant the assumption that they were not an inferior people, this was only part of the debunking scheme. The existence of superior Black cultures had to be presented as evidence that the proposition was false and a base emotion from the segment of mankind who profited at the expense of another had to be identified as its base.

Aside from this consideration, Mark and Kiona had to remember that they were now a family and had to consider this before they made any moves. They knew that any project in which they engaged would be demanding and would be a commitment for a long time. They would not consider leaving their baby for any length of time even though they knew that either grandparent would be more than happy to take Articulata. They also realized that any of these projects would mean leaving the USA for at least a two-year period. Along with the responsibility their life dreams flashed before their eyes: The impact their findings would make on the way people thought about one another, the thought patterns that would evolve to free humanity from the incapacity of mental imprisonment that stopped them from reaching out to one another. The choices were between raising a healthy child and opening up a world where a healthy child could be raised. Surely an area of compromise could be found! Yes, there was one. Career soldiers took their kids from country to country, from school system to school system, and normal kids came from this process.

Why shouldn't normal kids evolve out of a process in which they were exposed to fellow human beings that lived differently. After all it was only the Son of God that said, "Love one another, as I have loved you." Their daughter would be able to choose her culture as an adult because she would experience several as a child. Kiona and Mark were so excited to share this insight with each other that they ran to each other laughing and hugging. Mark said, "That's pretty good. Let's go make some more." Kiona laughed and socked him. She ran off and came back with her red nightie on.

The choice they had to make was a hard one to make. Three of the five choices were geographically close together. Being apart from their friends and loved ones, the loved ones they had worked so hard to rediscover, presented the problem. Kiona remembered how her parents feared her leaving the country to go to a land where Americans were not welcome. They and she found out just how much she could give back what she got. Fondly she remembered what she had to show Jonos to win his respect. He brought all the toughness that a Russian would bring to a Westerner at the negotiating table. However, he turned out to be a good and loyal friend. Secretly she hoped that he and Mattani would make it together. They seemed emotionally in tune with one another. This whole departure planning was beginning to assume the character of a De JA Vu. She shuddered when she remem-

bered how happy Helga and Henri were, and the misery Helga underwent after Henri's death. She sure didn't want that for Jonos and Mattani, despite the emergence of the relationship with Julio that brought
Helga back to life.

There was a fullness to her life, but there was an emptiness. She
was a mother and a wife. She had a career and a husband who was interested in helping her achieve the goals she had chosen for herself.
They had good friendships and a capacity to know how to initiate new
friendships, but there was now a crossroad in her life again. Friends
would be saying goodbye. As Amy and Rachel had told her years ago,
the friendships would be there, but the intensity would be less as their
lives became occupied with spouses and children. She was now feeling
like a teenager in search of new horizons but working none down to its
resolutions. . She thought of a therapist that presents opportunities to
their clients to resolve their dilemmas then moves on to never see if
their solutions ever work. It felt like being a spectator to life and not
living one of your own, like the Lone Ranger. This jangle of emotions
disquieted her. She decided to talk to Mark about it.

Mark was not entirely free of this conflict. From the Mayan experience he learned how civilizations rise and fall by losing that special
sense of oneness that comes from knowing God and knowing God's
expectation. Such knowledge was not based upon leaving behind
magnificent edifices but living a life that built a path to loving God by
loving man and the nature around man. From Gideon he learned that
the only victory we can claim is to fight not to impose ourselves or our
views on another, but for the right to go about obtaining this knowledge in our own way without hurting others. Having a family expanded those for whose welfare we were concerned and meant a dimension of selfishness had to be added to this search for knowledge of
the way of God. Gideon had battled for this right, and he did not forget
his own in this battle, but it meant he had to sacrifice himself so that
his own would be free to carry on their own version of the battle. As
Gideon had found out, those behind him took up their own version of
the fight.

Somehow word had gotten into the quiver documents about Fiery
and Ismalia growing old in Saskatchewan, but not tolerating any re-

minders of the old injustice, or of Komarovski becoming a huge bear of a mountain man, demanding to be left alone. There was even mention of Purple Flower sharing her life with a proud, independent White man, named Engler. There was even mention of a pirate, who sailed the seas with his Black woman raiding slavers and Spanish treasure ships. The document never mentioned what happened to Running Lion or Red Earth. Maybe they got lost in the pages of American History, maybe they were part of the network of men and women that led the battle for personal freedom unnamed and undiscovered.

# Chapter 2

Mark was exhilarated by the fact that he was even remotely connected with Gideon. He was more excited that a connection between Ericio and a Black woman, who may have been connected with Kiona may have provided a precursor to their own relationship. That the woman was a Mandingo was important because this tribe of Islamic Blacks were from the Mali, one of the African civilizations they were considering studying. The possibility so excited them about the potential of finding that there might be an intertwining of their cultural roots without an actual biological connection. Having any connection with these fighters was deemed an honor by both of them.

Aaron Don Leavy knew of Kiona's mission and that she had to answer its seductive call because it had the potential to break the back of an argument of an excuse that had been used to hold back Blacks for centuries. This was evil, senseless dogma that was at the root of much hatred and violent feeling. It had been the source for Klan activity. Motivation for violence against Blacks in the past and present, and a source of infecting disillusioned youth with the same purulent thought that had poisoned their forebears. History owed examination of this hurtful, sick doctrinaire excuse for persecuting an entire race of people for centuries, as well as a debunking of its validity. It was a huge task, and Aaron began to toy with the idea of the entire group becoming engaged in this project with Mark and Kiona. He decided to go ahead and discuss this proposal at the next meeting of the group.

Aaron addressed the group with his concerns: "We have established a unified pattern that threatens to be changed. We have successfully unearthed a big chunk of Western culture's past that has caused us to look at the motivations that lay hidden in our souls and have evolved to ugly and dangerous proportions. We need to hold up the mirror of what man is doing to himself. A couple amongst us is taking our discovery, which they have most admirably shared in reaching, to a more acute level of awareness. They want to attack the false proposition that has caused so much misery among humankind for all the centuries that a western culture has been in existence. The doctrine our couple is challenging is that Africa was peopled by a race that was inferior and subject to the iniquities heaped upon it by a White race, white to exemplify purity of soul.

It is my moral and professional opinion that we should join this couple in their quest because their quest is a morally right one and because they have proven to be friends when we needed them." Everyone rose and clapped their hands resoundingly. Mark and Kiona smiled through their tears. The company would bid a fond adieu to Durango and Mesa Verde and turn their heads to Western Africa. There would be much rearranging of plans. Fast friendships would erode into memories and all too infrequent get-togethers as distances and busy lives drew people farther and farther apart. It was real but sad to contemplate.

Julio and Helga had a community root established, in that they were active in working with the teen-aged population of Durango. They felt they owed it to the kids to see that their work continued. Yet they felt an intense loyalty to Mark and Kiona. They went to the social work and psychology departments at Boulder at the university. They were a couple that shared a commitment to archeology and a loyalty to two good friends, whose ideal they shared. However, they also believed in the kids and community they were helping and that someone devoted to the grass roots solution and that kids could find their own strengths to manage their own emotions to take a responsible role in their homes should replace them. In other words, they were looking for someone as talented and devoted as they were to take their place.

From out of the social work graduate school, came a young student, who had known the ravages of being the victim of a cocaine-addicted father and a mother, who was addicted to saving "her good man." She was the oldest of three girls and had been physically and sexually abused by her father while under the influence. Her mother had refused to believe her, and she had run away to Los Angeles to live in the street and make her own way. The ugliness of prostitution and other aspects of street life repelled her, and she acquired an alcohol habit. She had made the circuit of treatment centers, inpatient and outpatient, to effect a cure and found it was in her soul when a fellow addict tried to kill them both; she found she wanted to live. She also found she had to share the wonder of her recovery with others who had suffered from it to keep its spark alive. Her name was Guintera Aguinaldo after a reportedly beautiful relative from the past who was deported to Spain to pay a debt, and she was also related to a fighter against Spanish exploitation of the Pueblos. She brought two attributes with her: a pride and independent functioning coupled with a love for people. This proved to be the selling point that netted her the job. She attended the group with Julio and Helga, and she learned the skills that would help the group members attend to their issues. In addition, she was a martial arts expert and taught karate and Tai Kwon Do to the group. This came in handy because the former drug dealers were trying to make a comeback in the community in the guise of selling hate peddling weapons. She had plants among them locate their warehouse and manufactory and asked her new employers about a way of concentrating heat from afar on the buildings. Julio, who had no connection with technical aspects of the project, had remembered Helga telling him about the refractors, built by the Spaniards. She located the specifications in Da Vinci's writings and built one.

After hours a factory was burned down with an envelope containing photographs depicting various assembly line stages of weapons production and a photocopy of the charter granting permission to build a fertilizer plant with a note stating "lawns are not fertilized with magnums." The note was addressed to the Durango Police Department. The so-called hate group left their meeting hall due to a loud noise. Rushing out in the parking lot, they saw their cars in flames. One of them rushed at Guintera, who was part of a spectator crowd, only to have to seek help for his broken arm. The hoodlums quit the town once again. The kids in the group seemed to like this spunky lady, who had been where they had. Now Helga and Julio could leave the work they had started in capable hands. They would be able to join their friends in Northwest Africa.

Mark and Kiona also found a merging of their professional souls to match their marital vows. Mark had consistently pondered over what made Man tick in his relationships with others; from the Mayans he and Kiona had learned that the creation of a propaganda machine reached basic elements of people's psyche so that the masses could be shaped by telling them what their egos wanted to hear. National translations of the Bible left room for individual interpretations of vague or double meaning passages, according to the needs of the translator. Thus, could a man/woman be classed as a heretic, sinner, witch, or inferior being? The classification depended upon what axe the translator had to grind and how he/she presented his/her argument as that of the people. From Gideon and Dark Waters they learned that to create an adversarial argument, a diametrically opposed proposition must be believed with an equal, if not more intense fervor. The factual evidence would have to be presented at the same fundamental level, as which the propaganda was created and disseminated.

The task before them both was to gather the evidence they found and represent it in as basic a way as it was written. According to Genesis 9:6, Ham, the father of Canaan, saw his father's nakedness (Noah) while he was passed out from drunkenness and told his brothers, who covered him. Noah is said to have cursed Canaan, the youngest son of Ham, saying he would be "The lowest of slaves to his brothers." Ham' sons were: Cush, Mizraim, Put, and Canaan. The Hittites were said to be of Canaanite descent. They dominated the Fertile Crescent between 2000 and 1300 BC and were masters of fighting and working with iron. Another son of Canaan, Cush, was the father of a mighty warrior, Nimrod, according to Genesis 10:19. The ancient Kushite warrior, of Ethiopia may have been of this origin. Mizraim, was also a son of Ham; it also means Egypt in Hebrew. The Hittites were more a threat to Egypt than a slave to this nation. Nor was Canaan a slave to Cush. In fact Cush's grandson was Sheba, whose queen married Solomon, and whose son was the progenitor of the royal line of Ethiopia's Kushitic fighters. Thus the Hamitic curse was a fallacy from its inception, but emotional appeals had to be attached to the would be facts to render them credible.

Caucasians mistakenly lump African Blacks into one culture without realizing the multiplicity of civilizations that have comprised this continent.

The Mandingo's are different from the Kush warriors or the Nubian, who made up the Sudan as are the Songhai; the Nigerians also were a cultural group of Northwest Africa. To the South was the great Zimbabwean civilization, Zulus, Kikuyus, and Hottentots all had individual and productive civilizations. History cannot Lump Frankic and Slavic cultures into one culture called White, nor can it coalesce Mandingo and Zimbabwean civilizations into one culture, called Black. Yet this has been done. As Afro-Americans have been excluded from their significant roles in their own nation's history, so have meaningful contributions been overlooked and or minimized in the multiplicity of African cultures. Whether this oversight is deliberate or done for purposes of convenient handling of data is not certain. At any rate, Kiona and Mark decided to look at three cultures in Northern and Western Africa: the Nigerian, the Mali, and the Songhai. The group was willing to go along with this scheme, as long as they had a centrally located base.

The peripheral potential connection from the past motivated them to try and trace their roots. Did any descendants of Rafana's mingle with Tom Engler; was there a mysterious linkage that culturally bound their two families together? If so, there was more binding power than their just cleaving together. This would make them followers of an established progression, and more able to survive the resistance to introducing a change in the pattern.

In addition, they could easier face being separated from their good friends not associated with archeology. Although they still had their group friends, they still needed more cement to cleave together through this stressor. They decided to visit Arne and Rachel in Cleveland. Julio and Helga came along with them. They brought Artie along with them because Yusseff and she seemed to enjoy each other's company. They thoroughly enjoyed touring the Natural History Museum and The Art museum on their first day there and going through the West Side Market and the ride on the Good times, a boat that toured the Cuyahoga River and Lake Erie. When they went to Little Italy, they found the food was good, but they also found they were not wanted there. A group was there waiting for them outside the restaurant until Arne took out a magnum. Then they dispersed. They spent the next day at the zoo and also saw the tropical rain forest. They and Rachel and Arne, Ron and Amy, and Helga and Julio enjoyed a production of "The Glass Menagerie," followed by an evening of country sing a long and dancing at the Boot Scooting Saloon in a town sixty miles south of Cleveland, called Cuyahoga Falls. Mark kept teasing Kiona about her strong thighs showing through the wide country skirt she wore. She smiled at him and told him he better look long because it was pay for view.

That night alone in their room at Arne and Rachel's she wore the now famous and symbolic red nightie while started to drift off to sleep after their shower. As she caressed him awake, and he noted her attire, he began to become aroused. Gently he lowered the garment from her shoulders and began kissing her all over her body, beginning with her powerful, beautiful thighs. As he caressed them slowly and gently, he verbalized that pursuit of their beauty and powerful love would launch a thousand sampans across the Pacific or boats from Havana to Miami. He stroked them tenderly and gently kissed the inside of her knees before she let him enter her. He began to kiss and moan at the lushness of her breasts, and she began to moan in turn. They loved each other to an endless crescendo of feeling that soared to the height of passion and returned them to the plain of golden shimmering wheat fields ready for harvest. Kiona vowed she'd never let him loose from the warmth of her thighs again. Afterwards, as she lay in the crook in his arm, she murmured how beautiful their love for each other had grown. He took her hand in both of his and said that each time was one step closer to the Garden of Eden and began stroking her and kissing her again. Leaving those they loved behind was hard, but they would, at least have some of their friends with them; more important, they had each other. They felt the unbound love that Gideon and Dark Waters felt for one another. They knew that nothing could tear them apart. Nothing would!

The time to organize their goals and thoughts for the ensuing project was fast approaching. They began by locating the sites they wanted to see and about which they wanted to learn. Timbuktu, Jenne, and Niani along the Niger River seemed to attract their attention be-cause both the Mali and Songhai civilizations were connected with them, as well as the Nok and Ghanaian cultures. Their study would have to go back to the dawn of civilization.

Our history goes back beyond the Egyptians and Babylonian and Sumerian civilizations of which we are taught typically as the begin-ning stages of civilization. According to Genesis, Kush was the son of Noah that fathered Nimrod, a mighty warrior of the Ethiopic people, a brown skinned people that were already present at the inception of the Egyptian and Tigris/Euphrates cultures. These cultures are said to have learned to use iron implements, divert from nomadic existences, to de-velop stable food supplies and industries of peace and war from these non white predecessors. The path of existence these brown men cut has been said to be a band extending from Malaya to the western shores of Africa. Such a civilization is said to have sprung up from the Yorubans in the geographic area of the Senegal, and the Volta Rivers. This brown skinned race of people shared alphabet, architecture, and physical attributes of a Black race, which were in turn shared with Egyptians Babylonians, as well as a Dravidian culture of India. This Ethiopic people had expanded their control of the known world via trade and commerce. They were said to be the tail end of this Yoruban culture, who were the Atlanteans; the mysterious culture from land that broke off from the west coast of Africa, allegedly, sinking into the sea. Conjecturally, these Black men were progenitors of the Egyptian and Tigris/Euphrates cultures.

The first civilization of Whites was also from these western Ethio-pians. It was the Minoan culture of Crete, in the Aegean Sea. Aryan peoples from the mainland of Greece invaded and laid waste to this civilization. The island geography seemed to necessitate the growth of a sea faring culture that traded with the Kushitic culture to the South. Intermingling occurred where White people settled in areas controlled by these Kushitic warriors; the result was the addition of a Semitic component to the African population. The Whites from the Greek cul-ture also had their own version of the Atlantean phenomenon: Accord-ing to their version, an Aegean island, named Santorin, sank due to a series of volcanic explosions. They averred that these were the Atlan-

410

teans, of legend and that Quetzal coatl was one of them.

During the Roman years, a Kushite kingdom was established at Axum and dominated the area we now know as Ethiopia. Semitic peoples mingled with this kushite. Iron working was prominent at their capitol, Meroe. Much of Egyptian culture found its way to this nation, as the people in the area were beginning to show concern about themselves. They developed their own ideas of architecture, language, and religious worship. They carried on trade with Uganda, peoples of the Lake Chadd area, China, and India. Each of these areas contributed new ideas to their culture. At this time, Geez was developed as a religious language. In addition, some of their old ideas were transformed: The mingling with the Yemenites resulted in the establishment of trade routes; a matriarchal society was passed on from contact with Egypt.

As civilization evolved more, property became important and was no longer regarded as property of the tribe, which was matrilineal, as it was composed of brotherhoods from common female descent. Acquisition of wealth led to greed to keep it in the family instead of sharing it with the tribe, populated by a common mother figure. Therefore, inheritance shifted to a patrilineal line; a man could leave his wealth to his son, rather than to his brother or sisters. The Kushites expanded to the northwest to Nubia, which gave rise to a Sudanese empire that arose in the western lands south of the Sahara. The Ghanaian, Mali, and Songhai cultures arose from each other in the wake of militarism. To the south, in what we know as Rhodesia and Mozambique the Zimbabwean culture arose. Gold was abundant in this area and commerce and trade were the cornerstones of a culture that dated to bartering with Solomon who traded for gold, gemstones, and objects of art with a land he knew as Ophir. This culture was known for its feudal aristocracy, standing army, its lavish imperial palace, and two story apartments, lining its capitol, Mohomatopa.

These civilizations were magnificent, yet they reflected that in Eden, man sought to equate himself with God. This violated the contractual relationship with God, and Man had to be expelled from Eden to live by the sweat of his brow. This involved competition and striving. In turn, greed became instituted among men; with this came feelings of frustration that had to be released to the outside. The faculty humans have for this release is anger, an emotion that can either drive a person to use his/her abilities to their maximum or to eliminate the perceived threat to having more: We can go to war. Thus, did Cain slay Abel. Racism became an instrumentation for an excuse for the Cains of the world to slay the Abels.

Mark and Kiona became aware that the battle fought and materially lost but spiritually won by Gideon Retta was an instance of racism bringing about the cataclysm that cost him and his wife their earthly existence. Yet not a dent had been made in racist thought before or after that time. It was beginning to seem like the same dubious battle that Don Quixote carried on with the windmill. At length, Mark arose from his seat in the library and took Kiona by the hand. He took them both to the outside before he spoke. "Have you been having eerie feelings while we do this primal study after what we have learned about Gideon, Dark Water, and their struggle?" She asked her husband what kind of eerie feelings he meant, and he elaborated on the thoughts he had relating the struggle to the first murder and to Don Quixote's useless battle. She saw the look of anguish on his face, took his hand, and said, "Come on, Boy, we need a bike ride to the mountains!" With that, she led him away from the library home to embark on their tandem bike to Mesa Verde with Articulata in the bike seat and a packed lunch in a bag on the handlebars.

They parked the bike off of the road before the entrance to the cave where Gideon's remains lay. Mark knelt before the tomb, as if it were an altar and wept. Kiona knew instinctively what was troubling her man's soul. She sat next to where he knelt and pulled his head down to her lap. She began stroking his face and quoted from Corinthians 13:12, "When I was a child, I spoke as a child, but when I became a man I put the things of childhood behind me. Now we see through a glass darkly; then we shall see face to face. Now I know in part; then shall I know fully, even as I am fully known. And now these three remain: faith, hope, and love. But the greatest of these is love." The words penetrated Mark's soul. From his lips, escaped the words, "Getting frustrated was like Adam felt and Eve did when she ate of the fruit before he did. They wanted to know the world of God before they knew God. That is the child in me. I saw through a glass imperfectly and thought I saw clearly that racism won over change, but it is changing in minute amounts, the way a differential equation becomes an integral one, second by second. Only I can't see it happening because it's happening right in the middle of where I am. If I can maintain hope and faith, I can love God. Then I will know God and Know Man." Kiona looked with tears of happiness in her eyes at him and said, "It's a simple, yet a complex truth that if we love each other enough, the land that we are brought together upon becomes sacred, and we love it. Then it loves us and nurtures us. Through this mutual love, we come to love and know God, and he comes to know and love us." Then they heard Articulata's cry for attention and brought her into their embrace before the body of Gideon Retta. The light may have refracted at a peculiar angle, but Kiona thought she saw a smile move across the preserved face of the four hundred-year-old remains of the ancient warrior.

Needless to say the couple returned to their study with a new vigor. They learned how the art of war, introduced by Cain, tore them apart, led to another economic and militaristic rivalry, and, in the end, led to the degradation of the magnificent expression of God's love for the world. As in inquisitorial Spain. The rivals emerged as part of a melting pot. Arabs came to West Africa around 738 and brought together nomadic tribes and clans in the procurement of goods, trade. The Soninke clans were around Senegal, Guinea, Mauritania, and Mali around 300.

Berber invaders took them over until the Soninkes could gain strength through superior weaponry and gold, which the Arabs coveted. However, they were not able to defeat these clans, and they became the Ghanaian civilization that ushered in the golden age of West Africa. Salt and gold provided the sources of wealth that allowed the Ghanaians to maintain an empire with Arabs, Berbers, Moroccans and various other tribes waiting to pounce on them. A Moslem tribe laid siege to Ghana for ten years before their capital, of Kumbi fell. This occurred in 1077. All the states under Ghana declared themselves independent. Under the Mandinkas, the Mali developed at the Niger River. They initiated a program of agricultural expansion and gained control of the gold trade and salt mines. The Mandinkas were Moslem, and the Mali represented the first great Islamic state in the Sudan. The maximum achievement occurred under Musa I. A well ordered; just empire of great wealth and splendor existed. Merchants traveled freely about West Africa, Egypt, India, and China. Timbuktu boasted a great university and a grand mosque. Iron, tin, and copper were mined. In 1325, the Songhai stronghold of Gao was conquered. Taxes flourished, and the food supply was abundant. However with the death of Musa, the Mali declined, and the Songhai captured Timbuktu and made it an even greater city. By 1475, the Songhai rose to supremacy. They became masters of the soil and water, traded with the river people. The cities of Jenne, Gao, Timbuktu, all boasted universities. A well-known university was flourishing at Sankore. Moroccans, who became known as Moors, harassed this empire. They took over the salt mines under Judai Pasha, who took Timbuktu and Gao with the aid of Spanish gunpowder. The Hausa were independent states that were never brought under centralized control, but cooperated with in a loose federation with these empires. They are in what became Nigeria, where an important Black culture, known as the Nok culture is said to have had its beginnings from 800 BC These Moors conquered the Songhai with the help of Spanish and Portuguese mercenaries, the mercenaries that turned the Falasha's against the Moslems.

To the South a civil war caused a split into southern and northern factions in 1485. The northern emperor was unable to relate to southern chiefs, and he allied himself with the Portuguese because of their guns, which were turned on them. Thus, did White, Christian Europe begin its rape of what had excelled for centuries before they even showed their faces.

Other than the wanton exploitation and slaughter for resources, the main response of the world's White industrialized powers has been one of denial, degradation, and destruction. As early as 146 BC when Rome defeated Carthage, their memories were stirred by the Kushite civilization whose power they could not control or by Hannibal, who had the audacity to bring the war to their soil and almost defeat them. They so feared resurgence, that they had to destroy this Black culture, Carthage. The destruction had to be for all time. Hannibal was pursued until he committed suicide. The library at Carthage was destroyed and

500,000 volumes of learning destroyed. The Moors followed suit and destroyed the libraries at Sankore, Timbuktu. The most debasing of such knowledge destruction occurred at Alexandria. During the rise of the early Christians, Theophilus felt an urge to promote faith and to destroy pagan knowledge. An academy had been started at the library at Alexandria under the teachings of a woman philosopher, Hypatia. The writings of Plato and Aristotle were discussed. He led a mob against the center of learning, and his son, Cyril equally as zealous, found Hypatia, led a mob against her, and hacked her to pieces. For this pious act, sainthood was conferred upon him. This occurred in 414 AD. Slavery was inaugurated from the West Coast of Africa, now that the civilizations that would have stood against it were sacked. They would have arisen against it because of what it did to nations that were already ravaged by the greed of parasites. Farmers and craftsmen were taken from their own land, thus increasing the cost of production by creating difficulty in finding people with productive skills and reducing them to serfdom in the guise of cheap laborers, making production cheaper for a boor that did not realize the worth of a human being because an institutional structuring took place that condoned this by systematic lying. In America, the new nation built with old eyes, needed slaves. In the Spanish colonies indigenous populations were allowed graciously to work themselves to death in the silver and gold mines. A church official came to the rescue when a high death rate was hampering production. Bishop Bartolome De Las Casas proposed that each gentleman could import 12 African slaves.

How could Man blunt his sensitivity to this inhumanity in his midst? The start was the curse of Noah against the children of Ham for seeing his father naked. From there, a cover up took over because it was in harmony with a greedy hidden agenda: The rapers and ravagers of cultures did not want to look at themselves. Beginning with the curse. It seems only logical to ask what was Noah doing naked in the first place for Ham to see? Another sensible question that comes to mind is why are Ham's children supposed to pay for what Ham saw and what Noah did? The fact that such superlative civilizations arose makes the whole curse a lie. However, the obliteration of these cultures leaves a vacuum of protest. The European traders were able to picture the African Black as a barbarian that was half animal. For this reason, as late as the nineteenth century the right Reverend James Wilson was allowed to display his indifference to human suffering by referring to slavery as the gracious institution that elevated the heathen cannibal to the civilized contented domestic around them.

Mark was morally offended by the fact that such a lie could be perpetrated upon a segment of humanity for all the centuries it had been. What's more, how could the single voice with him and Kiona and their group behind them make in the narrow minded trappings modern day man used to hide from the truth of existence. The answer came to him suddenly. "If you save one human being, you save humanity." Only Gideon Retta had saved more than one human being. He had saved Fiery Water and Ismalia and Running Lion. He had saved Komarovski and Ericio De Pelunis, Purple Flower and Red Earth, and Rafana and Tom Engler. Would Mark and Kiona add themselves to the list?

# Chapter 3

The time had arrived for an organizational meeting. The decision had been made to go to Africa with Mark and Kiona; a central campsite had to be decided upon. Lagos, in Nigeria, was suggested because it was a big city and offered easy access; Dakar, in Senegal was suggested because several kingdoms that became part of the Sudanic Empire were within its bounds. For historical reasons Freetown, in Sierra Leone was considered. Slave ships were launched from this site, and, under British influence. Slavery was abolished there. It was reasoned that many descendants of slaves, who were freed by the Englishmen, would reside in the area. However, there was little of archeological significance in this country. Mattani was in favor of going further south to study the Zimbabwean ruins because she would be closer to home and family. She did come to realize that their mission would find a higher degree of data in the west. Dakar was decided upon as the campsite.

Aaron sent away for brochures from the Bureau in the Sengalese government that dealt with trade and commerce to get government permission for a site and for literature about their culture. Six tribes exist in a former French colony that is 80% Moslem. The nation of Gambia runs through the country. The country is about the size of Nebraska and houses about four million people. A rigid caste system divided the country into five castes. The area in south of the nation is known the Casamance. The country supports itself mainly through agriculture and a fishing industry. The main crop is peanuts, and several industries are derived from it; phosphate mining is important around the Dakar area. The country has Ghanaian, Mali, and Songhai roots. The nation has a republican form of government with a powerful president since an attempted coup d'états in 1962. The tribes in the

417

Dakar area are mainly Wolof and Serer. The coastal areas have a pleasant climate most of the year. A site was chosen near St. Louis at the mouth of the Senegal River because here Dutch, English, and French slave traders did their business and because the Portuguese had established a settlement at Goree, near the area. In deference to Mattani the group asked Aaron to look into starting a dig in the Zimbabwe area after they completed this one. The plans were being laid down.

Freddy Gauland was nervous. His connection with Tripod Productions was shaky. The leads he came up with never seemed to pan out. He was so excited about the project with Professors Horton and Owens for a movie about the Gideon Retta Saga. The focal point of his interest lay in his connection to the Sound People. He thought there might be a connection between him and Elk Horn, the husband of Fawn Eyes. The point of revelation of the connection was the phylacteries that were brought West from the Phoenician trader, who was his father, after the decimation of his tribe on the East Coast. Freddy was not the family success story. He had a dream about being a neuro-surgeon and tried a stiff pre-med course in college. He could not get through the anatomy course. His dissections resembled the work of Lizzie Borden. The final insult came when his instructor's suggestion for improving his technique was to paint portraits of the garbage scows on the Hudson River. His family was embarrassed and placed him in the obscurity of Tripod, an obscure holding company for a failed movie company that caved in during the Great Depression; he was given a generous allowance to keep the Gauland name out of the public eye by dealing in art objects. It was in this line of work that he found the phylacteries mentioned in an art journal. His relative in the larger company felt a big production would bring back the glamour of making movies to his family name. Freddy was instructed to bargain for the movie rights to the Gideon Retta Story. The bargaining team consisted of the two professors, the four other partners, and, the archeology group.

Needless to say, the bargaining meant several sessions with closed windows to prevent the language from heating up the mountain air of the community and causing long extinct volcanoes to erupt. Jonos brought up a very pertinent point. He felt that money could be saved by presenting the film as a documentary that showed the growth of man to a creature overcoming the ways of the world to find a natural sense of a supreme being in the same way the Soviets were learning that they had to return to an essence beyond themselves to keep the culture, established by the revolution, from crumbling. Mattani argued that getting this idea across required an emotional impact rather than just facts. This meant being drawn into a story, not just a presentation of facts; the evidence lay in the difference between two Russian writers: Aleksandr Solzhenitsin describes the criminal injustices of the Russian prison system in a long drawn out narrative that presents the brutal facts that occurred in "The Gulag Archipelago". In "Doctor Zhivago", Boris Pasternak created the story of a man that was robbed of the right to love and live and to be treated as an individual to the extent that pilfering fire wood was a state crime or that poetry that presented personal views was regarded as evil. The choking impact of totalitarianism is expressed more by being drawn into it and living it than by reading a factual description of it in action. Likewise, the robbery of resources, the expropriation of souls, and the misguided perception of God that colonialism brought to mankind had to be brought to public awareness on a feeling level by living through the experience vicariously through the eyes of another. One does not factually find a path to God; one feels his/her way there.

Another issue that Grady Almederson brought up was the changing character of the movie industry. Aside from the fact that more people are not attending movies frequently due to the availability of home videos at a lower cost, people needed to develop a capacity to relax while in the process of doing business. Hence, the growing tendencies to use talking books in auto cassettes, while enroute from one destination to another. It seemed that if the project was to be successful, these markets should be probed. Suddenly there was a gleam in Freddy's eye, such an idea could get his company out of the red, but he needed backing. "If we advertise share sales, as part of the introductory material in the movie, and I can get approval from my uncle to give you shares at a cut rate, we can turn this into a profitable venture for both of us. Immediately after the meeting, Freddy went to the pay phone and called his uncle. When his uncle heard the proposal, he wanted to check it out; he said he'd be on tomorrow's flight. Mark and Kiona agreed to meet the plane with him.

The plane landed at the Boulder airport; as the passengers descended the stairs, Freddy called out to a pudgy, little man, "Uncle, here, over here!" As he got a glimpse of his face, Mark thought there was something familiar about the figure approaching them. As the little man drew near, Mark screamed out, "Bartie," and ran up to the restaurant owner and hugged him. "My God!

Is this Mark Engler? I'd thought I never would see you again." They caught each other up on the years, and Mark introduced his wife and child. Bartie knew about Arne and Rachel: They had a stop in at his deli on the way back to Ohio, he also knew about Kiona and Articulata. However, he had no idea that Mark had grown into such a shrewd businessman. Mark laughed and said no such thing had happened; a committee made these decisions. Bartie, as kind as he was, also was a shrewd, tough businessman when he wanted to be. He dragged the committee through import/export considerations on the movie, the talking books, the videotapes, advertising royalties, protection against plagiarism, tax write off.

In the end, he agreed to put his full support behind the project and told Mark he could always have a job at the deli. They all smiled, but they all noticed the tear in his eye. Mark put his arm around him and asked him to spend a few days with them.

Bartie was very appreciative of the opportunity to spend some travel time away from the deli. It wasn't fun anymore. Students came, grew up a little, left, and came back for football weekends with a bunch of garbage talk about how Diamond's Deli was the life of the campus and how Bartie was the host of an infinite number of good times that involved beer, women, and the best link with home through kosher sandwiches. Mark and Kiona showed him their scrapbook from Yucatan and Rachel and Helga's translation of the scroll and quiver documents. Bartie wanted to be a part of this organization, an integral part of it. He was even more impressed with the fact that, through genetics, he might be connected to the history of the area of the country on which he now stood, and which he had never seen before in his entire life. That blew his mind completely.

Thus, continued the saga of Tripod Productions, with Bar Kochba

Fenzel and Freddy Gauland at its head, scheming on a way to buy controlling shares of common and preferred stock and sell them at the same time. Bartie sold his restaurant and began an earnest advertisement campaign in the local theaters to buy stock in a movie that actually took place on the sidewalks where they strolled, got into fights, campaigned for issues. The hulla baloo attracted politicians looking for issues, businessmen in the community looking for tax deductions and pro-social flows for monies that came from evading anti pollutant legislation, and a group of angry kids looking into ways to fit into the community rather than destroy it and themselves. They were angry because a couple leading them, for which there were strong bonds of attachment, was leaving them. True enough, they had worked hard to find a capable replacement, but she hadn't proven herself to them the way they had. As a result, Helga and Julio had to meet with their group and launch a plan to have the movie made in Durango. Guintera Aguinaldo accepted the challenge of battling to have youngsters engaged in a project that would provide a multitude of jobs to the community and give some angry kids a sense of their own history. To accomplish this, she had to join ranks with the business community and bring the angry youngsters into a sense of harmony with them. The truth of the statement: It takes a community to raise a child was about to come out.

In the choice of this commitment, Guintera connected herself with her group, connected herself to the archeology group, and connected her group and Grady, Ruthie, Bert and Jack, and the two professors, as they came to be called. In turn several inter-weavings led her to discover a connection to Gideon Retta and his war for recognition of individual right. She became acquainted with Mark and Kiona and learned of the scroll and quiver document translations through her relationship to Julio and Helga. In reading these translations, she discovered two names: Thomas Aguinaldo, the spy on Father Nico's ranch and fighter, killed by Trocadero and Guintera, the dancer, who fell in love with Gideon and was deported to Majorca, as a Jew. To bear out the connection she decided to create a family tree.

Guintera's simultaneous connection to the archeology group and the business structure also caused her a complication from which she had to extricate herself. After a meeting, she accidentally dropped her purse. When she bent down to pick it up, she found four appreciative eyes trying to look away from what had interested them a few seconds ago. She left the room, stifling an uproarious laugh while Freddy and Bartie attempted to recover their composure. There was a twinkle in Bartie's eye that, in all honesty, matched her own. He was in his seventies, but he was alive; he thought, he plotted, he played angles. "Geezer or no, I do believe, I like this man; we'll just see what happens." In the meantime, she had to cement a relationship to a group of youngsters whose needs she saw and whom she wanted to protect from the drug and street life on the West Coast. She shuddered when she thought of the horror to which she had exposed herself because no one was there to give enough of a damn to stop her.

Grady and Bartie came to the next meeting with her and the kids. Freddy also came but he had decided to listen more than talk. Grady asked the kids just what kind of interest they had. Some wanted to design and make sets, some wanted to learn how to operate the camera, and some wanted to act and learn to produce and direct. Some wanted to be in the advertising and money making end of the enterprise. These Bartie took aside to be schooled by him and Grady to work for Freddy. In addition, Jack was there to teach them ways to cut corners and save money. Guintera found ways to open up doors for the youngsters that had expressed interests in the actual making of the film. The youth of Durango were alive with the excitement of their new adventure. Julio and Helga were now relics of a distant past.

Now that Guintera had an interest in antiquity awakened, and her new charges were occupied with the growing industry, she turned her interest to the finer, more vintage areas of life. She invited Bartie to dinner at her apartment and instructed him to bring a flagon of Lambrusco wine, and a loaf of Italian bread. He did as ordered and brought a bouquet of Tiger Lilies he had stolen from a family flowerbed. He toasted her beauty and commented on the gorgeous tawny caste of her skin against the off white of her apartment. Soon their clothes were off, and they began a passionate night of making love. After several hours, she said, "Where do you get your energy? I am about thirty years younger than you, and I think you will destroy me by way of sexual expression." Bartie laughed, and she joined him in a chuckle

and added, "You're damn good! Did you hang around those coed ladies, when you served lunch? Of just what did your desserts consist?"
She did warn him to be careful around the kids because they were im-
pressionable and because she cared about them. They were more than
a job; they were a portion of the tortured experiences she had endured
and overcome. She was not reliving her life through them; she was
sharing her learning of coping skills with them. As she finished describing her relationship to her wards, he put his finger to her lips and
kissed her and said, "I love kids too, but I found out that we have to
lead our own lives apart from them. Otherwise, they'll think we belong
to them and devour us." Then they turned to each other again.

Freddy went through a period of depression because he also had an
interest awakened in Guintera, but he found an interesting way to
adapt to it. He remained attached to the movie project, but he became
increasingly attached to Grady and Ruthena. He expressed his obsession with tracing his roots from both the Phoenician and from Elk
Horn. In doing so, he found a process that took skill and patience to
unearth. He wanted to add this skill to the services offered to the clien-
tele, as well as to the kids in the group. From there he enrolled at the
university in family therapy courses and within a year had a license to
practice. Because of his linkage to retired businessmen via the family
trees, he was able to specialize in areas in which problems occurred
with generation gaps. Particularly in the conflicts that occurred in
moving from one culture to another. In the course of these transactions, he met many ladies and was able to pick and choose among
them. He maintained deep friendships with Grady and Ruthena and
Bartie and Guintera.

Both Grady and Ruthie and Jack and Bert were conscious that they
would not see their kids or Articulata for a long time. They began to
take Artie to the park and playground more often. Artie began to notice
how bigger boys would pick on smaller boys or how some crowds of
girls shunned other girls. One day she was with Grandpa Grady and
Grandpa Jack and asked them about why boys and girls got mean to
each other. Grady was the first to respond. Hugging her to him, he
answered thoughtfully, "Sometimes people get unhappy inside. They
don't always know about what they are unhappy, but they feel trapped

by their unhappiness. They think that they can get rid of it if they find someone or something to put it on." Jack added that someone that usually gets the unhappiness is usually smaller or weaker than the unhappy person is. The smaller or weaker person becomes unhappy and starts people hating each other and thinking that they deserve more of God's world than they have because they are better than the ones that made them feel unhappy. That's what makes people take from each other. Right now your mommy and daddy are working to show all of us how we learned to do this mean thing to other people." Artie took Grandpa Grady's hand and Grandpa Jack's hand and said, "How did my grandpas both get so smart?" Grady stopped and thought, then said, "I guess I had the meanness scrubbed off of me by a sea that was meaner and cleaner than I was." Jack paused awhile longer and stated as if he were just fitting something together now." A long time ago, a thirteen-year-old boy gave a raincoat to a bully, and I just learned how beautiful that was today. That boy was your daddy."

Mark thought to himself, as he rode his mountain bike on the road between Durango and Mesa Verde: "What have I learned about how Man has fit himself to the world of his Maker, and how has he approached the nearness to its reality that Gideon Retta and Dark Waters had. They were apparently able to sublimate a material loss into a spiritual victory. How much of the victories we claim are self defeats that keep us mentally incarcerated in a prison whose walls are of our own making? How long will we continue to build racial, religious, and cultural barriers between us that imprison us? Where is the magical formula that will allow us to say I am unique, but your uniqueness is as good as mine is? Let's use both of ours to get through the world."

Gideon, Dark Waters, and Fiery Water learned that they had to cling to each other and combine their uniqueness' to get through this world and to negotiate the next one. They had opportunities to build mental prisons that compartmentalized their ideas into who stood for them or against them in obtaining material resources; what they chose to do was to regard the life that God gave them as precious and fight to keep it alive for them instead of imposing their view of it on others. They did not eliminate killing and violence because human beings need a confirmation that they have an existence that will endure. They get this confirmation by belonging to a system of belief that they believe is right. The rightness is confirmed by bringing numbers to the fold. Hence, the push to cajole, impose, or otherwise prove we are right by the multitudes we bring into agreement. The result is a stagnation that blocks out those outside the pale of our agreed upon ideas. Mark digested these thoughts and tried to fit them into the pattern of exploration of life upon which he and Kiona were about to embark.

Mark remembered the nightmare he had from which Kiona had rescued him by getting him to fully understand the twenty-third Psalm. Now a version of the dream returned to him: He went inside the structure where a rarefied atmosphere enveloped him. He learned the hidden truth about all of Man. When he emerged he knew humanity, but the knowledge made him different. He was different physically and emotionally than he had been. His skin had become ashen, and his hair had turned white. Some had fallen out. The biggest difference was in the perceptive capacity. He felt knowledgeable the way Frankenstein's monster had. He loved mankind and wanted to give that love, but the information he gleaned made his fellow man look at him with revulsion. The love he had felt for mankind turned to hate because revulsion had fostered rejection. Suddenly he heard an inward voice, perhaps the same voice that had emerged from Kurilia so long ago, or maybe Moses heard it out of a burning bush, maybe Paul heard it on the road to Damascus. The voice that thundered an answer in his head roared, "Thou hast penetrated the mystery of my Word. You cannot go back to the ways of other Men. For thou art my prophet. This means you can no longer walk with others. You have to walk at a distance and guide them." To this he answered, "Nay, My Lord, indeed I have become knowledgeable, but I am but another man. Therefore, I will revere thee because I can never become thee.

Mark was fearful because he felt that the awareness that he could not share all knowledge with God made him covetous and envious. Once again, he shared his fears with his wife. Together they looked for an answer. They found the answer they sought in an unlikely place. They saw Guintera enter a church and to emerge with a serene look on her face. When they next saw her, they asked her about it. She told them that she attended AA meetings there to humble herself before

God: To remind herself that she was part of His plan, whose magnitude she could not fully understand because she was created in His image, not as Him. She went on to expound upon the idea of the capacity to surrender: In the Garden of Eden Adam came to want the same knowledge as God and was banned from the paradise which he had abused by seeking an intelligence he was not meant to have because he was not structured to be able to manage it. The findings of Tycho Brahe, Copernicus, and Johann Keplar shed much light on the ordering of the universe; they also, as a corollary, gave Man the idea that he was the center of the universe. Thus, he was supposedly able to master the world around him. Failure to do so would be an admission of weakness and allow others to take the powers from him by stealth or might. Therefore, an admission of inability to handle an area of life was a sign of vulnerability. Yet, Man is not structured to negotiate all areas of life or to reconstruct the world of God's creation to his liking. To be able to live in a society, Man must learn to harness the powers he can and give up what he cannot handle. Addiction maintained a delusional state, in which Man attempted to control all of life and run away from the fact that he couldn't handle all at the same time. To be strong for the kids, in the group, Guintera found that she had to humble herself before God so that she could concentrate her efforts in areas in which goals could be reached. She suggested that maybe Mark and Kiona had to gear their efforts to disproving Ham's curse, not connecting it to all knowledge, which they could not attain.

They wanted to know how this grappling for knowledge, as they were, could lead to an addiction, and how it led her to one. She related this tale: When she was living in the streets, she met a young man who was extremely bright, but extremely troubled. He was a former law student that had washed out of law school. He did not wash out because he did not study. To the contrary, he over studied because he did not believe in the brightness he had and felt he had to learn everything he could without organizing and prioritizing information. He came to the streets after his washout because he felt he had nowhere else to go. His family wrote him off as crippled emotionally and weak. He got a room and supported it by menial jobs, but he read and philosophized constantly trying to find a place in the world, in which he could fit.

She found him in a library one day when she was plying her wares. Having no one, they filled the vacuum in their lives by engaging in a kind of puppy love. For a while, they were happy, but the real world intruded upon them with demands to earn a living and start a family to show those that condemned them that they were stable. They were caught in the bind of living their free, unrestricted life with their peers and the guilt for not pleasing their families, in the end, he tried to kill himself and became a chronic mental patient. She went back to the streets, but she never forgot that he tried to handle what he couldn't manage and destroyed himself trying it. She did visit him, but seeing him as a shell of a person depressed her horribly. For a while she went back to drugs to run away from this episode, but the real addiction was to an impossible dream. She and Bartie shared their twilight/dawn love because it offered them both a comfort zone, but her real source of a stable relationship was the meetings that kept her strong for the kids that looked like they were headed along the same destructive path she had taken.

Guintera began to think more frequently about her origins since Bartie and Freddy felt a desire to learn more about their connection to Elk Horn. She began with Thomas Aguinaldo, who had been killed by Trocadero and whose ears had been sent back to Gideon with a cruel, sadistic note; he had joined the war because a reportedly beautiful older sister was sold into bondage to pay a debt in Portugal. He was of the Mestizo class, intermarried into the caste of colonizers. The stain on his pride to have one of his family seized and disrupted from her family moved him to fight against such oppression. Guintera went to the library to find bills of lading; passenger lists to and from Portugal during the time span between 1450 and 1500. She found a listing under a name, Escobar, which described a tall, Black prisoner brought to New Spain in chains. He had been transported with Falasha rabbi and a tall beige skinned woman, said to be a Jewess. They were let off at Majorca where they went their separate ways. The records seemed to disappear. Guintera asked Bartie if he would like to engage in a mutual project with her in seeking information about their genetic connections. She wrote to the Majorcan government Census Bureau to get information and was surprised to learn of a woman fitting the characteristics previously described who stowed away on a ship to the Americas. When she was discovered, she told the captain she was carrying his child and wanted to make a new start in the New World. The captain's logbook described a raid by a pirate with a Black woman, second in command, who took them and the crew prisoner. They were virtually dumped on an island off of the South Carolina coast. Because of the tawniness of her skin, she was labeled as non-white and sold into slavery.

Checking into old slave market records was not a difficult process to negotiate by mail. Guintera was sold to a shipping merchant, listed as A. Caduceus. He had a predilection for drink and was in need of a woman since he had never married. He was kind to the original Guintera, but he mistreated her daughter. When she entered puberty, he turned to her sexually. She stole a rowboat and made it to the Cajun Islands in the Gulf of Mexico. A descendant of hers is said to have served with Jean La Fitte in the War of 1812 disguised, as a boy. She was pregnant after the battle of New Orleans and ran away to what was to be Texas. Her daughter was a survivor at the Alamo. The records became spotty after this. A Phillipe Aqulnaldo was killed at Shiloh. He had fought a dozen rebel soldiers for five hours from a blacksmith shop; the remainder of his company had reached in inch by inch fighting. After the others were wiped out, and his ammo ran low, he held the rebels at bay by shooting molten metal from a furnace with a bellows until a bullet found its mark. Her great grandfather was a cook on the Titanic. He rowed himself to safety in a huge pot. He picked up three other survivors, and they lost their voices screaming for a cup of Mulligan Stew. Her grandfather flew barnstorming planes during the depression and fought with Claire Chennault in the Flying Tigers before the United States entered WW II. Her history took some digging out, but it held a richness of its own.

Bartie's history was traceable from Elk Horn and Fawn Eyes to their sons in Puget Sound country. After Long Branch's migration, the connection shifted to Mesa Verde. From this point a gap exists in explaining the transition from the Pueblo tribe to the Caucasian race in his genetics. Another, enigma lay at the other end of the Lineage tracing. How would a Phoenician trader bearing phylacteries show up on an East Coast American Shore? These riddles seemed to require the organization of a separate dig at a later date.

This need for further exploration became the basis of another advertising campaign. Grady got the idea from Bartie's dilemma to add a line about organizing digs to complete scanty knowledge about family histories to the commercial that appeared in the movie theaters. The result was an avalanche of inquiries about developing personal family digs. To meet the demands, Professors Horton and Owens started a training program in Archeology digging that would offer college credits in Guintera's group of adolescents. Bert and Ruthie began to do research in exploring the potential market in videotapes and talking books.

# Chapter 4

In the course of human events no movement or belief pattern develops without incurring criticism or making enemies. This also occurred with Kiona's plan of endeavor and about their public stance against racism, as shown by their union in matrimony. Minuscule hate movements seemed to coalesce around the couple. A member of the family that had cheated Professor Owens was one of the leaders in this White backlash activity. Signs were tacked to the trees in their neighborhood. A swastika was painted on their house. Mark was expecting an attempt to burn a cross on his lawn. He, Grady, Jack, Jonos, and Mattani were waiting for the little party on a Friday night. Around the block, Julio had made special arrangements for a paddy wagon to be dispatched. When the cross had been pounded into the ground and was about to be lit, lights flashed, and a group stood around holding gas cans and blow torches. At either end were two men with sawed off shotguns. "Anyone need help with a bonfire," called a voice. The perpetrators were given orders to anoint themselves with one of two gallon jugs and to follow the parade that was led by one shotgun bearer and followed up by the other. The others were in between them brandishing their torches. The leader was singled out and ordered to wash the swastika off of the house then told to drop his pants and have one painted on each cheek of his buttocks. The paint had been mixed with the anointing oil, which turned out to be stinkweed dissolved in formic acid and colored with prune juice. Before they joined the parade, they had to pour some of the anointing oil in their shoes and put them back on their feet. They had to join hands and sing Civil War songs at the top of their lungs, in order to add a disturbing the peace charge to any others brought against them. Once in the paddy wagon one stalwart shouted, "Racial Supremacy is not dead!" He was joined by several other people in the wagon that added with emphasis, "Yeah, you can tell it by its stink!" Unfortunately the Owens family harrasser was not present. The putrid robes were not discarded, but used as evidence. The residents of the holding cell also did not appreciate the scent that the racially pure brought with them, and several of them brought visible marks of their disapproval before the judge, who asked if they could identify any of their assailants. The reply was no because they wore masks. The judge smiled as he sentenced them and said, "What goes around comes around." The cross was burned at a hot dog roast, and the ashes were left on the front steps of the family that was leading the White Backlash activity.

A security guard at the South African embassy took it upon himself to chastise Mattani for being a "Cheeky Kaffir" in a super market with his billy club. He could not be brought to trial due to diplomatic immunity. He also worked as the embassy chauffeur. A call came for him to pickup dignitary at the airport. The dignitary's name was Madame Pickle Snatch Kovaboster. He could not locate her and had to have her paged several times over the loudspeaker. Someone would answer the page and designate a meeting place at which she would not appear. At one of these places he found five cages of Llamas being prepared for shipment to a zoo. At another, he found a convention of condom salesmen. The last site where he had a response to his page was a group of evolution students returning from a remarkable study of the development of advances in the prostate gland of the horse, as was demonstrated in sixteen progenitor specimens. It dawned on him that Madame Pickle Snatch Kovaboster was a fictitious name. When he got back to his car, he found a large circle of people avoiding it. There was a ring of male skunks around it attracted by the spray of female skunk on the car. A note was on the wind shield saying:

Dear Kaffir,
   You're in our country. We frown on beating ladies senselessly. Congratulations on winning by diplomatic immunity. Hope you learned something.
Some Americans
P.S: Have a nice bus trip home.

Mattani chuckled when she heard about the escapade; the message here was that racism would not be tolerated. The final note in this backlash activity occurred as a result of several articles going back and forth in the newspapers, written by both adversaries. The racists referred to the Curse of Ham, and Kiona and let loose with a barrage, in fact, of data disproving it, and the group presented corroborating data that demonstrated the results of racist thinking. They described the horror and hate with which the Pueblo war was fought. At a mountain park by a river, in fact it was the same river into which Fiery Water had plunged to save Joaquim so many centuries earlier, the archeology group spoke on their expedition.

The family member of the family that took the land promised to the Owens family was in a sailboat with a placard boycotting the archeologists as rabble-rousers. Suddenly a gust of wind caught in the sails and caused the boat to capsize. Mark heard a voice cry out: "Help, I can't swim." He dove in the water and pulled his adversary out of the water and brought the boat to shore. After this, the racist name calling, debates, and threatening gestures stopped. Whatever racist feelings were left in this community, they were not blatantly expressed, but the burial underground let them fester like a sore.

Knowing that people would use facts to fit their preconceived notions had become a discouraging thrust to Kiona. Mark and Articulata tried various strategies to cheer her up to no avail. In desperation, they asked Rachel and Arne to visit. They came that weekend.

Yusseff had grown by leaps and bounds. They seemed very happy together. In order to end hostilities, the man Mark had rescued proposed that the Owens family and the archeology group have a picnic in mesa Verde National Park. Reed Hymer and His family joined them as guests. One guest seemed to have a peculiar fascination with Rachel and Kiona, staring after them with an angry look in his eyes. Reed pointed him out to Mark and Arne, and all three began to note his meandering about the park, looking for quick exit sites, etc. Reed, at one point, recognized his face; he was the student they had dropped off at the police station, wearing a garbage can. He apprised Mark and Arne about who he was. The young man was surprised to see a familiar figure dressed in a trench coat and a Cary grant mask and another wearing a Mike Tyson mask. He smiled and said; "Don't you guys ever change your tactics?" With that said he tore one mask off then the other and found his parole officer and the chief of police under the disguises. They got on either side of him, took an arm, and escorted him to a police car in which he spent the afternoon locked up as a suspicious character. After this the chief gave him a ticket to tour a zoo in Phoenix, Arizona that was about to receive a shipment of Llamas. Due to a mix-up in the plane ticket office, he was seated in the freight compartment with the Llamas. Rachel, Arne, and the rapidly growing Yusseff enjoyed this train of events. As for the young man, who was not so young anymore, he was fast learning that vengeance was not the route to pursue.

The chain of events was a tonic for Kiona's depression and lifted her spirits tremendously. She and Mattani decided to have an unusual party.

They would knock on peoples' doors and start singing a song and ask them to help them finish it then ask them to join them in going to another neighbor's house and start another tune. Soon practically the whole town were marching through the streets singing. When they came to the high school, the marching band joined them. They began to stop at businesses that were still open. One man let himself be dragged from dinner, bringing a shish-ke-bab with him. Another man about to pick another man's pocket was handcuffed to a deputy and dragged along. The crowd became so massive that a police escort went along with it; some of them forgot themselves and joined in the singing. A couple hot dog vendors and peanut and popcorn salesmen joined in. The party ended at the South African Embassy with a rendition of "We Are Marching to Praetoria". Some of the staff wanted to join the singers. After all had returned home, Mark and Kiona, Rachel and Arne, Helga and Julio, and Reed and Michelle took a trip to Mesa Verde and stood opposite the cave where Gideon Retta was interred. They all joined hands and sang the old Woodie Guthrie song "So Long, It's Been Good To Know Yuh".

There were tears in Kiona's and Mark's eyes along with every one else there. They all knew what they had unearthed and what had to be done with it.

The leave taking with Arne and Rachel and Reed and Michelle was hard for the two of them. The softening blow was that their campaign against racism was beginning to show some positive effects. the facts that the family that had wronged Professor Owens' family stepped out of their racist cocoon, and the willingness of staff members from the South African Consulate to join in the singing might be an indication that mankind is willing to grow up. Time would tell the difference. What time would not change would be the friendships that had been brought together by the events that had bonded them together permanently. They were not fixed into the cultural norms that meant safety and security to a parental generation, but to the world of today without attacking the parental paradigms.

Mark was bothered by something that was causing him a lot of disquiet. He couldn't quite put his finger on it. A quotation kept coming to his mind: "God, grant me the serenity to let go of the things I cannot change, the courage to change the things I can, and the wisdom to know the difference." He could not fathom why this was preoccupying him, but he decided to think about it. He saw Kiona playing with Artie in the park and smiled for a moment. He went over to them smiling at his own little circle of serenity. His arm circled his wife, and he told her something is on his mind. She asked if it couldn't wait until later. She wanted to give their daughter some quality time. He said O.K. and proceeded to pick up Articulata and plant a kiss on her forehead then walk through the park alone and think a while. Whether or not he and Kiona presented factual information about the curse of Ham, those who were bent on myths of racial superiority would continue to believe in the curse or find other supporting data. Yet there were also large numbers of people that needed to be pushed into taking a stand that could be moved by presentation of facts to support this move. He had to have enough faith in God to be able to provide the data so that all men would at least think about the real world around them.

Mark's mind went back to the frieze, the team, had found and analyzed in the temple of the Mayans. He thought that the sacrifice of a potential threat to the Quiche rule was a devised way to eliminate threats based on a belief that worthy humans had to be presented to the

Gods as gifts. In order to render the concept of sacrifice as acceptable, a body of facts had to be presented to the people that tapped into their basic wants and did not expose the hidden agenda. These were the principles upon which propagandas were created. Now he and his wife were challenging a centuries old propaganda machine with facts about positive accomplishments of Black achievers in a culture prejudiced against them and evidence they would unearth of superlative Black civilizations throughout history. Would this be enough to turn the tides of men's thought, or would the haters find more compelling information for their racist thinking. This is the area that is blurry to man and must be left to God. A man can only expect to achieve serenity if he has perceived his task accurately and completed it as best he can. Mark did not know whether or not he and Kiona would be able to concentrate on building their family life after this series of digs or if they would have to steal moments between battles for knowledge that would liberate humanity from its mental prison.

When Mark got home Kiona was ready to listen to him. She felt proud of the way he had analyzed and reached a resolution to their dilemma. She admitted that this had also bothered her. She was not sure at what point she had to let go or let others carry the torch of freedom and dignity, or at what point she should stop to enjoy her husband and child. His groping had also given her some answers: She came to the conclusion that each person had to come to his/her balance of altruism and enhancement of his/her own life. The limiting factors were how much a person can spend of his/her own ego and see no return or a negative return on the investment. The would be fighter for justice had to not only engage the unjust majority, but those of the minority that are too devastated by the aspect of change to take up arms against an atrocity or those who receive benefit from it. The tribes who had trade agreements with Spain did not want to do battle with their benefactor; every colony is comprised of a minority who want someone to take care of them either because of a real or perceived inadequacy in their functioning. These people will resist change in a system, no matter how evil that system is. Another facet that she considered was that people become entrenched in habits to the extent that they fear that a change that destroys an established comfort zone without guaranteeing a more positive result than what they have is resisted. To do battle with the falsity and injustice of Noah's curse of Ham's children meant a re-education of these minorities within the larger minority that benefited from or were used to the existing evil. From the beginning she wondered to what extent was she her sister's keeper. She shared this dimension of frustration with her man, who was able to tune into it: He said that they were no one's keeper; the very step they had taken in building a life together belied the need for a keeper or subordination of the self to one. All they could do was to present the information that they found and some guiding principles for its use, then grit their teeth with their faith in God as their guide. The faith involved risk, but it was a risk based upon a belief.

From where did this belief come? It came from the precedent of Gideon Retta's experience. He and Dark Waters believed enough in their cause to take on the power of Imperial Spain knowing that physically and empirically they would lose, but spiritually they would win. Today we do not regard the edifices originating under enslavement as real accomplishments compared with the real prizes of dignity and self-respect. Can one honestly compare Ghandi's liberation of India with Hitler's autobahn in Germany? Somewhere a descendant of Fiery Water or perhaps Red Earth or Running Lion walks the planet and remembers that a tall warrior fought for the pride in himself he wears in himself today. He does not ponder upon Trocadero's genius in using forerunners of tanks in battle. The belief that sustained the fight for spirituality was based upon faith that if one loved the land it would love him/her because it was a proper use of what God had provided for the Earth and for Man; the love was the catalyst that brought both to God. Faith that Earth and Man were tied to God was based on the persistence of both despite the weaknesses of both that could've meant destruction if God had so willed it.

The philosophy of asking for serenity also had its roots in faith. When one has given his/her all, nothing remains to be given. Gideon and Dark Waters had given what they had to give for their cause. Their love was sent to the land with their ultimate sacrifice, as Abraham was willing to do to Isaac, as God did for Man. Now the land conveyed this love to God by providing nurturance to those who remained after the slaughter. Fiery Water and Ismalia survived in Saskatchewan, Ericio and Rafana sailed the seas marauding Spanish shipping, Komarovski survived alone in the mountains, arising against tyrants upon the need, Purple Flower survived to connect herself to Tom Engler and to bring the riddle of humanity's battle into the present with Mark and Kiona as its spokespersons. What, but faith that the Lord will provide could be passed onto Him after the Land passed on the love of these people via their sacrifices by providing nurturance to allow their progeny to survive. As a result their ideas survived and grew as the cultures grew. When one has done all that one can do, any more doing will break down the machine that is the human body. An obsession that drives a human being to do more than he/she can do denies that ultimate control is beyond mankind; it says that a man is in ultimate control of the universe and can never surrender to a greater power, lest a weakness is revealed, which leaves vulnerability to whoever is stronger. There is no point at which one can rest and replenish the energy to return to the job. This is what the war between Gideon and Trocadero was becoming. Trocadero could not tolerate defeat because he would look weak before an enemy that was pre-defined as weak. Gideon, on the other hand, knew that his spiritual victory would only come about if he showed his fellow man that dignity was earned by an ultimate show of unity for the right to work this land in the dignity of God's love, which provided it. In deed the land of Colorado did prosper, but not until men worked the land with love and cooperation with each other so that this could be given to the land and ultimately returned to God. Thus, the serenity prayer is a manifestation of faith and honesty with ourselves about how far we can go in marshaling God's resources to return our love for ourselves, our fellow man, and the resources he has provided for us, the energy to work the world.

# Chapter 5

The afternoon was warm and sunny. Artie was with her Uncle Bartie and Aunt Guintera. The group decided on an outing to the cave that housed Gideon Retta's remains. Each made an offer to him to bless their next digs in Dakar. They all had a spiritual feeling about him because his commitment to his cause was total. Jonos stepped up to the makeshift altar first; he offered the medallion his father had won at Stalingrad to liberate his land from the rapacious claws of Adolph Hitler. He had jumped on top of a panzer tank blowing it and himself to bits to misdirect a squadron of them into Russian machine gunfire. Helga dedicated a memento to Gideon from her scrap in the alley with the youth that had attacked her. In the struggle, she tore a pendant from his neck that identified him as Dragon Slayer. He was also a fighter that became dedicated to helping other youth find themselves as he had through the group after he had served his time in jail. She gave Gideon's spirit this to show love can come from hate. Mattani offered a song she had written about how Apartheid divided men from one another and created hatreds. Mark and Kiona took each other's hands and offered him their thanks for showing them that they could love each other. Qamar offered a prayer to Allah that the spirit of Gideon carries the wish to find God through finding each other to Him. Aaron addressed the spirit for the group: "O, Warrior of God's cause you have carried the Lord's message to us through writing the history you lived and leaving it for us to read. We know that your sacrifice brought the message home that we must love each other to use the world God created for us wisely and to show our love for Him. As men we are about to learn for ourselves and convey what we have learned to our fellows that God did not create an inferior race to be used as a scapegoat for the advancement of other men's greedy plans. Today we entreat you to help us strengthen ourselves to help us be one more instrument in carrying the Creator's message to man, as you once were." With that they hugged each other and left the cave, each bearing their own view of what their mission was.

Kiona began to have some mixed feelings about going to a country that was divided into castes. This meant to her that there could be only selective communication with people, and that learning about the past cultures would be fragmented. The others felt that fragments could be put together. They also felt that looking into a country's past did not give them the right to walk in and decide what was right or wrong about their way of life. As students of the world that was, they came to learn not to teach. Peoples' resistance in other experiences inhibited learning, and a way was found to overcome this resistance. Mattani even offered a solution to the dilemma. She proposed that one group member align him/herself with one caste, learn to communicate with people in this group, and convey their perspectives to the archeology group. Where caste lines and tribal lines interacted to cause conflict, the government could be consulted for appropriate intervention. Thus, communication had to be coordinated between castes, tribes, and with the government. Aaron could not handle this alone. Perhaps the church could be used as a communication, and Mattani agreed to work with the Christian segment. To establish the base of a friendly government, the in-laws agreed to work with the national assembly. Freddy decided to give up his private practice and go with them to be part of the government negotiations. Besides he was looking for additional markets for Tripod Productions.

Mark was becoming aware subtly and subconsciously, at first, of a pattern of survival a culture seemed to pass through in its evolution that carried near fatal aspects to it. There seemed to be a crumbling of the old followed by an impatient filling of the vacuum between the old and the new. In the wake of the substitution, suppressed groups struggle to become the new seat of power; a period of reshuffling and violent upheaval ensues. The Old Guard uses this unstable time to attempt to reestablish itself and back factions or create them that either promote them or maintain the disunity. Thus, the Rwandan war emerged in Africa, along with several other engineered civil wars, and the continual outbursts in India between Hindus and Moslems or Hindus and Sikhs. Mark's area of concern was how could the group protect itself from being made a victim or being put in the middle of such a conflict. What format could be devised to fight the discomfort of Disequilibrium's Librium? Had Gideon found a solution to this puzzle? The answer was what Gideon had found: that Man had to love the world he inhabited because God witnessed the use of the abundance he bestowed; and the life of Man was better because of this. When humans felt that the world centered around them, they took what other humans were returning to God. To make up for this greedy and unjust acquisition, they built magnificent monuments to God instead of using what He provided wisely and fruitfully. The simple formula for harmonious living had become a statement of elitism that stated a better of quality of Man now served God, as testified by leaving monuments behind them for God to cover up the stealing from other men that had taken place. The disrespect with which this elitist strain showed other men was perhaps, the reason a Gideon Retta arose in the first place. However, the cold hate and vengeance that dominated him had to be tempered. Thus, did Dark Waters enter his life.

Mark's musings seemed to unlock a cyclical phenomenon in the growth of Man. Adam and Eve wanted to have what God had and sought it from the tree of knowledge. Hence, work and child bearing were imposed upon Man. Mankind still had to produce for the common lot that shared a totem in nature, i.e. a tribe, springing from the line of a common earth mother. But Man was just as acquisitive as He was in the Garden, only the greed took on an altered form. "The Lord provides" became, "I want for me, not mine." For this reason Cain slew Abel and asked God if he was his brother's keeper. Men, who were inspired to acquire, wanted to acquire other men, as well as other material goods of the Earth. Thus, were war and slavery born. The possessor acquired the goods for which he would have had to contend with those he possessed. To create classes of possessors and possessed was to create the discomfort of having and not having. Those not having wanted a restoration to the state, in which those bound by a common mother figure prospered; they wanted a return to the tribal ways, by which all worked for the common good. In keeping with this philosophy, Moses cried out, "Let my people go." Governments were instituted among men to govern with the consent of the governed. Bolsheviks seized power from Mensheviks and propertied classes so that resources could be allotted to the working man to allow production from his abilities for his needs. This is another way of saying let us return to Mother Earth so that we can return to Father God what He gave us to show we cherish Him for the giving.

Mark could not sit still with the knowledge he felt he had unearthed. He ran to find Kiona to share what he thought was his discovery with her. Either his zeal became infectious or some of it was released in a zest that Kiona already had, but she applied the curse of Ham to this evolutionary cycle. The curse was an excuse for the covetousness that drove men to enslave other men that in turn would drive them all back to seek a return to the Matrilineal status of the tribe. Once again, it was the old adage; "Thou shalt have no other Gods before me." The racism that they had engaged in battle was nothing more than the acquisition phase of the cycle of Man reaching the peak of its depravity. Only, with modern weaponry the devastation would be far greater than in Gideon Retta's day.

A frightening aspect also crossed both their minds. Men do not like to change their habitual ways of thinking. It was obvious in a state of violence or its threat most times having to be initiated to begin fundamental changes in ways of behaving to one another. South Africa will not give up Apartheid without a war, despite the blatant violation of the right of peoples who were there for centuries before the Africaners even heard of the Zulu or Zimbabweans. By what miracle would they be able to turn the tide of reactionary battle that had been victorious since the greed of Europe had, with the deceitful wink of racism, talked of elevating the savage hordes?

To combat the resistance men would have to institute a fundamental change of thought and action; the outcome of such resistance's would have to be unearthed along with the falseness of the doctrine of the curse. History was full of these tales of the results of suppression. The mighty Roman Empire that gave us the Gracchi, as social reformers also brought Spartacus and the slave rebellion that kept the empire tottering for four years because its magnificence was built on the backs of the enslaved; the rot of using others was at its foundation. In spite of the awareness that the building of the South in the United States on the backs of those abducted from their homes was a moral wrong, slavery continued. When Nat Turner led a slave rebellion, it was put down by force and suppressed in the teaching of history in school because it meant the exposure of a fear of retaliation for an unjust violation of God's law. What of the hypocrisy of Vietnam: For centuries, other nations exploited the national aspirations of this people. It took one of the authors of the cradle of liberty, France, to exploit and abuse this country, and the Western spokesman for Democracy to turn its back on the plea to recognize its integrity to drive the nation to an unceasing war, every bit as bloody as the one Gideon and the Pueblos and waged. The unearthing of this truth about Noah's curse might be resisted with the same force as the other conflagrations. The saving grace is that Man is learning that he can destroy what has been built over thousands of years with one fell blow over the lies and pettiness' of the past. Maybe this will finally cause us to sit down with one another and empathize. Perhaps Mark and Kiona had found an answer that is workable. Perhaps Gideon and Dark Waters did not die in vain; the trading post of the past, where men could exchange cultures and ideas, may have had some use.

Mark and Kiona had made a momentous decision and had only to look around them to see that if people would stop and take a look at what others endured, they could help a community grow and serve God to serve themselves. Chasing the drug dealers out of Durango had unleashed an attitude of public pride and spiritedness that led the youth to join ranks with their forebears and create an industry around the archeological discoveries. The whole revolution in attitudes was based on restoring the abundance of the world to this creator to show respect for having given it. The exploiting drug pushers were not expelled by a plethora of laws and building expensive correctional facilities and/or programs, but by telling a bully that brought poison to a community to get out by making his/her entrance into their community to take over, painful to them. These youngsters, with the aid of Julio and Helga and the army base had shown the Drug Lords the same thing that Gideon and Dark Waters had shown the intrusive, exploitative Spaniards.

Yet there are those who do not learn to seek the resources for mutual communion with God. They had either real deficits or distorted thinking that led them to believe that they had a greater entitlement than other men did. They were obsessed with wrongs done to them or perceived as done to them. Mark pondered the distortions and thought about the youth he had given the raincoat so long ago. He had had a bitter life that ended in gunfire. He could have seen that, at least, one person cared enough about him to support his efforts in altering his belligerent stance to life. The habitual response assumes the character of an addiction because we become afraid to risk change. The risk became fearful, in part, due to not wanting to give up the comfort of an established pattern. One comes to believe the adage: if you fail to learn from history, you will repeat it. This becomes a rote rule. If the rule is established on the basis of an erroneous assumption and it is more than a harmless opinion, but a basis for defining a life pattern, it develops into an obsession. In "The Covenant," James Michener defined an obsession as poisoned thought. By use of propaganda, Mark learned that an obsession can come to be can come to be a national or international policy. In a sense, Mark and Kiona's mission was to excise one of the tumors of the tumors of distorted thought.

In excising these tumors of thoughts, we must keep free of their metastases. For each of us, a bitterness or inability to absorb pain has the potential of finding its mark of disillusionment upon our souls. The glue that binds us to the way to God has to be found in the reservoir of faith. The storage for this faith has to be replenished to be maintained. To test this maintenance of the fountain of faith, a tragedy may have to occur to disrupt the road we have chosen to tread. This process now entered the lives of Mark and Kiona Engler.

The autumn of the year brought memories with it. The Ma Trash episode always brought laughter to the group of friends. The sneaky way Amy presented a dead cat to a young man, that had hurt Rachel, at a fraternity party on Halloween had been a comical memory, a remembrance that brought them all together. Now they were gathering for their yearly party. Reed and Michelle Hymer, Amy and Ron, and Rachel and Arne with their families all got together with the Englers. Part of the festivities was to join the community in a Halloween parade followed by a costume-judging contest. A would be assailant also attended the parade and contest, the receiver of the cat. He was exposed by Reed and Ron and placed on probation and weekend jail time for two years. A condition of his probation was to do follow-up work on telephone harassment cases. Recently he was interrupted in carrying out another harassment plot and shipped to Phoenix, Arizona to a zoo with a plane full of Llamas. Needless to say, his heart was seething with a desire for revenge. He bought a telescopic rifle and rented a room in a sleazy hotel across the street from the parade under an assumed name, Emil McTavian. The room was on the third floor of a seven-floor building located next to a doorway leading to the roof of the building. The rifle was of a simple construction so that it could be easily disassembled. The room was rented several weeks ahead of time. The would be Mr. McTavian located trash cans and clothing hamper on the floor above. He also purchased a cheap used auto, which he parked in an alley alongside the hotel so that it would be a familiar sight to the neighborhood. He knew his tormentors would be in a pack together. He could shoot them one by one then descend the fire escape to his waiting car from last gun part dumping site on the fourth floor. He also equipped the rifle with a silencer to deaden the noise. He would wear a change of clothes under his outer garments, which could be discarded with parts of the gun. There would be no more dead cats, no more garbage can outfits, no more Llamas, and vengeance would be his.

While McTavian was rehearsing for his grisly task, the Halloween parade participants were busying themselves with their arrangements. Amy, Kiona, and Rachel prepared the same outfits they wore the night of the fraternity party. Ron and Reed wore the same Goofy and Barbara Streisand masks and trench coats that they were wearing the night they captured McTavian. He was spying on them so that he would know them by their costumes. The children's costumes were next on the agenda, along with Mark's, Arne's, and Michelle's.

Mark taped two toilet-plungers to his front and back, attached to ropes that were attached to a headband that he wore and two more ropes attached that went to his feet. He used tape to anchor a sheet to the ropes and toilet plungers and taped a strand of ribbon to his posterior. Resisting an impulse to hysterical laughter, Kiona asked him what this was supposed to represent; he told her he was dressed as a kite. Arne tied a rope around his waist with several fir branches protruding upward from it. Attached to the branches were several apples. He was dressed as the tree of knowledge. Michelle wore a rented tuxedo with a derby and mustache and cane, as Charlie Chaplin. Yusseff, Arti, and Reed's and Amy's twins crawled into a long piece of plastic tubing to be a giant worm. Holes were cut into the bottom to allow their feet to be free. McTavian was oblivious to the small children that would, at least, be witnesses to violence. The pathological lust for revenge had turned to a tunnel vision. The mirth of the costume preparation did not even distract him from his bizarre compulsion to get even.

Emil McTavian showed an extreme level of preoccupation with his vengeance. He even began to observe every move the Englers and their guests made. He was able to ascertain the depths of their friendship and loyalty to each other. He learned the foibles of the children and the child rearing practices of the parents. He knew that Yusseff felt protective towards Artie and that Amy's twins were partial to butter pecan ice cream. He knew that Reed's son was frightened at the sight of cicadas. He made use of these bits of information to discover weaknesses and flaws in their characters that would leave them vulnerable to his machinations if this attempt failed. He happened upon Artie watching the movements of a female oriole to attract a male and walked up to her describing the swift movements of the birds' flight, when he encountered Yusseff, who said to leave the girl alone or he would call his father and mother, who were picking leaves for their collection about five feet away. Thus, he found out that this was a close knit group of people who looked out for one another. Another time, he observed their protectiveness from a distance: A teenager was annoyed that Reed's son was taking too long at a drinking fountain and was teasing him with a cicada after inadvertently discovering his fear. Out of nowhere, Reed and Mark appeared with a policeman, who led him to a wooded area, and offered him the choice of trying to extricate his skateboard from a patch of poison ivy or sitting in a jail cell until his parents picked him up. This was a fan for McTavian's anger. He well remembered that he was punished with this, so called leniency, for his harassment of Amy and Rachel.

The entire group had to go, but he could not afford to use more complex weaponry for fear of attracting attention for the purchases; subsequently, he would proceed as planned.

When he saw the weird array of costuming they had arranged to use, he chuckled and felt a pang of remorse for his decision; but anger at the embarrassing situations in which they had placed him with their bizarre punishment methods egged him on. He developed a ritual to perfect his task: Two hours of practice a day at a rifle range plus another two hours of observing the movement of one or two people in a crowd from the rooftop to perfect his pinpointing skills followed by some relaxing activity constituted his day. He had begun this preparatory procedure about two weeks prior to the visit; he saw Kiona in the supermarket and had recognized her. He then began observing them and learned about plans for their get-together. His observations had actually begun at the picnic with the family that had cheated Professor Owens' family in the past.

Unfortunately, Reed's recognition had disrupted the planning stages of his plot. He vowed he would not get caught the next time. Hence, the indirect observation approach; he blanched at the thought of having to watch the eating habits of Llamas and putting up with their smell for an hour on the plane coupled with the boredom of listening to complaints about telephone harassment for two years and spending sunny week ends in jail. This brought his sense of humiliation to overboil. Oh well! These clowns would not be embarrassing him anymore. The time for reckoning was fast approaching. A burst of self-pride and satisfaction was immersing his wounded soul in a pool of settling calm.

The friends' growing enthusiasm and excitement about upcoming Halloween events compensated for McTavian's calm: the parade and costume contest. In fact, the entire Durango community appeared to be electrified by the celebration that was coming. The kids had figured out a way to put wheels on their huge worm costume so that they didn't have to stick their feet out. They took apart two bikes and used two mop handles for axles then rested the worm on the axles, with the bike wheels at either end. Mark always liked to eat sandwiches at a parade so he preoccupied his time making his kite costume in a way that would keep his hands and mouth free. Arne had to place the apples on the fir branches so that they did not hit him in the eyes. Rachel, at the last minute, decided to rent a puppy dog costume, and she kept raising her leg at Arne. Ron had contributed the dead cat and decided to dress like a cat.

Amy wore her old trash bag and pumpkin mask, and she had to endure her husband repeatedly running behind her and pinching her bottom. Mark also kept getting pestered by Kiona pulling on his kite tail and putting thumbtacks at its end to stick to his bottom. The axle idea did not work on the worm costume because the rigid mop handles did not allow the wheels to be turned. To allow turning to take place, the kids could either rest the worm on an auto frame from the junkyard or attach roller skates to the ends of the hole at the bottom via a screw and turn the skate when needed by a rope attached to it. They chose the latter method because there was less bulk and clumsy maneuverability to encumber them. Yusseff had reasoned out these concepts. Thus, did the friends prepare for the upcoming festivities, while a deranged mind plotted to try and turn the merriment to mayhem.

A pang of guilt crossed McTavian's mind. These innocent children were not part of his humiliation, why should they be kept from reaching their majority. After all, they had done nothing to him. Then he reminded himself of his resolve. The best way to cause a parent pain is to deprive him/her of the children. Any survivors would have to live with this loss because of the indignity he had suffered that had caused him to give up his name and present himself with an alias. He seethed with rage that he had to give up his honored family name to restore the respect due it. However, family dignity demanded the seeking of vengeance. He would reveal who he was when the time came. Just as Edmund Dantes had done in "The Count of Monte Cristo." He was of less noble bearing than McTavian.

447

# Chapter 6

A sense of family revenge motivated McTavian to find an excuse for unacceptable behavior. This excuse came from the sense of mutuality that comes from the common struggle for survival that a family undergoes. The concept that all a family has is each other encourages a pulling together through times of stress, but it also acts as a barrier to instituting changes. For instance, sometimes families pull apart when children achieve adulthood. Yet there is some bond then the bond becomes misused to promote selfish interests; growth is prevented. When a family extrapolates to a cultural group from these dogmatic postulations, the norms that are established are thought about as a return to the basics. The basics need to incorporate the need to grow as the world grows; else we are not "Loving the Land so it will love us." For the land has changed. Whether we maintain the basic tenets of what has meant survival for our families or "Go with the flow" remains a judgment call. We can either fight for McTavian's family honor or follow the paths of Grady Almederson and Jack Engler and allow the generations to learn from each other. The path we choose often depends upon the course we have struck as individuals. This will limit the response to a propaganda machine. By this means culture can be a flexible tool to guide Man, not a rigid controlling device.

Mark and Kiona had to deal with this concept in their decision to expose the fraudulence of the Curse of Ham. They had to search for a doctrine that could be substituted as a replacing norm to define role relationships between human beings. The new doctrine would have to preserve stability and, at the same time, keep an eye open for whatever changes needed to be instituted to assure survival. The sea scrubbed Grady clean to look at what his daughter wanted out of her life. He did not look at her as an extension of himself or as a being that was meant to live the life he wanted for himself. His one requirement was that she live responsibly as a person; this meant that she would have to be responsible about how she loved the world that God gave her to wend her way through: She would have to be responsible as a person. This meant that she would have to be responsible about how she loved the world that God gave her to wend her way through: She would have to be responsible about the love she carried for a man and every human being with whom she related. She would have to prepare her child to live in a world that might be very different from the one into which she was born.

The love and safety of her parents' home was a blanket of safety, a blanket that would be outgrown, but placed in a safe place to remember what was given. Mark and Kiona both hoped that opening the door, by debunking this propaganda tool, would be part of what every person would engage in: examining themselves in relation to their relationship to the whole world. By this self-proving, they could find their own path to their own paradise.

Regardless of their task, McTavian had a task of his own to organize. He timed the different events of the parade. He also made note of which events would create loud diversions for the gun shots. With this done, he tried to establish the timing pattern between events so that he could have an idea about how far apart he had to fire the bullets so that he would have enough time to escape. Suddenly an idea struck him; if he fired several guns at once, he might be able to fire only once and get the job done. However, this plan offered two disadvantages: One, there would be more guns to discard, which would make the project take longer; two, the purchase of several guns from one gun store would look suspicious. Purchasing from several stores would increase his traceability. Therefore, the plan of multiple gun use was discarded. Another consideration was which events would draw the group closer together, and which would spread them farther apart. He also had to figure out what would cause the police to bunch their forces together and what would spread them farther apart or whether they would use maximum or minimum manpower. Parking was also another consideration: how could he create or alleviate traffic jams, dependent upon escape needs. He thought of using smoke bombs to obscure vision and bought some goggles so that his visibility would not be impaired. In mapping his escape route, he planned to hide in a cave used to store men and weapons during one of the Pueblo Wars until the search for him had died down. He had already cached a supply of food and water, along with a biker's disguise. This might just turn out to be a perfect murder.

The feeling and response system that had triggered this plot was McTavian's deep hurt to Rachel as a foreign student by speaking of her as an Easy mark for an American. She was hurt to the quick and isolated herself from American men. Amy and Kiona plotted and implemented their revenge at the Halloween party. This was followed by the subsequent harassment and sentencing to allow him to complete his education and serve justice at the same time. However, His warped viewpoint took this to heart because he came from a historically well known family and believed he was meant for something special on this Earth. Hence, he felt he had to be treated with special attention, almost a reverence. Holding him responsible for his act was also telling him that he was a mere human being and no different than anyone else. To admit the insensitivity of his act would shatter the image so carefully cultivated by his family. His entire essence demanded revenge. His tunnel vision based on his distortion of thought and building a system of thought and action around it was a perfect example of an obsessive-compulsive neurosis.

To the three girls, this event was a humorous part of the past. Amy, whose costume had been a trash-bag and a pumpkin on her head was given the nickname, Ma Trash. In their get-togethers, opportunities arose for much teasing and banter. Even Ron and Reed were included in the merriment. Although the police chief and probation officer did not know Reed and Ron officially they had a good idea that they were the instigators of the protective action in the past. Since they did not make a public issue of McTavian's behavior, they went along with embarrassing him out of action, as long as no harm was done. They even engineered the last caper. The error was that a serious character disorder was present, and it was about to be brought into the realm of a serious crime with serious repercussions. The event at which McTavian chose to strike was at a picnic after the parade. A pumpkin pie-eating contest was to take place at a park across from the hotel. He chose this site, as opposed to the parade because the parade offered the public more freedom of movement to spread their panic and make escape more difficult. Moreover, the victims were packed into a smaller area.

Some of the vendors crowded into the picnic area hustling their wares. The cool of the late October season caused a demand for hot dogs, hot chocolate, etc. in the watchers of the pie-eating contest. Mark, Kiona, Reed, Ron, and Yusseff were all stuffing themselves with pie.

McTavian put the silencer in place and took aim in the cross hairs of the telescope. Reed just took a bite of pie and was smiling at something Michelle had said. Suddenly his head pitched forward, and he coughed. A bit of icing had gone down the wrong pipe. Kiona leaned forward to wipe a crumb off of Mark's nose. The gunner had her in his sights. A fly landed on the lens and obscured the cross hairs. An officer happened to turn his head toward the apartment building then the hotel. About halfway up he saw what appeared to be a glint. He nudged the officer next to him, and they began running toward the reflected light. Artie gagged on the large bite of pie she took, and Mark picked her up to slap her back. He was in the center of Emil's sights. He started as he saw two uniformed figures running toward him. The bullet whizzed by Mark's ear. He didn't hear it, but he felt it and knew what it was. He ducked down and jumped down from the platform to join the policemen in their run. He called to Kiona and Artie and anyone else to join them. At the same time Amy climbed up to give her husband a hug. She felt a hot flash of pain and fell to the ground. She looked down to see a spreading patch of red on her right shoulder. She screamed, and a physician called 911 on his cell phone and ran toward her. Frightened, McTavian saw that several other runners followed the two policemen. In a panic, he threw his weapon on the floor and ran to the back of the escalator stairs to descend to his car. He negotiated the position just ahead of the crowd and started his vehicle.

In the meantime, Ron jumped down to aid his wife. He grabbed his twins and headed Amy and them right toward the ambulance, which had just arrived. The doctor had put a bandage around his wife's shoulder and a splint on her arm.

They rushed off to the hospital, and Amy was admitted. Ron and their sons paced the floor while they worried. They heard Amy groan while they dug in her shoulder to get the bullet out. The staff also had to set her arm due to a break occurring in the fall. Then she had to get an air cast put on it. There was actual yelling going on during this process. She was a little weak from the surgery and bleeding. However, she was all right basically.

McTavian started his car with the runners at his heels. They started to pound on the doors and windows until he got it moving. A police car started pursuit, and the chase was begun. McTavian veered into a tree and was apprehended. In interrogation his honored family name was revealed; He was Anthony De Melo, scion of a house that had once served as chief inquisitor of Portugal. This time he would be indicted for attempted murder. The leniency of the past would no longer encumber the dignity of his family name. Unfortunately his new title did not have any special privilege or recognition attached to it. He was sentenced to ten years hard labor. The remorse he did not show was to be learned by isolation, moments of physical brutality, and by being treated as an impulsive child. This time, he would be held accountable for his acts. For all the pride he had bestowed upon his family name, no one visited him. He had made himself a hard bed. He was given ten years to learn how to get up out of it.

Amy emerged from this horror with a new knowledge about vengeance. Although her sense of vengeance was less violent than Gideon Retta's, it was a part of her, as much as his was a part of him. What made her stop and think about the subtle art she had learned so well? She thought about how she thought she had mastered the subtle nuances of getting even, only to become a victim of the same sort of thought processes. Yet when she pondered on it, Gideon had been far more adept at violence and revenge than she. He found that two phenomena emerged from preoccupation with this dark concept: Enactment of vengeful impulses led to the victim also becoming vengeful thus leading both parties to an endless chain of violent pursuits. The second phenomenon unleashed was a belief that the world is egocentric to Man. In other words, a poisoned thought entered the injured

party and became the dominant thought that motivated behavior to assume the right to punish a wrong. The assumption of this right was an
expression of Man's seizing a power that had destructive potential because it repeated itself in the victim. For this reason God took vengeance away from Man and placed upon His shoulders.

She brought this conceptualization to Kiona because she felt there
might be connection to the curse Noah had made. His outrage at being
caught undisposed would seek an outlet to feel a sense of release from
the sense of feeling trapped by the sin he had perpetrated before his
Lord. Hence, to draw attention away from his own sin, he created the
sin of being seen at his sin and held accountable for it by making
Ham's seeing him a sinful act. Shem and Japheth walked in backwards
with a blanket to cover their father, so as not to see him. By putting
emphasis on seeing Noah indisposed and not on the state of being indisposed, Noah took his anger at bringing his sin before God out on
the discoverer. This was an act of vengeance. A loving, omniscient
God would not hold the discoverer of sin accountable, but the sinner.
Therefore, God did not honor this decree of Noah, but Man had invented it as an excuse to plunder the Land that magnificent civilizations, which preceded White men, had built.

A further connection was made within Amy's mind because of the
depth of fear that was instilled by being forever separated from her
sons and husband, if De Melo had succeeded in killing her. It led up to
a connection between Gideon Retta and herself. She sought revenge
for the psychological injury heaped upon Rachel years ago. This led to
the incidents of harassment and punishment perpetrated by and suffered by De Melo. An ancestor of Anthony De Melo had tortured
Gideon and paid for it with his own life. Gideon pursued a bloody war
starting out with a vengeance principle. The initial victory was not the
final one, and it instilled a vengeance motif in the hearts of Imperial
Spaniards. Gideon had to motivate victims to fight a losing war to gain
a spiritual victory that was spelled out as a right to love God in their
own way by loving the Land He provided and restoring its produce to
Him. This made the Land mutually God's and Man's. The spiritual victory stood the test of time. When a tourist views the acropolis or the
coliseum, he/she thinks of the glory that was Rome or Greece. When

he/she sees Pueblo cliff dwellers selling trinkets made from minerals or clothing from hides of animals he/she recognizes that there is a glory that is in Colorado, Arizona, New Mexico. Etc., a glory for the integrity to maintain a right to live the way we feel is right. The Pueblos mission of the sciences of remembrance is to help us see that isolation and separation may have meant the survival of a culture, but humanity is a multicultural aggregation, and if we don't follow Ben Franklin's advice of pulling together, we'll all "hang separately." Hopefully, the knowledge to be gained by Mark and Kiona's project would help us to pull together. Amy certainly had the lesson brought home to her. At any rate vengeance belongs to the Lord because Man cannot handle it; the sum total of its expression is the destruction that Cain heaped upon Abel. As Gideon had learned, as Rachel had learned, and as Kiona and Mark had learned, life building involves a blend between isolation for singular survival and learning from each other for mutual survival. This component comes from having to go beyond cultural boundaries because mankind goes beyond cultural boundaries.

The message of hanging separately or surviving together was carried to an unexpected quarter, yet a predictable one. Jonos Tevrisz came to the project with a great mistrust for capitalist society. His father had perished at Stalingrad, the bloody battle in which Mother Russia, under Joseph Stalin, had kicked Hitler out of her Land. Hitler was regarded as the ultimate of Capitalist greed that had an earlier expression in the civil war between the Whites ad the Reds after the revolution. Jonos saw Russia as standing against its enemies, as Gideon saw his battle as identity for the Falasha against the Amhara. In reality, there was not just one Russia that threw out Hitler, but a unification of Russians composed of the nations taken to comprise the U.S.S.R, who chose to identify themselves under one banner to win over an invader. This phenomenon was not unlike Gideon's unifying the tribes in the area against Spain as well as rivals of Spain to throw out the usurper. Until Kiona and Mark showed him the treachery and futility of such mistrust, he never questioned the imperatives of his culture. The concurrent meshing of three phenomena in his own head concretized a break with his old way of thinking.

The first of these was his reading a book that was written by a Russian and had to be smuggled out of the country. It was Boris Pasternak's novel, "Doctor Zhivago." In this novel the writer discovered that the revolution attempted to destroy what was called the personal life to the extent that individuals were not allowed to enjoy the sensuality of poetry about nature or that stealing fire wood for one's family was a state crime. Such a philosophy was imposed in the name of justice for all and imposed on all much the same way that Imperial Spain imposed its version of Christianity on the Pueblos and other tribes they found in the New World. He was jarred to find that his beloved Mother Russia could treat her own with such emotional brutality to achieve what she called brotherhood.

The second phenomenon was the change in political viewpoints that drove communism from Russia after understanding that her survival was, after all tied in with that of other nations and cultures. As the United States and the USSR competed for world domination, they found they needed each other more and more. Some of the nation states within the USSR began to rebel against being part of Mother Russia, and the Kremlin was offended, as any capitalist nation had been wont to position itself. As food shortages, radioactive plants exploding, and other disasters occurred, East and west found they needed one another. A period of détente evolved, in which tensions eased, and in which a temporary period of trust would occur. This was followed by a period of Glasnost and by a period of Peristroika during which there were cultural exchanges, changes in government policies, allowing small capital industries to conduct business within the USSR Suddenly the Communist Party collapsed and was no more. If Russia were to survive, she would have to learn to love the land and see nature as a road to God, not as a nemesis of which the proletariat had to gain control. Life was more than enforced sharing of resources. It entailed loving the world which was bequeathed to us, either by the sweat of our brow, our conniving, or by simply being given to us. At any rate, redemption would come with love of self, love of society, and love of God.

The third phenomenon was the remembrance of one of Gideon's fighters, Komarovski. He left the barrenness of Tsarist Russia to build a new life for himself, but he found he had to fight for it.

He discovered that a Spanish Emperor could be as insensitive to the needs of other people s the Tsar of a cold, difficult Land to love. For this reason, he retreated to the mountains where loving work would be repaid with a yield, a yield that would make him feel he was returning the Lord's bounty so that his needs would be replenished by God in an act of good faith. Yet when a fellow, who had proven his sincerity to him brought his own need, the Russian stepped out of his isolation. If Komarovski could take a chance on Man, when he had seen a tangible reason to trust one man, he felt he could take the same chance with what he saw from Mark and Kiona. In other words, because he had witnessed behavior that demonstrated that having faith in God had merits, he was willing to try and develop this faith in a power beyond himself. If all of Russia was willing to look into the idea that man is more than an application of the theory of dialectic materialism, then maybe he could too.

Mark had tried to use the Serenity Prayer to free himself from the introspective nightmare that was tearing his insides apart. He wanted Kiona to enjoy her motherhood and started to try to keep to himself more to make some reality out of his thoughts. However, he found he had to turn to her. She sensed his need. They had taken Articulata to a playground in the cold November chill following the Halloween attempted violence. She noticed when he thought his two ladies weren't looking; he would shudder and look as if he had the weight of the world on his shoulders. She took his hand and said, "When Karl Marx formulated his theory of how to solve the riddle of the rich getting richer and the poor getting poorer, he would spend all day at the Library and wrestle with his thoughts. I think that all that rumination and pondering makes people crazy. I have a better suggestion of how to spend our time." "What's that," said Mark beginning to smile. Jonos and Mattani are on the next bench, and I think Artie needs a baby brother. Do I, have to say more?" She did not; Mark was over at the next bench very rapidly explaining that Kiona felt faint. He said it was probably nothing, but he wanted her doctor to check it out. They raced home, and she beat him sufficiently to have the red nightie on when he got there.

After their lovemaking, he stroked her face gently and asked her how she had learned to read him when he was trying to keep her from sharing his pain. She said to him that it was part of the old Tammy Wynette song. She stood by her man not due to an obligation invented by someone else, but because she knew him to be a good and loving man, a man that would not hurt anyone if he could avoid it. She pulled him down to her and kissed him, stroking his face, as he had stroked hers. They then hurriedly got dressed and went to get Artie from her Uncle Jonos and Aunt Mattani.

# Chapter 7

Kiona did not get pregnant, but she and Mark did want to have a little boy to help Artie grow up in a balanced family. As a result, they kept trying periodically. They really wanted to wait until they had returned from Africa because the project would take all their energy. They had decided to take Artie because they did not want a lengthy separation, or any separation from their daughter, but they also felt they had a vital mission that could not be postponed. They persisted because they liked making love with each other and because they did not want the other to lapse into depression or feelings of frustration. They had both experienced this state. Mark and his wife were both dedicated to exposing he falseness of the curse and their life together; fitting these two goals together was not exactly an incongruity, but it was a difficult task.

It was made more difficult by the imploring of Jack and Grady. They felt that the fluctuating status of many and the violence of the politics of the emerging African states would be dangerous for Artie. The arguments they used were countered by their son and daughter. With all the racial and other violence on the scene in America, where was the safety in staying at home. At least, three incidents had happened right in Durango in the last six months. Both Mark and Kiona wanted their daughter to be present at her brother or sister's birth. They would be connected as a family through all events. This is how a family grows. They did not want a gap to develop between sibs so that they would not know each other. In the end both father-in-laws shook each other's hand and shook their heads at their son and daughter.

They began taking Artie to the Library to look at slides to familiarize her with Dakar. This may have been premature because of how small and young she was, but they thought she would, at least be able to identify buildings by seeing them several times in the slides. Of course, they were wrong, but they all had fun. They even tried to teach her some words in French, but the effort was in vain. However, it gave both of them a chance to relive their own past travel experiences. Dakar was an important city because it is the westernmost city in Africa. It is not only the capitol of the nation, but also an industrial city and a port: European, American, and South American planes are to be frequently found at its airport. A railroad links it to the capitol of Mali.

Education is stressed, and 70% of the children attend school; there is a university in the city with a medical school of fine reputation. Through these studies, they began to learn the personality of the city.

European traders first made Westerners aware of this peninsular extension of land jutting into the Atlantic in the fifteenth century. They concentrated their settlement on the island of Goree. The name came from one of the tribes in the area, the Woloffs. It means tamarind tree or refuge. And a refuge it is for what is exotic and cultural and for what is evil. For along with storage hold below and living quarters above, on the Goree shoreway was the Maisson de Escalve, the slave house. Here slaves were sold into bondage or thrown into the sea through an open door. The French took it over from the original owners in 1677. From this island, the city grew and achieved its name in the latter part of the last century. The city is equally dynamic, culturally sophisticated, and ugly. Along with terra cotta roof tops and white buildings are hustling vendors, raucous noise, fumes, and thieves. The influence of the French is felt everywhere. The hub is the place Del Independence. Here are cultural centers where books and maps, as well as films are sold, performances are given. The Fan Museum has displays of masks and traditional dress of the entire Senegalese area, beautiful fabrics, carvings, and drums. These may go back to Songhai, Mali or ancient Nigerian civilizations. Sights also include a presidential palace with beautiful gardens and guards in colonial uniform, a Grand Mosque with a floodlit minaret, and the elegant hotel De Ville. Marketing is available for shippers for both local goods and tourist items, but they are ridden with hawkers, that negotiate in shrewd bargaining terms and thieves that may work in teams of two or three. Some of the vendors may sometimes be in league with them. Touring walks occur along the cornices, but there is danger of bag snatching. This is the setting to which the archeological group was migrating.

Having a population over a million also would create an industry that would give this million people plus tourists something to do. Dakar has not failed its public in this regard; all five castes and six tribes of the Senegal area, the strip of a nation that runs through there (Gamia) and the nests of tourists that hover there looking for activity are well entertained. Beaches and hotels are available for swimming and diving, fishing communities are around the area, kayaks are available to be rented. The sport of pirogue, or dugout canoe racing, is available. Each coastal village sends a team of twenty-five to an annual regatta at Sommebedioune. Bars, nightclubs, and discos abound for the wee hours of the weekend. Trinkets and memorabilia can be found at the village Articanal. Transportation is by airline, cab, or bus. A train connects Dakar with the Mali capitol, Bamako. However, there are no meters on cabs, and the cost of the trip is arrived at by haggling and negotiation. On buses, one must ask about destinations and routes. Because of these datas, the group decided to live in Dakar in opposition to Aaron's plan to live in the St. Louis area.

As with many other nations, the area is not free of political agitators and movements. The southern part of the country has been embroiled in a separatist movement, and bordering countries and a nation within its borders (Gambia) have supplied arms and other support to this movement. This is known as the Casamance separatist movement. In the northern part of Senegal Muslim fundamentalists agitate and are under surveillance, while more secular radicals and arch conservatives are under watch also. Unfortunately foreigners unintentionally become victims of these political outspringings.

Grady and Mark left to find a suitable place to stay in Dakar. On the plane Mark noticed a familiar face. He saw the face of a young boy that was in his early adolescent or pre-adolescent years. He knew he had seen that face before, but he couldn't place where. Next to him sat a woman of her middling years, who also looked familiar. Behind them sat a tall, dignified looking Black man. Mark sat up with a start as they young boy addressed him: "Aren't you the Man we met on a plane trip to Mexico about five years ago that started singing on the plane. I held my nose at your horrible singing voice, and my mother slapped me." Suddenly the memory came back to Mark, and he grinned about the Lad's giving his mother a loud raspberry in return for the slap. He addressed the issue with the young man, and they both laughed about it. Grady laughed after hearing this tidbit. This drew him into the conversation, and the boy introduced his mother, whom Mark now remembered. The tall Black man introduced himself as the boy's stepfather; he was a native Senegalese involved in the international trading of gold coins for collectors, operating out of New York. He was going home to visit his family for his yearly vacation. He was from a Muslim brotherhood, Mouridia. This brotherhood worked with the government to maintain a stable state and a conservative Muslim religious elite status. He was also instrumental in engineering stability in the Casamance, Gambian, and Mauritanian disputes for separatism and fights over boundaries. Grady explained the mission of the archeological group. The man gave his name as Habib Bourganye, and his son's name, as Tommy. He introduced his wife, as Elois Edmondton Bourganye. Grady and he exchanged business cards. There might be a future here for the corporation.

What Habib Bourganye did not tell Grady was about an international connection his family had with the Ethiopian culture. He only knew the barest rudiments of it, himself. His family had once done a genealogical study. They found a relationship to a Majorcan, who had converted to Muslim. He had been a fighter against Amharic rule, as a Falasha Jew and ran away from a defeat to Portugal. From there he was deported to Majorca with a woman he never saw again in some connection with some treacherous and violent behavior of a violent Falasha soldier. He had served as a rabbi to the Falasha community before his deportation. In order to seek obscurity, he became Muslim and took the name, Ahmet Bourgan. His former name had been Nahum of Gondar. He entered the realm of business, doing monetary exchanges. His grandson fought with Dutch separatists against Spain, became a Protestant, and was hanged. His son, to avoid the embarrassment moved to Morocco from Majorca. From there, the family migrated to Senegal.

Grady and Mark went about the business of locating the most inexpensive housing they could. They finally located a mid range hotel where they could get a reduction in rent if they rented for at least one year as a group. It was the Hotel Farid at 52 Rue De Vincens. The rooms were clean, all credit cards were accepted, the area was relatively safe, and there was a good Lebanese restaurant nearby. Habib had helped them locate it. He had also used humorous innuendoes to his power in the city to persuade the manager to give them a deal for long-term rental and a group rate. Grady also referred to negotiations on the other digs and hinted that the hotel might be possibly used for a future movie site with possible acting positions for locals. Now that the position had been secured, the two of them decided to relax a little and do some sight seeing.

Leisurely they toured the Fan Museum and its display of masks, cultural costumes, and carvings and drums. They went to both markets and were not so much intrigued by their wares, as they were by the behaviors of the people. They observed that some of the hawkers worked in collusion with the thieves, either acting as lookouts for the authorities or by pointing out tourists with large amounts of money on their person. Once a target had been selected, one person would bump into victim, and another would reach for his wallet. Grady and Mark decided to try a little counter intrigue. Grady had always kept the handcuffs with which he had stopped an attack on Ruthena years ago. Now he would have a use for them. They got the attention of the local policeman and had him watch their operation. Mark flashed his money, while an adorable, little girl begged him for money. A grown man bumped into Mark while a small man reached for his wallet. Grady deftly bent down and handcuffed the midget to his partner by the ankle with one cuff and to cart of the third accomplice while the policeman arrested the little girl. Mark and Grady agreed to drop charges in return for the four agreeing to work with the police to deter other thieves by exposure.

With this done, they continued their sight seeing expedition: They viewed the Presidential Palace and government buildings, along with the gardens. The last sight they saw was the Grand Mosque built in 1964. It had a floodlit minaret that allowed the evening sky to be dominated with Islamic spirituality. They spent the rest of the afternoon at the beach.

As they walked by the cabana, they noticed an attractive, bikini clad young lady saunter up to an older man emerging from the dressing room and snuggle against him, while a younger man bumped into him and took his watch. Grady sauntered up to the woman and flirted with her. As she took the bait, he took out his handcuffs and gave her hand to him; he handcuffed her to the handle of a trash container. In the meantime, Mark tackled the thief, and retrieved the gentleman's watch. He then yanked off his trunks and ran with them until a policeman stopped them. He then told the officer the story, and returned the elderly gentleman's timepiece, as he was standing nearby stunned by the attack upon his person. Grady saw all this and dragged the Lady over to them by grabbing the other handle of the trash can. The gentleman was Habib Bourganye's father; he was soon joined by his son and grandson, emerging from the cabana with looks of amazement at the hubbub around Grandpa Bourganye. Habib invited Grady and Mark to his home on Ile Goree. On the way there he told the tale of his genealogy; they told him the story of Gideon Retta and Nahum of Gondar's connection to him. He enthusiastically endorsed the corporation and emphatically stated he wanted to be a foreign office recruiter. A new partner had just entered the corporation.

The Bourganye home was situated on Le Castel, a rocky plateau overlooking Dakar. From a point across the water, Mark and Grady could see the beauty, the mystery, and the intrigue that was Dakar, the city where the Mali and Songhai had made their impressions upon the earth; where they had proven that Canaan's offspring were not a race of inferiors, but that formulations based upon this assumptions of inferiority were a crime upon humanity. The crime was no less vicious or shameful than that of Pharaoh or Hitler. What would it take for a safe world to evolve that would be safe for Articulata? As the inventor Samuel Morse had said, "What Hath God wrought?" These thoughts were interrupted by the serving of food: The national cuisine of Senegal, thieboudjiennel (Rice baked in a thick sauce of fish and vegetables), diomodah (A peanut based stew with meat or vegetables), and poulet yassa (grilled chicken in onion and lemon sauce) were choices of entrees. The desserts were mainly fruit mixtures of several berries with fresh milk poured over them. Beverages served were tea, made with green leaves, heavily sugared, Senegalese beer (Flag and Gazelle are brand names). Peanuts or groundnuts are the main crop and appeared in many of the dishes. Habib presented Mark and Grady with copies of English/Wolof dictionaries, since this was the main tribe that lived in the Dakar area. Habib explained the origin of the marabout system. In order to create an efficient means of delivering religion to the masses, certain religious leaders were ascribed with divine powers to act as a link between God and Man. These men became known as marabouts. Groups who followed the teachings of a singular marabout were known as brotherhoods. Amadou Bamba founded the brotherhood, to which Habib belonged, about 1850. It is the Mouride Brotherhood and appears to have taken a version of the Protestant ethos as its paradigm by stressing hard work as the road to salvation. The government endorsed the philosophy of this brotherhood until Bamba made public his anti-colonial political stance; as a consequence, he was exiled and returned in 1907 as a secret ally of France. A sect of Mouridia emerged under Ibra. Fall, which stressed time spent at labor, rather than prayer. The marabouts get their wealth from the groundnut, or peanut plantations. The work is considered salvation's for the Mouride and appears to create a collective work force. Herein another source of conflict is brought to the fore: The groundnut drains the soil, and constant expansions occur for new plantations. This growth crowds out game preserves, as well as land for semi nomadic tribes that inhabit the area encroached upon (the Fula, of Central Senegal).

Hence, this is a state about the geographic size of half of California into which seven million people are jammed with a narrow country running through it, plagued by border disputes, a separatist movement, and a dispute between farmers, game reservists, and nomads. A union between a religious brotherhood and a socialist republican government to create a nation molded from Ghanaian, Mali and Songhai roots. To this Grady would worry over his daughter, granddaughter, and son-in-law, while the son-in-law worried over his wife and daughter and himself.

In addition to what they had learned about the northern part of the country, they had to learn about the customs of five other tribes and five casts plus the rules for intermingling among them. They had to learn about other marabout brotherhoods and their relationships to their populations and the government. After this humongous task, they had to go on to learn about the Zimbabwean civilization. Then the hard task would begin: They would have to integrate what they found in both regions with what they had learned about a few outstanding Black giants in Western culture and put it all together to demonstrate that the curse of Ham was a lot of hooey. This could take another ten years of work.

# Chapter 8

They had accomplished their mission and found a place for the entire group. In addition to a group rate, the hotel manager granted them cooking privileges due to being a marabout brother to Habib. With this task done, they took a cab to the airport and boarded their flight. Grady could not make himself be contented with his son-in-law's move, but he held his silence. He knew that this mission had a strong bonding power for Mark and Kiona, as well as for the whole group; he also knew that the addition of Habib as a supporter made a significant gain for the corporation, but the danger of thievery and harassment, the border intrigues, and the restless tension between nomadic tribesmen and groundnut farmer, all, brought a fear for his loved ones to him. Once again thoughts of the murders in El Salvador and events of the Sandinista Wars crowded his mind. He knew that he did not have to say anything and that Mark could read his thoughts. As if in response to these thoughts, Mark put his arm around his father-in-law and said, "Dad, I know you and Mom, as well as my parents will feel alone while we're gone and fear for us. I also fear for us, but this mission is important to lift a false burden from the shoulders of a people that did not deserve it and to put the blame for it on the perpetrators. The chain of human bondage needs to be broken at its beginning. It may not be, but, at least, racists will have to admit their evil and be judged for what they are." Grady stated that enough proof had been provided centuries ago, but no one intervened to change the face of the South or the urban ghettoes in the North or the police brutality that occurred in every city in the nation. He asked his son what made him think that he and Kiona's thoroughness and commitment to exposing the truth would make a difference in the hearts of men.

Mark told him about his nightmare, and how Kiona had used the twenty-third Psalm to help him muster his faith in God to sustain him.

All at once another source of strength hit him: The sustaining force that had driven Gideon Retta. He knew the rightness of his cause, and he believed in the backing of the God of Nature. In turning from violence, he had turned to the immediate family he had and come to love the land so that it would love him. In doing this, he had experienced an intermeshing between Nature, Man, and God that was a union of faith that would survive the isolation Man imposed upon himself with his greed. This was the secret of life that Gideon had unlocked by sacrificing himself. This is what he had passed on through the centuries: Man sustains himself by living a natural life and using the world to restore the fruits of it to its creator and back to himself. Through the tunnels of Mesa Verde, echoed the message Gideon Retta had passed onto Kiona and himself: "Love God through loving the world, and the love will come back to you."

Love certainly had come to him. The attraction that drew them together, his willingness to face a log with a blow torch, and the forthright manner in which they both stood up to their parents demonstrated that their love was there to stay. To strengthen their connection, they looked at how Gideon and Dark Waters stood for each other, learned from each other, and developed a life philosophy together. This was their sign that a union, such as theirs, could survive; they only had to find their life and build toward it. It meant that a lot of ignorance and failure to understand real beauty had to be shut out to leave them room to cherish each other. Hence, a teacher helped their growth from the distant, yet not so distant past. That the evolution of their relationship was a step from the binding aspects of cultural norms was a loud and clear message that the patterns of building a family are derived from a pre-existent culture but are cast in the image of adaptation to a whole different set of survival skills. In other words, our habits are based on old ways we have learned, but they adapt to new information and must undergo a transformation to survive new conditions. If the older generation learns to be flexible by objectively observing the changes and survival of their progeny, the culture grows; if not, it extincts itself or allows a more forceful set of mores to destroy it and create a new culture in its wake that may or may not endure. Fortunately, both of the in-law couples had had the wherewithal to see the wisdom of being open to change and able to grow with their son and daughter.

The plane touched down at Boulder, and Kiona, Artie, Ruthena, Jack, and Bert were there to greet their prodigal sons. They all crowded around Mark and Grady to find out what they had experienced. They found the information about the social structure of the marabouts fascinating and were amazed that the peanut, brought to American South to restore nutrients by George Washing ton Carver was depleting these same substances in Senegal. All three in-laws were eager to meet Habib Bourganye and his family. All four wanted to relocate to Senegal, but they reconsidered because of the corporation. The two professors and Bartie and Freddy were capable managers, but they only had specific knowledge only about their areas of endeavor. Therefore, the original founders were needed for trouble shooting and could not go gallivanting off to Senegal. Kiona was interested in the different customs of the six tribes and how they related across caste lines. The development of the marabout system and its relation to the politics of the country also fascinated her. Most of all, she was glad to have her husband and father back safe and sound. The love that they all felt for one another was the love that went back to the God that put them in the world he created way back when he allowed Eden to be the home where Man dwelt. Noah, David, Jesus, of Nazareth, and Gideon Retta and Dark Waters each served as a link in the circular chain that led back to God. Now Mark and Kiona were marked to join this system joined through the ages.

Of what was this linkage composed? Maybe it was, in part, the curiosity that Mark felt about what made Man tick; maybe it was that final integrity that Kiona chased after that proved a human being was just that and shared the love of itself to bring back to the Lord. Maybe it is the realization that we can best relate to each other by using culture to find each other, rather than using it to divide us from each other because we are afraid of the consequences of loving: We have to take a risk.

Just what is this risk? It may mean stepping out of the safety nets and the stone walls of our isolator's castles to touch the naked soul of our fellow man with our bared soul. Maybe it could be what Jack Engler learned over the years between climbing the Japanese Zero to kill his nation's enemy and reaching out to embrace Kiona and her family as his family. Was it a move from isolation and separatism to union and blending that comes from being more than a father's son? Samuel Morse, the inventor of the telegraph, once said, "What hath God wrought." Perhaps we have reached the stage in our development, when we should be doing a little creating of our own. The leaning tower of Pisa, the Parthenon, the Pyramid of Ghizeh are monuments of the world that was; where are the monuments to the world that is? To build these, we have to step from the world that was to the world that is.

Mark and Kiona had a fierce longing for each other that night. He and Grady had been gone a week. As soon as they got in the door, they let Artie spend the night with her grandparents and ran to each other. She drew him to her and circled him with her arms. He kissed her breasts lovingly and murmured they were the grape of the wine of his life. His hands encircled her lush bottom, and he whispered into her ear that she was the Napa Valley of his life. Kiona moaned softly, as he said these words from his soul. She began to nibble at his lower lip and face. She began to kiss his throat and to play in the hairiness of his chest with her fingertips. He began to moan, as she had and picked her up and gently lay her on their bed. He began kissing her inner thighs and murmured over their loveliness. She whispered fiercely into his ear that he should take her and began to reach for him as he once again moved his lips to hers. As he entered her, he whispered, "Bring me a son from your holy temple." She moaned once more as if the longing inside her would burst, and they thrusted with each other until they felt as if they were in heaven. They awoke several times during through out the night and repeated their course of action. By morning they lay in each other's arms exhausted and blissful.

With their love renewed, they knew they were preparing for a tedious, exhausting, and potentially dangerous business. They also knew they would face it together. Their daughter would be their inspiration. For she was God's gift to them and the flourishing of her life was their gift to Him. Somewhere in God's house, a spirit of a tall, ebony warrior and a short, Pueblo princess took each other's hand and said, "Love the Land, and it will love you."

# Epilogue

This book is not a historical document, nor is it a biography of the author's street brawling life. What I meant it to be is a statement that we can create beauty by carving it out of the past and blending it with the present to move to what is an inherent purpose of our existence; to share the love that the ultimate figures of science or of religion have declared as our reason for being. I felt that my wife and I shared a part of this. At other times, I felt I shared it with my brother, and, at still other times, I felt I could share it with my children. I have also felt I shared it with a couple close friends. Now I see myself as sharing it with a companion. What appears frustrating to me is that love appears briefly, then disappears behind a cloud of safety and cultural identity.

Asian Indian, Chinese, Hebrew, European, African, Afro American, and Amer-Indian thinkers have not directed their ideas to their own kind only, even if that was the only model they knew how to address. Addressing multitudes of cultures assumes that a common thread runs between them that may be tapped for communication. Mark and Kiona's struggle and Gideon and Dark Waters' equally painstaking battle indicated that addressing these differing numbers of people means stepping out of the net, but not returning to it. Gideon could have stayed safe in his Father's house and kept turning the other cheek; Mark could have been satisfied to receive Cherie's favors in return for manipulation and domination. Kiona could have enjoyed the prestigious life of a doctor's wife if she would have manipulated Reed the right way. Everything could have been all comfortable and isolated. No one would have known about the pain of the nonconformists or the individualists, who refused to collectivize their farms for Joe Stalin. These men were heroes the way Gideon was. Who fought the battle was less important than remembrance of the ideal for which the engagement took place. Wars take place when provocation is sufficient. Provocation is enough when one entity has stepped away from a majority and enjoyed fruits, apart from the mass hulk of numbers, and didn't the uniqueness taken from them. In other words, they stepped out of the mold and wanted to live their own joy and not have it dictated by those that dictated their existence. These were not the carbon copies of their ancestors; there was a new genome; something new had evolved something that did not discard the old, but embellished it, separating the wheat from the chaff and saving the wheat.

Gideon Retta admired order as a soldier, but he knew that to have tolerance for a wise move by a tyrant, compassion would have to be installed as an ingredient. For this reason, he spared the lives of his prisoners and let them become part of his troops or die a fighting death if they refused.

When I wrote my acknowledgment, I made a few errors for which I now wish to offer my apologies. I stated that I had not altered the outcomes of history. This is not one hundred percent accurate. I kept the Pueblos in Colorado four hundred to eight hundred years after they had left the area for New Mexico because I wanted to make use of the mountains of Mesa Verde. John De Mello was the Grand inquisitor of Portugal, but I am not sure of the time period; I just used his name as a random source. I also do not know how or when he died. I do know that Leonardo Da Vinci left primitive drawings of tanks, but I do not know of armies that used them. The weaponry used was not anything verified in history to my knowledge nor were some of the modes of transportation. I do not know of any Puget Sound People, nor of any Russian settlements or explorers in the area during this time. The journeys of Long Branch, Kurilia, and Adolphus, and across Siberia and up the Pacific Coast of Russia are products of my imagination, as was the village of Vitoskva. If this does not cover all of my errors or distortions, the reader has my profound apologies for any other discrepancies he/she may find. Three names that I had forgotten to mention, among many other friends from my new job, who read and heard excerpts are Jan and Helen William's and Denise McDonald, who translated my typing into legible form. I also made a brief reference to an alliance with an Irish band that settled in Western Canada after withdrawing from the war. I have no historical evidence for this settlement or these people. Professor Owens' family and the Southern family that swindled him were not real people. I hope that I have not omitted anyone. The object of my writing was not to offend anyone.

I have saved this last space for thanking for my friend and neighbor, Ms. Emily Davis, because her help to me has been spiritual and factual. She has a tremendous fund of knowledge about the Bible, which she generously shared with me upon my asking. She also lives a truly Christian life and shares this willingly. Sometimes when my own anger and bitterness would be reawakened by something I wrote, or when I would become absorbed by hurts that were my own doing and get mentally blocked, she would remind me that I led myself astray and show me her idea of why I did so.

I have disagreed with some of her formulations, and I am stubborn; but her steadfastness forced me to listen and learn some things. For this she has my deepest thanks.

As human beings, we need not only to acknowledge that others have helped us grow, but to grow as a society from the interaction. This maturation comes, in part, from building from the bases that our forerunners lay down for us. The world of our parent's changes, and, to survive, we must change with it. The change does not mean scrapping the wisdom of the past. It means modifying it. In implementing this modification, we have to hold the bases in perspective. They were conceived by us to meet our own needs and subject to change by us. As Talmudic studies are subjected to rumination and re-digestion continually, so are the fundaments of our social structures. If we relegate the past cultural directives as not subject to debate, we are saying that the pyramids of the Mayans are all that they contributed to show that we were here. I say that our contribution is measured by how we use the bounty of the world that God provided to provide for our own continuation as an entity in this world, that is still here: Breathing, reproducing, striving, and loving. To do this we need to understand that the basic norms we established are not immutable laws handed down to us for enactment without debate or modification. They are theorems that get relegated to axioms without testing whether realities have changed or less than objective goals have been injected into their formats. They have been designed by us to establish order, but definitions of order can change. For our cultures to adapt to changes, we must assume responsibilities for defining, ruminating, and re-digesting the basic precepts we have organized to control us, not put their debating, reformulation beyond our reach. We can not afford the luxury of basking in the past wisdom of our mentors and not become our own teachers. With these concepts in mind, I created a Gideon Retta and a Mark Engler. Their responsibilities were to be more than their fathers' son's.